GONE SO LONG

GONE SO LONG

A NOVEL

ANDRE DUBUS III

W. W. NORTON & COMPANY

Independent Publishers Since 1923

NEW YORK LONDON

Gone So Long is a work of fiction. Names, characters, places, and incidents are the products of the author's imagination or are used fictitiously. Any resemblance to actual events, locales, or persons, living or dead, is entirely coincidental.

Copyright © 2018 by Andre Dubus III

Printed in the United States of America
First Edition

For information about permission to reproduce selections from this book, write to Permissions, W. W. Norton & Company, Inc., 500 Fifth Avenue, New York, NY 10110

For information about special discounts for bulk purchases, please contact W. W. Norton Special Sales at specialsales@wwnorton.com or 800-233-4830

Manufacturing by Quad Graphics Fairfield
Book design by Helene Berinsky
Production manager: Julia Druskin

ISBN 978-0-393-24410-6

W. W. Norton & Company, Inc.,
500 Fifth Avenue, New York, N.Y. 10110
www.wwnorton.com

W. W. Norton & Company Ltd., 15 Carlisle Street, London W1D 3BS

1 2 3 4 5 6 7 8 9 0

For Ariadne

Tell me.
Who was I when I used to call your name?
—From "Prayer," by Marie Howe

GONE SO LONG

My father's parole officer had an office above a shoe store in Lawrence, Massachusetts. The street was a wide two-lane of sparse traffic, cars parked in front of parking meters built in the 1950s, and the buildings on both sides were made of the same red brick as the mills along the river. There were rectangular blocks of granite above each window, the roofs flat, and on the first floors were one shop after another, leather goods and a bakery, an office supply next to an Army and Navy outlet next to a jewelry store, its display window a dusty glass case whose shelves held little.

A cop glanced at my bare legs and climbed behind the wheel of his cruiser and drove up the street. I stood there on the sidewalk a long time in the sun. Or maybe I went walking. I may have gone walking because so many of the shops and storefronts were closed, their doors shuttered, some of the windows cracked and taped or half covered with boards screwed into the bricks. It was the kind of street that existed before shopping malls and it reminded me so much of Arcadia, the Florida cattle town I'd grown up in, how it was stopped in time, that it was like I'd stepped into a dream I was having where I wasn't dressed and very soon I would get caught doing something I shouldn't be.

Three brown boys walked by me in baggy basketball shorts and shoes with the laces untied. One of them had a red pick in his hair, and they couldn't've been older than eleven or twelve, but as they passed me one of them said something in Spanish and all three laughed. A door opened and a man in a tie walked out, his eyes on me. There were the smells of coffee and cooking onions and cigarette smoke, and I walked through the door he'd just come out of. Italian music was playing. There was a row of booths, two of them filled, a flash of hair and faces, and a long counter with stools, but I was moving to a small table at the window. It had a dirty plate on it, and a half-empty coffee cup. I sat there anyway.

From the table I could look up the street and see the entryway to the interior stairwell of Parole Officer Xenakis's office. It was made of red brick, the steps granite, the bottom one in sunlight but the rest in shadow . . .

This opened something in the young woman that came as a surprise to her; once, when she was fifteen and had just begun to smoke, she had to hide it from her grandmother, Lois, who smoked herself but wouldn't allow her granddaughter to do the same, so Susan had to sneak outside. A few times she'd done it against the wall of the house, but she was afraid Lois would see her rising smoke through a window so she started doing it deeper in the trees near the river.

One afternoon it was so hot she could smell the rot in the dead branches on the banks. She could smell the wet sand and clay and the tiny crayfish. She could smell gator shit and Spanish moss and her own sweat. But what she never smelled were the brown and gold scales of the cottonmouth snake coiled a foot from her bare feet and legs. When she looked down and saw it, she'd just taken a deep drag of her cigarette and now she nearly coughed but did not move. The cottonmouth's triangular head was resting on its own coil, its eyes pointing at her ankles. How could she have been so stupid? How could she have allowed herself to be so exposed? She did not move. She slowly exhaled smoke through her nose, and maybe she'd made a noise of some kind, for the snake lifted its head and opened its white mouth and Susan was sprinting back through the trees and this is the moment that came to her as she watched the shadowed entryway of her father's parole officer's office.

It hadn't occurred to her that what she was doing could be dangerous. This came as much a surprise to her as the warmth of the smiling waitress who appeared at her table and began to clear away the dirty plate and fork and half-empty cup.

"Menu, sweetie?" The woman had dyed blond hair, brown eyebrows, and large breasts. Wrapped around her hips was a soiled apron like she did some of the cooking, too.

Susan said no thank you and ordered iced tea.

"You got it." The woman held the plate, fork, and cup in one hand and was wiping down the table with the other, but she kept staring at Susan, smiling at her. "Honey, you are gorgeous. You should be in the movies."

Susan had heard this before, but only from a few boys who wanted what some of them got from her, never from a woman the age her mother would have been. Susan may have thanked her for her compliment, or maybe she didn't. But she sat there feeling sorry for herself.

No, she sat there feeling the warm, fleshy presence of what she'd been denied. Her grandmother had never been big on compliments, and when it came to Susan's looks it was always words of warning about not looking too trashy. About spending too much time on her hair and makeup, which she rarely spent much time on at all. On how tight her tops were and she was too old to leave the house without wearing a bra.

But never just a sincere compliment from a woman who'd been her age only twenty years earlier.

Then through the window and up Canal Street, a man stepped out of that shadowed entryway into the sun. He was tall and thin and wore a tank top and sweatpants and sandals. From where Susan sat, he looked half black, too. She watched him turn and walk up the street.

The waitress brought her iced tea and set it in front of her with lemon and packets of sugar.

"Let me know if you need anything else, honey." She kept smiling down at her, taking her in as if she were a true gift to her day, and Susan smiled up at her and thanked her, and maybe that's when the anger started. There was how much she enjoyed this woman's attention, how surprised Susan was that she'd needed it.

Why was she even here?

It wasn't her father she'd needed at all.

For over an hour she sat at that table. The last of the lunch customers—

three old women speaking Greek or Italian on their way out the door—had gone, and Susan saw two more men come and go from Nicholas Xenakis's entryway. The first was obese and wore loose gold chains around his neck, his hips rolling as he labored his way up to the street corner. That couldn't be him, could it? No, she felt nothing seeing him. Nothing. The second was in a white shirt and tie and suit pants and was probably her father's parole officer himself. He'd stepped out onto the sidewalk and smoked a cigarette. He had black hair cut as close as a cop's, and every few drags he'd point his face up at the sun and close his eyes. It made her want a cigarette, too, and she ordered more tea and went out to the sidewalk and smoked one.

Cars passed. The sun felt good on her face and arms. The man went back up the entryway's stairs and she went back inside to her table. Two men in summer suits walked by soon after that. They looked like bankers, or maybe she's just remembering that now as her older self writes this. It doesn't matter. But every man she saw was beginning to feel predatory to her in some way.

A few minutes later a beefy man in a blue T-shirt walked up the sidewalk on the other side of the street. His hair was tied back in a short ponytail, and he had the heavy brows of a boxer, and she hated him. Even when he kept walking past Nicholas Xenakis's entryway.

The next morning she sat at that same table and that same warm waitress served her a poached egg and black coffee. Two men in a booth kept staring at her. They wore blue work shirts with the name of some company stitched onto the shirt pockets. The fatter of the two had a brushy mustache and he kept elbowing the man beside him, who laughed and said something to the two men across from them Susan could not see. This attention was not new. It was what she'd known since Gustavo, and she had come to expect it, to rely on it like money in an account she could draw on whenever she needed it. But that morning, hoping and not hoping to see her father, this part of her felt like one big debt and every man she saw was coming to collect.

This second morning was hot, the sky a gray haze. She kept imagining taking her cup of black coffee and carrying it over to that booth and dumping it into the face of the pig with the brushy mustache. She'd been there just under an hour, and her waitress was busier than she'd been the day before, though she still seemed so very happy to see her and kept calling her honey. Susan knew she called lots of customers that, but she was taking it in like cool water. She was just about to leave when up the street a man stepped out of Nicholas Xenakis's entryway onto the sidewalk.

Something sick and electric hummed through her. He had a hooked nose and long sideburns. His hair was combed back, and he seemed big even from where she sat, his hands big, his feet, his shoulders which sloped in a white T-shirt. He stood there a moment. It was like he wasn't sure where he was supposed to go next and he was waiting for someone to tell him. He looked up Canal Street then down it, and that's when she saw how close together his eyes were, how thick his forearms were. And then he started to walk, stepping off the curb into the street, and his arms hung still, or moved but did not move much, and she could smell fried clams and the ocean and she knew.

She felt like throwing up. She stood and rushed by the booth of men and the long counter, its stools taken up by people she'd never seen come in. Then she was in the locked bathroom, sitting on the toilet, her shorts and underwear around her ankles, breathing hard. A slick sweat came out on her forehead and throat, and there were the smells of floral deodorizer and old grease. The floor was linoleum. She stared at it. It was white with gray swirls, a faux-marble, and on the wall was tacked a poster of the Amalfi Coast of Italy. It must have been taken from a plane or helicopter, these cliffs of stone villas built along winding roads above a beach on the Tyrrhenian Sea, though she would not know the name of that water then. That would come years later when she'd fly to Naples for a week with Saul Fedelstein, when she'd stay in a hotel on those very cliffs overlooking that same beach.

Or maybe it was not that beach or that part of the Amalfi Coast, but what stays is that Susan emptied her bowels then, and if that man with the hooked nose and the big forearms had walked into that restaurant on

Canal Street, if he was somewhere on the other side of that bathroom door, the place may as well have been filled with writhing cottonmouths, for what stays, too, is the sting in her side, everything leaving her too fast, the linoleum at her feet, and she saw the young woman she knew had been her mother curled on that linoleum, and the sting in her side became a burn and then was gone as quickly as it had come, and Susan sat in her own stench feeling the soft open utility of her own organs, and my God, how could he have done it?

Those big hands and thick forearms. All that power and he still reached for what he reached for.

And so what was Susan to him? What was she to anyone?

PART

ONE

1

ONCE AGAIN her name moves through Daniel's blood like floating debris. It scrapes along his bones and pokes at his old organs and it is a steady, pulsing nudge in his head. For days now it has lodged itself in the searing ache in his hips and lower back, and he knows there's only one way to free it, but first he needs to finish these chairs he's caning under the sun. His eyes sting. His work glasses have slipped to the end of his nose. Daniel takes them off and lets them hang around his neck. He wipes the sweat off his forehead then stands to stretch his back, but the pain remains, the sickness deep inside him now, he can feel it. It's not going anywhere. He sits on his stool and puts his glasses on and gets back to work.

Today he notices his hands. They're his old man's—thick fingers, chipped and yellowed nails, though his father's always had carnival paint in his cuticles that never came out. Daniel reaches for the nail file he uses to weave the cane under and over itself. A warm wind kicks up from the east and brings with it beach sounds, or maybe it's just Daniel's memory of them—the creaking gears of the Ferris wheel and the popping water balloons and the cries of gulls. There's the tinny whine of the carousel organ and the rattling jerk of the roller-coaster cars, the shrieks of women and children hurled out over the hissing surf. But always there comes, rising up from inside him and getting louder, the blaring rock and roll of the Himalaya: "Sugar, Sugar," "Proud Mary," Tommy Roe singing he's so dizzy his head is spinning. Yesterday, after months of thinking about it, Daniel finally drove around the Midway, and it isn't half what it used to be. The wooden roller coaster was torn down years ago, and the Ferris wheel they have now is kiddie-sized, the Himalaya gone, though there's a strip club with tall white columns at the doors. Half a block down from that, in the front window of a souvenir shop, a male mannequin in swimming trunks stands among beach towels and hula hoops under a two-month-old hand-lettered sign: *Father's Day Sale/Half Price.* Daniel hasn't seen his daughter in forty years, and there is so much to tell her, but why would she listen?

There was her mother's brown skin, her long wet hair that smelled like the ocean and baby oil and made him want to kiss every part of her. There was her small face and straight back, her breasts and brown nipples. All these years later he can still see them, the tiny dark freckles around them, how white her breasts looked, the rest of her always so tanned because they were both amusement park kids who lived at the beach: Danny Ahearn, Liam's son, the artist's boy, though only a few called his father an artist. They called him Ahearn or Old Liam or the Magic Mick because he could take sea-air-beaten shit and make it new again: the giant clown's head on the roof of the Fun House, all the signage for joints up and down the Midway—the Five O'Clock Club, Willey's Hard and Soft Ice Cream, the Pavilion and Bath House and Shaheen's Fun O'Rama Park.

And Linda's father owned the Penny Arcade. Her family lived there too, though you wouldn't know it. Past the Skee-Ball and slot machines, the pinballs and billiard tables, was a black wall, and on the other side of that wall was the apartment Linda lived in with her mother and little brother Paul and her father, Gerry Dubie, who hated Danny because he could smell how much he wanted his Linda. Everybody wanted her, and that was the problem.

No, that's old thinking. The problem had always been Danny's. For him it was more than just wanting; it was a need so fierce his own body felt like a too-tight suit, like the blood in his veins was about to turn on him until he was with her again. And then when he did have her, that hot worm of possession burrowed into his heart. He'd never been one of the handsome boys, not like Jimmy Squeeze who got his name because he could hold a pencil between his chest muscles, or Tony Scarf with his long hair and five hundred Skee-Ball tickets hanging off one shoulder, or Manny Pina and his lean torso and face you could put on a cereal box. And there were so many others, beach raff from all the stinking mill towns of the Merrimack Valley, sometimes a few rich boys from Boston or New York who rented air-conditioned cottages on the sand past the barrooms at the edge of the strip. But Danny had something the others did not, something he never would have known about if Will Price hadn't told him that afternoon in May 1969, the season just about to kick into gear.

Cane likes wet heat, like this morning's. This is the sixth of eight chairs from a one-hundred-year-old dining set, and he'd had to refinish each one before the caning could even begin. The other seven are within easy reach, like everything, because he lives small.

His trailer rests against a stand of torch pines so overgrown the branches cover his tin roof, and when it's hot like today, the pitch goes soft and he can smell it and the ocean as he works in the yard. It's a forty-by-forty patch of ground he did not earn, but it's his anyway. Three years ago he hired a man to build him a tall plank fence, enclosing Daniel's single-wide in this square with a narrow gate for his Tacoma. He hired a carpenter to build him a small shop for his caning, one he framed on concrete against the west fence, and Daniel liked how much smaller that made his patch. He was paroled twenty-five years ago, but really, he's never been all the way out. His days and nights are as regimented now as they were then: awake at six, in the shop by seven, lunch at eleven, and the rest of the day—unless he's late with a piece of furniture—he drives over the river into Port City and the Council on Aging, picks a name, and drives an old man or woman to a doctor's appointment or to the plaza to shop for food and medicine. If he's not needed, it's his schooling time. Sometimes he lies on his bed in the trailer and listens to a book on tape, history mostly. He just finished a long one all about John Adams. Or he goes to the library, a one-story building in the town square where it's cool in the summer, warm in the winter, and he likes the three ladies who work behind the desk, though only one of them works there at a time. People might think he doesn't like women, but he does. He's never stopped, though there is one older one he stays away from. She's tall and her hair is gray like his, and she does her work standing up. A few times when he's come in, she's glanced at him over the rim of her glasses like she thinks she might know who he is but doesn't remember exactly, though she knows it isn't good. It may have been a mistake to come back here, but when his mother got sick he just had to, and now she's been gone three years, and nobody was more surprised than he was that she died with some money, leaving him—at this late age of sixty-three—with his first home, a shop, and this patch of ground he sweats on under the sun.

Daniel sticks the end of the cane into the next hole in the seat's frame and begins to weave it back across. He's thirsty. But that can wait. He needs more aspirin, but it doesn't do the job anyway, and that can wait too. Working on aging furniture, it's so easy to keep drifting back. He thinks about his old man and how quiet he always was and how that made Danny quiet, his mother doing the talking for all three of them. She was from New Jersey and had that accent from there, which made her sound less intelligent than she was. She had a high voice too, and it seemed to come from that hooked nose of hers, the one she gave Danny, and she was always talking to herself. She'd be washing the dishes, Danny's father sitting at the table slowly reading the *Boston Herald*, sipping his Bushmills, Danny sitting in front of his plate he'd wiped clean with a slice of bread, waiting to ask to be excused by his old man, then over the running water in the sink would come Ma's voice: "Yep, I said that to her. I *did*. Don't tell me I didn't." Or: "I know it. Three times in one day, the poor thing." And Danny's father would turn a page of his paper, and that was Danny's moment, the only time his father would tolerate an interruption, everything he did concentrated, focused, and solitary.

Three times Danny was in solitary, and it was strange how he became his father. Time was Danny's now. Time was wet concrete he had to wade through. Time was thick air and the buzz of fluorescent lights that never went out, and Danny lived those days by reading one word at a time out of the Bible, the only book they gave him, old words he couldn't even sound out in his head, and then, when he couldn't tell anymore what was morning or afternoon or night, even when the cold eggs on his plate told him, he became his mother, talking to himself, though he was really talking to his little girl Susan. He sat on his bunk and told her things out loud he needed her to hear. He knows he did, but what? What could he possibly have said?

The year he went down, 1973, Susan was three years old, and she used to sit on his lap and snuggle into his chest and listen to his heart. *It's so loud, Daddy.* Her hair was straight and brown like Linda's. She had Linda's small face, too, spared the hooked nose of her father and grandmother, spared Danny's badly spaced eyes.

It started with Will Price the spring of '69, what he'd shown Danny about himself when he was nineteen and working for his old man scraping signage his father would soon paint. Danny was on a twelve-foot ladder in front of the Five O'Clock Club, the big O a clock face whose numbers he'd just sanded, and now he was sanding the C, a cool wind from the ocean on him, the sun on him too, and his father called out to him from around the corner where he was painting the side door entrance. Danny couldn't hear him because of the wind, and he shouted back, "*What?* What did you say, Liam?!" Funny about that, how he called his own father by his name. Maybe he could tell Susan about that, too. But what was the story there? Was it a falling off of respect? Anger at his old man for raising him in amusement parks up and down the East Coast? Or was it how he left Danny's mother to talk to herself while washing dishes at the kitchen sink?

"What'd you say, Liam?!"

"Jesus, you got some *pipes*, kid." It was Will Price, looking up at him from behind his aviator sunglasses. He owned the Himalaya and the Frolics, and he was a man who never left home in anything but a pressed shirt, pleated pants, and shiny black Italian shoes. His shirt collar was open around a bolo tie like cowboys out West wear, and from where Danny had stood on the ladder above him, he could see Will's bald spot, too.

"How you doin', Mr. Price?"

"I says I'm almost done." Liam's voice in the wind. And he wouldn't be happy if his son was still prepping the sign when he was ready to paint, so Danny left the C the way it was and picked up his scraper and took it to the curled white paint of the l.

"You're Ahearn's kid, right?"

Danny said he was. And maybe he could feel the change that was coming, because this was new. No grown man or woman had ever taken notice of him before. No teachers in school, anyway, and he'd gone to a few, the first near the Palisades Amusement Park in New Jersey, the second up in Maine a mile from the Palace Playground in Old Orchard Beach, the third in York when they lived at Wild King-dom Animal Farm and where Danny's clothes—no matter how hard his mother scrubbed them in the tub—always smelled like hay dust and elephant and lion shit, and there were other schools, too, the final here on the coast north of Boston, Salisbury Beach, a sandy strip of carnival park where Danny lived with his mother and father in an uninsulated camp no larger than his trailer now. All the cottages had names, and theirs was Sea Spray.

At his new schools, other kids took notice of him for a while, the hooked nose he got from his mother, his eyes too close together, the acne on his face and upper back that began to erupt in the first of three high schools he drifted through like some hobo on an invisible train with no tracks. But whenever a few boys loudly pointed out his flaws he knew only too well, they always made a mistake, for there was something sickly hot in Daniel that sometimes needed to get out, his knuckles scraped and sore after, more than one boy's nose flattened to bloody cartilage, and Danny would get suspended again. He'd gotten plenty of that kind of attention, but not this, not somebody important staring up at him.

Will Price said: "Say 'real fast.' "

"Real fast."

"Christ, your voice is like a fuckin' bass drum."

And in no time Danny had become Danny "The Sound" Ahearn, head DJ in the glass booth on the Himalaya ride, the job every young man on the beach would bleed for. And even though he wasn't handsome like the ticket takers down below, he looked good in the red blazer and white pants Price had tailored special for him and the other boys. Every night the Himalaya had a line of people a hundred feet long, most of them girls, all of them beautiful with their long hair and unbuttoned blouses, their bright eyes and smooth skin, some of them laughing while they lit up cigarettes and blew smoke out their noses like movie stars. From where Danny sat in his glass booth, a fan on him, the smell of fried dough and popcorn and gear oil in his face, he could see them all, and that's when Linda first saw him, though she'd known him for two years already, or at least knew who he was, the way he knew who she was, though the wanting hadn't gotten inside him yet.

It was a Saturday night. The sun had been down an hour or more, and the strip was loud and crowded and lit with carnival lights. He had the mic to his mouth and had just flipped on "Build Me Up Buttercup" by the Foundations, Jimmy slowing the ride to switch gears and make it go backward, all those purple cars on curved tracks below him stuffed with kids his age or younger, half the girls thinking they were in love, the boys trying to hide the hard-ons in their jeans. Jimmy got them all going fast and Danny held the mic an inch from his lips and lowered his voice as low as it would go: "Now sit tight as we go backwards real, real, reeeal fast." But from behind the smudged glass of his booth, his eyes were on three girls in the front of the line. One was a tan and scrawny Puerto Rican, her hair wild and frizzy, the blonde beside her sunburned with a candy necklace around her neck, and they were both laughing and yelling in each other's ears over the music, but it was the one just behind them that caught him, Gerry Dubie's daughter. It wasn't her long brown hair or her small face. It wasn't her dark eyes or that gold chain at her throat. It was how she stood there in all that blasting music and carnival noise and talk and laughing as if she were alone somewhere quiet, just her. Then she looked off to the side like she'd remembered something important, and the Foundations were singing, "Build me up, build me up, Buttercup," and that's when she raised her eyes straight to Danny in his booth like he was Jesus on the cross. He had the mic to his lips, but he couldn't say anything; it was too much; it was like she'd been wanting something for so long and she didn't even know what it was till she looked up and saw him staring down at her, him, Danny "The Sound" Ahearn.

A TRUCK passes by. Daniel can't see it over his fence, but he knows from that feathering rattle of the diesel that it's a pickup, one of those big ones kids like to drive now. His mouth and throat are dry. He still punishes himself. He does. But nothing good is going to come from not drinking water when he should. He rests his file on the caning and goes inside.

In the hot trailer, he fills a glass under the kitchen faucet and drinks. The water tastes like iron, and he thinks of blood and hears the term his good doctor used over two years ago, *active surveillance*. At the library Daniel looked up "prostate" and "cancer" and saw that's the term they all use, but five appointments have come and gone without him.

This life of his is not something he fears ending. He threw it away with both hands years ago. But these past thirty-four months his daughter's last name has sat inside him like a shard of glass, and for too long he hated Liam and his mother for not taking her in. They lived in the same neighborhood as Lois and Gerry, and his daughter could have had his old room in the Ahearn house, so why didn't they take her in? Though Ma said she'd wanted to, that she begged Liam to do it. She told Daniel this a very long time ago and she said it again near the end.

Those last days, sitting beside his mother's bed for hours, different nurses coming and going, the morphine dreaming itself through his mother's blood, he stared at her sleeping face. She was past eighty, and for the first time she looked beautiful to him. Her cheeks were drawn and pale, but her nose seemed smaller, her lips more full, and though her hair was thin, it was the pure white of a woman who'd never once dyed it, not once. The word *lovely* came to him. She looked lovely.

"Danny." Sometimes she'd wake up and just start talking.

"Daniel."

"Who's Daniel?"

"Me, Ma."

"We never called you Daniel."

"I know, Ma, but I like it better now."

She turned her head and stared at him. The oxygen tube in her nose hooked around her ears and flattened her hair. "I was on the Flying Horses, Danny. Me and your father. I was on a stallion and he was on a mare. Isn't that funny?"

The Broadway Flying Horses. Liam's pride, maybe his only one, a carousel of four chariots and forty-six hand-carved wooden horses, three dogs, and three goats. Some Danish sculptor carved them in 1890, but for years Liam Ahearn kept them alive, using a different color of Japanese oil paint for each bridle, mane, saddle, and tail, not one horse like the next, each one a song. At one time his old man must have wanted to be a real artist, one of those guys who hang their paintings in fancy galleries where rich people stroll sipping wine and writing big checks. Maybe he wanted to be famous, Daniel doesn't know, because his father never talked. Ever. It was like living with a very old man years before he got old.

"Could I have some ice?"

Daniel filled a spoon with crushed ice from the Dixie cup on the stand. He placed it on his mother's tongue and she took it and pursed her lips and looked up at the ceiling, her eyes roving back and forth as if she were scanning a crowd. Outside her curtained window there was bright sun, and a nurse laughed on the other side of the open door behind him, and maybe that's what made his mother turn back to him then—that laugh, a cool trickle down her throat, she and her long-dead husband riding the Flying Horses.

"I wanted to raise her, Danny. Don't think I didn't because I did, honey."

"I know it, Ma." Though he did not know it. He'd never seen this woman ever fight for anything, even a scrap of attention from his father. But right then wasn't the time for fighting. Daniel was sixty years old. Sitting beside his mother's bed in that small room that smelled faintly of urine and cotton and old skin, he was thirteen again, fourteen, fifteen, home from school for days because he could never hold in all that lay so hotly inside him. He'd be kicked out once more, but his mother never scolded him, never yelled. She never told her husband, either. Liam left for work before Danny was supposed to leave for school anyway, and she'd make her son pancakes or eggs and bacon, and she'd let him lie on the couch and read his comic books: *The Avengers*, *Blue Beetle*, though *Enemy Ace* was his favorite because the hero was a World War I German fighter pilot named Hans von Hammer ("The Hammer of Hell"), and he was misunderstood by everyone but had a code of honor and never shot down an injured or helpless pilot. Sometimes his mother would sit beside Danny in her housecoat, smelling like coffee, Ajax, and sweat, and she'd ask him to read her an episode and he would. He could feel her watching him as he read, though, and when he'd turn to point out some action on the page he'd catch her staring at him, a love in her eyes so deep it made him feel shy and like going to another room, but there was only his bedroom or the bathroom, and now, forty-five years later, after all that had happened and all he had done, an oxygen tube hooked under his mother's nose, she turned her head on that hospital pillow and gave Daniel that same stare, her eyes so clear and steady with it that he had to look down at his hands.

"Her last name is done, Danny. That's all Lois would tell me."

His mother-in-law, Lois. He still thinks of her that way. And not "done" but *Dunn*, right? Susan on his lap, her small ear pressed to his chest, his hand completely covering both her knees.

"Why'd she tell you, Ma?"

"Ice, honey." Her eyes were on the Dixie cup. Daniel took the spoon and scooped crushed ice on it, dripping cold water onto his mother's wrist, IV, sheet, and chin. *Susan Dunn*. Not Susan Lori Ahearn. But Susan Dunn. Three when he disappeared, twenty when he was paroled (and not one visit from her), forty years old three years ago as Daniel tilted the spoonful of crushed ice into his old mother's open mouth.

"Did you tell her it was for me?"

His mother swallowed and shook her head.

Behind Daniel's eyes was a white sky. It was all you could see from the yard. No treetops. No telephone poles or wires. No roofs of buildings. Only the sky above the corner towers and twenty-two-foot concrete walls and razor wire flashing in the sun. That patch of sky, it was cruel in its hint of how big and endless it really was, and it was cruel how slowly the next words from his mother were coming.

"Where does she live, Ma?"

"She wouldn't tell me."

"Did you ask her?"

His mother nodded. Her eyes were on the ceiling again, scanning back and forth, back and forth. The oxygen tubes in her nose looked crooked, and she seemed more tired than she'd been only a minute ago, as if that minute had been years.

"What did she say, Ma?"

Her breathing was shallow. Her breasts lay slack beneath the sheet and johnny.

"Ma?"

There was more laughter from a nurse, the beeping of a distant machine in a distant room, his mother's breathing. She did not go that day, or the day after, or even a week later. It may have been three weeks, and they had other talks but never again about Daniel's and Linda's daughter Susan.

The morphine seemed to take his mother places she enjoyed: wolves in the snow who were friendly and covered her with branches to keep her warm; a gondola in Venice, Italy, a place his mother had never been, though now she was floating under stone bridges with Frank Sinatra "when he was young and skinny," then the gondola became a sleeper car on a train, and she talked a long time about farms and men with hands cracked from the sun and rain and wind. "Your father always worked so hard, Danny."

"I know, Ma."

"He was very talented."

"I know."

"He used to brush my hair."

"Liam?"

"The moon, Danny. I always thought about it."

Daniel can't remember the last thing she said to him, but it was not from the world he lived in. When she died Daniel was driving to see her late on a Sunday morning in March, dirty snow plowed up against the sidewalks.

Nailed to the pine trunk just inches from his trailer's kitchen window is a rusted metal thermometer in the shade. Ninety-four degrees. Daniel rinses his glass and sets it upside down on the drainboard and steps back outside. His trailer's door is slightly warped and racked out of square, and he has to lift upward before the latch clicks into place. The sun is as high as it will get all day. There isn't a shadow in the center of his yard, and his half-caned chair looks raw and undressed. It's from the Victorian era, a time when everyone seemed to want to live like dukes and duchesses, and it's part of a set for an antiques dealer down in Port City. He's a pipe-smoking bull of a guy who told Daniel if these came out right, he'd trust him with a core-reed rocker on a bentwood frame made just after the Civil War. Daniel had to go pick up the chairs in his truck, and he'd quoted the dealer $1.50 per caning hole for each seat, which didn't include refinishing them first. This is a big-money job that could lead to other big-money jobs, though Daniel's bills are minimal so what does he need the money for?

Susan Dunn. With each passing day, week, and month, those two words his mother gave him are rising to the surface of his skin like something infected. Susan Dunn. She's living out there somewhere. He'll need a nest egg to find her, won't he? And maybe she needs money. Maybe he can give her that.

The sun's too high now to keep working. Daniel carries the half-caned chair inside and sets it down alongside the others. His shop isn't much larger than a storage shed, and it smells like varnish and walnut dust and the galvanized metal of its roof flashing. Daniel swings the door shut and padlocks it. He's thinking of a cool shower, and he should eat something, too, but he has no appetite, just that ache he can't quite get used to, and it's only as he's walking under the sun to his trailer does he know that this is the day. Whether he's needed at the Council on Aging this afternoon or not, this is the day he's going to walk into the town's library, sit at one of the computer screens, and type onto the dusty keyboard her name, his grown daughter's name that does not sound at all like the one he and Linda had given her so very long ago: Susan Lori. Susan Lori Ahearn.

2

IT WAS close to dawn, and still, she could not sleep. She lay in the dark on her back, and it was as if she had no arms or legs, eyes or ears, her face an abstraction. Her husband was curled on his side, one hand between his knees, and he was snoring lightly, though she barely heard it. Nor could she quite hear the air-conditioning unit in their window, their room probably too cool, though she did not care or reach for the light blanket at her feet. She breathed deeply through her nose, but she smelled nothing—not the cotton sheets or pillowcases, not Bobby's dried sweat or the skin of his bald head inches away, not the sticky red wine at the bottom of her glass on the bedside table or the wax of the chamomile candle beside it she'd blown out hours ago—nothing. And she should be able to see the contours of their room, but it was like staring into the shadows of a shadow and she closed her eyes, but that left her floating alone in her own darkness and she opened them again to this nothingness she'd been inside of for weeks—at meals together at their small table in his red kitchen; working side by side in the study—her on the novel she'd resurrected with his help, him on the revision of his dissertation to make it more palatable to the masses; and later, making love, his breathy grunts in her ear, his tongue in her mouth, she seemed to be watching it all from far away, once again stuck alone in this non-feeling that now swung her legs off the bed and into the bathroom.

Plugged into the socket beneath the toilet paper dispenser was a night-light shaped like a saxophone, its dim glow spreading over the floor where Susan knelt rummaging under the sink for the scissors. They were cool and heavy and when she flicked on the overhead light, she squinted at a face she no longer seemed to recognize. It was small, her eyes dark, though she'd worn very little makeup for years, not even to cover the lines at the corners of her eyes and lips. The overall effect, she thought, was weariness. She was forty-three years old, and she'd grown weary.

Now she was holding her long hair between two fingers, and she began to cut into it, the snipping sound muffled in her ear. She dropped the hair into the wastebasket and kept cutting, then she turned off the light and walked into her writing room. Such a joke. She sat at her desk, and it occurred to her only then that she was naked. She ran her fingers over her shorn head, felt stray hairs fall to her shoulders and breasts. That was something at least, that she could feel that.

She ran the cursor to where she'd last left off: and she saw the young woman she knew had been her mother curled on that linoleum, and the sting in her side became a burn and then was gone as quickly as it had come, and Susan Lori sat in her own stench feeling the soft open utility of her own organs, and my God, how could he have done it?

Those big hands and thick forearms. All that power and he still reached for what he reached for.

And so what was Susan Lori to him? What was she to anyone?

Her fingers hovered. There was such ugliness to all this. But she remembered the toilet, and she remembered that image of her mother curled on the floor.

She pressed return until there was just a blank screen. Sweat came out on her forehead and the back of her neck. Her mouth tasted like ash. And as Susan Lori washed her hands with scalding water and pink liquid soap, she looked into a smudged mirror and saw the same dark beauty of her mother, but without the cheap insecurity in that Polaroid Susan had of her at fifteen, without the need for anything or anybody that would make her own reflection in the mirror look better to her in some way.

Susan Lori did not know if her mother had ever looked into a mirror like this, but leaving that bathroom and not caring whether her foul smell followed her or not, Susan Lori may as well have hoisted a shield and drawn a sword, for she scanned the room for the man with the big hands and thick forearms, but he was not there, and the men she passed in the booth were ghosts as dead to her as her own shit moving through the sewer pipes under the street of the parole officer of the father she no longer wanted to meet or talk to in any way.

Of course Susan Lori knew that man she saw could have been someone else. But in that hot factory town on that brown river that smelled vaguely like gasoline and dried mud, every man and boy looking so hungrily at her as she waited to see the one who had taken her mother from her, a part of Susan Lori began to see all men as invaders. And whether their intent was to give pleasure or to inflict pain, whether they used their

fingers or sharp objects never meant for a woman, she had been carried
to where she had never before allowed herself to go: the final moment of
her mother's suffering.

Susan stared at that last line. She felt the blood descend to her
fingertips, smelled the dusty throw rug under her bare feet, heard a
car pass by outside, saw the pale blue of daylight filtering through the
curtains.

Outside two warblers were calling to one another, and she crawled
back into bed beside Bobby and pulled the sheet up to her throat. She
could hear his rising and falling breath, could smell the hard wax of
the candle on the lamp table beside her. She grew too cold and pulled
the light blanket up over them both, then she closed her eyes, her
body sinking more deeply into the mattress, and soon she was floating down a brown river past mill buildings toward the sea, the kind
waitress in her dirty apron smiling and waving at her from the banks.
When Susan woke, bright sunlight lay across Bobby's side of the bed
and he'd been gone for hours.

In the bathroom she avoided the mirror, but her neck felt cool and
naked, and she dressed and walked down the dark hallway for the
kitchen. Propped against the coffee maker was a note written in Bobby's left-handed sprawl: *Baby, your **hair**. —LOVE, B*

This was his way of saying he was worried about her, which he'd
been for weeks now. She'd taken the semester off from teaching to
work on her "novel" and her MFA chores, but she spent most of her
days sleeping or trying to read or pretending she wanted to eat or to
make love to a man she felt so far away from, and the thing is she did
not know if it was him or just everything, for that was how it always
showed its leaving and its return, her no longer being able to take pleasure in the small pleasures: a glass of Malbec after a long day of work;
the smell of the bay blowing across the sunlit campus; a fresh sliced
tomato on blue porcelain; a student's inspired and well-written paper.

She'd begin to feel the slow drifting away from all of it, her anomie
back in her house, some black hook that lifted her then hung her just
out of reach of whatever it was she thought she loved. It had started
when she was very young, and she'd nearly grown used to it, like some
black birthmark across her face.

"Enemy?" Bobby had asked her the first time she'd opened that
window into herself. They were sitting together on the couch in his
study on a weekday afternoon, both their classes done for the day, and
he'd poured them some wine she did not want.

"No," she'd told him. "Anomie. Alienation. I don't know, estrange-
ment." But it had become their word for it, her enemy.

Outside the window the sun shone on the roof of her car, the dark
roast beginning to drip. It was a Saturday and she remembered vaguely
Bobby telling her he planned to spend the day cleaning and organizing
his office on campus. She'd made a life with Bobby Dunn. She had,
and so she could only hope that she was wrong about what she did not
feel. Maybe she was wrong.

She was tempted to read over what she'd written the night before,
but she was afraid she would do what she always did, which was to
judge it as shit then delete it and sit staring at nothing once again. No,
it was as if some small flame had been lit inside her, and it would take
very little to blow it out. Bobby loved the novel she'd been trying to
work on again. He thought it was "genius," but he was wrong. It was
shit, every word of it false. It was from the point of view of a Mexican
girl living in some tenement in Culiacán, but every time Susan tried to
be her with mere words, she kept seeing—not some Mexican city—
but the brick shops of Oak Street in Arcadia where Susan had grown
up, her grandmother's antique store on the first floor of the building
below her. And Susan wasn't up there alone, either. She was with Gustavo, his dark eyes and rough hands and straw cowboy hat he'd set
aside until they were done. The girl she was really writing about was
herself so why not just write about *herself*?

Because she'd never been very fond of her own company, that's why.

But she kept seeing her old room in their house in Arcadia, the pine bookcases her stepgrandfather had bought at an auction sale, her single bed in the corner where there was a wall lamp she'd lie under reading for days. There was her desk at the window overlooking the woods where she took pride writing essays on *Leaves of Grass* and *The Pearl* and *Jane Eyre*.

There was making love with Gustavo in that bed.

She needed to go back there, her memory of it a jumble of old dry pieces that could only feed the flame of this new writing, this sense that she was walking into some eternal room where someone she forgot she knew was sitting there waiting for her.

She poured her coffee into one of Bobby's black mugs and carried it down the hall into her office. Her laptop was open the way she'd left it, its screen dark. She sat down and tapped it bright again.

the final moment of her mother's suffering.

It was a weekday afternoon, and she and Bobby had just made love on their unmade bed. She lay on her side facing him, the late sun through the window across his face and shoulders, his big hand on her hip. From his study spilled Ornette Coleman's *The Shape of Jazz to Come*, and Susan had grown used to its discordant noise, the way you do the sounds of construction in a house next door to you, the hammer taps and whirring saws and wood dropping onto wood. She'd smiled at him. "You and Ornette, I'll never get it."

"It's easy. There's no tonal center."

She just stared at him.

"Nothing's predetermined. There are no harmonic *rules*. Look, life's one big fucking mess, Susan. To shape it too much is a lie." He smiled back at her, and maybe it was what he'd just said and then his smile in that light that did it, the rest of the room in shadow.

"Bobby?"

"Yeah?"

"I'm not really an orphan."

"No?"

"No."

And so she told him of the mother she'd lost the way she had and the father who still lived. She told him of finding all this out just days before going back to college her senior year. She told him about driving up north to find her father.

"Jesus Christ."

"Yep."

"You don't remember him at all?"

"No, not really. Glimpses here and there. And maybe his shoulders. I don't know. Something about his shoulders."

Bobby began to look at her differently. He began to look at her as if she were broken and in need of fixing. He'd always been attentive, but now he was more so, calling her to ask what she wanted for dinner. Walking up behind her at the kitchen sink and massaging her shoulders, making love with her like she'd been sick a long time and he didn't want her to have a relapse. She hadn't been sick, but telling Bobby had brought shame back to the surface of her skin like a fever she'd never quite shaken, and this was why she'd never told anyone before and now she regretted having done it.

Jesus Christ. She opened her email and wrote in Lois's address, then, in the subject line, *Coming for a visit?*

But what was she going to tell her? That she was writing a *book* about herself? Lois would consider that airing their family's dirty laundry, and she would use that cliché too, and she would want no part of it. No, Susan couldn't tell her that, but maybe she could tell her the partial truth.

Hi, Noni,

Would it be all right if I stayed with you for a little while? (Bobby and I are taking a break right now. I can explain when I see you.)
Love, Susan

Her face heated at this small betrayal of her husband, who knew nothing of this "break," but she pressed send before she could change her mind.

3

IT WAS just after dawn and already fossil hunters were out on Bone River. From where she sat on her screened porch, smoking her first Carlton of the day, sipping a hazelnut coffee with cream and two Splendas, Lois could see their canoe slip along behind the live oaks and dangling Spanish moss, and she could hear their low, expectant voices too. It put her off, this intrusion into her solitude. They called this northern part of the river Bone Alley because of all the mastodon and shark's teeth you could find, but that wasn't Lois's thing, and she never understood it.

She inhaled deeply on her cigarette and let the smoke out slowly. She was tired from yesterday's Antiques Fair, walking up and down Oak Street inspecting the vendors' tables, making sure they weren't peddling any Tupperware or guns, books or CDs or handmade jewelry. Everything had to be dated no later than 1950, and she'd only caught one item, a hardcover published in 1951, *The Catcher in the Rye*. The vendor was a small woman who wore a Devil Rays cap perched low over cataract sunglasses. Around her wrist was a medical bracelet of some kind, and that may have softened another volunteer inspector but not Lois.

"You can't sell this one. Pre-1950 only."

"It's a classic."

"It's from '51. Put it away or I'll have to ask you to pack your things and leave."

The woman put her hands on her narrow hips. She had the knobby elbows of a bar drinker, and Lois didn't like her.

"You're Lois Dubie, aren't you?"

"Maybe."

"I've heard about you." The woman snatched the book from Lois's hand and dropped it into a bin at her feet. "I've heard about you, all right."

Lois knew her reputation. Not long ago, checking her business emails, she found one from her only employee, Marianne, defending her. *Her life hasn't been easy, you know. Why don't you all cut her some slack.*

Lois had scrolled down. It was a group email from other antique shop owners in town. The subject was *This 4th Saturday Antiques Fair*, and most of it was logistical, but Ann Barlow of Ye Olde Treasures chimed in that someone *other than the ever-so-warm Lois Dubie should be the vendor inspector.* Others had agreed in their mousy ways, and Lois couldn't give two shits.

You're bitter, honey. It's made you mean. Those were Don's words in her head. Sometimes a floorboard would creak on its own, and Lois would turn her head and expect to see him. Tall, bearded Don who even in his sixties pulled his hair back in a short ponytail. When she was young, she never would have looked at him twice. She would've thought him a hippie, one of those stoned boys lying half naked on some blanket on the beach, losers who weren't man enough to fight for their country. But Don was the first antiques picker she'd met right after she and Suzie moved down here, and he stood in her shop she'd only bought and opened three days earlier when she hadn't known a damn thing about antiques other than that they were old. Something about the way he stood there on the floorboards made her trust him. Or maybe it was what he'd said, "You need a specialty. This shop's never had enough of a *focus*. I bet she sold it to you cheap." He'd smiled at her and handed her his card:

Donald Lamson, Jr.
Antiques Acquisition

Specializing in Auctions and Private Sales
Arcadia, Florida

A sparrow alighted on the clothesline. It had gray wings with some yellow in them, a seaside bird of some kind, too far inland from its own. The fossil hunters' canoe was out of sight, though Lois could still hear their damned voices, and she stubbed out her cigarette and opened the computer in her lap. She was eighty-two and swore she'd never buy one for herself, but you couldn't be in business these days without one, especially when you specialized in the selling of period furniture and vintage toys. What would've taken months to find years ago could now be found in half a minute. Don died before seeing this. She didn't know if he would have liked it or not. He was a man who came alive when he was face-to-face with others, a born salesman. He might have appreciated how easy it was now to find auctions and estate sales, but that's it, she was sure. Then he'd be off in his pressed khakis and plaid shirt, his sloping shoulders and gray ponytail, his warm, mostly honest smile.

Lois sipped her coffee and logged into her email. She wanted another cigarette but thought the better of it. She'd cut down to six a day, and her sense of smell was returning. The sun had risen only an hour ago, but its heat already carried the scents of the river—its sandy banks and dead wood and dried Spanish moss, its gator and turtle shit. It was going to be another baking day, and she thought about calling in sick to the shop, but no, Sundays were busy and she didn't want to drive Marianne too hard.

Opening bright on the screen was a stack of unopened emails. She squinted at them all. She'd left her reading glasses back in the house somewhere, though she didn't really need them as much as she used to. It was the only thing about getting old that had come as a pleasant surprise. Her eyes had begun to correct themselves.

Lois ignored all the self-congratulatory emails from the other shop owners lauding *Another Successful Fourth Saturday!* and she scrolled down looking for anything from her son or daughter-in-law. Paul had gained so much weight over the years. She worried about him. He was in his fifties now and that air freight job of his had him sitting at a desk all day and into the night. His son, Paul Jr., was husky too, but he worked in construction, which helped him keep it off.

There was nothing. Just junk the filter hadn't caught, and some mass mailings from toy archives she didn't want to open: E. T. Burrows, Fritzel, Halsam, and Wyandotte. Between the last two was: *Coming for a visit?* Lois tapped it open. Suzie.

Hi, Noni. She only called her that when she needed something. The rest of the time it was Lois. *Would it be all right if I stayed with you for a little while? (Bobby and I are taking a break right now. I can explain when I see you.) Love, Susan*

"Taking a break"? Jesus, Mary, and Joseph. Lois peered closer to the screen. She'd sent this yesterday. Now Susan would think she was giving her the cold shoulder. But then again, why shouldn't she? Hadn't her granddaughter been doing that to *her* for years? Only calling when she needed something? A loan? A place to stay? That one time she and the commercial fisherman with the long red hair wanted to borrow her only car "just for *two* days, Noni. *Please.*"

That's when Susan was twenty-five or twenty-six, her beauty truly striking, something dark and bright at the same time. It had begun when she was in high school, and that's when all the trouble started.

But they'd had good times before this. When Lois had just sold the arcade, they drove to Florida for Susan's eighth-grade spring vacation. Suzie was twelve and hadn't blossomed yet, which made her a bear to live with. Bad skin. No breasts. Her face still round with baby fat. She still only called Lois Noni, and though Lois did not know this then, they were ending a time when they were close in a way that never quite happened again.

But that was such a happy trip. Susan kept talking about how new their car smelled, how she hoped they'd see some alligators. Lois had been without a man for years, Gerry dead for all she knew, and she often asked her granddaughter to read to her, which she did, though Lois had no memory of any of the stories. But she could still see her granddaughter's profile on that long trip south as she read from a thick paperback novel with her knees braced against the glove box, her brown hair pulled behind her ears. Her nose was small and she had the same splash of acne on her cheeks Linda had had and she was going to look so much like her mother that it made Lois want to pull her in tighter than ever, and it made her want to push her away.

They had spent a week at Disney, and it had made Lois feel that her entire life had been small and trashy, her old arcade and the strip back home an insult to what amusement parks should really be. For this place was endless and clean with sky trams and guided boat tours and life-sized mechanical dogs barking at life-sized jumping fish; there were deep swamps and real tropical forests in an Adventure-land of gators and snakes that looked more real than real; every kid-die ride was polished and gleaming and upbeat music was pumped in you so you could hear no gears creaking and Dumbo the Elephant would carry children safely away then back again and a polite young woman dressed in a plaid skirt and vest guided Lois and Suzie and a dozen others all over the kingdom and its neighborhoods—yes, *neighborhoods*: worlds gone by with their cobbled streets and shops with scrolled columns at their doors that looked like they came from old England; or the future where every low white building of glass seemed to come from some astro station on the moon; or the boutiques where Lois bought her and her granddaughter floppy sun hats they wore to the Fantasy Faire where professional actors, dancers, and singers performed under a grand tent, their costumes the colors of cake and ice cream and summer balloons, all the families watching like they were being pulled into someone else's dream and it was better than any they could have on their own, that magic castle rising above them all as if God Himself must live there. Throughout that hot, lovely week, Suzie beside her in a halter top and shorts and flip-flops, her eyes taking it all in, every bit of it, Lois felt over and over again, *Yes, this is it. This is it.*

But she wasn't thinking only of places where people paid good money to be amused. It was something else, and she did not know what it was until she and Susan were back in their new Reliant driving west on I-70 through country that surprised Lois. Only thirty miles inland and they were in cattle country, no telephone poles or gas stations or houses anywhere. Instead, on both sides of the two-lane highway lay pastures of St. Augustine grass, black and brown cows grazing under the sun or dozing in the shade of oak and hickory trees. There were prairies of palmetto scrub and flatwoods of yellow pine, beneath them soft-looking beds of goldenrod and thistle. As they got deeper inland, the pastures became a floodplain, its shallow sloughs draining into Bone River, whose banks were thick with ferns.

"Noni, look."

Off to the south, a red-tailed hawk glided in a slow downward spiral before flapping its long wings and drifting east. Then they were in Arcadia, driving slowly down Oak Street past its brick and block buildings built in the early 1900s. Most of them had ornate spires mortared into their walls and rising high above flat roofs. There was an opera house and a saloon, and all the sidewalks were in the shade of porticoes, iron posts holding them up so you could stroll out of the sun and peer into the front windows of the antique shops and coffee and tea houses and rare book stores or bars, though there were not too many of those. It was as if she and Suzie had gone back to a time before either of them had come to earth, a simpler time, a safer time.

How long had Lois been afraid? A dark presence at her back that never let up, a lack of oxygen in the air, getting up twice in the middle of the night to check on Paul and Suzie in their room? And then, when Paul enlisted in the Air Force and it was just Lois and her granddaughter, it got worse. Lois paid a locksmith to install two more dead bolts on both doors of their arcade apartment. She paid him to put extra latches on the windows, too, and then she hired a carpenter to install iron mesh over the windows on the outside. She promised herself she'd hang flower boxes under them so she could grow ivy to snake up around the metal so it would look less like what it did—but she never got around to it.

One fall afternoon, pulling into their spot behind the arcade from the school bus stop half a mile down Beach Road, Susan said, "Noni, our house looks like a jail."

"It looks *safe* to me, honey. Now help me with these grocery bags."

But Lois never quite felt safe there. Growing up outside Boston in that waterfront town with her Italian aunts and uncles, three brothers, and eleven cousins, her mother and father seemingly in love all the way to the day her mother found her husband dead on the bathroom floor, Lois believed the world to be a good and loving place. Yes, you had to shout to be heard, and somewhere along the way she became the loudest of them all. Not just her voice, but her hair, her breasts that by seventeen were larger than anyone's she knew, her hips and rump. That's the word Gerry had used. Gerry Dubie, a pipe fitter who worked with her brother, Gio. Gerry, who she first saw rising up out of her brother's Chevy in the sunlight, all pompadour and slits-for-eyes and French good looks. Gerry, who wanted to go into business for himself one day. Gerry, who made Lois feel not just loud and loved but prized. Gerry, who gave her Linda and Paul and a life on the ocean.

But Gerry prized other things too, didn't he? He prized the High Hat, and fine suits like Will Price and the other owners wore. He prized convertible Cadillacs and wristwatches with gold bands. And so he started skimming from the slot machines that Lois did not even know were owned by bad men from Rhode Island. There was that morning when it burned her to pee, and the doctor told her it was no bladder infection and he stared down at her through thick glasses with his lips pursed in judgment of her, this married whore. There was throwing a toaster at Gerry's head. There was throwing him out and letting him come home again. Then there was Linda and that ugly boy from the Himalaya and all that happened that never ever should have. But that was a bad road to travel. That's where Lois had begun to lose her very self. No one could go back and change *anything*—not what you said and wished you had not, not what you did or did not do, not what someone else did that you would have stopped if only you'd known. There *was* no knowing.

All those beach bums and barflies starting to sniff the air around Linda only one hour, it seemed, after she'd bloomed at fourteen. But by the time Lois noticed this, it was too late. She'd been too busy worrying about Gerry and running the arcade, little Paul needing her attention, food needing to be bought and cooked, their small, cluttered apartment needing constant care to keep it livable, and—just like that—Linda had slipped away. She'd loved the beach so much and that loud trashy strip, and then Lois was holding her baby's baby in her arms.

Even now, over forty years later, Lois can still see the father as she saw him for the first time. It was one of those gray days when the air was so heavy it was like breathing through a wet sheet. It was August, and the strip was still crowded with families trying to buy some fun wherever they could, and Lois had left Linda in charge of Paul and the arcade while she drove to the IGA for groceries. When she got home and unloaded them, her hair had fallen and her blouse was sticking to her breasts and she needed to change out of it and sprinkle baby powder on her skin. She needed to spray her hair and find something clean and dry to put on. But Paul wasn't sitting in front of the TV where she'd left him, so she opened the door to the arcade and there, amid all the blinking lights and whirring pinballs and clinking slot machines, was her son at the controls of his favorite game shooting men dead, and there was his older sister being held by a grown man.

He was so much larger than she was. He wore a red suit jacket the Himalaya workers wore, and he had both his arms around Linda's narrow back, the strings of her coin apron low across her rear, and it was the way she let him hold her that did something to Lois, like this man was in charge now, like her daughter would do whatever he told her to. Then he glanced up at Lois, and she could see how young he was, barely twenty, with a big nose and eyes set too close together. His face flushed red as if Lois had just caught him doing something shameful, and he looked away and whispered something to Linda then turned and walked back through the arcade out into the gray of the strip, and it was like washing your hands at the sink of a public toilet then raising your eyes to the mirror, but there is no mirror and so you're staring at a wall that for a brief moment has erased your entire existence and you feel robbed and then warned that there'll be more of this kind of thing coming and there's nothing whatsoever you can do about it.

But that feeling lifted here in Arcadia. Standing with Suzie in the shade of that portico in this old cattle town surrounded by pastures and floodplains, Lois knew one thing: Here, she could keep bad things from happening to Susan Lori. Here, only one hour's drive from the Magic Kingdom and its endless lesson in doing things right, she could do for Susan what she had not done for her mother Linda.

The screen came back to life and Lois typed: *I'm sorry, honey. I just opened this today. Of course—*

She stopped. What was she going to write? *Of course you can stay as long as you like? This is your home?* But why this hesitation? Why wouldn't she want Susan to stay as long as she needed to?

Because she brought out the worst in Lois, that's why. Because seeing Susan at forty-three was never having seen Linda at that age. Because to love Susan was to pull her in with one hand and push her away with the other. Because Lois liked herself better when Susan was not living with her.

She typed: *Of course you can stay as long as you like. This is your* **home**.

Love,

She wrote *Lois*, then she deleted it and wrote *Noni*.

Out on Bone River a blue canoe moved swiftly behind the trees. Two men paddled hard from the bow and stern, and a child in an orange life vest sat low in the middle, shouting: "Faster, you guys. Go faster, *faster*."

4

YESTERDAY, SUSAN still hadn't heard from Lois and so she'd told Bobby nothing of what she was planning to do. But while he'd cleaned his office on the campus, she packed her suitcase and pushed it into the back of the closet, then she called him and asked what he wanted for dinner. She felt like cooking.

"You *do*?"

It was Bobby who cooked. It was Bobby who nurtured or tried to, especially when her enemy was sitting in her lap.

"Whatever you want, baby." He took a half breath. "Why'd you cut your hair?"

"I don't know, but I like it."

And she did. Before leaving the house yesterday to shop she didn't even wash it, for it left her feeling reckless in a good way, like she truly did not care what people would think, the same way she did not care whether or not anyone would want to read what had come out of her onto her keyboard as the sun began to rise. And as she pushed her cart down the aisles of the Kroger's, she'd felt set adrift on some current she knew nothing about, but she knew she was going to let it take her anyway.

What she felt was light, some freed bird moving easily now between the trees. Back home, there was the sustaining smell of the chickens cooking in hot olive oil, the cool wet tomatoes and olives beneath her fingertips, then Bobby's big hands on her shoulders as he lightly kissed the top of her head.

She turned and kissed his thumb, and as she lifted the cutting board and scraped the herbs and tomatoes and black olives over the chicken, she knew they would make love later and that she might even enjoy it.

Out on their patio, she and Bobby ate her chicken Provençal on a bed of green beans, the citronella candles flickering beneath their two palm trees. Bobby poured her more wine. "Your enemy on the run?"

"I think so. Yeah, it feels like it."

Later, making love, it was like having been away for a very long time then walking through a door that swings open easily on hinges that no longer creak.

This morning, while Bobby still slept, she went into her writing room and found Lois's email. She'd written it before six a.m. *Of course you can stay as long as you like. This is your* **home.** Something warm opened inside Susan, but it was followed by the cool draft of betrayal, and she moved quickly back into their bedroom and into bed, snuggling in close to her husband.

She woke to Bobby looking at her, giving her that sideways smile of his. "I do like your hair like that, baby."

She could see in his eyes that he was happy she was feeling better, but that he wasn't going to go on and on about it. It was what she appreciated most about him, his giving her room to move. She got up and peed and made coffee. Soon they were sitting across from one another at the kitchen table, her husband pulling out the Arts section of the Sunday *New York Times*. He was talking about how his classes hadn't even begun yet and already one of his students had emailed him to say that he hated the free jazz of Ornette Coleman. It was the man whose work Bobby had been writing about for years, and as he spoke now about his defense of Coleman's theory of harmolodics she watched him, this man she'd married three years ago, this tall, kind, and attentive man whose bald head had a sheen of sweat on it he didn't seem to notice or care about.

"Bobby."

"Yeah, baby."

"I'm going to go live with Lois for a little while."

"Is she all *right*?"

"I think so. I don't know. I guess so." Susan's face felt hot. "It's for my writing." She reached for her cup of coffee but did not pick it up. "I might be writing a memoir, I don't know."

He looked like he wanted her to say more about this, but she did not.

"So why go live with your grandmother?"

"I need to start at the beginning, Bobby."

"But why *live* there again? Won't a little research be enough?"

"Maybe. Probably. I don't know." She looked at him. His stubble was white, his lips parted slightly. He was fifty-three years old, but he appeared to her now as twelve or thirteen, a big, friendly, gangly boy who was preparing himself to be hurt. She felt unworthy of him, and maybe he could see that because now he shook his head and reached across the table and laid his big hand over her wrist. "Follow yourself, baby. Just come home when you're done, okay?" He was smiling at her, though his eyes were not, and it made her want to reassure him in some way, but she could not deny the relief she felt, something big driving by outside in the street.

5

DANIEL WISHES he had never called the Council on Aging today because they're sending him to pick up Rudy Schwartz in Port City and take him food shopping. Rudy is eighty-seven and gets around in a wheelchair. He was a high school mathematics teacher and does everything slowly and precisely, especially when he shops, studying the unit price of each soup can or package of frozen chickens he may put in the cart Daniel pushes alongside him. Rudy is also a cranky son of a bitch who treats Daniel like a paid employee, snapping at him if the cart isn't inches from him and his chair. Daniel prefers some of the old ladies he drives to doctors' appointments. Most of them are warm and chatty, grateful to him for his help and company, and many of them remind him of his mother.

Rudy's apartment complex is on High Street, and Daniel drives slowly down it, the sun high, the sky a deep blue above the maples and roof ridges and telephone lines. He passes all the three-story Federalist restorations, their clapboards as narrow as they were two hundred years ago, though they're four or five years old and painted white and yellow and owned by bankers, doctors, and businessmen. When Daniel was a kid, he knew this town existed five miles south of the beach, that they called it Schooner City because a hundred years earlier it held shipyards that built schooners with tall masts and billowing white sails. But when the world no longer needed clipper ships, they no longer needed this town, and so it had weeds growing up through broken concrete in the sidewalks, the brick buildings along the streets left empty, their windows gone or boarded up. There was no reason to drive over the bridge across the river then, though he still carries with him the flint of a dream of riding with his father in his yellow Impala, the backseat weighted with folded canvas tarps and paint cans and boxes of brushes.

The river stank like sewage then. The paint store was small and dark, but the bar next to it was even darker, and Danny remembers eating two hard-boiled eggs, cold and sour from the jar. His father sat on the stool beside him in a white T-shirt, sipping what Daniel now knows was a glass of Bushmills. Near the door was a narrow window. The sun slanted through it and cast a thin, bright shaft across Liam's hands.

But Port City got reclaimed by professional men and women who knew a good thing when they saw it—narrow streets of old houses on a river three miles from the Atlantic Ocean—and these good people did what good people do, they turned a shithole into a picnic ground, one too expensive for the natives who'd never left it but then had to. Many summer nights, though, Daniel likes to drive down here. He'll back his Tacoma out of his fenced-in lot. He'll head west on Beach

Road past the motels and their one-room cabins and fenced-in pools nobody seems to ever use. He'll pass the camps that were there in his youth, though now people live in them year-round and they have vinyl siding and paved driveways. Where there used to be pine woods, there are now apartment complexes and massive parking lots, and Daniel will ignore these as he turns south on Route 1, passing a seafood restaurant and boat repair shop, a karate studio and fish store and tattoo parlor. Beyond them stretches the salt marsh the sun will be setting into, and as he crosses the bridge over the river, the spangled water below dotted with white motorboats, he'll see on the bank the Harborside Restaurant, its deck filled with families eating at tables beneath striped umbrellas, the men in short sleeves and the women in skirts, some sitting at the outdoor bar sipping drinks and listening to the jazz ensemble in the corner, none of them looking up at the bridge as Daniel Ahearn's ten-year-old red Tacoma passes by, its driver feeling like an interloper, a word he learned only recently when the author of the Adams book had used it and Daniel paused the CD and wrote the word down, pulling his Webster's dictionary from the lamp table beside his bed and looking it up.

Interloper: One that interferes in the affairs of others, often for selfish reasons. One that intrudes in a place, situation, or activity.

On those nights when he parks his truck in the municipal lot of minivans and glossy black SUVs, he does not believe he is intruding on anyone, but as he steps onto the brick walkway for the main thoroughfare of strolling tourists and taxpaying residents, there's the thin-skinned sense that he's snuck in the back door of a party to which he was never invited. And it's in moments like these that he studies his own reflection in the plate-glass windows of pubs and boutiques and sees an aging man with a slight paunch and big hands, a man in a clean button-down shirt and khakis, both of which he ironed earlier in his trailer on the Formica table of his kitchenette. He sees a man wearing eyeglasses, his thinning hair combed back, his face lined in a way that somehow has lessened the prominence of his hooked nose, a tuft of gray hair visible just beneath his clavicle. He could be a retired schoolteacher or an accountant, maybe even a lawyer, a grandfather. *Is* he a grandfather? Or even a *great*-grandfather? These questions are not new.

Your children need your presence more than your presents. These were the words of the Reverend Jesse Jackson, and they were typed on a sheet of paper behind framed glass fixed between two posts in the ground. This was in front of the white clapboard Unitarian church. It was the highest structure in town, its bell tower taller than the Methodist church's shingled cupola in the south end, taller than Immaculate Conception's cross two blocks west, taller than the domed roof of the Greek church to the north.

Daniel had driven over the river into town one night last fall to go walking. From the bridge he could see that all the boats had been stored in marina yards for the winter and the docks had been pulled in, the water flat and gray as it flowed east to the dark lip of ocean at the river's mouth. When he parked his truck in the lot, a young family in matching sweaters walked by. The wife and mother had the curly blond hair of a young girl, and she smiled at him and he smiled back, but still, there was the feeling he was creeping into a good town of nice people where he would never be truly welcome. He tried to ignore this, for a lifetime ago he had accepted that all his invitations were forever canceled, that he was simply no longer *here* at all, which was only right, and that was when he walked by the Unitarian church, *Your children need your presence more than your presents.*

Daniel heard those written words in Jesse Jackson's voice, and it made him think of Pee Wee Jones. It'd been years since Daniel had thought of him. Jones was black, and he stayed away from the Panthers because they were too disciplined for him; the Panthers didn't drink hooch or smoke cigarettes, they wore clean denims and white T-shirts and studied books they discussed in small groups in the yard. But Pee Wee could draw and paint, and one time he did this sketch of a peasant woman he copied out of a book on Russian history. He lived in the Fives and Danny was in the Threes, but one night just before lights-out, Danny was shooting the shit with him in his cell and that's when he saw that sketch taped to his wall just above Pee Wee's bunk. It was the profile of a woman bending low over some task or another, her hair thin and pulled back in a tight bun. She had a hooked nose and her eyes were set deep into her face. Danny said, "Pee Wee, you just drew my *mother*."

Pee Wee knelt on his bunk, untaped that sketch from his wall, rolled it up, and handed it to him. Two days later was May 5, 1980, Susan's tenth birthday. Daniel had been gone over half her lifetime. He never knew if anybody ever read her the letters he sent her, and now he wanted to send her something more. In his own cell, he wrote on the back of Pee Wee's sketch: *This is a picture of your grandmother. I hope you like it. You're **ten** years old! Love, Daddy.*

Or something close to that. He didn't want to ruin the sketch by folding it, but there was nothing else he could do so he folded it carefully and sealed it into an envelope, stamped it, wrote his mother's and father's address on it, and carried it down to Polaski, a screw no one liked because he pushed his weight around and got joy making cons more miserable than they already were. When Polaski found out Willie Teague had a pretty wife, he'd stop Teague whenever he saw him and say, "Your wife's fucking your best buddy right this second, Teague. I mean right *now*. How do you like that?"

Polaski was big, well over six feet and two hundred fifty pounds. Like all the CO's he kept his head nearly shaved, a red stubble smeared across his shiny scalp. He had flat blue eyes and a wide face, and even when he was not tormenting Teague or dropping another con's mail in the mud on purpose or putting a ticket on somebody for insolence if they didn't give him the "proper attitude," then his thin smile always said he was about to and what are you going to do about it?

Danny did not want to give his daughter's gift to Polaski, but he had no choice. It was minutes from lights-out, and Polaski was locking up the steel mesh door at the bottom of the stairs. Danny had to stop on the last step and hold the envelope out to him.

"The fuck is that?"

"For tomorrow's mail."

"For tomorrow's mail, *what*?"

"Sir."

Polaski unlocked the mesh door and snatched the envelope from Danny and stuffed it into his back pocket. "It's lights-out, Ahearn. I could fuckin' write you up."

"I'm going now. Thank you."

"Thank you, *what*?"

"Thank you, sir."

Less than a year later, Polaski would bleed to death not four feet from where he was standing then.

Your children need your presence more than your presents.

On another day, Daniel might have felt unfairly stripped down and admonished by this sign, but that fall evening, the streetlamps flickering on, the smell of pizza dough and woodsmoke in the air, he felt only a melancholy gratitude for the memory of Pee Wee it gave him.

The following Sunday morning was cold and bright, and he was on his way to the German bakery that sold strong coffee and walnut scones. Now there was a new quote fixed to the sign: *Moses said to God, "Where can I find you?" God said, "If you are looking for me, you have already found me."*

Daniel stopped and read it again. A boy on a skateboard passed by so closely Daniel could smell his hair gel and the wool of his sweater. Moses's question: "Where can I find you?" From inside the church came singing, something choral and triumphant. A red beer truck rumbled by in the street. *Where can I find you?* It was as if a sentence that had lain as deeply inside him as the marrow of his own bones had just been pulled from him and tacked to that sign in the sunlight. But it wasn't God he was looking for—there was no God—it was Susan, and it was her mother Linda, and it was even Danny before he became Daniel reading that sign.

The singing stopped. Soon enough the front door of the church

opened, and Daniel stayed where he was and watched the congrega-
tion leave. Grown men and women. A lot of corduroy and sweater
vests, reading glasses and colorful skirts and long gray hair and even
a plump girl carrying a sleeping infant wrapped in a white blanket.

Later, after he'd sat in the bakery sipping his coffee and eating his
scone, he walked up to the tall doors of the church, pulled one open,
and stepped inside. He stood in a plank-floored entryway. One of the
interior doors to the church was open, and he could see empty whitewashed pews, could hear male voices coming from an anteroom off to
the right. Daniel did not know why he'd entered this building. It was
not for God, nor for any of His followers. But what was written on
that sign out front had gone inside him, and now he was slipping on
his reading glasses to peer at a list taped to the wall.

People Helping People
Volunteer Opportunities in the Greater Port City Area

Daniel read the list of agencies and halfway houses. Help for alcoholics
and drug addicts, for poor people and sick people and women raising
kids alone. He thought of all those years ago and his mother-in-law
raising her young son, Paul, and now her granddaughter, Susan. Gerry
ran off after only a year of that. That's what Daniel's mother had told
him in Visiting anyway, though it clearly pained her to talk about the
Dubies at all, so Daniel stopped asking. But he knew Gerry had owed
money to the owners of his poker and pinball machines, serious men
from Providence, and before Danny went down he'd heard something
about a waitress, too, a big-breasted brunette over at the High Hat.

Port City Youth Services*

Daniel began to see some beleaguered woman and her wild kids.
He began to see himself cutting her grass for her, hauling in groceries, sitting down at her kitchen table and helping her son or daughter

do their homework. But of course there was an asterisk beside this agency, and he leaned in closer and saw he'd have to be given a CORI check. Where there were kids, there was this, and even though he'd never been a danger to kids, Daniel knew his history would be discovered and he'd be denied.

He kept reading until he was near the bottom of the sheet: *Elder Services*, no asterisks, the Council on Aging the first one he saw. He studied the phone number, committed it to memory, and left the church before anyone saw him and tried to rope him in.

Just past the State Street intersection, Daniel takes a right and accelerates up the asphalt lane to Rudy's building. The old man is sitting in his wheelchair at the end of the ramp, his shoulders hunched, a scowl on his lined face like Daniel's late when he's at least ten minutes early. Daniel waves, that jagged heat in his hips shooting down both legs.

NOW DANIEL sits at the computer table, sweating from hurrying here from his truck. He feels weak from skipping lunch, and he can feel his heart beating in his dry throat, and he moves the mouse until the screen lights up, and he waits. By the time Daniel pulled up to Rudy's apartment complex and lifted the old man's wheelchair from the bed of his Tacoma it was well after five, and the library closes at six. Two monitors over, an overweight girl with a streak of green hair is tapping away at the keyboard. The older librarian is on duty, standing at the circulation desk reading something on a laptop computer. When he walked in, she glanced up and studied him as if she knew all about him, then she smiled automatically before going back to the small screen. "We close in forty minutes." Part of Daniel was relieved to hear this. He would never be able to find his daughter in forty minutes, but then his face warmed with shame for feeling this relief. But why wouldn't he feel it? If he ever does find her, what then?

The room is cool. He smells the spearmint gum the girl near him is chewing. She keeps tapping one key over and over, and he knows she's playing a video game of some kind. He's stalling and knows that too. He types in Google and waits. But that bright page comes up faster than he expected and now its long, empty bar wants him to fill it with words. There's an aching pressure in his groin that when he was healthy would send him to the toilet, but now he just looks out the window at the lawn, how it narrows into the town's center green where there's a granite monument to those killed when young.

He types *Susan*. Then he types *Dunn*. He presses the enter button and in half a breath one Susan Dunn after another presents herself to him: *Susan Dunn—Interior Designer*; *Susan Dunn—LinkedIn*; *Susan Dunn, Nursing School Faculty, Wideman Community College*. Daniel's heart is a lost fish swimming through his chest. Can that be her? That same little girl who'd pressed her ear to his chest? Daniel sees her as a woman, a stethoscope around her neck as she lectures a classroom full of earnest students. His fingertips have gone numb, and he taps the mouse and opens the file for Susan Dunn the nursing teacher: There's a résumé. A Ph.D. A photograph of a red-haired woman with warm green eyes and a wide smile. Fifty years old, at least. The kind of woman Daniel would want at his hospital bedside, though it is not his Susan, and now he is being pulled down a cold black river, and he begins tapping his way back to the others. There's one who's a psychiatrist in Minnesota. A head doctor. That would make sense too, but when he opens her file there's no photo, and this Susan's résumé has her going to college in the forties. He taps back to the list and scrolls down to a Susan Dunn Facebook page. He clicks it open. There's a photograph of an empty Adirondack chair on a dock on some lake. Beneath that is this Susan's *Favorites*:

Music: *Bobby Vinton, Tony Bennett, Dean Martin, Luciano Pavarotti*
Books: The Bridges of Madison County, *and* The Notebook
Movies: Gone With the Wind

He does not need to read more. This cannot be his Susan. He knows so little about her, but he knows this: she was a teenager in the 1980s, not in the 1950s or '60s, the time this Susan has to come from.

Daniel's tongue feels thick. He needs water. He taps back to all the other Susan Dunns in the world and scrolls below this one's Facebook page and sees: *Susan Dunn—Images.* He tries to swallow but can't. Under this are photographs of six women, but not one of them can be her. Too old, too fair, three of them blond, though his brown-haired daughter could have dyed it, couldn't she? He peers closer at one of them, but she has to be sixty, at least. He clicks the mouse too hard, and the screen freezes. Something loud is rumbling by out in the town square, motorcycles, eight or nine of them. He glances at his watch. Twenty minutes to six. He takes a breath, swallows clammy spit he can feel his heart beating in. He taps the mouse again, this time slowly, the screen opening up into dozens of photographs of Susan Dunn.

His eyes fill. They are all, every single one, women, not a young girl anywhere, but why would there be?

She's forty-three years old. She's forty-three years of age.

He pulls away his reading glasses, but they're his work glasses, still attached to the thin cord around his neck, and he has to wipe at each eye with a forefinger. He lets out a long breath that's louder than he intended. He puts his glasses back on, leans closer, and begins to study one Susan Dunn after another.

Most of the pictures are posed portraits, and Daniel's eyes pass over them too quickly. He has to force himself to slow down and take in each one. There is a blond woman in a dark business suit, staring into the camera with a smile so cold Daniel assumes her to be a state prosecutor. There is a younger woman, her hair short and black, two fingers under her chin like she's just finished writing a book and is still reflecting on it. There are women only in profile, some wearing earrings and some with pearl necklaces, and almost all of them have their hair newly done. There is a Susan Dunn standing at a podium, glasses at the end of her nose as she reads from her speech. On the wall behind her is a blue and gold banner: *National Real Estate Appraisers.* She is the right age, and Daniel squints at the screen then thinks to click the image itself, and yes, it gets bigger, but no, that can't be his Susan because this one's eyes are blue and her nose is too small. He clicks the woman's face, and it gets smaller and he scrolls slowly down, more faces rising up to him, so many Susan Dunns, too many.

"We'll be closing in fifteen minutes."

The older one at the desk. Daniel nods at her over his computer screen. The heavy girl next to him keeps tapping away.

He is thinking about tomorrow. How he will take a day off and come back here first thing in the morning. How he'll stay all day looking at these pictures. There are so many of them. How can there be so many? And now there are a few men, too. A man in a suit and tie. Another in a T-shirt under the sun on a boat. There is a Susan staring at him from a family photograph of her and her husband and five kids, all of them obese. She's the right age. Can they be his? Five fat grandchildren? He clicks the picture and narrows on the woman's face. No, too German. Or Swedish. Even under all that weight, it can't be his daughter. He clicks the picture small again. That word in his head, *daughter*, like a blade all these years, and there, just one row down from the big woman and her big family, is Linda.

The blood inside him stops moving. The tapping of the keys to his left becomes muffled and far away. It is his wife as she would have been if she'd lived another fifteen or twenty years. She is standing outside under the sun in front of a concrete building. Her hair is long and most of it is swept around to hang over her left shoulder. She isn't smiling, but she isn't not smiling, either. She wears a sleeveless cotton dress and no jewelry, her tanned arms hanging at her sides as if she's about to lift them and start running. A hand rests on her shoulder, a group portrait. Daniel's fingertip clicks the mouse. She becomes larger and more beautiful. It is Linda looking up at him in his glass booth at the Himalaya's gate. And it is Susan just before she ran from him to play hide-and-seek. Or just before she would climb up into his lap, her expression unsure but game. It is the daughter he hasn't seen in forty years, and he's found her in less than twenty minutes. The screen becomes a foggy blur. He pulls his work glasses over his head and wipes his eyes against his upper arms and puts his glasses back on. At the bottom of the picture, in small yellow print is: *Susan Dunn, Adjunct Faculty, English.* A teacher. His daughter has become a teacher, a little girl who loved books though Daniel was slow in reading them to her. She preferred Linda to do it, she and her mother lying in bed together, both their heads on the pillow while they stared up at the open book in Linda's hands.

But when was this taken? Where is Susan a teacher? Beside the picture is a small tab: *Visit page.* He moves the cursor to it and taps. The screen turns bright: *Eckerd College, St. Petersburg, Florida.*

Florida. Where Lois moved her after Paul moved out and Gerry left. Where Daniel's parole officer wouldn't let him go, even for a weekend, in August 1988. But why would he have gone south anyway? That letter from Lois the week he got paroled, he kept it for years. It was short and as clear as a bullet, and he'd committed it to memory without wanting to:

Danny,

    It is a crime they're letting you out. I hope they hurt you in there. If you come looking for Susan, you will be sorry. I own a gun and I will use it. Your daughter does not remember you, thank God. She only remembers her loving mother you took from her.

                                          Lois

It was one of the only letters he'd ever gotten behind the walls that did not come from his mother, and it came just days before his release. He'd read it in the yard under the sun. To his right and left, cons came and went. There were the smells of cigarette smoke and dirty hair and sweat. He was not a bad man, but he was. Everything that was in that letter should have been in that letter. He read it three times. He folded it twice and pushed it into the front pocket of his jeans, and he walked through the yard for the Threes and his room and bunk and concrete ceiling on which he would watch his life play out. *I hope they hurt you in there.* That bruised him, not because she wanted him to suffer, but because he had made *her* suffer. Sometimes he forgot about Lois. When he thought of the suffering he'd caused, he thought mainly of Linda's, and he thought of Susan's. And he thought of his own.

"Five minutes, sir." The librarian's voice is closer now. She's flicking off a light switch near the first shelf of books. The video-playing girl is gone, and he seems to be the only one there. On the windowsill to his left is a Salisbury Public Library coffee cup of pencils, beside it a notepad. He takes a pencil and the pad then writes down the main number for Eckerd College. He rips the paper free, folds it into his front shirt pocket, and taps the screen to return to Susan's picture. But the screen stays on Eckerd College and won't move. He slides the cursor to the small arrow at the top of the page and taps that, but nothing happens. There's the smell of perfume. The chair beside him is being pushed squarely to the edge of the table. "I have to shut these down now. We open again at ten tomorrow morning."

He taps the mouse once more, the screen frozen, his beautiful grown daughter just a page away, staring at him, not smiling but not *not* smiling, either, like it's okay to come looking for her. It is.

6

LOIS SAT in her deep chair behind the register craving a cigarette. On the desk beside her notepad a small fan blew warm air directly at her face, though every spring and summer Marianne would nearly beg her for air-conditioning. That was the last thing fine furniture needed. What it needed was a consistent lack of moisture from the five dehumidifiers Don had placed throughout the shop. Their constant humming had become as familiar to Lois as her own breathing, and she leaned back and watched Marianne up front helping a woman decide whether or not she should buy and ship back to Ohio a Biedermeier gilt mirror. Lois was asking $4,500 for it, which would leave her an $1,800 profit, which would be a good Sunday indeed. The woman was pushing sixty, and she was handsome the way wealthy women get, her hair newly done and stiff-looking, her alligator-skin handbag hanging from one wrist like some kind of pesky financial decision. Lois didn't like her, and she was glad Marianne was dealing with her.

The only other customer in the store was a young man in shorts and a polo shirt studying a Wyandotte circus truck from the late 1930s. Its bed was surrounded by a lacquered wooden cage for lions, and it had tiny lettering painted along the top rails that read: *The Greatest Show on Earth*. It also had spoked wheels and had come from an original set, and it was fairly rare. She'd gotten it on eBay for $350, but she wasn't letting it go for less than $450. This boy couldn't be more than twenty-five, a first-time uncle, maybe. That polo shirt of his looked thin at the collar, and she doubted he had the money, so she stayed where she was.

She kept eyeing the pack of Carltons in the folds of her handbag at her feet. She'd had two with her coffee, but it was still only late morning and she liked to have one after lunch, then another two with her wine at the end of the day, and her final one watching TV after dinner. She had to wait.

Out the window past the hot shade of the portico, Oak Street lay fully under the sun. A woman and a teenage girl crossed the asphalt, making Lois think of Susan, and she opened her email again. But there was nothing. She checked her sent file to make sure she did, in fact, answer her this morning, and there it was, that sweet lie. But it wasn't all a lie. She hadn't seen Suzie since Christmas in St. Pete. With her husband Bobby and his bald head and that chaotic jazz music Lois hated. But the way he looked at Susan always put Lois at ease, and he could cook, too, his savory turkey the best she'd had, really. It was a shame they were having trouble, but when did that girl *not* have trouble with men?

"Pardon me."

Up close, the young man looked a bit older, a worn look around the eyes. "How much are you asking for this?"

Not how much *is* this, but how much are you asking? Which meant antiquing wasn't new to him, and he was prepared to negotiate.

"Five hundred dollars."

"Seriously?"

"As a heart attack."

"It's strange you say that."

"Just an expression."

"My grandfather—" The young man looked away, his eyes on the woman from Ohio, though he didn't seem to see her. "My grandfather's sick, he—"

Oh, here it comes. Lois leaned forward.

"His mind is gone, and he only plays with toys."

"That's an expensive toy, honey."

"Can I give you two hundred for it?"

It sometimes came as a surprise to Lois how her body would slip into gear before she'd even made a decision about someone, but here she was up and out of her chair, grabbing the circus truck from the young man's hand and striding behind him to the toy shelves and placing it back beside a Rin Tin Tin Fort Apache play set. From here she could see a stain on the man's front shorts pocket, the kind that comes from carelessness and sloth, but she'd stood a bit too quickly and the floor of her shop felt like a boat on open water. She took a breath and talked right through the swells.

"Save your sob story for someone else, all right? Five hundred means five hundred."

It was the way he blinked at her with both eyes that made her think she might have been wrong about him. Or maybe he just wasn't used to being so easily seen for what he was, a picker or shop owner himself, in from one of the coasts and trying to steal a deal for a handsome profit later. The Sunday after every Fourth Saturday Antiques Fair, there were always stragglers doing that kind of thing, though Lois's Fine Furniture and Toys was the only shop in town worth poaching. No other owner dared to have the word "Fine" over their doors because every other store in Arcadia sold cheap bric-a-brac, the overwhelming heap of it under $300. It's the first thing her fellow antiquers began to resent about her.

"That's cold." The young man shook his head and walked out the front door. The shop righted itself again. Lois settled back into her chair and pictured an old man her age, his liver-spotted hands fumbling with toy soldiers and cars and trucks. Yes, she may have been mistaken this time, but she shrugged it off. It was always better to come off too hard rather than too soft. Always.

Marianne leaned the mirror up against the wall and began to tell the good woman from Ohio all about the Biedermeier period, how it wouldn't have come about if Prince Metternich of the Austrian Empire hadn't cracked down on artists and writers and musicians in the early 1800s.

"So, you see, the creative community turned itself to safer subjects, like the domestic arts and this lovely gilt frame."

Marianne was good, and Lois knew she was lucky to have her. Twenty years younger than Lois and twenty years older than Susan, she was about the age Linda would have been now, sixty-one or -two. Marianne had been married for forty years to the same man, a retired cattle rancher who'd given her a good life in a large post-and-beam house on eight hundred acres of land. They'd raised two sons, one of whom was a lawyer in Miami, the other a musician in Los Angeles, both married with happy kids, and every spring Marianne and Walter flew to Europe and stayed there for a month. Italy one year, Spain the next. Last year it was the French countryside. Marianne, like Lois, had no college, but she was a reader, and whenever Lois acquired something new from an estate or an auction or online, Marianne would do research on it on the Internet. She'd even drive into Tampa or St. Petersburg and check out books from their libraries. It's the thing she said she loved the most about selling objects from the past, how much they taught her about human history.

Lois couldn't disagree with this. She, too, had grown to appreciate what her antiques could tell her. Like her 1920s Sue Herschel collection of marionettes. They were on shelves beside the tin toys across from Lois's desk, and she found herself staring at them quite a bit. She owned eleven of them, six men and five women, the men in wool pants with suspenders, or baggy three-piece suits and straw boaters. Her women, on a shelf of their own, were all flapper girls with gloved hands and cigarette holders and cloche hats. Just before the Depression, Herschel wrote and directed plays but got tired of putting up with drunk actors, so she started making puppets and ended up years later running a crew of over fifty artists who made close to three thousand Herschel marionettes. They were used by dozens of theater companies around the country and even performed at the White House for Dwight D. Eisenhower. But most of them got lost along the way, or burned, or eaten by beetles and termites, and there were only a few left, and they were the first "fine" things Don had acquired for Lois's Fine Furniture and Toys.

"Wonderful, I'll just wrap this up for you, then."

That a girl.

Marianne brushed a strand of gray from her eyes and carried the Biedermeir mirror past Lois, winking at her on the way to the back room and the bubble wrap and tape. Lois nodded and closed her laptop. She waited for the woman from Ohio to make her way to the register, though she was taking her sweet time doing it. It's what antiques did to people. Whether you thought you were interested or not, they were as hard to ignore as your own aging face in the mirror. The woman's handbag hung at her side. She was running two fingers along the oilskin surface of a walnut plantation desk. It was made sometime during the Civil War, and its back had secret cubbyholes, and there were still scorch marks beneath the varnish from the candles its owners used while writing letters late into the night. Lois's shop was filled with hundreds of these objects, and how many hours and hours over the years had she sat alone with them? She had bought this business to make a living for her and Suzie, but she never could have known that old things would give her far more than a sale here and there. For years it was just enough to get by and build her collection one piece at a time, but then word finally spread and she had to hire Marianne to help, and even when real money started coming in, it was something else altogether that Lois enjoyed: Sitting in the heart of her pedestal tables and Viennese armchairs, her Biedermeir chests and nightstands and side tables, her ebonized commodes and miniature vitrines, her walnut writing trumeaus and hand-carved nesting tables and rosewood settees, her shelves of children's toys loaded with Kilgore trucks and Schoenhut dark horses, a Cox Shrike gas-powered tether car, cast-iron wagons and horses and a windup musical doghouse made in Switzerland, it was like sitting in front of a fire while someone old and strong told you one story after another, each as good as the one before it, each different but somehow the same, too. And how many of these beautiful things had been made during times of war? In times of mass sickness and death and floods and droughts? And yet, men and women still made them. That did something to Lois. She wasn't sure what it was, but that thought always stopped her, and often after closing she'd linger in her chair behind the register in no hurry to go home, especially when Susan was a teenager, especially then. For here, surrounded by so many fine things made by the dead, Lois could for once breathe easy, and she no longer felt afraid.

"To whom do I write the check?"

It was living people who ruined everything.

"No checks. Cash or credit only, please."

The woman had been pulling a leather-bound checkbook from her purse. She paused and raised her eyes to Lois. "Pardon me?"

"We don't take checks. Cash or credit."

Lois could hear her own tone, and she knew she should warm it up or she could very well lose this sale, but she did not like this woman from Ohio. She didn't like how the emerald studs in her ears matched the emerald pendant over her sun-freckled chest. She didn't like her manicured nails or her gold bracelets, and she certainly did not like how new it seemed for this lady to be denied *anything.*

"But, I assure you—"

"Cash or credit only."

The woman pursed her lips and narrowed her eyes slightly. In her scrutinizing presence Lois felt just like what she was: coarse, uneducated, and a little cruel. She also felt fat and old and without a man, which was how it would probably always be now, wouldn't it? She also felt right, and she wasn't budging.

"Very well, then." The woman pulled out an alligator-skin wallet and opened it to a compartment holding ten or twelve credit cards. She slid out a platinum one and handed it to Lois just as Marianne came around the corner from out back, the Biedermeier mirror completely taped up in bubble wrap.

"Here you are." Marianne was smiling widely, a sheen of sweat along her hairline.

"But won't you be shipping it?"

Does this look like the post office? Those were the words in Lois's head, but she was running the card through, and an $1,800 profit didn't come every day. She could feel the blood go tight in her veins, though, her mouth go dry, and she wanted that Carlton right now. Marianne was explaining that we're not set up to do that kind of thing. "But there are two UPS stores in Port Charlotte about twenty miles south of us. Do you have a GPS?"

"Of course I have a GPS. I just thought for what I'm spending, shipping was included."

Lois could feel her heart beating in her earlobes. "Nope." She ripped the receipt from the machine and pushed it and a pen to the woman. "'Fraid not."

The woman, whose name on her credit card was Anne Langely, glanced down at the receipt as if Lois were displaying something obscene.

I don't work for this rich bitch. If I lose this sale, then I lose this sale.

Anne Langely snatched up the pen and scribbled her name and put her hand out for her credit card. Lois handed it to her, smiling.

Anne Langely stuffed it back in with the others. "I don't like your tone."

"That makes two of us."

Again the pursed lips and slightly narrowed eyes. *Would she or wouldn't she?* Then Anne Langely hooked her alligator-skin bag over one shoulder. She turned to Marianne and lifted the wrapped mirror with both hands and held it close to her chest like a good schoolgirl. She said to her: "You shouldn't have this woman working for you. She's a disgrace."

"It's my shop, not hers." Lois grabbed her Carltons. "You have a nice day, now." She brushed by Marianne, through the back room and outside. The heat smelled like grill smoke, and as she lit her cigarette she could hear tinny mariachi music from two or three blocks over. Anne Langely could very well reach her car with that Biedermeier mirror then change her mind and bring it back and cancel her purchase, but so what? It had been a good month. Marianne would lose a commission, but who else in town paid their help 10 percent commissions in the first place? Nobody. So Lois would have to take a loss and then write Marianne a check for $180, big deal. But she'd be damned if she was going to get patronized by anyone.

You scare people away, Lois. You act like they're barging into your house. Don again. It'd been years since she visited his grave. He was buried in the Lamson family plot up north in Ocala, a depressing

spit of land under some mangy pine trees, his big body wedged into a
box just a few feet from his mother and father who he swore despised
one another their entire sixty years together. His little brother Arthur
was buried there, too, killed in Vietnam, that war the whole country
was fighting about when Lois was raising Paul and Linda. It saddened
her that that's where Don wanted to be, but where else could he go? In
back of their house under her oaks near Bone River?

And where was *she* going to go? Not in Ocala, and not beside her
lousy ex-husband up north, nor beside her mother and father. No, it
would be with Linda. It would be where her daughter went, though
just the thought of those ocean waves lifted the ground beneath Lois's
feet, and she had to sit quickly in her lawn chair under the rusted iron
landing above.

Resting on one of its flaking steps was the empty coffee can she
used as an ashtray. Lois stared at it, saw her husband Gerry wading
into the surf in his suit, that obscenely small can under his arm. She
shook her head and flicked her ash. Across the dirt lot, smoke drifted
through the hickory trees, and she could smell grilling pork or bris-
ket, the mariachi music changing over to that Tejano all the Mexicans
here liked. It had accordions in it and electric guitar too, a woman
singing in Spanish, and then an engine revved, one of those low-riding
trucks the young kids would work on when they weren't picking citrus out in the groves. When she and Suzie got here thirty years ago,
there were only a handful of Mexican pickers and their families, but
now Lois and Marianne and most of the white shop owners here were
a minority, especially on a Sunday, the only day the Mexicans didn't
work and Arcadia became a Mexican village and Lois didn't like it.
Don said she was a racist, but he was wrong. Lois was afraid they'd
scare away deep-pocketed customers, that's all. Other shop owners
were, too. They'd had meetings about it. Don had argued that the only
crime here was between *white* ranch hands shooting at each other
when they were drunk. Lois couldn't disagree with that, really.

But that Soto boy. Gustavo Soto. His high cheekbones and dark eyes and scuffed, pointed boots. He'd come to their house only once. It was a Sunday, and he'd pulled up in a battered El Camino. He wore a straw cowboy hat, his best western shirt tucked into his jeans, a single blue violet between two fingers, and when he stepped up to their front door he took his hat off and held it low in front of him, his chin down but his eyes on the door for Suzie.

Susan was sixteen but looked twenty. She'd started wearing sundresses, which nobody her age wore. She'd let her brown hair grow long, and she wore too much eye makeup and too many bangles on her wrist, and she'd been sitting in the den with one of her books, chewing gum and acting like it was normal to be all dolled up on a Sunday. Lois opened their front door before Suzie did.

"How *old* are you?"

He didn't say a word. Just looked at her the way you would look at a dog you weren't sure was about to bite or not.

"Do you speak English? I asked you a question."

"Yes, he speaks English, Lois. Jesus Christ." And Susan was stepping past her and hooking her arm in Soto's, taking the violet from him as he turned and nodded once at Lois and put his hat back on as they hit the ground, and he might as well have been that big ugly boy in a red Himalaya suit jacket holding Linda in the arcade, his eyes on Lois over her daughter's shoulder, and— No. Just *no*.

Lois's blood began to hum. "Hey! Where do you think you're *going*?"

Lois was in her mid-fifties then, heavy and smoking heavy, but she was running around the hood of the El Camino before the boy had started his engine. She reached inside and tried to yank the keys from his hand, but he held on tight and Suzie was screaming, "Let go, Noni! We're just going for a fucking *ride*!"

"No you don't." Lois had both hands on his wrist, but he was strong and jerked free of her and she almost fell on her rump as the engine sprang to life and shot into gear and the El Camino drove off, spitting dirt and dead pine needles under its tires onto the county road.

It was war after that.

One exhausting battle after another.

Lois inhaled deeply on her Carlton. She was sweating and thirsty and knew her blood pressure was up. She was also still tired. It had been a good morning. Maybe she'd close early for the day. Give Marianne her bonus and just go home for lunch and a nap.

"Lois, can I talk to you about something?"

Oh, Jesus, what now? "Was I too much of a bitch to that bitch?"

"Well, . . ." Marianne folded her arms beneath her breasts. She wore a yellow-and-white-striped blouse with pearls, and today she looked old.

"Marianne." Lois exhaled smoke. "I've had to work my whole life. I won't have some tourist from Ohio talking down to me in my own shop."

"I didn't think she was that bad."

"Well, she was."

"But, Lois, that was my sale, and—"

"You know I'd pay your bonus anyway. Haven't I done that before?"

"It's not just that. I—"

"Come out with it." Lois stubbed her cigarette out on the step and dropped the butt into the coffee can.

"People talk."

"So let them."

"But Lois, our rating has dropped from four stars to two, and it's—"

"Look." Lois braced her hands on the arm of the chair and stood slowly this time. "I'm pooped from yesterday, and I need to rest. If you want to stay open, feel free."

"Lois." Marianne still had her arms crossed. She looked frustrated and disappointed, and, truthfully, she was probably Lois's only real friend.

"Our business isn't down, is it?"

"No, but—"

"Enough said. I'm going home."

Somewhere in the neighborhood off Oak Street a man and woman were laughing. The Tejano singer seemed to be singing a ballad now, her voice nearly breaking with sadness, and Lois knew she should congratulate Marianne on her sale today, but she moved by her without saying another word. She didn't like being scolded. She never had. But once she was back in the old-wood-smelling dimness of the shop, she hoped Susan really would come visit this time. She hoped that she wasn't just talking.

7

BOBBY WAS leaning against the stove in one of his faded Hawaiian shirts. He held an empty coffee cup in his hand and still hadn't shaved. It was midafternoon, and the gray light coming in from the window made his skin bluish. He looked pathetic to her. God, what was she doing? But wasn't this a good sign? That she was starting to care again?

"I'm afraid you won't come back." He smiled down at her and shook his head and she stepped to him and he hugged her too hard for too long, his cup clattering to the floor. The skin of his neck smelled vaguely sweet, like fruit right before it starts to turn. It was a scent that had never pulled her closer to him or pushed her away, either, and there was the floating sense that she was watching this moment rather than living it. She pulled back, but her husband's big hands were still on her hips. He was staring at her shorn hair. "My muskrat."

She kissed his cheek. She grabbed her computer bag and stepped through the open doorway, the smells of dried palm fronds in the air, her tall, stoop-shouldered husband standing on the threshold, watching her walk quickly to her car.

Soon she was driving onto the Skyway Bridge, Tampa Bay stretched out to her left and right. A freighter ship was moving slowly out to sea, its cargo containers yellow-and-rust-colored under the sun. There were Lois's words to her. *This is your home.* But leaving her husband behind, driving toward the floodplains and cattle country of Arcadia, her laptop zipped up in its case in the backseat, it was as if Susan were on that freighter ship herself, curled up in the dark in a steel container heading who knows where. But at least she wasn't giving in this time. At least she was trying to do something about it.

SUSAN SAT on the top step of her grandmother's front porch, waiting for her. It was close to five but still hot, the air heavy with the smells of dead pine needles and the long dirt driveway she'd steered down nearly thirty minutes ago. She was sweating and wished she hadn't worn jeans and, of course, the front door was locked, as was the one to the back screened porch. When she'd checked it a few minutes ago, she was tempted to walk down through the pine and oak trees to the clay banks of Bone River, but there was that cottonmouth she'd written about yesterday morning, the ghost of her fifteen-year-old self dropping her smoking cigarette and running barefoot back home.

Home. It had never really felt like that to her. Living with her grandmother in this glorified camp in the woods from twelve to eighteen had felt strangely temporary, as if they were both on the run and it was only a matter of time before they would get caught.

She should write that down. She'd pulled her Honda up onto the grass to give Lois her parking space, and now Susan leaned into it and pulled her notepad and pencil off the passenger's seat. She drank warm water from a plastic bottle, the taste of it like the bottle itself. She flipped the pad to the notes she'd already begun to take, impressions, really.

- the high school is the same yellow brick and looks like a prison
- the Taco Bell is now a Lowe's. All the palm and acacia trees are gone

- Gustavo's old house is just a field of weeds behind a rusted chain-link fence. Half of it is leaning toward the ground like a car drove into it and drove off
- The citrus workers' houses still look like shit, though some of them don't
- The Bone River Campgrounds? Doing it w/Gustavo in his car? Getting caught by Lois
- The orange and lemon groves stretching out around this shit town on all sides? How beauty is free unless you can't see it? I could see beauty, but I always felt so trapped.
- By Noni? Yes. And by my enemy.
- Books helped. Books always helped

Susan wrote: *Living with Noni felt like living on the run. No, not on the run. In exile. Like we'd both been exiled.*

Susan set her notepad back on the passenger's seat. She needed to pee. Some kind of bird shrieked out in the woods behind the house. If Lois didn't turn down that driveway soon, she was going to call her. No, she shouldn't be too pushy or expectant in any way. With Lois it was best to lie low and let her direct things. It's what Lois did. It's what she always did best.

8

DANIEL LIES on his bed in front of the fan staring at the photograph of Susan Dunn. Right after work and before a lunch he did not want, he drove to the library and found her image again, printed it out, and taped it to the trailer wall, the photo's lower corners flapping softly in the electric breeze. Its colors are faded and the features of her face are not as clear as they were on the computer screen, but it's still what Linda would have become, it's still their Susan. At the bottom of the page, he tacked the phone number for Eckerd College he'd written down the day before, but he doesn't look at it.

For a moment, Daniel considers just letting it go, the way he has again and again for years. But there has always been the shadow-weight of her small cheek and ear pressed to his chest, her high, loving voice: *It's so loud, Daddy.* He was a young man then, just a kid, really, twenty-two or -three, and he needs to tell her that before he's gone. He needs her to know that he's no longer the boy who did what he did. He needs his daughter to know that there was always more to his heart than whatever she heard there.

Your daughter does not remember you.

Of course he had more than considered this, worried it like a sore on his tongue. Why *would* she remember him? When *he* was three, what did he remember of Liam? His bony lap? The hot paint colors under his nails? His silence as he sat at the table and ate whatever Daniel's mother had cooked for him? If Liam had disappeared when Danny was three, he would be only the ghost of a dream and no more.

She only remembers her loving mother you took from her.

Did she? He hoped so. Linda had been a good mother. The best. Daniel hoped Susan remembered her: the heart-shaped pancakes Linda made for her, the way she called her Suzie Woo Woo, the way she washed and combed and braided her hair, the reading to her at night, and how, if they were walking into the carnival noise of the beach after supper, Linda would carry Susan and would only let her walk if she and Danny were both holding her hands.

Danny carried her a lot too. He'd lift her onto his shoulders and press one hand up against her back, Susan's sticky palms on his fore-head and sometimes in his eyes. When Susan laughed or yelled over the noise of the crowd and the rides and the arcade machines, Danny would feel the vibration of her voice through her chest at the back of his head. Like the inside of his head was her home.

There were so many moments like that one. Once, playing hide-and-seek in their three-room cottage two streets from the water, Daniel had taken his time finding her behind the couch. He kept calling her name, calling it and calling it, Susan giggling in her hiding place. He lifted the chair and put it noisily back down. He did the same to the potted plant on the windowsill. "Susan? Suzie Woo Woo?"

Then he sat heavily on the couch and covered his face and pretended to cry. In seconds a small hand was touching his arm. "Daddy? Don't be sad. I'm here. *See?* I'm *here!*"

Lying on his bunk back at the Threes, that old question kept turning in him like a rusty auger. Did they ever tell her what he'd done? Not when she was still a child, because that would have been an abuse Lois and even Gerry weren't capable of, but what about when she got older? Fifteen, sixteen years old? Gerry was long gone then, but Daniel pictured Lois sitting Susan down at some table or on her living room sofa. Lois was where the beauty came from. She'd always been a big woman, but everything in her face lined up just right, eyes to nose to cheekbones to mouth. When Danny and Linda started out, Lois wore her hair up high the way women did then, and she wore heavy black eyeliner and black shit in her lashes, her lipstick a pink that would fade to white. But it would have been the mid-eighties when Susan was fifteen or sixteen, and what words would have come out of Lois?

Honey, there's something you should know.

What, Noni?

It's almost what Italians called their grandmothers, but when Susan was two she couldn't say Nonna, only Noni, and it'd stuck. Daniel tried to see his daughter in this scene. Her hair and face. Braces, maybe? Loose jeans like he heard they wore then? Maybe polish on her fingernails? Thin bracelets on her wrist? Did she have a boyfriend? Did he treat her right? This question inside him so right but so goddamned wrong, coming from him, that when he thought it he broke out in a sweat as instantly as if he were sick.

But the thing is, he could not picture Susan like this at all. Instead he saw her only as he'd last seen her. In her red shorts, getting jerked from his arms by one of the cops standing in his bedroom.

That afternoon of Lois's letter in 1988, Daniel still did not know she'd raised Susan in Florida, so Daniel pictured Gerry and Lois's apartment in the rear of the Penny Arcade. It was one big open room with two bedrooms in the opposite ends. A long black Naugahyde couch separated the TV area from the kitchen, which was small, not enough cabinets, the rear of the counters lined with cans of Spam and soup, tuna and sardines, boxes of crackers and dried spaghetti, cellophane-wrapped loaves of bread. There was a green Formica table with chrome legs and matching chairs, and in the middle of it was the large clamshell ashtray overflowing with Chesterfield butts from Gerry, Carltons from Lois. Next to this was a hula girls set of salt and pepper shakers, tiny holes in the tops of both their heads just above a hot-pink garland of flowers.

Did Lois allow Susan to keep his name? Daniel doubted it. Maybe before she was this beautiful Susan Dunn staring at him from her college in St. Petersburg, Florida, she was Susan Dubie. And maybe that's where Lois began.

What, Noni?

Your first last name was Ahearn. It would be hard for Lois to utter his name, but she would do it, blowing smoke out the side of her mouth like a curse. *It belonged to your father.* But Daniel could never or would never allow the rest of this moment to unfold on the ceiling above him. Because if Lois did tell Susan where he was, then that would mean his daughter did not want to see him or have contact with him in any way because she never came to visit and she never wrote him a letter.

He did not blame her for this. How could he?

He should write all this out for her. He has tried before, but then he had no solid notion of where she might be. The act had felt as useless as writing something he'd seal in a bottle and throw into the Atlantic. But he knows where she is. And so he should write something first, then send it to her, then call her. He can't just be some voice on the wire after so long. Whole lives have come and gone since he last saw her.

He sits up too quickly, spinning brown plates crowding his vision. He inhales deeply through his nose, smells the burned butter from his grilled cheese sandwich he only stared at, the pine sap through his screened windows. It's another hot day and his T-shirt sticks to his back, the revolving fan pushing around nothing but warm air.

In the drawer beneath the toaster, under loose pens and pencil stubs and the broken calculator, is the small pad on which he multiplies his price times the number of chair holes, and he pulls out the pad and one of the newer pens and sits at the table. He stares at the straight blue lines and all that empty space between them. He gets up slowly and fills himself a glass of water. He sits back down.

The whir of the fan, the shriek of a crow in the trees. He leans forward and writes:

Dear Susan

He crosses this out.

My dear Susan

No, this sounds too much like she's his. That he deserves her.

Susan

No. Too cold.

My daughter Susan

Yes, that's better. It's the truth. But it's still too cold.

My dear daughter Susan

That's right, isn't it? All four words in that order? Though there's still the feeling he's claiming something that is no longer rightfully his. Then start with that. Why not start with that?

*Ive got no right to call you these things. But even with everything that happened you **are** my daughter. Our daughter.*

Your mother was a very good mother. I hope you remember that about her. She did not deserve

He stops.

That hot, smoky kitchen. The overhead light missing one bulb so it was never bright enough in there. And Linda, she had had it. She was screaming and she was leaving and it was like being told your heart and organs are about to go for a little ride and you have no say in it. None whatsoever.

Forty years have passed and Daniel still wonders if they had been in any other room if things might have gone differently. Didn't she know what her leaving would do to him? But how could she? In their four years he had tried to tell her, but words had never come easy for him, and everything he did tell her sounded to his own ears like weak wind through a cardboard box. They'd be lying naked side by side in their narrow bed, her back to him, Danny's arm over her shoulder, his penis softening, his face in her hair. He'd say: "I wasn't alive till you." Or, "What I feel for you is, I don't know, so damn *big*." Did he tell her that? Did he tell her that daily he was afraid he couldn't hold it all?

Jimmy Squeeze's brother Bill. He didn't have Jimmy's muscles, but he was taller than all of them and he had a deep voice like Danny's, and he smiled a lot. Two times Danny had passed the Penny Arcade, pushing his old man's cart full of paint buckets and rollers and brushes and tarps and rags, and he caught Linda smiling up at Jimmy's brother, her small hands in the canvas pockets of her change-and-token apron, Bill telling her some private little story or joke that, seeing them like that, Danny just knew was about him and wasn't good.

Though what could Bill have told her? Danny had always stayed to himself, and so there wasn't much that could be said. Even when he became "The Sound" of the Himalaya. He would dress and climb up into the plexiglass booth and take to the microphone, but he never went drinking with the ticket takers later. There might be trouble and Danny had never liked trouble. Maybe it was from all those days he was sent home from school with swollen knuckles, his mother waiting for him with food and his comic books and that loving look in her eyes, like she somehow knew her son was going to have one of the hard lives, and she had to give him strength any way she could.

Until the Himalaya, Danny had begun to feel that, too. That his life would be lived on the edge of things, that he wasn't going to get what the others would. But when the rides shut down around midnight he took his time walking back to the Sea Spray because he still had on his white pants and red jacket and people nodded respectfully in his direction or smiled at him just because of what he'd done all night over the Himalaya's gate, all the beach rats acknowledging him like he was somebody, it was like when a fever breaks and you're sitting on your couch and you can feel the strength come back into your arms and legs; maybe he'd just moved too much from town to town and there was nothing wrong with him at all. Maybe he just needed to stay still long enough for somebody to notice him, an important man like Will Price.

And a girl like Linda Dubie.

Because there she was just after midnight only hours after she'd stared up at him in his booth. She was smoking a Camel under the orange light of Joe's Playland, one arm folded under her breasts, her hair loose over her shoulders. There were always a couple of police cruisers parked in front of the Frolics. Still, she shouldn't have been there alone. She was wearing that thin gold chain, and her bell-bottoms were tight and flaring out wide over leather sandals and her bare toes. When she saw him, she seemed to straighten a little. She held her burning cigarette low at her hip, one arm still crossed in front of her. Was she *waiting* for him? *Him?* The boy with the bad skin and hooked nose and eyes too close together? Because that's all that came to him as he slowed and looked over his shoulder for who she must really be waiting for. But there was only the wooden railing that bikers would park their Harleys and Nortons against during the day, the littered sand and black surf beyond, a drunk lying faceup mouthing words in the air.

"You Danny Ahearn?"

"Yeah." His voice sounded too cold to himself, testy and wrong. He stopped and stepped into the warm light of Joe's Playland. "And you live behind the arcade."

"How'd you know that?"

"I seen you making change there."

"That don't mean I live there." Her tone was tough, like most of the girls in these beach towns, but there was a softness behind it and some kind of tiredness, like she'd had it being one way and was hungry for another.

"It's the strip. Everybody knows everybody's business, right?"

He may have said something like that, Daniel doesn't remember, but he remembers Linda's small face under those orange bulbs over the sign for Joe's Playland. He remembers how dark that made her eyes, how long her throat looked, the dull glint of that thin gold chain resting on her clavicle. And he remembers what she said: "You're the best one they ever had."

She took a last drag of her cigarette, dropped the butt, and stubbed it under her sandaled foot. She blew the smoke out her nose and stepped off the sidewalk into the Midway that cars cruised around day and night. On the other side was the cluster of shops and kiddie rides and arcades, and Danny fell into step alongside her.

"I'll walk you home."

Weeks later, curled on his couch together, Danny's mother and father in bed hours earlier, Linda told him that's what did it for her, that he didn't ask if he could walk her home, he just told her he was going to.

That was her big mistake. She thought he was strong, and for a while, because she believed this about him, he did too. Out of all the boys on the strip, Linda Dubie had chosen him, Danny Ahearn, who at nineteen was already saving to rent or buy a cottage of his own. And the thing is—and how could Daniel ever write this to their grown daughter?—he and Linda couldn't stay away from each other.

Their first kiss was under the Frolics at high noon. The beach was crowded with the flesh of families, transistor radios playing rock and roll or baseball out of Boston, Frisbees spinning through the air, some hitting an umbrella or the open mouth of a running dog, the endless pounding surf, the sand too bright under the sun to look at without squinting, but there, under the Frolics, Linda's back against one of the wooden piers, a ring of dried barnacles above her head like a crown, it was cooler there and except for two hippies sleeping on an Indian blanket thirty feet away, Danny and Linda were alone. She leaned toward him and parted her lips, and though he had never kissed anyone before, kissing her then had felt like something he'd done every single day of his life with her and her only but a thousand years ago and they were picking up where they had left off so it felt new: her taste and her smell, they were kind of sweet the way pine is sweet, something with roots that go into you and spread out, and there was no end to wanting more of it, their tongues going deep, and she seemed to need him as much as he needed her, but there was nowhere to go. Both their mothers would be at home, so Danny was leading her through the bright sun and screeching of gears and yelling, laughing kids and tinny canned music, the smells of fried clams and hot asphalt and car exhaust, her small hand in his, his hardness an ache he tried to cover with his other hand. He was probably wearing cutoff jeans and she was too—they all did then—and because it was a Saturday the Himalaya was open and Price's son Ricky was up in the DJ booth, his voice okay but not deep enough, the purple cars full of happy faces whizzing around their track, and Ricky was playing "Sugar, Sugar" because he only played the top three hits on the charts over and over again, then Danny was ducking under the chain with Linda, her brown hair falling across her face, her eyes curious and eager, then under the Himalaya itself, the music buried now under the muffled rumble of the cars above them, the screams muffled too, and in the dark corner there, Danny's back against the plywood wall, their thousand-year-old kisses began again and he has no memory of either of them pulling off their shorts and underwear, just Linda's warm soft bottom under his hands, his sinking into her a homecoming somehow, her tongue in his mouth as they rocked, the rattle and rumble and screams above, just a wisp of "Sugar, Sugar, honey, honey" as he filled her with the only thing he could give her and maybe the only thing she'd ever really wanted from him.

Daniel writes: *What is done cannot be undone.*

He reads it, then crosses it out three times. Ronnie Dee used to say something like that all the time. He was a con in the Twos, and he was skinny and white and chain-smoked Lucky Strikes. He also had the book on hockey, but then one of the Italians from Springfield, Tommy Gardino, lost ten cartons of cigarettes on a Flyers game and Dee made the mistake of trying to collect. At Norfolk, they called the yard "the quad," clipped grass between sidewalks cons weren't supposed to step off of or congregate on, and that cold afternoon between schooling and work, Danny heading down to the barbershop, Dee was standing in front of Gardino and one of his boys, pulling hard on a cigarette, pointing his finger at Gardino's face. "What's done is done, Tommy. That's it." And when Dee walked away, Danny knew Ronnie Dee had probably just smoked his last cigarette, stood under his last patch of sky, smelled his last hit of grass and dirt and his own sweat. Two nights before, they'd been served cold pork chops in the mess hall, and there was still some gristle left on the long bone they found in Ronnie's chest less than one hour after he told Gardino what is done is done.

Daniel stares at the sentence he just crossed out. He writes: *undone.* There is little he does not know about that word. He has lain down with it since he was twenty-four years old, or no, it has lain with him, a thick chain around his neck pinning him to the bottom of a black sea. Nothing can be reversed. This he knows.

Susan, I used to be Danny.

You're a grown woman now so maybe I can tell you this. Danny was all blood and body. Danny didn't know how to think or sit back. Danny was a reactor. When he was a kid he used to read comic books but he could of been a hero of one himself and you could call it "The Reactor." His family moved around a lot and Danny was always the new kid and you may know what happens to new kids. But Danny would only take it for a half-minute or two maybe less and then the meltdown would start inside him though nobody could see it until it was too late. It was like the inside of him was white heat at all times and any slight that came his way and a button would get pressed by a part of him Danny couldn't seem to control and the walls would come down and the white heat would gush out and people would get burned.

Daniel reads over what he's just written. He doesn't like it. But he doesn't like it because it's true, so he keeps writing.

Your grandmother knew that about Danny and she was always trying to keep him cooled down. She loved him see? She loved him so much and she thought if she just kept covering him with coats of love it would dry into a hard shiny shell and no more heat could escape. But then I—but then Danny found another kind of love and every-thing got messed up. Your mother—

Daniel crosses out those last two words. He writes: *Linda Dubie was the most beautiful woman on the strip except she didn't know this. I don't know what she thought. Even now I wish I could tell you what she thought of herself. She was quiet like my old man was quiet. (Your grandfather Liam was an artist you probably know. The man who kept the beach magic looking.) But Linda's quiet wasn't cold it was warm. It was always warm. She smiled at us a lot. You and me. You'd be on my lap on the couch in front of the TV and Linda—your mother—wouldn't be watching the show. She'd be sitting in that hard chair against the wall just smiling at us. She had these dark eyes. Like yours. Like your picture I got off the computer at the library. You have her beauty that's the thing. She was a looker and I was too weak to allow that.*

Daniel stops. He's sweating, and his mouth is dry, and he glances behind him to his bed and Susan Dunn's picture taped to his wall. It doesn't feel right to be telling her all this, but it doesn't feel wrong, either. She's not a kid anymore. Maybe she never was because of him.

He writes: *We'd be out walking the strip. Sometimes I put you on my shoulders or when you were still a baby your mother held you in one of those slings the hippie girls liked to carry their babies in back in those days.*

Daniel pauses. He can still feel baby Susan in his palms, her tiny bottom and legs. Where he's going with his pencil right now can only get bad, and he wants to shield that baby from it, but it comes to Daniel that if he's learned nothing else he's learned one thing: the truth is the truth and whether you want to dig it up or not, it always makes its way back to the surface.

He writes: *Even out as a family like that the men would give your mother the twice-over. Sometimes we'd leave you with Lois and Gerry and that's when it really got to me. When men see a good looking woman with another man it's different. She's all woman to them then and they want her to themselves and now I was getting looks like I didn't deserve your mother. This one afternoon. It was the end of the season right before Labor Day and your mother and you had been on the beach while I worked with your grandfather painting. No. Maybe by then I was out on my own. I'd bought a shit box truck and I was trying to build my own painting business down in Port City. Anyways it was a Friday afternoon and I was done early and your mother had just put you down for a nap at Lois and Gerrys place behind the arcade. Linda was wearing flip flops and a skirt and just a bikini top. Her skin was brown and her stomach was flat and the way she carried herself with her long hair down her back well I shouldn't be writing these things to you but she had a beauty that could crack your heart. And she must of seen the looks she got from the strip boys and from the family men sneaking a second or third look when their own wives who seemed invisible to me were busy buying fried dough or a cheap t-shirt. But I don't think she did. Linda liked to hold Danny's hand and she liked to get a slice and sit on one of the benches on the Midway and eat it and watch the loud sunburned world go by.*

Like I said she didn't talk much but when she did it was all about you. Suzie Woo Woo. That's what she liked to call you. She said you were smarter than she was and she was proud of that. That's one thing you should know too. Linda quit school when she was 16. Gerry and Lois weren't happy but Linda couldn't do it anymore. She used to tell me. She used to tell Danny she didn't see the point. Anything she wanted to learn she could get from books and anyways she was going to run the arcade. See she loved the beach and the strip. Even the off-season when the cottages were boarded up and the rides were locked and snow blew in drifts down the Midway. I think she also got shit from other girls at the high school. Don't forget Linda was quiet and if you're beautiful and quiet other girls that age think you're stuck up and then your on the outs. Plus Linda thought she was dumb. Even though she could read books faster than anybody I knew. I blame her old man. He was no good. I'm sorry. I know he was your grandfather but he called her and Paul names. Shit for brains. Fathead. Stupid. Fuckwad if he'd been drinking. That shit goes in like poison. I know it does and I never got that from my own. No. What I got were strip rats looking at me like I didn't deserve Linda Dubie. See Danny believed that too. Deep down he did. Which is why he started doing what he did that day you were napping and he and Linda were sharing a slice on a bench under the sun.

It was Jimmy Squeeze's brother Bill. He walks by in one of them v-neck t-shirts he was always wearing and he had one of those leather wallets on a chain stuck in his back pocket and that's what caught my attention first. The sun was flashing off that chain. Then a station wagon full of sticky faced kids cruised in front of us and that's when I saw Bill glance over at Linda with this smile on his face like they both had a secret and maybe I could of let it go if he also didn't glance at me but he did and it was his mouth. Like this—I don't know the word. Sneer. And to this day I don't remember jumping off that bench or getting to the other side of the street right after that station wagon passed. Only the surprise in Bill's eyes before I hit him in the face then I was on top of him swinging and swinging. That white heat flowing and flowing. And the funny thing is—no it's not funny. The strange thing is I'd been married to Linda for two years then but I'd never heard her scream but now that's all I could hear—**Danny! Danny!** She kept yelling my name over and over but that did something worse *to me because how come she's defending Squeeze's brother like this? And I think that's when the worm started to grow. That's what I call it. That digging squirming burning that she was lying to me somehow and maybe always had been. And I'd never hurt anybody like I just did to Jimmy Squeeze's brother. Even when I was the new kid my whole life punching kids who called me names.*

*Two cops pulled me off and I got arrested for disorderly and a few other things and the thing is I hated trouble and had never given the cops any but as they cuffed my hands behind my back—people staring—I didn't even care because all I could hear were your quiet mother's screams in my head. It had so much—I don't know—**caring** in it. Bill was out cold and his face looked real bad but I wanted to hit him again. I'm not proud of saying this. But I did. And this was different. This kind of white heat was new. With them boys from all those schools the heat cooled almost as soon as I got it out of me. But now—well it just got hotter.*

*I was on a really bad road then but it had just started and I didn't know it. The station house was only two blocks away built up against the fence around the wooden roller coaster so the two cops walked me down there. One was on each side and they were pissed off and walking me fast so it was hard for Danny to turn around and look back at your mother. That's when he knew. Or that's when he thought he knew. Because why wasn't she coming with him? Her **husband**? How come she was standing on the sidewalk where Jimmy Squeeze's brother was getting attention from some EMT?*

You know there are some pictures that stay in your head like somebody burned them in with a pack of lit cigarettes and this is one I have of Linda Ahearn. Because that was her name then. I forgot to tell you that. She took my name and liked the sound of it. She said her old name was for a little doll you play with but now she had a woman's name.

She was standing there watching me go. That wind off the beach was blowing her skirt around her legs—her hair half in her face and *half out of it. One night she looked up at me when I was working in the DJ booth of The Himalaya (that's another story. I was somebody at the beach because of my deep voice. My boss Will Price called me The Sound.) Anyways your mother looked up at me like God had made me or something good and special like that. But now—just before I couldn't see her anymore—she looked like maybe she'd been wrong and it was the devil who made me. No. It wasn't that bad. I just remember she was standing so still watching me go and she raised two fingers to her mouth which was open a little and I'd never seen her look like that. She looked scared. Then I was in a cell till Liam bailed me out without a word though I could see the Irish pride in him and the shame too. All he said to me was: **You owe me every penny, hot head.***

Hot head. The way he said it seemed to explain everything to me. I was just a hot head. Except it didn't explain it. The heat wasn't in my head. It was in my chest and gut. My blood really. And after that day is when I—is when Danny started to slowly go crazy because he didn't trust her anymore. He had never trusted the strip rats but it never came to him not to trust her. She had chosen him. She and Danny and how from day one they could never hold back from each other.

Daniel stops. He looks out his small window to his yard and shop. Beyond his Tacoma, a crow is perched on one of his fence posts. Its small black head looks to the right and to the left. Then it lifts its wings and is gone.

9

JUST AFTER the Bone River campgrounds, Lois turned her VW Bug onto North West County Road. She had the air-conditioning going full blast, and as she drove onto the concrete bridge over the water she glanced out at all the tents and RVs, smoking grills and upside-down canoes on roof racks or in the dirt. A woman in a camo vest and wet shorts stood near her tent smiling down at her two children squatting on the riverbank. There was so much unguarded love in her face that Lois despised her, and she stepped on the gas and put the campground behind her. To her left stretched groves of orange trees, and she knew she should feel guilty about hating that mother but she didn't. Lois felt what she felt, and it wasn't the woman she hated anyway. It was how ignorant she was. That's what Lois hated more than anything. That young mother's joy. How long did she think she'd be able to keep it?

Lois was shaking her head and driving too fast, but she didn't care. One of her spells was coming on, and there was nothing to do about it. Especially as the county road curved north and she could see the hurricane fence and coiled barbed wire of the road prison, its paved parking lot filled with pickup trucks and cars and work vans. Alongside the concrete buildings of the facility, behind a triple layer of chain-link fences, the outdoor visitors' area was crowded with families. They'd built this place nearly twenty years ago. At the time, Lois had read in the paper how a hundred men were "housed" in three "dorms," that they had air-conditioning and their own TVs and vending machines, too. There were a dozen concrete tables under umbrellas and at each one sat a woman and kids sharing a meal with their criminal in blue. For years now, Lois would see these men in work crews in town, cutting grass in front of municipal buildings or trimming tree branches from power lines or picking trash on either side of the highway. Some were black, others white, and they all wore the same prison-issued blue shirts and blue pants with a dark stripe running down the sides. Some were just kids, nineteen or twenty years old, and others could be their degenerate fathers or uncles, and she hated them all. Hated that she had to see them or think about them. Hated that here in Arcadia of all places, this island in the heart of cattle pastures and floodplains, the state of Florida had built a road prison just three miles south of her house.

And now she had to drive by and see them having a Sunday din-

ner with their families. One of them—young and white with a shaved
head—held his toddler on his lap while he shoveled food into his mouth.

Lois stepped on the gas harder than she'd meant to, the county
road straightening out fast before her, acres of orange trees falling
away to her left and right. She stared at the oncoming road with an
awakened hatred that had reached her skin, her fingertips and eyelids,
the exposed flesh of her old throat. How many times had she pictured
shooting him in the face? No, stabbing him. Again and again. Over
and over and over. He'd done only fifteen years, and when he got out
over twenty years ago she'd bought the gun she still owns. Then six
years later they built this prison, and her fears that had begun to sub-
side with time and her fine antiques began to return, and she kept that
pistol loaded day and night.

That's what I don't understand. Did Donald say this to her face?
How such a loving woman can turn into such a beast.

You know why.

I do. But darlin'—

Darling nothing. He would never understand. Only other mothers
and, she supposed, fathers could understand, though Gerry took his
grief and used it as fuel for the car that drove him away. These days
there were support groups for women like her, but if there were any in
1973 Lois did not know about them, nor did she think she'd ever go to
any of them anyway. What had happened to Linda seemed to strand
Lois out on some ice floe in the center of an ocean. This three-year-
old girl with her, too. This miniature Linda who called her Noni and
brought her the promise of comfort when there really was none to be
had. The Ahearns did not fight her on raising the child, their shame
too great, and the mother was a simpleton anyway, the father a loner
and boozer like so many of the Irish Lois had known. Until Susan was
ten or eleven she slept with Lois in Lois's bed. It's just what they did.
A small voice inside Lois told her that the child needed her own bed
in her own room, but why? Why should she let her go like that? She
knew all too well what would happen when you let go. But one Fri-

day or Saturday night, Susan wanted her friend from school to sleep over, a skinny girl with an overbite whose clothes were too small for her, and they'd slept in Susan's room, the place she used to only use for reading or doing her homework in, and that was it; the following night Susan wanted to sleep in her own bed. And as Lois lay in her queen-sized bed alone, there was the feeling that she was adrift again in waters that could turn lethal if she wasn't vigilant.

Her mouth was dry now and she felt lightheaded and knew her pressure was up again. She needed to calm down. She needed to eat and drink something, and she needed to rest. But Susan was on her way, so how much rest would she get? Just before leaving the shop, Lois checked her email one last time, and there was a new one from Susan. *Thank you, Noni. I'll be there tonight. Love, Suzie*

"Noni" *and* "Suzie." She was really laying it on thick, wasn't she? Did she want money, too? She was probably getting a divorce. Maybe she needed a good lawyer, though her husband Bobby was as agreeable a man as Lois had ever met, so why would Susan need one?

Tonight? She typed back: *Drive carefully. I'll put fresh sheets on your bed! —Love, Noni*

She'd pressed send and closed her laptop and pushed it aside. She *would* have to put fresh sheets on her bed. She'd have to go food shopping, too. Susan drank regular coffee, not the hazelnut Lois preferred. Susan also ate a lot of fruits and vegetables, especially celery and green apples, as Lois recalled. Yogurt, too. The Greek kind with no fat. Last Christmas in St. Pete, that's all she ate every morning while Lois and Bobby made eggs and bacon, French toast, one morning strawberry-and-banana pancakes. But Susan also liked red wine and so did Lois, and she imagined the two of them sitting together on the screened porch sharing a bottle of Cabernet and talking as easily about things as they had last Christmas. Without that cheerful husband of Susan's here too, though, would it be as easy between them? Or would they fall back into their old ways?

But oh, shit, she'd been using Susan's room as storage for years.

Between her bed and desk were two unfinished Chippendale book-cases stuffed with vintage toys Lois hadn't been able to move in the shop. The last time Lois had walked in there it had been stifling hot, the air smelling of old stuffing and dried wood. Why hadn't there been an air conditioner in the window? She had the flash of a memory of Don putting one in there. Or did Lois remember him pulling it out because it had shorted? Either way, she would now have to clean that crap out of there and install a new goddamn air conditioner too. All before "tonight," whenever that was.

Maybe Susan could help her with that. She was certainly going to have to help Lois clear her own room out, that was clear. It'd be nice to have it all ready for her, to have it cooled down for her too, but why should Lois cushion her granddaughter from the realities like this? The woman who'd raised her was eighty-two years old. Climbing those stairs every day had become a chore, and she was seriously considering turning the front parlor into her bedroom. She was heavy and probably diabetic. Rooms tilted on her and she had trouble getting air into her lungs, and on a good day she still smoked six cigarettes and ate whatever the hell she felt like eating. For a few years now, Marianne, in her warm but indirect way, would ask Lois about the future of her business, a question that Lois knew had little to do with profit forecasts and more to do with who will own Lois's Fine Furniture and Toys after you're gone, dear Lois?

Dear Lois, my foot. Marianne would love to own the business. Well, maybe Lois should sell it to her. Marianne and Walter could afford it. But then what would Lois do? Sit on her screened porch day and night watching fossil hunters through the trees? Travel? Visit family?

Of her brothers, only Gio was still alive, his wife Kathy long buried, and his kids were neglectful shits who'd put him in a home off Route 1 in Peabody. It was an old brick facility on an asphalt lot wedged between an Applebee's and a Range Rover dealership, and he told her he had a good view of the parking lots and liked to watch people come and go.

No, thank you.

She could leave the business to Paul, but he'd always been all thumbs at everything he did. He'd wanted to fly jets but left the Air Force after only eighteen months and ended up working in air freight warehouses instead, loading who knew what into the holds of those planes he would never fly. He'd married a woman so cold she made Lois feel she was the warm one in the room, and Paul's wife was one of those churchgoers who slowly over the years had turned him into one, too. In their small living room in their small house on that narrow paved road crowded with other small houses was a color television nearly the size of a movie theater's screen. Beneath that was a shelf of Bibles, each in a different-colored binding and each bearing Lois's daughter-in-law's careful penmanship on the family signature page: *The Dubie Family Bible*

Terry Dubie
Paul Dubie
Paul Dubie Jr.

But all religion seemed to have done for Paul was make him fatter and angrier. How many times had she had to ask him to change the subject whenever it came around to blacks or Jews or Cubans, who he called "beach spics"? He believed we should have electrified fences erected along our country's entire coastline, which he told Lois was just under eleven thousand miles, though the shore of every bay, peninsula, and island had to be included, which brought our country's unprotected perimeter to just over fifty-four thousand miles. Then Paul Jr., sitting back on the sofa with one of his many Mountain Dews, reminded his father about airplanes and 9/11, and this got Paul back on the subject Lois could tolerate the least, which was that our own government had slaughtered three thousand of us and the entire tragedy had been a conspiracy.

No, Paul would turn Lois's Fine Furniture and Toys into something sinister and strange, selling paranoid pamphlets instead of toys made for small children so long ago.

But Lois could not leave it to Susan, either. To do so would be to leave it to whatever man she happened to be with at the time. She hated to think this way, but she couldn't help it. She did.

And so who was left but—Linda? Her daughter Linda. That's who Lois should be leaving her business to.

As Lois got closer to her own end, she could feel her out there in a way she had not in the years after losing her. *Would* she see her again? Some days, this question floated through her more like an answer in the affirmative, and there was a lightness to everything, the sharp corners of the day dulled, all the shadows lighted away. But there were other days, too, and she seemed to live through more of these, when the answer was, no, Lois, because when you're gone you're gone, and when you go, your memories of Linda will go with you, too.

Those hours were the blackest. Lois would find herself thinking just who, besides her, would remember her daughter, Linda Dubie? There had been her father, Gerry, but before Lois learned what actually became of him it had been so long since she had heard anything of him she suspected he had crossed paths with the men in Providence he had stolen from, and that was that. Then years ago Susan had typed his name into her computer and found out more, but when she sent Lois his obituary saying he'd died of a heart attack in Rhode Island, it was like reading about a stranger. Her last contact with Gerry were divorce papers she'd received by certified mail from his lawyer, papers she happily signed because all he'd wanted were his clothes and his Cadillac.

There were *Paul's* memories of Linda, though Lois had little idea what they were. On the subject of his older sister, he had always been a closed book. Though there was that one Thanksgiving at his house. Paul Jr. was still a teenager. He was sitting next to his father at the dinner table, Lois seated across from him, and Paul's wife had gone into the living room for a Bible to read them all a prayer and Paul

Jr. reached out for a roll and his father said: *My sister would have slapped the hell out of me if I did something like that.*

She would, too. Somewhere along the way, Linda had become the manners keeper in the house. At least when it came to her little brother.

Don't talk with your mouth full, Paul. That's gross.

Paul? Did you wash your hands after you peed? Go back and wash them right this minute. I mean it.

Paul, if you don't clean up this popcorn off the floor, I'm gonna make you do it.

Ma, Mr. Price bought Paul a slice today and he didn't even say thank you.

It was strange how this would come back to Lois in pieces, and sometimes only as sound. She could hear Linda's voice, so much like her own, high but with an edge, cotton candy with a rusty nail in it. *Ma, Paul's such a pig. I hate him. I really hate him.*

That was one of Lois's smaller regrets, a dark stream leading to a darker ocean of it, Linda having to share a room with her little brother. That was fine when he was a toddler and she was ten, eleven, twelve years old. It helped her get over her first hatred of him, this surprise baby who had come along to take her mother's attention away from her. But with Paul in the same room as Linda, she quickly began to see him as hers, or maybe as part of her, and those were the years Gerry began to roam and Lois was smoking too much, staying up late in front of a TV she wasn't watching, trying not to think of her man fucking another woman. How could it have ever been a surprise to Lois that Linda would want to flee just as soon as she possibly could?

Linda's cottage was only three streets south of the Midway. Her husband and father-in-law had painted every room white, and Linda had hung curtains and bought throw rugs. Lois had driven her to flea markets down in Port City for perfectly good furniture the rich people no longer wanted. That was a piece Lois could *see*. Linda in the sunlight in shorts and a light blue maternity blouse she'd bought herself, her brown hair pulled back in a single braid, a red stud in each ear her husband had won for her in the water gun booth. She and Lois were standing in the driveway of a rich woman's house on High Street, looking over the table of knickknacks and paperbacks, area rugs laid out on the lawn, the cane rockers and bureaus and hope chests. Linda was thumbing through a cardboard box full of albums. She rested one hand on her protruding belly while she flipped through records with the other. A strand of hair had come loose near her cheek and from the corner of her lips she blew the hair back and that did something to Lois. It was like watching a horse use her tail to swat at a fly on her flank, this thing the body did to protect itself without thinking. That protruding belly, Linda's hand on it. Lois felt less like a mother then and more like a sister in an infinite line of sisters, their wombs full, an older one whose job now was to guide and to instruct.

That baby girl came on a cool spring day, the sun high over the Atlantic, and Lois had been so swept up in the surprising joy of holding and helping to care for her daughter's daughter that she just did not see the signs she should have: Linda's ugly husband telling her she could not even say hello to any men on the strip. Linda's ugly husband leaving his painting jobs in the middle of the day and showing up at the arcade just to check on his wife. Linda's ugly husband scanning the strip for boys and men while he walked too close to Linda.

Gerry had made Linda second in charge then, and while Lois watched after baby Susan in the apartment out back, Linda made change in her apron like she always had, but she also ordered more Skee-Ball tickets when they ran low and popcorn for the popping machine and she kept track of maintenance records on the video games and slots, and she hired a slow boy with three fingers on one hand to keep the place swept and clean all shift long.

Linda loved the strip and she was a natural at running a business and she would have—

Would-have-beens. Could-have-beens. Should-have-beens. These were nothing but skeletal hands shoving Lois under cold murky water and holding her down, down, down. She craved a cigarette and she needed a drink and now she breathed deeply and turned into her dirt driveway under the shade of her live oaks. From here, her porch roof seemed to sag in the center, and her clapboards looked moldy, and there was Susan's car, her grown granddaughter standing beside it like she was getting ready to climb inside and drive away. But then she smiled and waved, and Lois took her hand off the wheel and waved back, and Jesus, Mary, and Joseph, what did she do to her *hair*?

10

SUSAN SET down her things and stood in the doorway of her old bedroom, its heat thick in her face. In the center of the room were two bookcases filled with old cars and trucks and dolls, one of them lying on her side and staring at her with one dead eye. On Susan's single bed, still made and covered with a quilted spread, lay an old fan, its blades looking like propellers from a plane that had flown in World War II. The windows were closed, and there was no air conditioner, and there were the depressing smells of dried wood and metal and straw stuffing. Above her bureau still hung her faded reproduction poster of a Renoir painting she'd tacked to the wall when she was fifteen, an image of young men and women under a striped canopy sipping wine and eating, talking, and smoking. They looked like they belonged in each other's company, and that this good time they were having was just one of many.

"*Well?*" Lois called from the bottom of the stairs. "It's a mess, isn't it?"

"Yeah, but I can clean it."

"I won't be able to help you, you do know that." There was an edge to Lois's voice Susan hadn't heard in a while, not when Bobby was around anyway.

"Where should I put it all?"

"Beats me," Lois called up. "Down here in the front parlor for now, I suppose."

"I'm sorry, Noni. I don't want to be a nuisance."

"Leftovers all right? That's all I've got."

"Yeah, of course, Noni. I can go shopping for us tomorrow."

"Good, we need a new AC for that *room*."

Susan could hear her grandmother's heavy steps to the kitchen. Outside her window was still that same live oak, its leaves big and green in the last of the sunlight. And there, behind the shelves of junk, was her small desk with nothing on it, like she was meant to come back to this room one more time, whether she wanted to or not. She grabbed the doll and a plastic helmet and three metal trucks and carried them quickly down the stairs, Lois calling to her from the kitchen, "We'll have to get *boxes* for that crap."

SUSAN'S HAIR was still damp from her shower, and she sat across from her grandmother at the same small table they had always owned in the same place it had always been, up against the kitchen wall beneath the window that looked out at the woods. That same lace curtain hung in front of it, too, but on the sill was a carton of Carltons and Lois's ashtray and a stack of coupons and a white Bic lighter. The sun was down and Lois had turned on the overhead bulb, which was still too bright and so often had made Susan feel—if she'd eaten with Lois at all—that she was strapped down and being interrogated. And now her grandmother kept looking over at her. She'd warmed up their lasagna in the microwave, and even though it was dry and cool in places, Susan was glad to see that she was still cooking for herself. Lois sat back and sipped from her glass of Cabernet. "You cut it yourself?"

"Yeah." Susan made herself smile. "Does it look like it?"

Lois seemed to want to say more on the subject, but she waved her hand in the air and said, "It's none of my damn business, Suzie, but if you're going to be here shouldn't I know more about you and your husband?"

"Yes."

"Well?"

Susan sipped her own wine. It was bitter and had begun to lose its flavor. Pushed into the center of the table between them was her old chair. When Don was alive, that's where she used to sit, and it was strange how she never thought of him much, this kind man who so often had tried to be a buffer between her and Lois. If he was here Susan could probably just tell her grandmother the truth. *I'm writing about my childhood, and I needed to come home and I don't know if I've ever loved anyone, Noni.*

"He's the best one you ever had. You do know that."

"Yeah."

Lois stared at her a moment. Her grandmother's hair had thinned so much over the years, and now she wore very little makeup and she had pockets of flesh under each eye that seemed to droop. It made her look more resigned about things.

"Well." Lois pushed herself up and out of her chair. "I need a cigarette."

"How much are you smoking, Noni?"

"Six a day. So what?" She picked up her wine glass and grabbed her ashtray and lighter. "Come out with me, if you want." She disappeared into the rear hallway, and there came the opening of the door to the screened porch then the closing of it. Susan sat there feeling as if Lois hadn't really meant for her to join her out there at all.

Now she lay in the dark in the narrow bed of her girlhood. She was naked and sweating. Earlier she'd rested that World War II fan on her desk, plugged it in, and pointed it at her mattress, but it wobbled loudly and she was afraid the blades would come flying off. From the open windows came the smell of pine and jasmine. It was a night bloomer that Don had planted too close to their house, and Lois told him to cut it down because it *stinks*, though he never did. But Lois rarely went outside anyway, and she kept the windows closed and locked, the air conditioner on until those few months when she needed warmth.

Susan could hear the quiet hum of Lois's air conditioner now. Lying in this heat, it was hard not to feel neglected or punished in some way, though just before they'd both gone to bed Lois had stood in the open doorway of her bedroom and said, "You can sleep in here tonight, if you want." Behind Lois was the dim light of her bedside lamp, that dark comforter on her bed, and that even darker carpet on the floor. Until she was ten or eleven, Susan had slept in the same bed with her, her grandmother's comforting warmth and weight beside her, the smells of cold cream and cigarette smoke. But to do so now, for even one night, would feel like a regression of some kind.

"That's okay, Noni. I've got the fan."

Lois had shrugged. "Suit yourself." Then she closed the door behind her and called through it, "Good *night*."

And it had been a good night. Out on the porch after dinner, they'd sipped their wine and Lois smoked two cigarettes and talked about the "mousy little bitches" who complained about her being this month's inspector for yesterday's Fourth Saturday Antiques Fair.

"They think I'm bossy when I'm just doing my damn job. At least Marianne sticks up for me."

Then Lois talked about her awhile, her employee Susan had yet to meet. "She's the best help I ever had, but she's a prissy missy, I don't know." Lois waved her hand in the air again. It was a mannerism she'd always had. Like she was shrugging off not what she just said but anything that someone else might say back. It used to make Susan furious, as if she were forever being shut up before she could say a word. But tonight, it did not. They were both sitting in the near-dark, only the dim yellow light on over the door behind them, and watching and listening to Lois, her cigarette smoke wafting out the black screen into the night, Susan felt as if she were in a museum and the woman who'd raised her was some talking exhibit of what had once been but had really never changed. And the younger Susan would have been hurt by what Noni had just said, that Marianne was "the best help" she'd ever had, because how many hours, weeks, *years* had Susan spent behind the register of that depressing shop? But Lois was right too. All Susan had ever done was read there. She rarely dusted or greeted the customers or even looked up when one walked in, the bell over the door jangling. *Smile at them, Suzie. You can at least do **that**.*

Though she could not, and did not, and as Lois went from criticizing Marianne to telling Susan how she'd run off a young picker today who was trying to "steal" from her, Susan just sipped her wine and listened, grateful that Lois was leaving her alone for now, something she'd gotten surprisingly good at over the years.

But it was too hot in this room. Susan swung her legs off the mattress and turned the old fan back on. Its engine moaned just before the blades began to turn, and as she lay back down on her back, the warm moving air felt old too, like the past itself was making her sweat.

11

ELAINE MUIR is ninety-one years old and has her blood pressure checked twice a month. It's three in the afternoon, the sun a high haze, and as Daniel opens the passenger door for her and helps her out of his truck, her hands small but strong in his, he can smell her lipstick and perfume and he does not let go until both her feet are flat on the asphalt. Daniel is sweating under his short-sleeved shirt, but she's wearing soft-soled shoes, a gray wool skirt, and a white cardigan over a white blouse.

"Nobody's like you, Daniel."

"Don't kid a kidder, Elaine." Daniel takes her arm and begins to walk her across the lot. It's newly paved, the white lines of the parking spaces too bright, and it gives off the hard industrial scent of black oil that begins to squeeze Daniel's empty stomach. He's tempted to hurry, but he won't.

Elaine says, "Oh, if I were only thirty years younger."

"Promises, promises."

It's the kind of flirtation Daniel can almost enjoy, though it sometimes leaves him feeling like a reformed arsonist reaching for a can of gasoline while eyeing the matches.

Elaine was still talking. "Were you, Daniel? You must have been."

"I'm sorry, Elaine. Was I what?"

"Married."

They are moving into the shade of the entrance now. An obese woman sits in a wheelchair near the glass doors smoking a cigarette. Her pant cuffs are rolled up, and her ankles and lower legs are swollen and purple and Daniel thinks of Tommy Banks at Norfolk having both his feet amputated because of his diabetes. After that, he got around in a wheelchair, and any con who owed him had to push him wherever he needed to go.

"No, Elaine. I never was."

"That's hard to believe, Daniel." There's a smile in her voice when she says it, but her words enter him like a gold coin dropped into a dank well. Elaine grips his hand harder as they take the one step up onto concrete. She raises her head and smiles at the obese woman. "Good afternoon."

The woman exhales smoke and nods and flicks ash at her feet. Her toes are nearly black, and Daniel can't look at them. He pushes the blue handicapped button on the wall.

"Don't you agree, Daniel?" He and Elaine are in the elevator now. She's been saying something about appetites—food and nicotine. "I try not to judge, but the addiction must be very strong indeed."

"It is."

"Did you ever smoke?"

"When I was young." He'd started in Walpole at twenty-four. Why not?

"Was it difficult to quit?"

"Yes." But it was a suffering he welcomed.

"Do you think he'll be here today?"

"He usually is."

"Oh, good."

The elevator doors open, and Daniel takes Elaine's arm and walks her across a shining corridor into the waiting room of a doctor who's fifty years younger than she is, but her hair is set, her lipstick fresh, her skirt, blouse, and sweater pressed and matching. Daniel signs her in and soon a young nurse comes for her. She's a hefty girl, and she smiles warmly at Elaine and compliments her hair and leads her slowly around a corner to the examination rooms.

Daniel sits in an empty chair and picks up a magazine without looking at its cover. A TV is suspended high in the corner of the waiting area, the volume turned low. It's an afternoon talk show hosted by some psychologist in a blue suit, a big balding man with a mustache. He's leaning forward in his chair talking to a young couple sitting across from him, two pale kids who look as if he's just told them they do not really love one another and never have.

Daniel glances around the room. Five patients, all of them female, four women and one girl. Two are closer to Elaine's age, and they sit side by side reading magazines through thick glasses. Near the door sits a woman from Daniel's time, though she's dyed her thinning hair brown, and a long varicose vein runs up her right calf. She has one of those small screens in her hand, and she's squinting at it without reading glasses, flicking her finger across the glass over and over. Up against the wall have to be a mother and her daughter. The mother's nice-looking, one of those minivan-driving women he sees so regularly in downtown Port City; they have the good skin and straight postures of the educated, but their hair always looks a bit frayed, and if you look closer you see they're wearing tight gym clothing they haven't had time to change out of before rushing to pick up their various children at their various activities. These mothers are always carrying water bottles or cardboard cups of coffee or tea, and they sip from them as they chat cheerfully with other women just like them, women at the height of their powers who seem to be giving all of it to everyone else at all times. This one's wearing a sleeveless top, jeans, and sandals, her bare shoulders and arms lean and muscled as she studies the TV up in the corner as if it were revealing an important secret. Her daughter, in shorts and a Dartmouth T-shirt, is showing too much of her legs and she's chewing gum while flipping the pages of a magazine so quickly she can't possibly be seeing anything long enough to decide it isn't for her.

The mother looks over at him. Daniel opens his magazine and puts on his glasses and reads whatever he first sees, though he isn't reading at all. He can feel the woman's eyes on him, and he's aware of the skin of his own face, how thin it is, how it masks nothing, really. But can she see it? That he means her and her daughter no harm? And now there's a burning weight on his bladder, but he stays where he is.

Behind the walls it was a joke if somebody said they didn't belong there. Everybody who was there belonged there. And if you whined about your trial or your sentence you weren't stand-up, so you just put your head down and did your fucking time. Even if it was for the rest of your life. But at Norfolk, smoking on the concrete stairs of the Twos or Threes after evening chow, guys would talk. One was Jay McGonigle. He had hair black as an Indian's, and he kept it combed back with Vitalis when most of the cons were letting theirs grow out like kids did on the outside. McGonigle had meticulous sideburns and was always working the sliver of a fingernail between his teeth. He was handsome too, with the deep eyes and strong jaw of a film star. It was easy to see how he'd gotten women out on the street.

Except he hated them.

Another con would be talking about his wife or girlfriend back home, how she was a cold bitch for letting him down or she was a saint for putting up with him but now she was a fucking whore who couldn't wait for him, and McGonigle said one time, "They're *all* fuckin' whores. Every last one of them." It was the way he said it, his eyes on the steel mesh of the cage alongside the steps, though he seemed to be seeing beyond it to something he savored. His hatred. A dozen years earlier he'd killed three young women in ten days. He'd strangled them after he couldn't get it up. That was the word about McGonigle, that he couldn't get hard with a woman though he didn't like boys, either. Something was dead in him and so he'd murdered those three girls for reminding him of it. Danny was smoking then. He remembers looking away from McGonigle and stubbing out his cigarette and walking up the steps past him to his room on the second floor of the Threes. Up the hill in Walpole, they called your cell your house. But at Norfolk, it was a room, and yes, Danny Ahearn belonged where he was, but not like McGonigle did. The only hatred Danny ever had was for himself. Especially those first years after Linda. Especially up the hill where there were no programs like at Norfolk, no morning schooling, no trade work in the afternoon, no house reps for each block house, no Debate Club or Quiz Club, the smartest or most educated cons competing against college kids who came in every few Saturday nights, the auditorium packed with inmates rooting for the Norfolk boys, who regularly beat brainy kids from Boston College and Northeastern, even Dartmouth and Harvard. It was a thing to see, and for days after a win there'd be a better feeling in the air of the shops and the schoolroom, the mess hall and quad, that maybe they weren't a bunch of hopeless degenerates after all, that maybe something good could come from something bad.

"Good news, Daniel." Elaine's smiling down at him, the young nurse at her side. "One-thirty over ninety."

"That's great, hon. That's real good." He begins to close his magazine and sees for the first time what he'd been staring at. A man his age is fly-fishing on the bank of a stream under cottonwood trees. He's graying, his eyes narrowed and his chin up, his line a whip out on the water, just a man relaxing in the setting sun of all his accomplishments.

Daniel sets the magazine back on the table. He stands and takes Elaine's arm and thanks the young nurse, but as he leads Elaine out of the waiting room of women to the elevators, pretending to listen to all the nice things the handsome young doctor told her, there is the picture of Susan Dunn burned into Daniel's head, her small lovely face, and he knows that as much as he does not want to, he needs to finish writing her that letter; he needs to finish it and then he needs to mail it to Professor Susan Dunn, Eckerd College, St. Petersburg, Florida. And this should happen sooner rather than later, for his bladder feels full when he knows it's not, just another symptom of what his own doctor told him before Daniel stopped going to see him. And those Victorian chairs. He has to get those done too.

The elevator doors open, and Daniel guides Elaine into it, this old woman for whom each afternoon like this is a small gift she prefers to unwrap as slowly as she possibly can.

THE RAIN begins as Daniel is getting ready to cook supper. There's a sudden drumming on his tin roof, then the smell of ozone coming through his casement screens. Out his kitchen's front window a puddle is already pooling in the yard, and he kneels on his bed and rolls that window shut. Back at the stove, he dumps a can of beans into a pot over blue flames. He should boil a hot dog too, maybe some peas or corn, but he's not up to it. On his Formica table sits his letter to Susan. He'd come home from dropping off Elaine Muir and just stared at it. Then he read it over and it felt to him like the truth. But who the hell really wants to hear it?

Daniel grabs his wooden spoon and stirs the beans. He can smell the bacon and molasses in it, and he thinks of Willie Teague. It was Teague's favorite meal, but Polaski would make him lie facedown on the floor before he could eat it. Polaski tortured Willie. If Teague even grunted something under his breath, Polaski would punish him for it.

He'd cut his TV privileges. He'd crank up the heat in Teague's room, or if it was winter, he'd shut it off. He'd take his shower privileges or yank access to the commissary, especially when Teague was out of TP. He'd throw away Teague's mail or tell him he had a visitor when he had none. When Teague's meals came, Polaski would order a rectal search just for the fuck of it.

This went on for months because Polaski just didn't like Teague, his sunken chest and underbite and gray eyes, this foster kid who went on to become a professional car thief. And so Teague just snapped. The day his wife smuggled in the gun, the metal detector was broken and there was no female screw on duty to pat her down. She had the .38 strapped up against her crotch under a loose dress, her cleavage showing up top.

When the shooting started Daniel was down in the barbershop cutting a CO's hair. It was Johnny Sills, and when Sills heard the first shots he was up and running out into the quad right when Willie was coming out of the Threes, Polaski bleeding to death at the door to the cage. Danny saw the next part, he and a bunch of other cons. Sills had both hands up like he was trying to talk Willie into giving up the gun, but Willie pointed it and shot and the slug ripped through Sills's heart and Willie was running into the Fives and seconds later came the last shot of that afternoon and Willie Teague was free of the place.

Daniel always felt bad about Sills. He was stand-up and treated him and the others with consistent respect. They should've named the new prison out in western Mass. after him only, not him and Polaski. Now, all these years later, it's the Sills/Polaski Correctional Center, and Polaski has gone down in history as some kind of hero who gave the ultimate sacrifice in corrections when he was a bully and a sadist.

Daniel grabs the pot handle and stirs the beans and turns down the heat. The rain is coming down so hard his trailer is like the inside of a can being beaten on by sticks. He glances down at his letter to Susan. He can write to her all he wants, but she'll never get her mother back. Why not just write his daughter a short note instead?

Susan,

    I'd like to see you before I go.

The rain begins to let up. His trailer smells like beans. He picks up Susan's letter and reads where he last left off. *He had never trusted the strip rats but it never came to him not to trust **her**. She had chosen him. She and Danny and how from day one they could never hold back from each other.*

There were so many places where they'd done it: under the Himalaya, on the beach on a blanket in the dunes at night, once under a pinball machine in the arcade at three in the morning when he ached for her and scratched on the window screen of her bedroom. It was low and faced the parking lot, and it was a hot night and they'd already made love earlier in the backseat of Liam's Impala, paint cans and rollers on the floor, Linda's bottom on a tarp Danny had pulled there for her while jerking down his shorts. It was only four or five hours later and he couldn't sleep and then Linda's beautiful small face was a shadow against the screen, but it had a rusted aluminum track and would make too much noise to open, Paul's bed just across the tiny room, so Linda whispered, "Out front." And then her hand was in his hand and she was spreading a T-shirt out under the pinball game because it was dark and hidden there and Daniel can still smell the dusty concrete and her hair and skin—salt from the ocean and soap and her faint pine taste as she let him push himself all the way into her. This gift from her. What else could he call it? No one else had ever been so good to him like this. No one had ever made him feel like a one and only like this. But the burning worm had come to life now. Even before Liam came to bail him out for the twenty-five dollars Danny paid him back that night. (And why hadn't *she* bailed him out? "I was with *Susan*! I didn't want to bring her *there*, Danny!") The real story, Daniel knows now and has known for too long, is that, sitting in that concrete cell on a steel bench waiting to get bailed out, the worm began to make him see things he hadn't seen before. How fast that first long kiss under the Frolics led to her giving all of herself to him under the Himalaya. How they never even talked about it before or after. How it was his first time, but it couldn't be hers. No pain. No blood. Only this slick rising and falling hunger he now had to have the way he used to need water and sleep and air. It never even occurred to him to wear a rubber. Because in those early months with Linda Dubie he was so damn high and happy, *nothing* occurred to him. He wasn't thinking at all. Neither of them were. To stop and talk and to think about things like pregnancy were as far away as a man being hurled down a white river pausing to ask the time.

The concrete walls of the cell were painted yellow and someone must've smuggled in a pen because a few inches from the barred door was the drawing of a vagina with something dripping out of it. Beneath that was one word: *slut*. It was a word the worm loved. It seemed to be its only food. How could Danny have been so *slow*? That smile she gave Bill in the arcade, that look on his face when he'd glanced at her sitting beside her husband in the sun. He'd been with her, too. He *had*.

That was bad enough. The thought that Linda had given Jimmy Squeeze's brother what she'd also given to Danny. But then the worm squirmed deeper and began to burn. Had she done it with Bill while she was *with Danny*? While she was Danny's *wife*? Danny stared at that jailhouse drawing and he thought of all the times she could have done it. When Susan was napping. Or maybe when Lois was taking care of Susan, and Linda was working the arcade. She smoked a lot of Camels, and she was always taking a cigarette break. One afternoon Danny and Liam were up on the roof of the Frolics patching the flat roof with tar, and Danny had looked over the edge and seen his very own Linda Ahearn standing in the shade of the entrance to the arcade smoking a cigarette, one arm crossed under her breasts like when they first met, her coin apron around her hips. She looked so beautiful and so alone and she was his, the mother of their baby, and then she got a long look from a big man walking by with his kids. But what if it was Bill passing by right then? Who's to say he couldn't flash that smile and lead her to some dark corner real fast? Who's to say he didn't? That *she* didn't? Then Danny had pictured his wife's legs spread as she let in Bill and stared into his eyes the way she stared into his, like he was the only one for her, and that's when the cell tilted and he threw up on the concrete floor, the worm burrowing from his head and heart into his guts, where it would stay until it was too late.

Daniel stands and walks over to the stove and turns the flames off under the beans. He sits back down and writes: *Susan. Danny lost his way. That's not the right way to put it really because it looks like I'm making excuses for him. I'm not. He deserved everything he got and more. But he went crazy for a while. That's what I'm trying to say. And when people are crazy it's like being around a drunk or somebody so high on something your conversation with them is from another planet. You can't talk to them. Linda couldn't—*

You should know that I went crazier behind the walls. You may know they put me in Walpole first and I was on Suicide Watch from things I kept saying I guess though I don't remember any of that. What I remember is wanting some con to kill me. I kept seeing

Daniel squeezes his eyes shut. Linda's face, her hair, her eyes, the way she stared right into his after, the surprise and the fear fading to a knowing he would do this. And there was the fading that did not look unlike love, an echo of it, though it was a love for who she'd been, a love she was trying to hold on to but couldn't.

I wasn't strong enough to take my own life.

I was a fish. That's what they call a first timer. And the sharks don't even circle a fish. They just go right for him but Danny went after the first shark that looked at him wrong. His name was Chucky Finn and he was from Charlestown. I had my tray of baloney and mashed potatoes made from water and powder from a box and

Why is he writing this? How can any of this be something she needs to read? He hasn't earned *the right* to tell her this. But she needs to know, doesn't she? She needs to know that even in max lockup he was so out of his mind by what he did that he feared no one, starting with two-hundred-sixty-pound Chucky Finn, who glanced up at Danny across the table just long enough to say, "No fuckin' fish," and Danny was on him faster than he'd ever been on anybody. He'd always had big hands and now they carried only blackness, and after he put Finn there with punches he still doesn't remember throwing, Danny straddled Finn's chest and his hands were squeezing Finn's bald head and he kept slamming it onto the concrete floor, three screws on him, cons staring at him like he was either an annoyance or a welcome distraction from the endlessly narrow days they'd been living for so long.

Can't he just tell her he was crazy and leave it at that? No, because if he leaves it there, that one word will just sound like an excuse. If he leaves it there, Susan won't really know any more than she may know now. And she needs to know that for the past twenty years, Daniel has abstained from women. He would like to say that Danny became Daniel behind the walls, but that isn't true. Danny was a young man, and that hunger Linda lit inside him didn't go away, though it did for months right after because the only picture in his head of Linda was the bad one, a slow nightmare of what he'd done playing over and over. He'd squeeze his eyes shut and press his face into his bunk, but that only made it worse. He saw what he saw and he felt it, too, and how could he have done it? How could that have been *him*?

It was that sound she'd made. Like she'd just burned her finger on the stove then yanked it back. The way she stared into his face, that black knowing about him, a curse on him.

He was twenty-four or twenty-five, but each morning he woke as soft as an old man. Even in solitary, his first trip to Block Nine for Chucky Finn, then his second for stomping the head of Chico Perez who'd pulled a shiv on him in the laundry room just because Danny's shoulder had brushed his. But the Reactor's core spewed its reckless heat, and Perez's shiv was in Danny's sliced palm and he stomped and stomped. But even all those days and nights in solitary, if his mind went anywhere good, it was only to little Susan, to holding her and playing with her, and, when she was a baby, feeding her in her high chair and patting her tiny back till she burped near his ear.

It wasn't until Norfolk, maybe six or eight months in the Threes, that Danny woke hard. It was a sign of life he hadn't seen coming because he'd stopped thinking of ever feeling alive again. But now this. A sign of good health in a healthy young man, and it wasn't right. It wasn't right that he was healthy, but at the same time he felt grateful for it. And there came a memory of him and Linda. They'd only been married a week or two and Linda was a few months pregnant, her belly just beginning to swell. It was late September but warm, and they'd slept with the bedroom windows open. Linda had hung white curtains, and when he woke on his side up against her back, his arm around her, a breeze blew in, billowing the curtains out before they fell to the side and their room smelled like the ocean. Linda said, as if they'd both been awake a long time: "That's so pretty."

Then they were making love and Danny, lying in his bunk back on the second floor of the Threes, began to jerk on himself and it didn't take long at all and no one on this earth was worse than he was.

Some of the guys went gay in there, though they never called it that. A mouth was a mouth, a hole was a hole, and you did what you had to do. What Danny did was go back to when it was just him and Linda. He'd picture them doing it in the sand and in Liam's Impala and on their couch with just the light of the TV on them. He'd picture it and start to smell her smell and hear her breaths and then it would all drop to his center and out into his hand and the TP he used, and there was the feeling he was trying to make dried flowers bloom again.

The rain has stopped. Daniel dumps some beans onto his plate and sits at the table. He moves aside his letter to Susan. She won't be hearing any of that. He spoons some beans into his mouth, but they may as well be a clump of melted wax he makes himself swallow. He pushes aside his plate and thinks again of that summer of 1988, outside for the first time since '73. Danny was thirty-eight years old but felt like a young kid who didn't know enough about the world to be in it.

His father was dead by then. Because of Danny's accrued good time, he was offered a furlough to Liam's funeral, but Danny didn't go. At visiting, he told his mother he was denied. His father had lived a small life, and Danny knew it would be a small funeral and he would stand out. There might be his mother's sister and her husband from New Jersey, some grown cousins, a few tradesmen from over the years, maybe Will Price and another owner or manager from one of the amusement parks Danny's old man had helped to look magic, but that's it. And Danny would not be the one in the cheap suit his mother would have to go out and buy for him, greeting people at the casket of this man who hadn't visited him even once.

Danny's mother wanted him to live with her, but after only a few months Danny's parole officer let him move to Boston. That first full summer out was hot, and he lived in a one-room a block from the barbershop where he worked in the shadow of the highway overpass across from North Station. At Norfolk he'd learned caning and he'd learned how to cut hair, and the owner of the shop knew Danny's PO and that was that. All day long, five days a week, it was men's heads and hair and talking faces in the mirror, a cotton clothes protector over their shoulders and chests, the rise and fall of their voices and laughter and jokes and talk of whatever was in the news. That August it was Bush and Dukakis. When Danny went down, Nixon was still president and we were in Vietnam.

At sundown he'd go walking. He was still smoking then, Winstons he kept in the front pocket of his T-shirt or rolled up into his sleeve. He'd gained some weight too. He'd never been one of those guys to lift barbells or play basketball in the shadows of the walls, and sometimes he'd see his reflection in the window of a package store or clothes shop, this guy with a gut and long sideburns nobody seemed to have anymore, his hair combed back, his hooked nose and big hands. The thing is, he looked like an ex-con, and he didn't like it. He also looked like he came from another time, and he felt that way too. He didn't expect the outside to be so bright and loud and full of motion, either.

All the college kids were moving back into the city, and he'd pass a couple of girls on the sidewalk with their clean hair and bare legs, their slapping flip-flops and naked toes. He'd smile at them as if he were still the age he'd been when he went down, but they'd pass by him as if he weren't there; and why wouldn't they? He was the age of their fathers and so he was invisible to them, which is how it should be, he thought. He *should* be invisible to women. And he thought of his Susan being the exact same age these college kids were, eighteen years old or so.

Walking along the brownstones of Back Bay, he'd see a father in a sweat-soaked T-shirt and shorts and running shoes unloading a U-Haul or station wagon, carrying a table lamp or rolled rug or a taped box up the steps and out of sight. Once down near Fenway Park, one of these men glanced over at him and winked at Danny as if he were one of them, just another middle-aged tuition payer doing his happy fatherly duty, helping move a kid who was going to college or getting a first apartment.

It was too much.

Danny began to take routes away from neighborhoods with colleges in them. In Boston this was hard to do, but he'd leave his one-room near the tracks of North Station and head east along Commercial Street to the wharfs jutting out into Boston Harbor. On the other side was Charlestown, and he could see the Bunker Hill Monument and thought of guys he met in Norfolk from that neighborhood, men who robbed banks like it was just another trade like plumbing or carpentry other guys might learn from their fathers and uncles. Out on the water were big gray freighter ships and much smaller pleasure boats and a few white motor yachts cruising along. When he got to Hanover Street, he'd walk up to Prince and the narrow cobbled streets of the North End. It'd be crowded with short-sleeved tourists and little kids, and sometimes he'd sit at a table in one of the open-air restaurants and order an espresso and sip it and watch cars drive slowly by, people stepping in front of them like they weren't there, horns honking, uniformed cops on horseback, a thin Italian man smoking a cigar in the doorway of his gelato shop, the stringed lights hanging over the street from one brick walk-up to another, the smells of fried squid and lemon and smoke and bubble gum and the perfume of the women walking by with their men. He couldn't stop staring at them, their faces and hair and bare shoulders, their small wrists and painted nails, their soft-looking rears behind shorts or skirts he wanted to touch and kiss but also run away from as fast as he possibly could.

That first stretch in the Hole, the voice that came into Danny's head was: *You did this, Linda.*

He knew he was wrong to even begin to think this, but he'd never been crazy before her. He had a temper, and he never took any shit from anyone for more than a heartbeat or two, but after the Reactor's heat had cooled he never thought any more about the boy he'd punched or kicked or both just to make him stop. That was the thing. Danny had never started anything with anybody. He never looked for trouble any-where, so why was he here in this cell with the light that never went off and a steel bunk bolted into the wall and a Bible with its cover torn off?

Because of you, Linda. But those words in his head made his face burn and he knew it wasn't her but it *was* her, or at least it was what she'd done to him; she'd made him feel he was one of God's chosen kings when all along she was doing the same to beach shit like Squeeze's brother Bill, though after over a year of this, he began to consider, like slivers of ice pushed into his veins, that he'd been as "sick in the head" as Linda had said he was, that she'd never done any of the things he said she had, and so what he'd done he'd done to a completely innocent woman. And even if she did do it, what he'd done was so wrong, so very wrong, and those fifteen years passed as slowly as an entire ocean drying up under the sun.

One late sundown that first fall outside, he saw a big woman across the street talking to a cop. She looked to be in her sixties, and she wore a pants suit and too much eye makeup, her graying hair done up with a lot of hair spray. When she lit a cigarette, it was like Danny's heart just tapped up against an electric fence because she looked so much like his mother-in-law he threw a five onto his table and walked down Prince and out of that neighborhood for good.

Why didn't he think of this? Lois came from a big Italian family only a few miles north of Boston. Why wouldn't she or one of her brothers show up in the North End? It hadn't been her, but that didn't matter. Of all the people he'd known on the outside, she was the very last he hoped to ever see again.

Ever.

Daniel feels a bit queasy now. There's an ache in his hips and groin, and a Coke might help, but he doesn't have any. He scrapes his plate and rinses it off in the sink and leaves his trailer. Sometimes he locks it, and sometimes he does not. But now, standing in the smells of pine pitch and wet sheet metal and damp dirt, he thinks of his letter to Susan on the kitchen table, and he lifts his front door till it clicks into place and he locks it. He steps around the pooled water in the middle of his yard and starts up his truck. For the past forty years he has lived his life alone. It's a condition you get used to, the way a one-legged man gets used to his cane and hopping from one resting place to the next. But this wanting to see his daughter once more seems to have opened up more wanting inside him. All this time he has kept those wants small: a warm bed, three meals a day, clean clothes, and just enough money to live. His only indulgences have been an occasional beer or ice-cream cone or movie, his trips to the library for books on tape. But as he backs out onto Beach Road on this wet night just to go looking for a Coke, he can feel that bigger wanting, his shame for this rising to his face as he steps on the gas and moves swiftly down through the dark pines and lighted trailers and cottages, families living inside them, each and every one.

PART

TWO

12

IN THE Lowe's parking lot, Susan sat behind the wheel of Lois's VW, the driver's door wide open, her notepad resting against the steering wheel. They'd already picked out their new air conditioner, which Susan had offered to pay for, but Lois had waved her hand in the air and told her to bring the car around. Susan wrote: *Noni's smell.* She always forgot it, but how could she? It was that obscene combination of baby powder and cigarette smoke Lois had had ever since Susan was a little girl, her grandmother's Carlton between her lips as she patted the powder under and between her breasts. Up north Lois only did this in the summer, but once they moved down here it became her morning ritual. Maybe Susan could begin with that. She could start with a description of Noni's large breasts, how, as a girl, they were pendulous and lovely to her. There was also the sticky sweetness of Noni's hair spray, her strong floral perfume, the rose tang of lipstick. Even at her fattest Lois had always been a pretty woman, but now that she was in her eighties she'd begun to let herself go. Her hair was thinning and she didn't bother coloring it anymore, and if she put on any makeup at all, Susan didn't see it. Today she wore dark sunglasses that covered most of her face, some kind of boxy cotton sundress covering the rest of her except for her arms. She was raising one of them now and calling Susan over, the underside of her arm jiggling as she stood there in the shaded doorway of the Lowe's store. A young employee stood beside her with the cart that held the air conditioner for Susan's old room, and she pushed her notebook onto the backseat, started the VW, and drove up to the entryway and climbed out to help.

Inland here, the air was too hot and thick to breathe. The asphalt felt soft under her sandals.

"Pop the trunk, Suzie." Nobody but Noni called her that. Hearing it now was as comforting as it was belittling. She'd have to write that down later, too: *Suzie.* That could even be her title. No, it sounded too much like a Barbie doll or a porn star, something both saccharine and tawdry about it, which was probably why she never liked it in the first place. She opened the trunk. It was stuffed with toy and furniture catalogues.

"Just toss those in the back."

Susan was wearing denim shorts and a fitted T-shirt, and as she leaned into Lois's car she could feel the invading eyes of the young man at his cart. He was twenty or twenty-one and held the fixed stare of so many of her students, his lips parted as if life were one long movie unfolding inside his head just for him. She turned to him and said, "There's enough room now. Thank you."

The young man lifted the air conditioner into the trunk. He pulled the lid down and turned to leave, but Lois surprised him with a two-dollar tip, and he thanked her and glanced down at Susan's flat belly and bare thighs before pushing his cart back through the opening glass doors of the store.

"Jesus, Mary, and Joseph, let's get out of this *heat.*"

Jesus, Mary, and Joseph. It was how people talked up north. Susan would write that down, too.

Back behind the wheel, Lois pulled out of the Lowe's lot onto DeSoto. She turned the air up to max, but its cold wind blew directly against Susan's chest and she pointed the air vent up and away.

"Any idea how we're going to carry that damn thing up the stairs, Suzie, never mind install it?"

"I think I can do it."

"No, you can't. You did enough yesterday. I'll call Marianne.

Those Mexicans keep their place up all year long." Lois glanced at her and accelerated.

It was the word *Mexican*: Gustavo all these years later.

"It can't be that heavy, Lois."

"Well, you're on your own, then. I can't do much anymore, you should know that. I'm not gonna live forever, you know."

It was her tone from the old days when her words were sharp and hurled through the air and could break skin if you weren't careful. If you weren't fast enough.

That was a word Noni used to use a lot—*fast*. "You're going to be one of those *fast* girls, aren't you?"

MotherGrandmother, she was both in one, and Susan did not really want to stay with her now. Things were already coming back to her that she'd long ago dug a hole for and buried. Like Lois's magisterial wave of the hand, that scrutinizing overhead light in the kitchen, how in the mornings, like today, she and Lois made two different kinds of coffee and were overly polite to one another when both would rather not have to talk so early at all.

Lois turned onto Pinellas for the historic district. She was humming a song from the fifties, something she did to make the air softer after she'd hardened it up.

Noni's smell and Jesus, Mary, and Joseph and how she never ever said she was sorry about anything.

"I need to swing by the store a sec. You can finally meet Marianne."

They were passing the one-story homes of citrus workers and ranch hands. Susan had driven by these yesterday, but now that she wasn't driving she could look closer, and she did. Some were run-down, with dog shit and faded plastic kids' toys spread around their front stoops, an upside-down motorcycle in one driveway, a torn couch in another. But others were well kept, their stucco sides hosed down, their cracked concrete driveways spotted with oil but swept clean. Beneath corrugated fiberglass carports, trash cans stood side by side, and it made

Susan think of her husband's kitchen knives, how Bobby kept them ordered by size in their butcher block holders, from the short paring knives to the long carvers and bread knives. Susan thought of last Christmas and how good he'd been to Lois, how he took her food-shopping with him and, when they got home, how he made her a Cuba libre with dark rum while Lois chopped celery and onions, and he peeled potatoes, Coleman's chaos turned off for once, Ella Fitzgerald singing, *Baby, it's cold outside*. Susan could see them from Bobby's office and living room where she draped strings of dried cranberries over the potted palm they'd used for their Christmas tree. She'd also wrapped tiny blue and white lights around its trunk and the bases of its thicker branches, and as she watched Noni working in their small red kitchen, sometimes smiling or laughing, her double chin jiggling merrily, Susan thought Noni's skin looked bad, not enough color in her face, and she felt a stab of love for her so deep she nearly had to sit down.

"Look the same to you?"

"Yeah, it does." Susan answered before she'd even taken in what she was seeing. They were in the historic district now, and except for the late-model cars parked up against the curbs, Oak Street still looked to be from a century earlier. Scrolled columns still held up the long porticoes shading the sidewalks in front of the shops, and between their glass display windows were heavy cypress doors that opened to stairwells to upper floors where Susan had never been, though when she was sixteen she and Gustavo had climbed the iron stairs behind Noni's store to the flat roof.

Gustavo. Maybe she should start with him.

Lois pulled her VW into the lot behind the shop and parked in front of a cluster of hickory trees. The exterior stairs were rusted now, yellow paint flaking off the rails. In their stippled shade sat an empty lawn chair, cigarette ash on one of its arms.

"Six a day, Noni?"

"That's what I said, didn't I?"

Susan followed Lois for the rear door of the shop. She was thirsty and a little hungry, and as she glanced at those iron stairs above the door of her grandmother's business, squinting her eyes in the sun, she felt like the dried-up ghost of the girl she'd been.

The inside of the store was too warm and smelled like mahogany, cast iron, and dust. It was such a familiar smell that it put her instantly back behind the register working through her stack of paperbacks, sipping warm Cokes and bouncing one leg on the ball of her foot. There was the hum of the dehumidifiers, the store still too dark and filled with dressers and chairs and bed frames, shelves of old toys that when Susan was a teenager made her sad to look at because she'd done the math and the kids who'd once played with those toys were very old or dead. Why in the world would anyone want what these long-gone little kids had left behind?

"Here she is, Marianne. Here's my Suzie."

"Oh, my, you're even prettier in person." Marianne walked around from behind the register, smiling and extending her hand. Her graying hair was newly styled, and she wore light pearls and a lime-colored blouse and matching skirt, her eyes genuinely warm. Susan liked her right away. She took her hand and squeezed.

"And a professor, too, no less. My goodness."

"Well, sort of—"

"Any action, Marianne?"

"Adjunct."

"Part-time?"

"Yes, it gives me more time for my own work."

"Marianne, anything?"

Marianne glanced over at Lois. "No, honey, just a browser or two. Nobody serious. And what *is* your work, Susan? My God, you could've been a movie star. Just look at her, Lois."

"She looks better with long hair. I don't know why she cut it."

Susan could feel those heavy scissors back in her hands, could see her small face in the mirror as she held strands of her hair and cut. "I'm a writer." She felt like a liar saying it.

"A *writer*, Lois. You never told me that."

Lois shrugged. "She's never shown me anything." Her tone was indifferent with just a touch of hurt, and she was walking down the narrow aisle between furniture of all kinds to the front of the shop and the two large windows facing the shade of the portico and the bright sun on Oak Street. "We need to display all our mirrors in these windows, Marianne. It was an accident that that bitch from Ohio found the Biedermeier."

Marianne smiled and winked at Susan. "We did that last fall, but sure, we can do it again."

"We did?"

"Yes, you remember."

Lois stared at them both. With the light of the street behind her, she was just a shadow and looked smaller than she was. "Did we sell any?"

"Now *I* don't remember." Marianne laughed and touched Susan's arm. Susan smiled at her. She and Noni seemed to have the easy rapport of old friends, and she was surprised at this.

"We need one of your Mexicans to help us with a new air conditioner, Marianne. Can you have Walter send one over? I'll pay cash."

"I really think I can do it myself, Noni."

"Don't be silly." Marianne reached into her purse on the desk and pulled out her cell phone. "I'll call my husband. God, he's going to love you. Are you staying long?"

Susan's face flushed warm. She turned to a shelf and ran her fingers along the top of a cast-iron statuette of a cowboy on one knee playing a guitar. "Not too long, no."

"Well, we'd love to have you both over to dinner at least once before you go."

"Hey, she might be here awhile, who knows?" Lois walked behind the register. It was the same one Susan had sat in front of so long ago, brass with ivory buttons for the numbers, and Lois popped it open and pulled out a twenty. "Mark this as petty cash, Marianne."

"What time should I have Walter send someone over?" Marianne held her phone to her chest. She had her eyes on Susan. They were attentive and motherly, and this made Susan want to stay and it made her want to leave.

"The faster, the better, honey." Lois was already stepping through the back door. Marianne punched a button on her cell phone and pressed it to her ear and smiled brightly at Susan, waving at her as Susan left Lois's old store full of old things feeling that old shyness that so often came up when she was around any woman who could have been her mother.

13

IT'S MIDMORNING, the sun on him, and Daniel wants to get this job done. In front of him is the last of the dealer's eight chairs and even here outside it still gives off the smell of the walnut stain he'd used on it last week. Daniel squeezes a few drops of glycerin into a bucket of warm water then stirs it with a short length of pine. He takes up three coils of cane, clamps them with clothespins, and pushes them down into the bucket where he'll let them soak for ten minutes. When he first started caning, he would weave the strands too tightly from chair rail to rail and when the cane dried and tightened it would fray. But no more. He takes pride in weaving his cane just right so that when it dries it's firm and level front to back with just the right amount of give in it. He keeps thinking of his letter to his daughter still sitting on the kitchen table where he last left it. *I'd like to see you before I go.*

A crow caws from the torch pines behind him. Last night he dreamed he'd slept nude beside a woman who was nude too. He had the body of a small boy, and he lay on his side with one leg over the woman's bare belly, his cheek against her breast. There was the feeling she belonged to him and always had, that part of him had come from her and that he would never fully be himself without her. He was aware of his penis touching the skin of her hip, and there was his full bladder too, and the sound that came from the woman's lips was like an old song she was singing to him, rain falling on his tin roof, then he was awake and alone on his mattress and he rose to piss for the fourth time.

How long had he stood there in his trailer's bathroom? How long had he waited for the two or three drops that burned as they released themselves? This was a worsening symptom, Daniel knew.

The crow caws then flaps its wings a dozen feet over Daniel's head. He counts the cane holes in the back rail of the chair. He finds the one in the center, then pushes a golf tee into it to mark it and does the same with the front rail. He reaches into the bucket for a coil of cane and pulls it dripping to him and releases the clothespin and runs his fingers a foot and a half down the length. That printout of Susan's face tacked onto the wall, she's a beauty like her mother, and he can only wonder if that has brought her trouble. He pulls the golf tee from the center hole in the front rail and weaves the cane through it and now, as if from a wind tunnel deep in the ground, comes Linda's voice and she's screaming at him, "You don't *own* me! I don't fucking *belong* to you!"

There was the way her long brown hair fell in front of her face, how small and dark her eyes got, her teeth flashing while flecks of spit flew from her mouth. Danny and Linda had been together for five and a half years, and since that hot afternoon making love standing up under the Himalaya, all that loud happy noise rumbling inches above their heads, they had never spent one day or night apart. Daniel had to have hundreds of moving pictures of her in his head, yet the same dozen or so keep circling, and this is one of them, though it has not come to him in many years.

He pulls the golf tee from the center hole of the back rail, but he can feel his letter to his daughter behind him like a cooling spirit only he can warm back to life and he better get to it while what's in his head is still there. He leaves the cane hanging where it is and soon he is sitting at his kitchen table in the heat of his trailer, a pen in his hand as he reads where he last left off.

His name was Chucky Finn and he was from Charlestown. I had my tray of baloney and mashed potatoes made from water and powder from a box and

Why the hell is he writing her *this*? The crazy that matters is the crazy *before* going down, not after. Daniel draws a large X over his handwritten words and writes:

I see you're a professor and I'm very proud of you for that. I used to love comic books but I wasn't a reader till I found books on tape.

Daniel's mouth is dry. His eyes burn. He pulls off his work glasses and wipes away the sweat with the back of his arm. He fits his glasses back on. Who the hell is *he* to tell her so casually about himself?

He crosses out what he's just written.

That worm I talked to you about? Well it became a black snake and it filled Danny's veins so he was scared all the time. But what could he do with this? He was The Reactor. When Danny got a bad feeling he shot it out of himself like a bullet from a gun. But now he was like one of the heroes in his comic books when two super powers come together in one man. Like flying and being invisible too. But this second power for Danny was no power at all. The worm had crawled into The Reactor and become the snake and the snake was Captain Suspicion and he never slept and he never got tired and he never believed a word anyone ever said especially your mother Linda.

Danny started coming home in the middle of the day. He wasn't working with Liam anymore so he could do it. Danny would just wrap his wet paint brush or roller in cellophane and climb down his ladder and start up his Datsun and drive too fast over the river and east to the strip. The whole way he wasn't seeing the road. Only Linda doing it with someone else and the thing is he was almost dis-

appointed when he never caught her doing anything but working the
arcade or taking care of you.

Daniel stops. He reads over the last few lines. He gets up and fills
a glass with tap water and drinks it. Outside his casement window
the dealer's chair sits directly under the midday sun, the cane he'd left
there drying out. That isn't good, but what lies on his table pulls him
more and he rests his glass in the sink and sits back down.

His fingertips are shaking. His heart feels flat in his chest, like it's
been run over by the past. That's what it feels like. How is it possible
that after all these years—decades—that memory brings the feelings
that went with it? It's as if the past is not past at all but just layers inside
us that are no more dead and gone than an old song on the radio. The
crow is back. It caws up in the trees outside Daniel's window. If Daniel
had a pellet gun he'd walk out there, take aim, and shoot it quiet.

And that bad afternoon only last year. Daniel was getting ready
to pull into a handicapped parking spot for Rudy Schwartz. He had
Rudy's handicapped card hanging from the mirror of his Tacoma too.
Rudy always handed it to Daniel before he even said hello, which he
didn't say often. It was one of those bright cool days in the fall, and
Rudy needed paper towels and pomegranate juice. Daniel had his indicator on and was taking the turn when a gray SUV swung into the
spot and a man in a tie and tasseled loafers climbed out talking on
his cell phone and walking toward the store pointing his key remote
behind him to lock his doors.

Daniel leaned on his horn, but the man kept walking. Daniel
doesn't remember climbing out of his Tacoma, but very soon there
was the man's back only a few feet in front of him, a wrinkled button-
down, and words were coming out of Daniel and the man was turning
around, his phone still pressed to his ear, his eyebrows rising as he
pulled his phone away.

"Excuse me?"

"I said you took my fuckin' spot and that's handicapped parking.
Now fuckin' *move* it."

The man, tall and deep-chested and under fifty, some kind of businessman, Daniel was sure, glanced over Daniel's shoulder to his old Tacoma and old Rudy hunched in the passenger's side, maybe the wheel of his chair visible in the bed, and the man raised his palm to the words that kept coming out of Daniel, this spewing heat.

"I'm sorry, I'll move it, all right?"

More words kept tumbling out of Daniel. He was aware of being watched, of a woman pausing at her open car door, of a man behind the wheel of a sedan cruising slowly by and staring out at him as Daniel followed the businessman to his SUV. Daniel's truck door still was open and he climbed behind the wheel and watched the SUV back out of the parking space Daniel pulled into a bit too quickly, Rudy's chair bumping up against the cab.

"Lookit," Rudy said. "He's driving off to shop somewhere else."

That's all Rudy said, and he looked at Daniel no differently than he had before, but for the rest of the day Daniel kept seeing over and over again the surprise on the businessman's face, that phone still pressed to his ear. It was the same look Danny had gotten from Squeeze's brother Bill, the same Danny had gotten from Chucky Finn and Chico Perez and all the boys and men down through the years who had tripped the switch of the Reactor, their expressions those of anyone who's just stepped into it. It was the look cobras and rattlesnakes must get all the time—a dark, rising fear while searching for a way out and seeing it's already too late—all in less than a heartbeat.

And there was Linda's face, too. Always, there was her face.

That was not a good week, for it left Daniel believing he had not changed at all, that the only reason the Reactor had remained dormant was because Daniel had for years kept to himself.

He writes: *Everything I'm writing to you now Susan is the story of a changed man.*

Daniel's cheeks heat up, and he knows it's not the weather. *Is he a changed man?* Because he still has a temper, doesn't he? But Danny would've thrown punches, he shouldn't forget that. He would've walked up to that rich sonofabitch and punched him in the face. He lost his cool, but he didn't do that.

A car passes by on the other side of his fence, and their windows must be open because he can hear rap music. It is the sound of angry young men and he hates it and always will. He puts down his pen. There's the feeling he's climbed back into a very old boat, one with no engine or oars or paddles, and he's letting the current take him to a place he'd walked away from so long ago, each step away better than the last.

Can't he focus on the good parts now? Being with his young daughter? How much he loved her? But ever since that night in that jail cell when the worm crawled into his guts where it grew into the Captain who ruled him, the air of Danny's house had been poisoned and even two- and three-year-old Susan was breathing it.

But no, he isn't going to tell her everything. How can he? That hunger he and Linda used to have for each other was gone, and what replaced it was another kind of hunger, at least for him. What he needed from her was a confession, and what did Linda need?

She needed to get the hell away from him, that's what.

Dear Susan,

The sickness I had has been gone a long time now, that's all I'm trying to tell you. Captain Suspicion. That snake in my guts. All that—none of it had anything to do with you.

He underlines that last word three times.

You should know that I tried to find you too. After five years on parole I was cleared to go out of state and I quit my barbering job and

That Greyhound down to Fort Lauderdale, a three-day trip. He had no idea where in Florida she was, but his mother had heard Lois owned an antiques store. If he had to, he would make his way to every town and city, searching through every set of yellow pages and visiting every shop he found.

The bus was half full, mostly black women and their little kids. One of the mothers was riding with a teenage boy, a skinny kid in a tracksuit, and if those two weren't napping or eating some kind of snack she pulled from a paper bag—apples and nuts and beef jerky—then they were talking quietly, smiling a lot, sometimes laughing out loud. And it became clear to Daniel that this woman had raised this young man alone, that she was probably escorting him down to some college where he'd earned some scholarship. Sitting on that bus heading south, Daniel pictured his mother-in-law Lois, her pretty face and big breasts and sprayed hair. Susan would be twenty-three years old, raised by one woman like that polite young man had been two rows in front of him. Who the hell was Daniel Ahearn to show up now? His daughter was who she was going to be, and how would his showing up be good for anybody but him?

At a rest stop in Savannah, he stepped off the bus into a hazy heat and he walked across the highway and the median strip of cracked red clay to the northbound lanes, where he put his thumb out.

. . . and I quit my barbering job and took a bus as far as Georgia. But I changed my mind and went back home Susan. I didn't want to bother you and I don't want to bother you now but I'm coming to see you in a few days just this one time and I hope that's all right with you.

Love,
Your Dad

No, that doesn't look right. He hasn't earned the right to use that last word. Daniel crosses out *Dad* and writes *Father*. Then he capitalizes the word LOVE and he signs his full name: *Daniel Patrick Ahearn*.

He rips out each page of his letter and numbers them and folds them together. Then he stands, lets his work glasses hang, and walks back out under the sun to this chair entrusted to him to mend. The coil of cane droops from the golf tee in the front rail, and he can see how dry it's gotten. This gnaws at him far more than he knows it should. He pulls the tee away and reclips the cane and pushes the coil back into the water that is its natural home. There's the ground-tilting sense that time and space are whirring by too fast, that he had better bear down and get something done or he'll be flung someplace where it is forever too late. He needs to get his daughter's college's address off the Internet, and he needs to mail that letter. There's a queasiness rising, and his back and hips ache, and it occurs to him he should get the oil changed in his Tacoma too. But first he has to get this job done, and he wants to get right back to work but can't. He must wait for the cane to moisten up. And so he waits. He cleans the lenses of his glasses on his shirt, puts them back on, and Daniel—he, and Danny, too—they wait.

14

IT WAS late afternoon. Susan sat at the desk of her girlhood in her newly cooled room staring at the screen of her open laptop. She ran the cursor to where she'd last left off: And whether their intent was to give pleasure or to inflict pain, whether they used their fingers or sharp objects never meant for a woman, she had been carried to where she had never before allowed herself to go: the final moment of her mother's suffering.

Now what?

Failure. It was an iron wall pressed against your face. You step to the right or to the left, and it's still there. If you turn and run in the other direction, it's there too. At least that's how it had felt to her for years. Then Bobby—and yes, Phil, her thesis advisor, even though he clearly wanted to fuck her—they had cut a window in that wall, one that looked out over a deep valley of wildflowers, and just when Susan had summoned the nerve to climb through it and leap, she no longer believed a word Phil had told her about her novel, and she could feel her enemy approaching, her love for her husband fading like an old photograph on a sunlit wall.

Three soft knocks on her door. Lois stuck her head in. She'd been taking a nap. The hem of her boxy dress was wrinkled, and her left bra strap had slipped halfway down her shoulder.

"Want a glass of wine?"

"I need to work first. Can I help you with dinner later?"

Noni waved her hand in the air. "Do your work. Doesn't your school start soon?"

"I'm on sabbatical." Which really meant she hadn't signed her contract to teach three composition courses this fall, behind her a long line of adjuncts happy to take them instead. Lois took in Susan's bare feet and legs, her denim shorts and cut hair. She narrowed her eyes at her and looked like she wanted to say more but then pulled the door closed.

That blank screen was bright and empty and all it said to her was, "You can't." *Shit.* Maybe she was wrong about her Culiacán novel. And maybe Phil was right, that it was good and she should stick with it.

This was last winter over coffee in the Student Union. It was her second residency toward her second graduate degree, and she hated how thin and cold Vermont air was in January, how it made her lungs ache even when she'd been back in the warmth for hours. It was late afternoon, and Phil was dressed in a black sweater and an open-collared shirt, curls of silver hair poking out the front buttons. He pulled a pint of brandy from a paper bag and poured some into his coffee and hers. "I think it's the violence," he'd told her. "It's your subject matter, I'm sure of it."

She'd felt naked and ugly and of course he was probably right. Should she be surprised? "Why do you say that?"

"With your other work, Susan, it's as if you're clearing your throat.

But this Mexico novel, all that brutality, well, this is your *song*, I'm sure of it."

That was a phrase Phil Bradford used a lot. In class he would say, "There's more to this passage than we're getting, I'm sure of it." Or—and this to James Cobb, a former hedge fund manager writing an espionage thriller, "Throw this shit out, Jimmy. There's a real artist in you somewhere, I'm sure of it."

Susan wasn't so sure of that at all. James was a rich, self-absorbed asshole who spoke to everyone about their work as if *he* were their teacher, his patronizing tone having far more to do with his hundred-thousand-dollar Mercedes parked in the campus lot than anything else. But he was an anomaly. So many of Susan's fellow writing students seemed to be far more like her: middle-aged or older and trying yet again to find a way to write something substantial and accomplished enough to move a stranger. Some of these writers had become her friends, a new turn of events Susan had somehow gone most of her life without, for these new friends were women. Most of them had children and husbands or ex-husbands. Many of them had always had jobs, too, and now that they were fifty, sixty, sixty-five, it was *their* time and they were stealing it to write a novel or memoir, a collection of stories or poems. The woman Susan felt closest to was Diana Clark.

She was sixty-two, the mother of three and the grandmother of seven. She had short white hair and wore loud colors all year long—blazing flowered blouses in the summer, bright red and yellow scarves and sweaters in the winter. In July she drank gin. Come January, she switched to straight bourbon. From her ears hung earrings she made herself, most of them silver hoops with some kind of cheap gem soldered into the bottom center, and in workshops she said just what she thought about a piece but in a way that was somehow still encouraging. "Mary, honey, you're a good-hearted soul, but your sweetness is killing your stories because you're trying to rescue your characters from their own damn trouble."

Mary was a retired fifth-grade teacher from Illinois. She'd blushed and glanced over at Phil Bradford, who was studying her over the rims of his reading glasses, her manuscript pages laid out on the desk before him like plans for a house he'd decided not to build. "I can't disagree with that, Mary. I really can't."

Mary's eyes had filled. She dabbed at them with her fingertips then looked around the room at the eleven other writers looking back at her. "But, how do I fix *that*?"

Diana had leaned forward in her chair, her hoop earring swaying. "Just let the shit hit the fan, honey, and get the hell out of the way."

There was laughter, and Mary smiled weakly and Phil began to make some point about characters' actions being their destiny and hours later Mary was drunk in Diana's room, her head in her lap as she thanked her over and over again for telling her "the truth."

That was a word that showed up quite a lot in those residencies.

"This line doesn't ring true to me. I think you're lying." Or, "This entire story captures the messy truth of domestic life, as far as I'm concerned." Or, "Truth and beauty. Isn't that why we're *here*?"

Yes, she'd thought, and because Bobby had nudged and encouraged her to go. Because ever since meeting Bobby Dunn just over three years ago and marrying him not long after, her life felt less like an airless room and more like an open field of fertile ground and all she had to do was dig and plant and something good would grow.

Tall and bald, one eye blue, the other brown, how Bobby would dip his head and smile at her sideways. Fifty when they'd met, ten years older than her. It was a mixer for adjunct faculty in the Student Union, and they were standing side by side at the bar waiting to order a drink. He'd winked down at her and said, "How do like being a member of the Migrant Farmworkers of Academia?"

She'd shrugged. "No meetings."

"No benefits, either."

"But there's freedom." That's when she'd noticed what he was wearing, a linen jacket with frayed sleeves over a T-shirt. In fiery letters over black was: *HARMOLODICS = FREE JAZZ*.

"Harmolodics?"

"Ornette Coleman. Harmony, melody, and rhythm all share the same value." He winked at her again, and she was surprised she didn't like it.

She never really knew what Coleman's theory meant, and she never grew to like his music, either. Painted on the study wall of Bobby's one-story house across from campus were Coleman's words: *That's how I have always wanted musicians to play with me: on a multiple level. I don't want them to follow me. I want them to follow themself, but to be with me.*

She and Bobby had made love for the first time with Coleman's frenetic saxophone playing over them, the discordant bass and meandering drums. They had known each other for three consecutive days—a drink together at the Eckerd Student Union that first night, a shared crab salad in downtown St. Petersburg the next day, another lunch, this time at his house the day after that. It was a Sunday, and Bobby, in that same T-shirt, stood in the small kitchen whose walls he'd painted red, the window and door trim black, and he kept refilling their wine glasses from a jug of cheap Sauvignon Blanc while he explained to her his thesis about modern jazz, that by the 1960s it had fallen into patterns as controlled and repetitive as classical music and it was Ornette Coleman, "this poor black fucker from Texas with a plastic fucking sax, who set jazz free again."

Bobby had stood there at the stove sautéing spinach in olive oil, smiling down at her sideways. He was barefoot in baggy shorts, his legs pale and thin, his shoulders slightly stooped. His bald head glistened with sweat, and she liked how his passion was directed not toward her eyes and hair and breasts, but to *her.*

Only two weeks earlier Alan had asked her to marry him. Usually he'd leave for work at six and let her sleep, but that morning he brought her coffee and nudged her awake. He sat on the edge of the bed in one of his white T-shirts stretched tightly across his back. He'd shaved his cheeks and throat, which made his mustache look thicker than ever, some gray in it, and outside her window the trunk of her sable palm looked gold in the first light of this day she knew would come, for they always did; boys became men and men seemed to need nests to work for and without a woman in it there could be no nest.

What she'd loved about Alan was his physical strength, his callused hands and fingers. She'd admired his quiet, discerning confidence, the kind that came from years of building iron and concrete buildings rising into the sky. She liked how gently he made love to her and what a good father he was to his two sons in college, one in the East, the other out West, how she and Alan would be driving to a restaurant in his truck and he'd pick up his cell phone and call them both. Ask about school. Ask if they were taking care of themselves. Ask if they needed any money. And she loved how he'd always sign off with, *Love you, pal.*

And now here Alan was sitting on the edge of her bed at dawn on a Wednesday, his eyes on the carpet, telling her how much he'd learned from being married once before and how he was going to bring all those skills to her. That's the word he'd used, too—*skills.* Then he'd raised his head and looked at her, and in that moment she resented him for giving her so much power over him.

Let me think about it.

I'm sorry you have to.

There was need in his voice, and just the shadow of an edge of aggression. He was, after all, a man who willed things into place that had never been there before. He leaned over and kissed her, and she kissed him back, though she could already feel herself looking for the door.

Then came this Bobby Dunn and his love of harmolodics. He'd written his Ph.D. dissertation on it and was confident it would be published, though his confidence was different from Alan's. Alan's came from directing earth movers and cement trucks and towering cranes hauling iron. Bobby's seemed to come from years of loving a sound that not many did, of wrestling with the right words, sentence after sentence and page after page, that might compel the reader to listen more deeply, to open her mind and her heart, which she found herself giving to Bobby Dunn in that hot red kitchen and its smells of smoking olive oil and cooking spinach. He was a talker, so she sipped her wine and she listened to his story of Coleman dispensing with recurring chord patterns altogether, and she could not say she no longer loved Alan Chenier, only that she had clearly packed her bags once again and now she was stepping through yet another door held open for her, this one by Dr. Bobby Dunn and his free jazz and sideways smile.

I don't want them to follow me. I want them to follow themself, but to be with me. Bobby played his own chords and let her do whatever she needed to do. He never expected her to shop for food or to cook. He never expected her to keep their nest clean and colorful and nurturing. He never expected her to fuck just because he wanted to. Instead, Bobby shopped for food and Bobby cooked. He hung paintings on the walls and he watered the plants and Bobby made love with her when *she* wanted to. Bobby liked when she read to him, and when they were at an Eckerd party, a male colleague standing too close to her or lingering too long beside her, there was Bobby's trusting sideways smile at her. *Go on, follow yourself but be with me.* This freedom was new, not one boy or man like this before. Once each of their doors closed behind her, she became a possession in a bright room, which left her feeling prized, then kept, then confined. But even that was better than being alone. For when she was alone, soon there came a muffled starkness to everything, a shadowed stillness that felt dangerous, though there was also the feeling that whatever bad thing was coming she deserved it.

The last night of her residency in July, two of Phil Bradford's fingers resting on her hip, he had leaned in close to her at loud, drunken Charlie O's and said: "Girl, you can *write*. Now you just need to believe that."

But she didn't. What she really believed, yet one more debilitating time, was that she was not a writer but a reader. That year she discovered books at Arcadia High. Only two miles away, it was still there, a one-story brick-and-glass hole teeming with the children of cattle ranchers and citrus tree farmers, kids who seemed to be passing through that place as if it and even their teen years were inconveniences they had to tolerate on their way to sitting in saddles or behind tractor wheels. And Susan Dubie was the girl with the Yankee accent and bad skin who from eleven to fourteen was shunned. But by her fifteenth birthday her skin had cleared and she grew breasts and hips, and it was like when Noni sold the Penny Arcade and bought them their first new car, a red 1981 Plymouth Reliant. There was that Chrysler star on the hood, those cream-colored seats, and that smell—like the world had changed its mind and from now on everything would be good.

People looked at them differently. In the grocery store parking lot when Noni would unlock the trunk and load it with groceries, Susan would see a man or woman passing by, maybe pushing an empty or full cart, and there would be respect in their eyes, an acknowledgment that here was something good in front of them that belonged to somebody else who must be doing something right.

Those first boys her sophomore year, they looked at her and her new body the same way. But after years of being ignored or called zit face or fucking Yankee, they could just keep looking and only look and she quickly tired of being their show. On free periods when too many of them all were milling about, she'd go to the library because that was where she found the first book that did something substantial to her. It was by a man with three names, and it was about a rich boy in Los Angeles, his girlfriends and boyfriends, the parties in big houses with expensive liquor and cocaine and the stolen sports cars of mothers and fathers who were never around. In one scene, he and some friends find the body of a young woman in the alley behind a restaurant, and they don't do anything; they just stare at it and smoke cigarettes, then drive off to another party. The last scene is of the young man throwing up in his father's office at dawn, sitting in his black leather chair waiting for him to come home just so they can talk, though he has no idea about what or why.

Susan hadn't known there *were* books like that. Noni only read magazines and watched TV. The only book in their house was *The Thirst for War*, a thick military history Paul had left behind. Susan's life was nothing like this rich boy's in Los Angeles, but going inside his head and heart for three hundred pages made her feel less alone and somehow more alive, and every afternoon during her free period she'd be in the Arcadia High School library reading novels, most of which she knew now were deeply adolescent but that she'd loved anyway— tales of dead girls in love with live boys, of horses and thieves and men carrying straight razors in dark attics and a few young women who could rise out of all this by their wits alone. Then there was her first year up at Gainesville, her dorm mate bright and blond, a tennis player and swimmer whose father lived in New York and sent her three hundred dollars a month for "extras," which too often became white lines laid out on the glass coffee table of their suite, tequila shots, Valiums for the morning after.

Her name was Andrea, and she called Susan "the Dark One" because all she did the first few weeks of the first semester was read novels on her bed, her headphones on to block out Andrea's stereo. But now Susan was reading books written for grown people, and the first was Hemingway's *The Sun Also Rises*, a book so heartbreaking that days after finishing it she was still under its influence, young Jake Barnes and his war wound that would forever keep him from making love with a woman, though he's in love with the beautiful and fallen Brett Ashley who loves him too and is fucking all his friends.

One night, as Susan walked through campus under palm trees and security lamps, the happy, oblivious sounds of other students seeped from open dorm windows and the air itself felt tender, the people in it cruel. She drifted back to her room, where she drank too much vodka with Andrea and three tanned boys from Miami, and then it was two in the morning and the boy moving inside her was the first since Gustavo, her legs around him as he clenched and froze and moaned into her ear, and her eyes filled with tears she hid from him, not because he wasn't Gustavo, but because he would always have what Jake would never have and did he even deserve it? Did any of them?

She read more novels, those assigned in her classes and those she found at the used bookstore downtown: Faulkner and Willa Cather and Saul Bellow, F. Scott Fitzgerald and more Hemingway, Zora Neale Hurston and Richard Wright and Virginia Woolf. She stayed up late in her room writing papers until her eyes burned, though what she wrote never seemed to do any justice to what these novels kept doing to her: it was like being penetrated and opened up and pulled into layered parts of herself she hadn't even suspected existed. And even for those books she did not love, there was still this sense that the dark parts inside her no one would ever truly know were now blossoming like night flowers. She felt grateful and almost too alive, all this blossoming ready for the next thing. Soon, sitting alone on her bed reading another book seemed redundant. It was time to move, time to *do* something. But what?

All those boys. Five her first year, the third her favorite. Peter Wilke. His narrow shoulders and white skin. The pink-tinted glasses he wore. His smell—sweat and sage and American Spirits. How he only wanted to make love if she let him feed her first, walk her downtown to Raul's for a taco and beer. And he liked to sit on her bed before and after and listen to her read to him. It was her idea to do this. It's what she'd done with Gustavo, though with Peter it wasn't the same.

"You read like it's you."

"What?"

"Like you *are* those people in that story."

"I am."

"You are?"

She explained that that's what happened to her, that when she was reading a great book she and her life disappeared completely. He asked if that was good and she was surprised he'd asked that, for she'd always felt that any life other than one's own had to be better in some way, at least for a while, because it would be new. Like the tall, dark boy she drifted from Peter for—Chad from New Jersey. Big shoulders, skin the color of cinnamon, his loud laugh and white teeth and the way people in rooms parted for him like he was an approaching king. When he was inside her, it was always too fast and too hard, which felt good in a way.

But Peter sent her heartbroken letters that made her hate herself and then she began to hate him for making her feel that way, something Chad never noticed at all, so she was on to the next boy, then the next, and she wasn't even sure which boy's it was she had vacuumed out of her in that cold windowless room, the fluorescent light above her so bright but far away, like it was time for her to be judged but no one really had the time.

This was the first thing she'd ever written about. It was late fall, just days before Thanksgiving. That afternoon she'd put her feet in stirrups for an aging doctor who talked to her like she was a pet dog ("That's it, good girl."), it was fifty degrees and a wind off the ocean blew dead pine needles across campus. Andrea had taken care of her that day, bringing her Tylenol and a glass of water. She even made her brownies, and Susan could not say she felt remorse for doing what she had, but her relief was that of someone who'd gotten away with something and she just knew one day she would have to pay for it.

The next morning, Andrea gone, Susan skipped her algebra class and sat on her bed with a notebook and pencil. She wasn't sure what she was doing or why, but she was trying to capture how that fluorescent light had looked above her, how it seemed so close while also being so far away. She wrote. *When Peter was inside me, he might as well have been in Canada.* She wrote about Chad, and Sanjit, the shy boy from India whose penis was long and thin and curved so much to the left she thought something was wrong. She wrote about how much she loved words, but how she never seemed able to use them much when talking to boys, or how maybe she just wouldn't. Then, of course, she began writing about Gustavo, his smell opening up inside her—cigarette smoke and orange rinds and worn denim. The first time she saw him was the first time he saw her.

It was a Sunday afternoon, the one day Susan sat behind the register at Lois's store earning pocket money that she spent mainly on paperbacks. Sunday was Gustavo's only day off from the citrus plant, and because he did not go to the clapboard Catholic church on Pinellas with the rest of the Mexican families, he'd sleep late and pull on his cowboy boots and walk to the Sawgrass Saloon, where they served breakfast all day. He'd order cold beer and steak and eggs. Sometimes he'd shoot pool by himself and play songs on the jukebox—Freddy Fender and the Mavericks and he liked the high plaintive voice of Patsy Cline. He never even knew she'd died young in a plane crash. What he'd done was drink three shots of Jim Beam that Sunday, because he was the loneliest man in the world. This was Susan's idea of him anyway. This was the story she'd written about him that day, and the one that followed, so she could forgive him because she had to forgive him.

In 1986 she was sixteen and she'd started reading the Brontë sisters. When Gustavo had stepped out into the flat bright sun on Oak Street, she was sitting behind the register with a novel in her lap, being pulled into a desire she had not yet felt for a man: Heathcliff, standing in a frock coat under a heavy gray sky, one boot propped on a peat-covered stone.

Don had just cleaned up at an estate auction. He'd brought back brass lamps and a gleaming chestnut armoire for rifles and shotguns. There were three western saddles etched with engravings, and a collection of Stetson cowboy hats that had hardly ever been worn. Lois liked the saddles and Stetsons so much she displayed them in the front window, resting the cowboy hats against the saddles like the men who owned them were off bathing in a river.

Gustavo needed shade. He was half drunk in the sun and so far from home and he stepped up onto the sidewalk under the portico. It was one of the Stetsons that stopped him. It was the only black one, its headband tiny beads of turquoise. It was the hat of a man who'd worked and sweated his way to his dreams coming true, and Gustavo wanted it but did not have to look at its price to know it would never be his. Every Friday he sent half his pay home to Culiacán, and the only way he would ever wear a hat like that would be if he stole it. But then he saw her, Susan Dubie, in her halter top and jean shorts reading a book, "and, well, he forgot about that hat."

That was the last line Susan wrote that morning when she didn't go to class. She knew there was so much more to their story than that, but she wasn't up to writing it then, and besides, she seemed to have written herself into something big and invisible and important. Its blooming presence made her put down her pencil and close her notebook. It made her take a long deep breath and let it out. She was staring at a jagged scratch in the door casing, seeing it for the very first time, and it was as if every cell in her legs and arms and face, in her chest and stomach and all the organs within it had her name on it and that name was Susan Dubie and she was a writer.

Maybe that had been a mistake. Maybe she should have just kept writing without putting a title to herself.

"*Susan?* Come and *eat!*" Noni's voice flew up from the bottom of the stairs and into this room as if twenty-five years had not passed since they'd shared this house. Susan yelled back that she'd be right down.

She could smell frying chicken. Her bare shins were cold in the air from the new window unit. That line she wrote down yesterday waiting for Lois. Susan picked it up and read it again: *Living with Noni felt like living on the run. No, not on the run. In exile. Like we'd both been exiled.*

And then they'd begun to fight each other, and so what was left but a terrible aloneness? Her grandmother had no friends, none, though once, one night maybe, she and Don had another couple over for drinks out on the screened porch. Another man in antique "acquisitions," fat and balding, with a booming laugh and a thin, quiet wife who was the only one dressed up and looked disappointed as she stepped out of their Lincoln in front of the house. Susan watched her from the second-floor window, and she'd despised that woman for being disappointed, though why wouldn't she be? Susan had stayed up in her room and tried to read, even when Lois called up for her to come down and "show yourself."

And what had become of that girl? She'd come back here at forty-three with absolutely nothing to show, that's what. What lay behind her other than a long trail of abandoned writing and aborted pregnancies and severed relationships, the sole constant her enemy, though she never called it that then or put a name to it all, and the only thing she'd ever been able to see through to its end was the reading of a good book and the teaching of one semester at a time, and now her one sliver of hope was that she felt called, yes, *called*, to finally write the kind of book she truly hated.

"Don't let it get *cold*!"

"I'm *coming*."

Susan closed the file to her novel and quickly logged on to her email. There were two from Bobby, which she knew she should read, but she couldn't bring herself to do that just yet. Beneath his was one from Phil Bradford. She tapped it open:

*Remember, I'll need at least **twenty** new pages by next month, Susan. And no more Kundera! Nobody wrote better about violence than Hemingway. —PB*

Susan wrote: *I'm working on something new. (Sorry.) But don't expect too much from me. My track record is bad. —S*

She pressed send and shut her laptop. Outside her window a small bird landed on an oak branch, its tiny claws embedded in a clump of Spanish moss. Its beak was long and yellow and pointing directly at her. Susan took this as a sign, but as she walked out of her old room and down the narrow wooden stairs into the welcoming smells of smoking fry oil and cooked chicken, she couldn't say whether it was a sign of something good or bad, only that she was hungry and looking forward to eating with her grandmother, her mother, the source of the story she would most likely fail at writing, too.

15

IT WAS nice sitting out here with Susan and their glasses of red wine. The night had cooled and through the screens came the sharp and honeyed scent of jasmine, the wood rot of the riverbanks. In the light from the kitchen window Susan's short hair made her neck look long and lovely, her profile her mother's, her wrists too. At dinner she'd seemed down and distracted, and she'd eaten two pieces of chicken one after the other.

Lois tapped out a Carlton and lit it with her Bic. She inhaled deeply and savored it for a heartbeat before letting it out.

Susan glanced over at her. "Six?"

"No more, no less. How the hell'd *you* quit?"

"Vanity."

"Your teeth?"

"And my skin and hair and stinky breath."

"That never stopped any of them."

Susan kept her eyes on the screen and the night on the other side, and Lois knew she'd just stumbled over a line she hadn't seen was so close.

"You going to tell me about you and Bobby?"

Susan raised her glass to her lips. "You ever miss Don?"

"Why do you ask?"

Susan shrugged. She sipped her wine. "Have you dated anyone since he died?"

"Nope."

"Don't you get lonely out here?"

"I was thinking of getting another dog." Lois took a hit off her cigarette. Now that she'd said it out loud, she just might.

"I admire that about you."

"What, dogs?"

"No, that you can be alone so easily."

"I didn't say it was easy."

"But you do it."

"Honey, was it your idea to 'take this break' or his?"

Susan glanced over at her. She looked sixteen again: decisive but unsure of herself. "He doesn't know I feel this way. He thinks I came out here to write."

"That man loves you."

Her eyes seemed to darken and she looked back out at whatever was beyond those screens. "Have you ever had it just *stop*, Noni?"

"What? The feeling?"

"Yes."

"The sex part or the other?"

"The other."

"I did with your grandfather, but he killed it off himself."

"What about with Don?"

"I didn't like him sometimes, but I always loved him."

Susan seemed to go real still in her chair. She shook her head.

"Then maybe you never did, Suzie. You always jumped in too fast, you know." Lois flicked her cigarette ash into the seashell tray on the table beside her. She knew she'd just run right over that line, but the hell with it. If they were going to have a talk then they should damn well have one.

Susan was staring at her. "Something's wrong with me." Her voice sounded small and naked. It had been years and years since her granddaughter had allowed herself to be like this in front of Lois, not since she was eleven or twelve years old. Its unexpected arrival felt like both a gift and burden.

"Join the club, honey. I haven't met anyone perfect yet, have you?"

"You know what I mean."

"I know self-pity when I hear it. What good will that do you? You don't think I've had reasons to feel sorry for myself? Living with a man is a job, Suzie. You go to work whether you *feel* like it or not."

"You don't think I work?"

"I didn't say that."

Susan reached for the bottle and filled her glass almost to the rim.

"In my time we didn't put a lot of stock in feelings. We just did what we had to do."

Susan sipped her wine, swallowing twice. She kept her eyes on the screen and the black shadows beyond. From far off, a dog barked. Something *was* wrong with Susan, Lois had always known that. But why wouldn't there be? My God, she'd seen it with her own two eyes. At three. Three years old, for Christ's sake.

"You gonna divorce him?"

"I don't know."

"Can I ask you why you married him, then, Suzie? I mean, you've been with so many. There must've been something different about Bobby."

"I'm trying to figure that out."

"Some things you shouldn't have to think about."

"Like what?"

"Love, you either feel it or you don't."

"I thought you didn't put stock in feelings."

Lois could feel the smile in Susan's voice. "Don't be a wiseass." The dog kept barking. It sounded farther away now, on the trail of something. "How come you've never shown me any of your writings? I *do* read, you know."

"Like what?"

"The paper. Things on the Internet. Magazines. That's reading."

Susan sipped her wine. She seemed to be listening to that barking dog getting farther and farther away. "I'm not very good at it, Noni, and I never finish anything, either."

"Why not?"

"Why aren't I any good?"

"Oh, I don't buy that. After all those books you've read your whole life? If someone else can write one, then so can you."

"I wish it were that simple."

"Some things *are* simple, honey, which doesn't make them easy."

Again, another crossing of the line, though Susan didn't seem to care. The dog had gone quiet, and she was tilting her head and looking off to the south. "You think he's chasing something?"

"Some fox or a bobcat, probably." Lois stubbed out her cigarette, but she pictured an inmate from the road prison flailing through the woods, his face scratched and slick with sweat, the dog on its trail. An old fear welled up cold inside her and she couldn't remember the last time she'd pulled her pistol from her bedside table drawer and held it.

She reached for the wine bottle and filled her glass. "You'll write a book someday, Suzie."

Susan smiled over at her. She looked sad and resigned but also determined in some way. "I'm going to load the dishwasher."

"Leave it."

"Nope, I'm going to earn my keep." She stood and grabbed the wine bottle and Lois's ashtray Lois hadn't dumped in days. She was about to ask her granddaughter how long she was thinking of staying, but she didn't want it to come out wrong so she stayed quiet. She turned and watched Susan balance the ashtray and bottle in her left hand so she could open the door with her right. In the kitchen's light she was a tall lean shadow with spiked hair and narrow hips, her mother's body down to her toes.

16

It's just after nine in the morning, the sky a deepening blue, and Daniel drives slowly down Old Route 1. Every few seconds he glances in his rear and side mirrors at the dealer's chairs. He'd fastened them down tight, each one separated by cardboard so there'd be no scratches, and even going thirty-five they do not waver.

He finished the final one late last night in his shed under the glare of a halogen work lamp. He'd worked in silence, just the occasional dripping of rainwater off the pines onto the roof of his shed and the hood of his Tacoma he'd parked under his lone elm. It was one of the last ones standing from that Dutch disease years ago, and there was the feeling when he'd gone to bed that some of us live long past when we're supposed to, his guilt about this so old it had hardened into something broken and rusted but still able to cut.

This morning, while he stood at his toilet and waited, the smell of brewing coffee filling his trailer, there had been more burning than normal and when he was finally able to summon a few drops, the water in the bowl turned the color of roses. His doctor had asked him to be on the lookout for this kind of thing and here it was and it wasn't good and it was about time.

A car horn goes off behind him. In his rearview he can see a blond woman in a black Range Rover, and he should probably pull to the shoulder and let her pass, but what's her fucking hurry? He eases up on the gas till she's right on his bumper, her pretty face contorted the way they get, then he flicks on his blinker and pulls into the asphalt lot of the fish shop where he sometimes buys himself a salmon steak he'll later grill on his small hibachi at the foot of his trailer under the pines. But his appetite isn't what it used to be. He hardly feels like eating anything at all these days.

The lady in the Rover leans on her horn as she accelerates past him. Daniel sits there feeling calm yet up against the clock. There were quite a few years when he'd thought about doing it himself. That day back in Boston when he almost did. It was a Sunday in late spring, the barbershop closed, and he'd walked himself under a rising sun to the top tier of the Tobin Bridge and stared down at the swirling water far below. The bridge had no sidewalk, just a thin ribbon of concrete for past and future workers, and behind him the traffic was light but fast, their exhaust wind pulsing at his back, the speeding roll of their tires a refrain in his head: *Do it or don't do it, we don't care. Do it or don't do it, we don't care.*

On both sides of the river were industrial docks and acres of empty cargo containers from all over the world. There were hangar-sized buildings and hundreds of parked cars and a massive mountain of sand for city trucks, and maybe that's what began to give him pause, the thought that he wouldn't see snow again. Or maybe he was just a chickenshit piece of trash who didn't even have the balls to climb over that steel railing and jump off. That was what cons said inside when something bad was going down. *Hey, somethin's jumping off.* And standing at that railing, there came to Daniel the flash of his first cell near the trap to the Visitors' Room. Visiting hours had just finished, and he was sitting on his bunk when he saw Queenie and Diaz hurry by, a dark intent in their faces that made him stand and walk to his doorway and glance down toward the trap just as Mike White left it. His face was pale from all he'd ingested, one of the screws in on it because there was no way Mike could have swallowed so many coke balloons in Visiting in any other way. He was famous for it, this skinny kid from Bunker Hill who would shit out and clean fifteen or sixteen of them for the Charlestown boys, but now Queenie walked up and threw a right into Mike's face, dropping him, and Diaz pulled a shank and straddled White and tore open White's shirt and stabbed him in the abdomen, ripping upward, Queenie reaching into White's gut and yanking out as many bloody balloons as he could, stuffing them into his pockets, Mike lying there with his mouth open, staring up at the tiers he could no longer see.

"Jesus saves, brother." It's what Mike White said all the time, the way others said, "How's it hanging?" or "Catch you later." *Jesus saves*, but of course Jesus did not save Mike. Nor did his "father," and Daniel had always had little patience for anyone who believed otherwise. No, each of us gets spit out into a life as random as rushing gutter water after a long rain nobody saw coming, and you should count yourself lucky if you land someplace dry at all, no matter how small and dirty that place may be.

But he was still here, wasn't he? Alive on that bridge on that Sunday morning? He had no right to be, he knew that. Nor had he any right to be living back on the outside. But he *was* on the outside, the river below glinting the morning sun back at him, the smells of engine exhaust and rusted steel and pigeon shit, the men and women behind the wheels of those rushing cars at his back maybe driving off to church somewhere but ignoring the poor bastard at the railing only feet away. *I'm still here, motherfuckers. I'm still here.* And so it was his hatred of his life that made him stay.

But now he has grown to like his life too much—his small caning business, the trailer he owns under the pines, his shop and fenced-in yard and driving old people around and listening to books on tape till late into the night. The truth is he's ashamed he ever went to a doctor in the first place. His time was coming for him, and he went running. But if he's stand-up, he'll do the right thing and he'll let his body do to him what it aims to do because there's still enough time to drive south, and there's still enough time to deliver and get paid for these eight Victorian chairs strapped into the bed of his truck.

Daniel waits for the traffic to clear, then he pulls slowly back out onto Route 1. He picks up speed and passes the tattoo parlor and auto

body shop, a lone gull hovering over the salt marshes and dropping out of sight.

THE DEALER'S shop is in an old warehouse on the river, its parking lot half asphalt, half rain-rutted gravel, and Daniel stays on the asphalt as he backs his Tacoma slowly into the bay. The dealer steps out of his small office. He's nearly as wide as he is tall, his white beard needing a trim at the throat and neck, his pipe stem sticking out the front pocket of his work shirt. Daniel unhooks the last of the bungee cords, and the dealer takes the first two chairs from Daniel and looks over the rest. "You do good work, Ahearn."

Daniel says nothing, just climbs up into the bed of his Tacoma and starts setting the rest of the chairs onto the tailgate for the dealer to set down next to the others.

"Just sold that rattan you did for me."

"That's good."

"Got a set of split rails coming in. You good with Danish?"

"I've done it." Daniel's not sure he has, but there's the library and the Internet and that's all he'll need.

"This week?"

"Can't. I'm going on a trip." He feels as if he's just told a lie, though he has not. His work glasses dangle from his neck, and there are the smells of fresh cane and varnish.

"How long?"

"Don't know."

"A week? A month?"

"The first one."

The dealer writes him a check and tells him he'll be in touch, and Daniel climbs into his Tacoma and drives out of the warehouse into the sun. At Water Street, he waits for a city truck to rumble by, then he turns right and follows it deeper into downtown Port City, both

windows cracked, the dealer's check in his front shirt pocket. Daniel keeps hearing what he told him back there in his cool, dim warehouse. *Can't. I'm going on a trip.*

Now that these words were said out loud, they seem like a declaration that both binds him and lets him go. Or maybe it was that blood in his toilet water early this morning, or that he has finished his letter to his daughter.

At the teller counter of the bank, Daniel asks a young woman whose nameplate says *Laura* to give him his checking balance too. She nods at him and smiles and taps her keyboard as quickly as if she were part of the machine herself. She smiles automatically at him and pushes toward him his blue deposit slip, Daniel thanking her and walking outside into the sunlight. For years that was the kind of smile he'd taken all he could from. It came from bank tellers like that young Laura. It came from waitresses and middle-aged women behind convenience store registers; it came from busy mothers on the streets of Port City and the women who worked at his library and old women through the Council on Aging like Elaine Muir and a few others. Those brief flashes of warmth, sincere or not, they were better than nothing ever again, and he took them in like air through a straw. But, standing here on the sidewalk and pulling on his slightly bent work glasses to read his deposit slip, there comes a tilting, in-between feeling that those years are ending, that things are about to get better or worse and in no particular order.

$12,647.43.

The trailer and land are paid off. But who knows how long he'll be gone? He should pay the next quarter's property taxes ahead of schedule, then throw some extra to the electric company, water, and propane too.

And he should take some out to give to Susan, if she'll take it. If she'll even see him.

A man and woman are laughing. Daniel peers over his glasses across the street. They're standing in front of the Starbucks, the man in a shirt

and tie, the woman in blue jeans and a light sweater, a pocketbook over her shoulder. The man holds a cup of coffee and leather satchel, and he's clearly making time with this woman, but he also looks like a lawyer and why hadn't Daniel given that any thought before? A will. He needs to put into writing where his property should go.

A burning weight has dropped into his groin, and he needs to find a damn toilet.

A Port City cruiser drives slowly past. The cop is looking straight ahead and not even glancing in his direction. Daniel takes this as an encouraging sign, and he stuffs his deposit slip into his shirt pocket, lets his work glasses drop back around his neck, and crosses the street for the lawyer and the pretty woman and a piss in a coffee shop toilet bowl he will not look into or even think much about.

17

To sit alone in the empty house of your youth, it was like having died years earlier and nobody remembered you any longer. After Lois drove off to the shop, Susan dumped her grandmother's hazelnut and brewed some dark roast and carried a cup up to her air-conditioned bedroom. Outside her window the sky was gray, the air thick and heavy. Earlier, she'd eaten yogurt on the screened porch while Noni drank her sweetened coffee and smoked her Carltons and told her a dream she'd had about her old dog Lilly.

"She was carrying a gun in her mouth and she dropped it at my feet. Strange, huh?"

Susan nodded, though she hadn't told her her own dream. She and Gustavo were making love again. In the dream she was no longer sixteen but forty-three and Gustavo was also Bobby with Phil Bradford's gray tufts of chest hair, this man who was three men. She opened the new file on her laptop. She sipped her coffee and began to read:

My father's parole officer had an office above a shoe store in Lawrence, Massachusetts. The street was a wide two-lane of sparse traffic, cars parked in front of parking meters built in the 1950s, and the buildings on both sides were made of the same red brick as the mills along the river.

There was her long description of the town and her sitting at the window seat of that greasy spoon for two days, of boys and men staring at her, her growing hatred of them, and then the moment she finally saw him, stepping off the curb into the street, and his arms hung still, or moved but did not move much, and she could smell fried clams and the ocean and she knew.

She did not want to read the rest, but she did anyway, quickly, and it was like parting a cut in your skin with two fingers and peering inside. She scrolled to the last line.

she had been carried to where she had never before allowed herself to go: the final moment of her mother's suffering.

No, there was so much more to this. Other things behind this and before it. She had started too late. She needed to go back. Susan began to see the palm trees of her campus, the way the sunlight made them look so green, even when they were dry.

My college senior year was my time of two Dannys.

I was living off campus with my friend Andrea then. We were renting a condo across the street from another complex where one of the Gainesville Five had been murdered. She was a girl my age, and after raping her, the killer, Danny Rolling, made her kneel on the floor of the bathroom and he stabbed her in the back and then he cut off her head.

Those murders were all anyone talked about. A thousand students left the campus and over seven hundred never came back. There were counselors everywhere, and professors encouraged us to talk about it in class, and there were symposiums on the causes of violence, on serial killers, on violence against girls and women, in particular. A lot of the boys offered to walk us wherever we wanted to go, though it became just another way to get into our pants.

I never took any of them up on walking me home. I was too angry to be scared.

Susan stared at that last line. Was that true? Yes, at everything and everyone. And it had begun as she stood on the bank of Bone River only minutes after Noni had finally told her the truth.

All summer Lois had been acting strange anyway. They'd both be watching TV and Susan would glance over and catch Noni staring at her, her expression hard and mournful.

"What?"

"Nothing, honey."

Then that smile of hers Susan had never trusted because sometimes she'd feel loved by it, but other times it would precede Lois saying something cruel, like the shorts Susan was wearing made her look like a slut. Or she should wear a bra. "Nipples are advertisements, you know." Over the years, Noni smoked more and ate less. For all of Susan's life she'd been a big woman—fleshy arms and hips and legs, her breasts generous pillows Susan would lay her head on when she was very young. That August, Lois was still a big woman but her skin seemed loose and there was less of her somehow and in this diminishment lay waiting something she did not want to do but had to.

Then, just days before Susan was supposed to take the bus back to Gainesville, a boy and four girls were murdered off campus and the killer hadn't been caught. Noni did not want Susan to go back.

"I'm going back to school, Noni."

"No you're not."

They were sitting at the table out on the back screened porch. Lois had baked manicotti and garlic bread, and Susan had tossed the salad, both of them sipping the Diet Cokes they both drank too much of.

"I'm twenty years old. You can't really stop me, you know."

"Christ, do you even *know* how many times you've said that to me?" Noni had taken only two bites of manicotti, and now she pushed herself away from the table and lit up a cigarette. She'd just had her hair done in a perm and colored darker, the brown ringlets around her cheeks making her face look rounder than it was. She was in her sixties but looked younger. A day or two before, Susan had told her she didn't have to worry about her going back to Gainesville, that lightning had a better chance of hitting her. She did not know if this was true or not, but living with Noni had become suffocating and so she would just take her chances.

"I bought a gun yesterday, Suzie."

"What? *Why?*"

"It's a pistol. I'm gonna learn how to shoot it, too." Her grandmother blew smoke out the side of her mouth. She said, "You're old enough to hear this."

And then what Susan had dreamed and daydreamed since she was a girl fell away—no more late night and the Ahearn car going over the railing of a bridge, her mother and father knocked into one another as they hit the river, cold water rushing in and pulling their car down deep, the air leaving them, their next breaths water, and Susan had prayed again and again that they did not suffer that part too badly, that soon they were both rising up out of that black river into the air, that they'd drifted over their house on the beach for a long time as she, three years old, slept in her bed, Noni reading a magazine in the living room one door away, that from time to time they still drifted over her. Inside Susan somewhere was the memory of her mother's long brown hair, her smile and her laughter. There was a Ferris wheel and the smell of cotton candy and riding high above all the people.

"He's *alive?*"

Lois nodded. Her eyes were so dark and still and scrutinizing. It was the way someone must look when they have to put down a beloved dog, watching and waiting for the poison to reach the heart and do what it's going to do. Susan's stomach seemed to lift and flip inside her. She stood and walked out their back door, letting it slam shut behind her as she ran down to the river. Spanish moss hung from the oak trees and just missed her face.

Anger wasn't the right word. Rage, maybe. Though that wasn't quite it, either. Susan remembered seeing across the river an exposed root in the clay bank. It was curved and deep brown, its beginning and end in the earth where she couldn't see it. It was grotesque to her, a malevolent glimpse of the lie she'd been eating since she was a little girl and she was screaming at it, shrieking at it, and she snatched up pieces of shale from the ground and threw them at it. Everything she saw she detested: the brown river and its sandy banks, the oak trees and their creepy fucking Spanish moss, her and Lois's house through the trees on the county road, the screened porch where her grand-mother stood in shadow watching her.

Susan hated every passenger on the bus back to Gainesville. She hated the floodplains and cattle and the small shit towns and rusted pickups and box houses with TV antennas on the roofs. She hated the fishing boats on trailers and the billboards of cheerful smiling mothers selling cleaning products or serious men selling Jesus or fat happy men selling cars or insurance or guns. She hated seeing Andrea again because Andrea was still rich and oblivious and all she wanted to do was talk about the "Gainesville Ripper." Susan hated that that was all anyone wanted to talk about. Hadn't they read *anything*? Didn't they know that this fucking planet of ours was *saturated* with blood? Didn't they know she had her own problems? She even hated that she felt this way, and when someone painted the names of all five victims on the Thirty-fourth Street Wall, she hated that she didn't rest a flower or note or votive candle on the shrine pile beneath their names. But she hated even more every young man to glance over at her and smile, and for the first time since she was sixteen, she stayed away from them all. Even when Andrea would drag her to a party and Susan would drink too much. Even then. And she hated whatever music was blasting—the Black Crowes, Alice in Chains, Jane's Addiction. She hated the pretty girls and the homely girls who wanted to be the pretty girls, and she hated that Chad from New Jersey tried to talk her into a back bedroom "for old times' sake." She hated that Andrea noticed all this and told Susan over coffee one Sunday afternoon, "You should get counseling. These murders have fucked you up."

No, Susan wanted to tell her, *What fucks me up is something I'll never tell **you**.*

But why not? Andrea was her friend. Andrea had driven her to that bright fluorescent room. Andrea had walked her back to the dorm room after, too. She pulled her sheets back and told her to lie down, and she brought her water and Tylenol, and later made her brownies. Eating them together in the late afternoon light, Andrea told her she'd gone through that twice herself. That she shouldn't think too much about it. "Fucking *guys* don't." Then, drunk one night, Andrea cried with her face in Susan's lap, her nose pressed into Susan's belly: "My dad's fucking some whore *my* age."

Susan had comforted her as best she could. She stroked Andrea's hair, and smoothed it past her damp cheek. She could hear the pain in her friend's voice, and it wasn't just one kind of pain, either: there was confusion and disgust, shock and grief; there was even a flash of jealousy, but above and beneath all these there was shame.

Andrea was just so *ashamed.*

And it was as if Susan's roommate had tapped a tuning fork against steel, its low vibration moving past the Susan everyone thought they knew into the real Susan, the one who now detested the very blood moving through her, for it was half her father's, half her mother's, one a killer, the other his victim, and so Susan herself was really nothing more than the living reminder of an unforgivable crime.

No, I was too shamed to be scared.

Everywhere I went on or off campus I felt naked and ugly, a thousand mirrors and cameras pointing at me. Then they caught the Gainesville Ripper and his name was Danny, too, and I couldn't read enough about him.

This felt like a sickness. Like one weekend her junior year when she'd slept with three boys separately and only hours apart. Part of her wanted to and part of her didn't, and she gave in to the part that did.

Danny Rolling had grown up abused. His father was a cop who beat Danny at age one when he didn't like how Danny crawled. By the time Danny was five his father had tied him up or handcuffed him over a dozen times. Danny's father tortured the family dog, and it died in six-year-old Danny's arms. When Danny was ten, his father tried to teach him how to drive and called him names and slapped him for not knowing how to handle the clutch. All this time his father had been beating up Danny's mother, too. One night when Danny was eleven, he tried to protect her, stepping between her and his father, and his father beat him almost unconscious. His mother locked herself in the bathroom and slit her wrists but didn't die. Before he turned thirteen, Danny started stealing liquor and getting drunk in the woods near his house. He taught himself how to play the guitar and he'd sing his prayers, but he also started daydreaming about hurting people and he couldn't stop. It was turning him on.

Susan read over what she'd just written. She sipped her coffee. Of course her obsession with Rolling was clear to see. She needed to believe that his evil was caused by others. She needed to believe that the other Danny, her father, had somehow been a victim, too.

That late August afternoon when she took the bus back to Gainesville and her senior year, she and her grandmother had not parted well. Ever since Noni had told her, there'd been a coolness between them, and Susan knew it wasn't Lois's fault; she probably shouldn't have told her any sooner than she did, but it had felt good and right for Susan to pack her clothes and buy the bus ticket back to Gainesville, back to a city of murdered young women.

"Why'd you fucking tell me this?"

"Because he might try to find you, honey."

Which was why Noni bought that little silver gun. Lois never showed it to Susan, but while looking for her other duffel bag, Susan had found the pistol in Lois's closet. Under Noni's shoe rack lay a gray plastic case and Susan opened it, this shiny revolver sunk in blue velvet. It made her think of coffins. She closed it and snapped it shut and pushed it back under the shoes.

Back in Gainesville those first months, Susan walked through her life as a new girl, for she had a different history now, one that changed a view of herself she hadn't known she'd been living: she'd been the orphan raised by her sometimes cruel grandmother, her story as tragic as a fairy tale, which left her feeling—though she'd only felt this faintly before—that she'd been wronged by fate and now the dark spirits that ruled over these things owed her something good.

For too long that goodness lay in books and in the boy who would love her the way she was meant to be loved, whatever that meant, for she still did not know, and now, sitting in front of her laptop, she was back at her commencement under the sun, the bleachers full of men in ties and ironed short-sleeves, women in light dresses, kids in Gator T-shirts, and so many people holding bouquets of roses and baby's breath. Noni sat under a small umbrella Paul held over her. It was sweet of her uncle/brother to come, for that's how Susan had always felt about him, that he was both. He'd gained a lot of weight and still kept his hair short, though the Air Force had released him early, and now he worked as an air freight operator at Miami International Airport. His wife Terry sat beside him, a diminutive smoker who handled their six-year old son, Paul Jr., as if *he* were air freight.

Susan Lori Dubie.

Under her robe she'd worn a cotton top and skirt, but everything had stuck to her skin. Her mouth and throat were dry, the mortarboard heavy on her head as she climbed those five steps of the temporary stage. Paul's voice carried over the crowd, "Yo, *Susan*!" and she was shaking the dean's hand, the university photographer kneeling just feet away, and was she really squinting out into the crowd under the sun in the bleachers looking for *him*? Was she really hoping to see a man standing or sitting alone staring only at *her*?

Susan read her last sentence: It was turning him on.

She and Gustavo. They were sitting in the front seat of his El Camino. It was late on a school night, Noni's ten p.m. curfew long behind them, and Gustavo had parked his car deep in the oaks of the Bone River Campground. They'd been kissing, and rubbing hard against one another, and she let him unbutton her blouse and unhook her bra. He had his radio on low, a rock station from Tampa playing hits Susan felt far away from because the kids in her school liked them. In the dim light of the radio panel, she could see Gustavo's face as he stared at what she'd just offered him. It was something she had never done for anyone before and she felt exposed but not vulnerable, not the way she'd thought she might. Instead, seeing the hunger and gratitude in his parted lips, it was as if she'd just opened a bureau drawer in her own room and there was a loaded pistol she could take out and wield whenever she felt like it.

Then he'd touched and kissed them both. He began sucking on one nipple, a tingling heat shooting into her crotch his hand was now rubbing over her jeans, and she pushed him away. She buttoned her blouse and told him she wanted a cigarette. He sat quietly a moment. Then he turned off the radio and pulled his Bic lighter from his front shirt pocket and lit a filtered Camel and they shared it.

"You are different." He took a short hit off the cigarette and passed it to her. He let the smoke out his nostrils so fast it was as if he didn't smoke and was just pretending to. She took it from him and inhaled deeply because she did smoke, had ever since last year when she'd read a novel set in sun-blinding Morocco, its men and women smoking beside unused swimming pools and in dark lounges sipping chartreuse.

"What do you mean?"

He nodded. With the radio and its light off, he was just a shadow in deeper shadows and she could feel the wetness between her legs caused by him.

"How many years have you?"

"I told you, seventeen." She had only added one year, so it didn't feel like a lie. His hand reached for hers and held it. She could feel his calluses, the skin of his palm and fingers like old rubber.

"When I had your ages I made tunnels for La Alianza de Sangre."

"Drugs?"

"We made tunnels under the streets from one casa to another."

He went on to tell her about trying to avoid doing anything else for them, but then he was given a gun and a heavy pack he was to carry through one of the very tunnels he'd helped to build. He crawled half-way through then left the gun and the pack in the dirt and crawled out and ran back to his family's two-room home not far from the Humaya River. Later in the night, he walked to a telephone and called his uncle who had work in Florida in a village with a name that sounded to Gustavo like a bonita girl. Now he was safe and earning honest money and he'd met a girl named Susandubie. That's how he'd always pronounced her name, like it was one word: *Susandubie*.

"Each week I send home my money."

"Your family?"

He'd stared at her. "Si, for my madre and sister."

"That's nice of you."

He shrugged. "I am a man, Susandubie."

Susan opened the file to her Culiacán novel. She ran the cursor to where she last left off. On Pedro Infante Blvd. a low rider rumbles by, and she can hear American rap music and a young man shouting over it as they drive for the Humaya River. She hopes Adelmo isn't with them. She hopes she's wrong about him, and the bloody shirt she found at the foot of his bed is from anything other than what she fears it is. Through the wall comes her father's labored breathing, his puta's cries, and Corina rises from her bed and wraps herself in her robe and climbs through her window to the iron stairs leading to the flat roof.

Susan tapped her fingers on the corner of her laptop. This had been so hard to write. Not just because she felt she was pretending to be this Mexican girl Corina, but it was something else too. She'd write a sentence then cut it, write another then delete that one too. She'd thought that maybe her problem was not knowing enough about Mexico. What did she know about it except for what Gustavo had told her? That's when she began to open links about "narcotrafficking," how five or six years ago the Sinaloa Cartel broke up into warring factions, roaming clans of young men and women who often filmed and posted online what they had done to their fellow human beings. One video showed the execution of five women who were simply the sisters, wives, or mothers to men of a rival gang.

The women were forced to kneel on the ground, their hands tied behind their backs. Most of them were heavy and middle-aged and wore oversized T-shirts or cheaply made blouses that had been ripped open, their bras torn off. Behind them, leaning against a dusty pickup truck, were three young men in black paramilitary pants and boots, one shirtless, the other two in faded T-shirts. Each held a rifle or a handgun or both, their eyes on a fourth man walking behind the women, speaking in fast loud Spanish, clearly performing for the camera. He was older, short and squat, and he wore an American baseball cap and held a long knife in his right hand. Every few seconds he'd lean down and lower his voice and whisper something into one of the women's ears. Then he'd straighten up and slap the back of her head and keep pacing with that knife, and Susan could feel her insides begin to twist inside her, her finger trembling over the laptop button that would stop this video, but she didn't stop it and then it was too late and she couldn't stab that button fast enough. She'd seen what she'd seen, and its stark and utter darkness carried her back to the Gainesville murders and her Year of Two Dannys. That was the time and place that began to insist on itself. But she did not want to write about that, or maybe she just wasn't ready to, so she stared and stared and what came was watching her father's parole officer's office, and waiting.

Susan sipped her cool coffee. Through the oak branches the sky had no color at all. She closed the file and her laptop, Bobby's unopened emails still inside it. With him, something happened she hadn't seen coming. Because she was welcome to follow herself there also came the pull back to what she'd been trying to do for years. No warm body in bed beside her. No loving or grasping gaze on her. Her enemy, for now anyway, at bay.

But now her room felt too small. Too quiet and still. She needed to run.

Then she was walking down her old driveway in her sleeveless top, shorts, and running shoes. It was hot and she could smell pine and eucalyptus, the sun almost directly over her head, a stupid time to run. But here she was doing it anyway, stepping onto the asphalt of the county road and running south.

18

DANIEL WAKES behind the wheel of his Tacoma. He'd reclined his seat back and from here there is only the sky through the windshield, a strip of cloud like a torn sheet. He thinks of that con in the Sixes who hanged himself from his sink. This rich prick who'd beaten his wife and kids for years then went down for embezzlement.

Daniel is hot and sweating. His windows are cracked, and he can hear the whoosh of air brakes, the rattle of a tractor trailer chassis as it rumbles by. He's thirsty and needs to piss, and he should try to eat something, too. Taped to his dash is the picture of Susan. He stares at it. She seems to be looking right at him, and she's far more beautiful than her mother ever got to be. He sits up. There across the New Jersey Turnpike and the wide Hudson River are the sun-baked high-rises of New York City, a place he's never been. From here, in the parking lot of the biggest rest stop he's ever seen, the lower tip of Manhattan looks like a glass-and-concrete cluster fuck of commerce, the highest building rising out of where the two fallen towers had been. Daniel had seen a photo of it in the paper, and this close it looks like long wide panes of glass fitted together, the top a spire at least another thousand feet on top of that, maybe more.

There were those months right after when American flags were everywhere—hanging from new poles mounted on people's porches, or as decals on their car bumpers, or bungeed to pickup truck racks and flapping in the wind. And it was good to be united in hatred for a while. It was good to walk into a store or the library weeks later and have people glance over at him and know right away that he was not one of the bad men. Not him.

Yesterday, Daniel sat at the library keyboard and typed in: *how to write your own will*. On the desk to his right was his letter to Susan. He'd folded it twice so it would be narrow enough to fit into an envelope, but it was a few pages long and thicker than he'd thought. He could feel the sweat drying under his shirt from the walk from the garage. He usually used the one down in Port City so he could wander downtown for coffee while his truck was getting tuned up, but Angie's Repairs was close to the library and post office, and now the screen lit up with a page giving him eight steps to complete. He moved the clicker to the print button and tapped it hard.

After the bank, when Daniel had asked that man in front of the Starbucks if he was a lawyer and did he know anything about writing a will, the man laughed and said he'd never be a lawyer, but he was also stand-up and he'd looked at Daniel with the respect good citizens give the old and the dying.

"It's cheaper to do it yourself. Just go online."

"God," the pretty woman had said. "I wish my husband had known that." She laughed and touched the man's shoulder and smiled at him and Daniel before she disappeared around the corner and was gone.

At his keyboard Daniel typed in *Eckerd College*, and before he could even type in where it was, it showed up and he tapped it open and there was a color photograph of the entire campus taken from a helicopter or airplane. There were buildings and a long athletic field and a white sand beach on blue water. There were the green dots of palm trees and glass and chrome flecks of cars, and there was the feeling that he was looking at something far more profound than he was—like a picture of a place where people were happy long before you were born.

Then pictures of students popped up. Boys and girls. They were tanned and wearing white T-shirts, and they looked so damn young and healthy that to know his own Susan was among them, well, it made him feel low and dirty and deeply wrong and he almost stopped everything—the letter, the trip, all of it. But there, at the bottom left corner of the screen, in big black letters on white, were the words: *CONTACT US*. The center of his bones may as well have been a magnet, those words metal, and he could only take this as a sign. He pulled a pencil from the cup on the windowsill and wrote the address. It occurred to him he had no map, but there was that time he had to drive Rudy Schwartz down to West Roxbury for Thanksgiving, and the lady at the Council on Aging had shown him Google Maps on her computer. Daniel went to that. He did not know where his daughter lived, but he knew where she worked, and he typed that address in as his destination. Then he typed in his own: 26 Butler Place, Salisbury, Massachusetts. He tapped the back of the mouse and there, in less than a full second, was his highlighted route out of Massachusetts, down through Connecticut, New York, and New Jersey, the route cutting west and south through Maryland and Virginia into the Carolinas then Georgia to Jacksonville and a straight shot down the west coast of Florida. At the top of the page was: 1,402 miles. He could do it in two long days, seven hundred miles each, twelve or so hours of driving each day. But with his condition he'd have to stop more often than he would like. Maybe he'd do it in three, give her more time to get his letter and know he was coming. In fact, he should pay extra and send it overnight. And he should do that before the post office across the street closed, which was soon.

He pressed print then read more about writing your own will. It said that if he didn't have one then all he owned would go to his next of kin anyway, but it would also go to probate and his "beneficiary" would have a "waiting period," and he did not want Susan thinking that he had not thought this through for her. He glanced down at the list of things he had to do for his will. It looked long and like a lot of trouble, but so be it. Step number five said *you cannot handwrite your will*. Step number seven said he had to sign it in front of two witnesses. Who would that be? The final step, number eight, said he had to give the original to "a person who will execute the will on your behalf." What, Rudy Schwartz? Elaine Muir? They'd probably be gone before he was. He'd have to think about this, and he'd have fourteen hundred miles to do it in, too, because he was not going to slow down now.

Daniel opens his truck door and presses two fingers to the wad of cash in his front pants pocket. For eighteen dollars and change, the postman said Daniel's letter would be in St. Petersburg by three p.m. today, a Wednesday. When Daniel paid him, he'd pulled out what he'd withdrawn from the bank, four thousand in C-notes. He peeled one off and handed it to him, a short guy with thick glasses and fat cheeks he hadn't shaved all the way up.

"What'd you, win the lottery?"

Daniel had never been any good at that kind of talk. He wanted to say it was none of his business, but it felt good to be finally sending that letter and the man was being friendly, so he made himself smile and said nothing and waited for his change.

He rises out of the Tacoma and locks the door. His hips and back burn, and there's a queasiness deep in his gut he needs to feed to get rid of. When he'd backed out of his fenced-in yard at dawn, the siding of his shed looked the color of peaches and he'd like one now. A cool ripe peach. Maybe a cold Coke and some crackers.

The sun is still not directly overhead, and he glances at his watch. He's been on the road just over five hours, his nap in this parking lot twenty minutes, and he's still an hour from noon.

19

LOIS SAT in one of Marianne's stuffed chairs sipping a brandy. It had been a good evening all around, and even though she would like just one more cigarette, she was content to sit here and watch how captivated Walter and Marianne were by Suzie. She sat between them on a leather sofa that had to be twelve feet long. Behind them lay a glass wall separated by wooden posts holding up the high wooden ceilings, and Lois kept admiring the view. Under the last light of the sun lay acres and acres of St. Augustine pasture and palmetto scrub and islands of oak and hickory trees that appeared purple-brown and reminded her of the autumns up north she still missed.

Susan, beautiful in earrings and a print dress (even with her short hair), was talking about the writings of some Russian doctor Walter had apparently just discovered in his retirement. All night long Walter had drunk in Susan as greedily as a man fresh off the wagon, his smile a bit too constant, his eyes passing over her granddaughter's face and body like he couldn't believe his good fortune in having a woman of this caliber inside his home. And now that this woman was speaking so intelligently about books, well, he was past gone.

It made Lois feel both proud and, yes, admit it, a little jealous too. Walter seemed as good and handsome a man as she'd ever met. At sixty-eight, he was tall and had let his white hair grow long enough to curl at the nape of his lined and sunburned neck. His blue eyes were deep-set and gave off the pragmatic light of a born businessman, yet they were warm too, always up for a good time, and tonight he wore an open-collared shirt, pressed khakis, and brown cowboy boots that were broken in but newly shined. Since Lois and Susan had arrived three hours earlier he'd been sipping tequila on the rocks with a squeeze of lime, though you'd never know it.

He didn't slur his words or get stupid the way Gerry had. If anything, the more he sipped, the more he seemed to concentrate on whatever the hell Suzie was talking about. Marianne, looking worn and lovely in her navy blue dress, her legs crossed at the knee like the lady she was, kept nodding her head like she had read those same Russian stories when Lois knew she was just being polite. Every few seconds she would glance over at Lois and smile and Lois would smile back, though she wasn't going to be a phony and pretend she knew anything she didn't.

"Seriously." Walter's voice was low, a bit thickened now, it was true. "He treated peasants pro bono?"

"I don't know if he ever charged *anyone*." Susan laughed. She sipped her own brandy, and then Marianne asked her a question about her writing, and Lois could see how taken Walter was with this thought of the Russian doctor who just gave away all his training. Over the years Marianne had told her about how good Walter had been to his help, how when one of his hands got drunk and drove and killed a man, Walter had bailed him out and paid for his lawyer and even supported the hand's wife and kids for the three years he was in prison. There was one of Walter's Mexican cattlemen who had a sick mother back home, Walter paying all her medical bills. There were a few stories like that. And there was the way he talked to whomever he met, whether it was an elderly antiques picker in a wheelchair out on Oak Street, or the bank president he went marlin fishing with, Walter looked everyone in the eyes as if they were just as important as anyone else.

He was too good to be true, frankly, and now Lois could see the chink in his perfect wall she'd suspected for years anyway. Women. If he was given the okay to start making love to Susan right now, there would be no holding him back. And while Suzie talked about the novel she was writing, her face turned toward Marianne, Lois could see how her friend and employee was indeed listening but how she also kept glancing past Susan at Walter on the other side of her, Marianne registering just where Walter's eyes were aiming, which was Susan's exposed knees and thighs. Lois could see how much history was in that look, and it made her feel closer to Marianne in a way that surprised her.

"So, it's set in Mexico?" Marianne said.

"Yes, in Culiacán." Suzie glanced over at Lois and she knew why, but that Mexican boy was old water under a rusty bridge.

Walter rested his empty glass on the low table in front of them. "Did you fly down there for research?"

"No, just a lot of reading. And, you know, I grew up with people from there." Susan sounded apologetic. Spots of blush bloomed at the base of her throat and collarbone. It was what happened to her as a kid when she was ashamed or caught lying, and Lois said, "That girl's read more books than anyone."

Walter looked over at her and smiled as if she were a child. He stood and picked up his empty glass and hovered over Susan. "I've been to Culiacán quite a few times. If you ever want to hear more about it, I'm happy to help."

Lois just bet he was. Susan thanked him, and Marianne smiled at her, but her eyes were on Walter walking into the kitchen and dropping ice cubes into his glass.

Lois set her brandy down on the side table and pushed herself out of her chair. Limit or no limit, it was time for that cigarette. The room tilted a bit before it righted itself, and she picked up her bag. "Excuse me, girls. I'm going to smoke."

"Haven't you had your six, Noni?"

"Who asked *you*?"

"I love that you call her that. Have you always?"

"My whole life."

It was a phrase Lois took with her out onto the deck. *My whole life.* The sun was down now, the sky streaked embers above the pastures and yellow pine. It was warmer out here than she'd expected. Maybe because of the brandy and the earlier light over Walter's land that had brought her back to the autumns of her girlhood and womanhood and spinsterhood.

My whole life. Hers was winding down, she could feel it, though there was little sadness about this, just a clear-eyed knowledge. She shook out a Carlton and lit it up and leaned against the high railing and took a deep, luxurious drag. There were still small pleasures like this. There was how surprisingly good these first few days with Suzie were going. Even late this afternoon when Lois had walked into the kitchen to see Susan preparing a marinade for their night's dinner and she told her no, honey, Marianne's invited us to her place tonight, there was none of the old drama.

*What do you mean? Were you going to fucking **tell** me?*

*How was I supposed to know you'd cook something? You never lift a damn **finger** around here—*

Fuck off, Lois. And then the younger Susan would have thrown her wooden spoon against the wall and stomped out of the room as loudly as she could. But tonight there'd been none of that. Susan had simply stopped stirring and shrugged and said, "No problem, I can cook all this tomorrow night."

What a pleasant change this was.

But her granddaughter did have problems, didn't she? Her fading marriage to a very good man (better than Walter, apparently), her lack of belief in her writings, the way she'd lived her entire life like a wanderer. Lois turned and blew out smoke and watched through the glass as Walter sat back down on the sofa. Susan was listening to Marianne, nodding at whatever she was saying, and Lois felt bad about not having heard much of what Suzie had said about her novel.

But *who* writes novels anyway? For his entire life Lois's father had worked first shift at Malden Mills, helping to make everything from Army uniforms to fake fur coats. Her mother was a housewife. Lois's uncles and aunts were cops and nurses, a few tradesmen and two fire-fighters. Her cousin up in New Hampshire had become a high school librarian, but that's as close as anyone from Lois's family had ever gotten to rooms full of books and the people who read them, never mind wrote them.

It was Linda who first loved to read and write. She learned how to do it earlier than the rest of the kids, too. She went from picture books to chapter books in less than a year. Until she'd had Linda, Lois could not remember ever stepping foot inside a public library. But when Linda turned eight or nine that changed. They'd started taking out the limit allowed, which might have been six books at a time, and Linda would be done with them all in less than a week. When she hit middle school and high school her favorite class was English and she actually liked getting assigned an essay to write. Lois still had some of them, her journal too, though there was very little in it and Lois had never been able to sit down and read it more than once. The way Linda had written it, it was with a tone she'd never had in life, and it made Lois feel as if she'd never known her own daughter.

There was one good thing, though. Until she'd found that journal, Lois had never fully understood Linda's quitting high school. Her daughter's grades were better than anyone's until they weren't, and there was her love for the written word. Why leave school? But the answer was on the first or second page.

Being smart only gets you lonely.

But it wasn't just being smart. It was being smart and beautiful. It's what high-class people wanted for their daughters. At least that's what the night soaps had always shown. If you're the daughter of a lawyer or doctor or CEO, you'd better be smart and beautiful just to

get through those private high schools and colleges and cocktail parties where you could snag your own CEO if you didn't become one
yourself. But where Lois and Gerry were from, a girl who had both
was pegged as thinking she was better than everybody else, and she
got shunned.

And so Linda shunned *them* and left school and—

Jesus Christ.

Lois stubbed her cigarette out on the railing. It was some kind of
exotic hardwood, and she thought the better of it and brushed away
the ash with her bare hand.

I need someone who's different like me. This was written on only
page one or two. Linda's journal was one of those speckled composition notebooks, and on the cover she'd taped a picture from some
magazine of a sunset over the ocean. Off to the side of it she had
drawn a peace sign and a cross, though Lois and Gerry had never
taken the kids to church.

Lois found it between the mattress and box spring of Linda's bed
in her and Paul's old room. Maybe she hadn't taken it with her because
down deep she'd known she wouldn't be able to keep anything private
from that Ahearn. It had only been a few months, and it took a lot for
Lois to even walk in there, the room blurry as she began ripping off
the sheets to wash them. That's when she found it. She sat on the edge
of the mattress and opened the notebook and saw her daughter's neat
handwriting—half print, half cursive—and, no. Lois closed it and did
not open it again until at least a year had passed.

I need someone different like me. Then Linda went on to describe
seeing Ahearn for the first time up in the DJ's booth of the Himalaya
ride. It was his voice that got her, something about his goddamned *voice.*

"I thought you might need an ashtray." Marianne was stepping
through the French doorway holding a flat seashell for Lois to put her butt
in, a gesture Lois found both thoughtful and insulting. "Thank you."

On the other side of the glass wall, Walter was leaning toward

Susan on the sofa as if he were telling her something he'd never told anyone else.

"Susan is a gem, Lois. Just a *gem*."

"Walter sure likes her."

"I knew he would." Marianne glanced back at them. She crossed her arms and looked out at the darkened pasture, just a lip of red over the flatwoods.

"You should've seen her ten years ago."

"Do you like her husband?"

"He's the best she's ever had and, believe me, she's had a lot."

Marianne nodded, though she didn't seem to be listening. She pulled her arms in as close as if it were chilly instead of the Florida-muggy Lois had never quite gotten used to.

"He's roamed before, hasn't he?"

"Oh, Lois."

"Hey, listen, my husband gave me the clap, for Christ's sake."

Marianne shook her head. "Not for a long time." She turned back to the window. Walter was nodding at something Susan was saying, and Marianne looked at Lois then out at the night. "Susan looks a bit like her, I'm afraid. I saw it as soon as she walked into the shop."

"Then why invite us over, honey?"

"I think I just like to punish myself."

"For *what*?"

She shrugged. "I don't know. Not being good enough." Marianne waved her hand in front of her face, and Lois knew she should move toward her to comfort her, but the night had been going so well and she didn't want this to turn into a scene. It ticked her off that her friend felt this way, but this unquestioning loyalty to her husband, it was what made her such a good employee.

"Sorry I asked, honey. It's none of my damn business anyway."

"No, I'm glad you did. I've never talked to anyone about it before."

"Who was she? His secretary?"

"No, *I've* always been his secretary." Marianne glanced back through the window. Susan was listening to Walter, but she looked distracted, ready to stand and join the women outside. Marianne lowered her voice. "She was some woman he met on a plane."

"Oh, *please.*"

"It went on for three years."

"Christ, how'd you find out?"

"A credit card bill."

"When was this?"

"The boys were in high school. But it wasn't all his fault, I—"

"You *what*? Don't give me that, honey."

Susan's voice was nearer now. She had stood and was nodding her head at Walter still on the sofa, then she was moving through the doorway out onto the deck. She held her empty glass but didn't seem to notice it was empty.

"You have a beautiful home, Marianne. Thank you for such a great dinner."

It *was* good, though Lois found the pork roast to be a bit dry and in need of garlic. Marianne was thanking Susan, her voice as warm and cheerful as it had been all night. Lois had seen her do this many times at the shop, too, switch herself on and off like that. Lois would be in her chair behind the register, her laptop open, looking for new estate sales or deleting junk emails, and Marianne would be dusting all their furniture, looking pensive, sad even, which always irked Lois because what did *she* have to be sad about? Then the bell over the front door would jangle, some potential customer walking in, and Marianne would smile immediately and her back would straighten up and she'd drop her duster and welcome whoever was standing there like she'd been waiting for her and her only, all day long.

Her little story of her husband and the woman on the plane, it surprised Lois yet it did not surprise her, for men were men, after all, but it also made her wonder, once again, if anyone could ever truly know anyone else. Everyone's heart was so close to the skin, yet also dark and infinite and a million miles away.

THE ROAD prison was lit up like a strip mall's parking lot. Four towering lamps shone down on the fenced-in visiting area and on the
one-story concrete buildings that made up the cells, and it was good
not to have to drive at night. Sitting behind the wheel in the dim glow
of the VW's dashboard, Susan's face looked as old as it was, a fading
middle-aged beauty, and Lois felt a tenderness for her she had not in a
very long while. It seemed the moment to tell her how happy she was
to have her here, that she loved her very much. But those words never
came easy, if at all, even for Paul and Linda. How many nights had
Lois lain awake aching to have said those words to her daughter more
than she ever had? And here was Linda's daughter, Lois's very own
Suzie, and all Lois could say was: "Guess what Marianne told me out
on the deck?"

"She's such a sweet woman, Noni."

"Yeah, well, apparently not sweet enough."

"What do you mean?"

"Walter had an affair on her."

"No, when?"

"Years ago. Some woman he met on a plane."

Susan shook her head and downshifted past the road prison and
into the curve, her headlights sweeping through the dark orange grove
then over a lump of matted fur, half on the asphalt, half off it.

"Oh, it's a dog." Susan slowed and steered around what was a German shepherd lying on its side as if it were sleeping, a spray of blood
around its head and snout. Lois looked away.

"She looks like my Lilly."

"You should get another dog."

"No, they die too soon."

"I wish you hadn't told me about Marianne and Walter."

"Why?"

"I'd like to think that there's at least *one* good marriage out there."

"There is, honey. You and Bobby."

Susan accelerated and upshifted, and Lois could see her tall husband's face last Christmas, the way he stood at the kitchen stove smiling over at Susan with such love in his eyes. It was as if he really knew her and accepted all that she was and all that she was not and would never be, but Suzie, she seemed to smile back only halfway. It was like what he was aiming at her was a bright light and she was meant for the damn shadows.

"Don't be like me, Susan."

"Yeah? What's that?"

Lois had to swallow and her eyes welled and, shit, what *was* this? "Don't push the good away. Don't be afraid of it."

Susan flicked on the blinker and pulled onto Lois's long driveway. The air in the car felt thick and too close, and Lois pressed her window button and breathed in the warmer air of the outdoors.

"You need to let your husband love you, Suzie."

Susan pulled in front of the house and turned off the engine and lights. "Why do you say that?"

"Because you're not getting any younger, and I see what I see, that's why."

"But don't I need to love him too?"

Lois pulled on her door handle and swung out her leg. "One follows the other, honey. It's a two-way street." Lois pushed herself up and out of her car. There were the smells of dead pine needles and oak bark and the banks of the river behind her house. She'd grown to love this place of hers, though for her, home would always be back north, the fast-talking men and women who would seem rude down here, the ocean too cold to swim in, though Gerry had waded into it in his best suit holding their daughter's ashes.

She'd left the light on above her front door. Her porch steps were shadowed and empty, and yes, in need of a dog bounding down them to greet her.

20

SUSAN LAY curled in bed on her side, her knees drawn up, and she kept seeing last night's pork roast on her plate, that dead dog in the road, then she was off the bed and rushing into the bathroom, flipping up the toilet lid and dropping to her knees, her abdomen jerked from the inside as last night's dinner shot out of her into the clear, waiting water.

She spat into the toilet, thought of the guacamole in a wooden bowl on Marianne and Walter's coffee table, how quickly its surface had begun to go brown. Maybe this was from *that*? But the image made her heave again, and she spat once more then flushed and stood, her nipples tender against her T-shirt.

No. Not that. It couldn't be that. But when she reached up and touched one of them, a shiver shot into her belly and hips, and, *shit*, this was just how it had felt two times before. A hot wave rolled through her abdomen. She'd brought her pills with her and took one every morning, dry-swallowing it then sipping her coffee, but had she missed any mornings back in St. Petersburg? Those horrible weeks when she'd felt nothing? For her husband, for Corina Soto, for that second graduate degree and all she'd at first thought she'd wanted to learn from it? Because this was how it had happened before. All she had to do was miss a day or two and her body would offer up a willing egg so fast it was like a barking dog straining and straining against his leash until it snapped.

Susan brushed her teeth then washed her face and hands. She dried them quickly on the towel on the rack then walked down the hall past the stairwell to the small window overlooking the driveway. She parted the curtains, but there was only her Honda parked below, the mid-morning sun already on it. If Noni had gotten sick too, she wouldn't be at the shop, and Susan let the curtain fall. She stared down the hallway. Noni's door was closed like always to keep her room cold, but her own was wide open, sunlight spilling from it onto the floor. People get sick all the time. Maybe this was just a bug. Maybe that's all this was.

But Noni's car was gone and all morning Susan sat on the screened porch, her bare feet on the sash, her laptop braced against her knees, and she couldn't work. Already her old room had become claustrophobic, and even the memory of what she'd written the day before opened a vein of self-hatred inside her that robbed her of just the kind of will she was trying to summon regularly. She should eat something, but the thought of food, even yogurt, made her stomach clench up, and she didn't even want coffee. Beside her was a glass of water she should drink more of, but she didn't. She needed to get back to work, but instead of writing, she checked her emails, opening the oldest, Bobby's. The first one read:

Play that plastic sax and then come home. Love, your husband, Bobby

Bobby leaning against the stove in his faded Hawaiian shirt, an empty coffee cup in his hand, his gray and white stubble and worried eyes.

Bobby's second email was the exact same, and she pictured his long fingers tapping the send button twice.

Noni last night telling her not to be afraid of the good. Don't push it away. Something like that.

But when had Lois been afraid of the good?

There was an email from Phil Bradford, but Susan wasn't going to open that one yet. It would be about her abandoned Corina, and she wasn't up to a scolding from a mediocre novelist who wanted to get her between the sheets. It's the last thing she needed from her "mentor," the same kind of one-dimensional attention she'd been getting from men for years. And she wished she'd heard the rumors about him before she'd signed on to work with him, but she hadn't and what Lois said had loosened some damp pebble that now began to roll, taking two or three more with it, and Susan knew if she didn't start writing right this second she wouldn't write at all. She opened her file and ignored her last sentence about Danny Rolling.

When Lois told me about my family, I'd known all along without knowing I knew. We left the strip when I was twelve, but before this, sometimes in an aisle of the IGA, a man or woman would look over at me like they knew something from a long time ago when I was a little kid and their kids were little kids and they could tell I had not been told yet and they wondered when I would be, but I'd felt it anyway.

Sometimes Noni would stop pushing the cart and she'd chat with some of them, especially the men. She'd pat her hair and stand straighter, pushing her breasts out just a bit, smiling hard when I knew she didn't feel like doing that. It was like she was always on the lookout for the next man, a better man, and that she would never be completely safe and sound without one.

But what I'd always felt in my family was trouble, that there was something bad in me, though if this ever came to me as a full thought I'd see Noni yelling at me, calling me a slut or an ungrateful bitch, and I'd blame her that I felt this way.

I blamed her for everything.

I blamed her when my skin was bad, my cheeks peppered with zits. I blamed her when one minute I loved everything—the gurgle of Bone River, the way the sunlight lay on the pine needles, the smell of Crisco melting in Noni's frying pan on the stove—and then hated everything: my face; our small house on the county road; Lois's old cigarette smoke in all the drapes and furniture; and that same gurgle of Bone River; the same damn sunlight and melting fucking Crisco—it all disgusted me and she disgusted me, and when she'd call me down to supper I'd yell down that I wasn't fucking hungry. "Not everybody has to eat like you, you know!"

Sometimes Lois would take this, but most times she wouldn't. She'd come rushing up the stairs and barge in, her hair coming undone, sweat ruining her foundation, her voice shaky because she couldn't quite get her breath. "Don't you dare talk to me like that, you spoiled little bitch! You think you're too big to spank? Well, you're not. Now get your ass down to dinner right this damn minute." Sometimes I would and sometimes I wouldn't, but she'd be done with it all and would eat down there alone.

Once I got my door locked before Noni could get up the stairs, but she busted it open, splintering the wood. "I've had it. You want to live with your father's family? Do you? Because I'll pack your bags right now!"

It was something I'd thought about many times.

I had one photograph of my mother but none of my father. Whenever I'd ask Lois about it, she'd go all quiet and say something about my father's family being poor and not owning a camera. This made me love him more. He'd died young with the woman he'd loved when his life was just starting to get good. Noni had a lot of pictures of my mother, a whole album full of them.

When I was fifteen or sixteen I came home from school and found a photograph propped on my bureau. It was a picture of my mother I'd never seen before, and Lois had put it in a wooden frame that looked new for once. In the picture, my mother is outside on the strip I still remembered. It was a close-up of her face. Behind her right shoulder are the blurred white lights of a cotton candy vendor, and above that just the corner of a pink sky. My mother's hair is long and dark and swept off her shoulders, which are bare because she's wearing a halter top. Around her neck is a thin gold chain. She's wearing eye shadow and too much mascara, and her cheeks are fake rosy with blush she applied to hide her bad skin the way I used to hide my bad skin. She's smiling, but it's an embarrassed, barely tolerant smile.

My mother was beautiful, but the thing is she looked poor and cheap and like she'd sleep with any boy who would talk nice to her.

But I couldn't stop staring at the photo. In it, she was fifteen or sixteen, and I was fifteen or sixteen. When Noni got home from the shop, carrying in two bags of groceries, I thanked her for the picture and at first she looked at me like she didn't know what I was talking about. Then she smiled and said, "You look just like her, you know."

That may have been one of the rare times I didn't say what I was thinking: *But she looks cheap, Noni.*

I helped her put away milk and butter and cans of soup, and I asked her questions about my mother I must have asked before, but now, that picture of her up in my room like some dark twin of me, I wanted to hear more.

Things Noni told me about my mother:

She loved the beach. Once, when she was six or seven, she ran into the waves and a rip current caught her and my grandfather barely grabbed her in time.

She hated rain and the fall, though she liked snow. She said the strip looked soft and clean then.

When her little brother was born she liked to hold him, though when he got older she started bossing him around. Telling him to wash his face. To pick up his toys. "Don't talk when you eat." Noni said she said that all the time.

People's mouths disgusted her. She couldn't stand when her father chewed gum or brushed his teeth standing in the kitchen. She would tell him he was "gross."

She didn't eat much. "Like you," Noni said. "You eat like a bird."

She hated it when Noni and Gerry fought. She'd come running from her bedroom and yell at them to stop. Just stop it!

Noni said that Gerry would disappear for a few days and when he came home my mother would sit really close to him on the sofa in front of the TV. She would bring him a can of beer if he asked for it.

She stayed in her room a lot, and she hated that she had to share it with Paul. The floor was concrete, and she painted a red line between their beds. One side was Paul's, the other was hers, and if even one of Paul's socks fell over the line she started screaming.

She screamed a lot. Noni said "she went from ice to fire" just like that. But mainly at them. Outside the house she was quiet.

She loved to read, but she hated school, then she quit school, though she never told Noni or Gerry. Every morning for a week she'd walk to the bus stop then keep walking. She'd sit on the covered porch of one of the summer rentals that had closed for the season and read all day. When a notice from the school came in the mail a week later, Lois confronted her daughter about it, and my mother said, "You need help with the arcade, Ma."

Noni's eyes welled up telling me that. And she told me that more than once. My grandfather was sleeping with another woman then and was doing business with bad men. That's what Noni called them. She also called them shady. She always believed that's how he'd met his end, but in my thirties, hungover on a Sunday and living with Brian Heney or Tony Riccio, I spent some time on the Internet and found my grandfather's obituary. He'd died not long after Noni and I moved down here. Gerard L. Dubie, formerly of Salisbury, Massachusetts . . . he was fifty-nine and died of a heart attack in his home in Woonsocket, Rhode Island. He had a wife named Jean Marie. They listed his three stepchildren, and then they named Paul and my mother, the daughter who had "predeceased" him, then his four grandchildren. I wondered if I was counted in one of those four. I printed it out and sent it to Noni. A few days later I got an email from her:

You'd think somebody would of told me.

When I moved to Gainesville when I was eighteen, I took that framed photograph of my young mother, and I also packed a Polaroid of me and Noni at Disneyland. I was twelve, all baby fat and the wrong hair under an oversized straw sun hat my grandmother had just bought me. She bought one for herself, too. Then she asked some father walking by with his wife and kids to take our picture with Lois's camera. In the picture we're in front of a water fountain, and Noni looks huge and pretty, and she's pulling me in close and we both look so very happy, and I suppose we were.

It was before my body began to change. Before I would hate my new school and myself and Noni for moving us down here. What was wrong with where we were?

What I remember about living in my mother's old apartment behind the arcade:

Sleeping in Noni's bed. Her room was dark, and the sheets smelled like hair and lipstick and cigarette smoke. At the foot of the bed was a black-and-white TV. The channels never came in too well, but Noni wrapped the antennas in aluminum foil, and Mr. Rogers always smiled through a snowstorm.

Noni cried a lot.

Paul was gone a lot.

Grandpa Gerry was a tall shadow in the doorway to the arcade and all its clanging bells and rolling balls and rising and falling voices.

In Paul's room, which used to be my mother's too, there was that red line painted on the floor between the beds, but it was under Paul's dirty clothes and empty Coke bottles and comic books with charging, stern-faced soldiers on the covers.

There was eating off a plate on my lap in front of the big TV.

There was how Noni's face grew rounder and rounder, her hair thinner, her eyes swollen.

There was the afternoon after school when a man was screwing steel bars over our windows.

There was Paul doing push-ups and sit-ups in his room. How he cut his hair short.

There was that fight between him and Grandpa Gerry. Yelling in the arcade early on a Saturday morning. I was watching cartoons in my pajamas, eating from a box of Honeycomb, and something slammed against the other side of the door to the arcade, then it flew open and Paul ran inside. His mouth was bleeding, and if I ever saw Gerry again after that morning, I don't remember.

There was never enough room to move, and there weren't enough windows and the ones we had Noni covered with heavy curtains. It was like living in a submarine and one of the sailors had drowned and nobody knew who'd be next.

There was the dim light of our kitchen. There was a man's voice, though he wasn't talking to me. It was low and seemed to vibrate the air like it was coming from underwater.

There was a hairy arm and a yellow telephone cord and—this voice. Like a whale in the house. Hurt. That was a word I knew, and it was in the air like a bubble rising. And wife. Or was it life?

It could have been life.

21

THE PHONE had been ringing. Susan looked up and out the screen at the shade of the oaks, the hanging moss, the bed of dead pine needles stretching to the river. It should be a beach and an ocean but wasn't.

The ringing stopped. There was the cry of some bird deep in the woods, then the ringing again, and Susan swung her laptop to the side table and stood and rushed into the kitchen to answer her grandmother's phone. There was an insistent pulsing between her ears, and if there was bad news on the other end of the phone it could only be this morning's writing that had caused it.

"Hello?"

"Good, you're home. Listen, honey, I know you're doing your work, but I need you to go borrow Walter's truck. There's an auction I have to get to in Punta Gorda, and the damn preview started an hour ago."

For a moment it was as if she were hovering outside herself. Who was Walter? And how could she drive a truck? She was just a kid, though no, there on the kitchen table was a stack of Lois's bills, a half-empty carton of Carltons, a full ashtray and her coffee cup, a spot on its rim smeared with lipstick. There was a box of saltines and cellophane-wrapped lemon cookies and a stack of toy catalogues leaning against the wall under dark drapes parted just enough to let in a bar of light that was speaking to her now.

"Is that a yes, Suzie? *Susan?*"

"Yeah?"

"Well, are you going to go get the truck or what?"

Susan wanted to ask why Marianne couldn't do that, or why retired Walter couldn't drive it over, or Lois herself. But the questions themselves felt wrong; she was staying here free of charge and Noni was asking for a favor and that should be that. "All right. I'm leaving now, Noni."

"Don't let him give you the old truck. The new one has a bigger bed."

Susan told her she wouldn't and she would, and she hung up and walked back out to the screened porch, her open laptop on the side table like evidence of something obscene. She felt a little weak. She sipped from her glass of water and swallowed twice, but it dropped into her stomach like something solid and heavy. But she could feel that she was still under the spell of that girl, like some echo she felt pulled to hear. The thing was, Susan actually *wanted* to keep writing, and she would do this thing for Lois and get back to work just as fast as she could.

LOIS WAS having one of those rare moments when she missed Don in a way that nearly ached. Estate sales were his specialty. He liked nothing better than chatting up the ladies at the registration table, picking up his bidder card, then strolling through the merchandise. But after all these years she still wasn't sure what was truly valuable and what was not. The older, the better, of course, as long as it was in good condition or not too pricey to restore. But Don read books and articles on whatever he was looking for. He drove to seminars taught by experts. When he showed up at an auction, he already had a good idea what he was looking for and how much he was willing to pay for it. With Lois, she went by her instincts and winged it and she was lucky to have done as well over the years as she had. She largely had Marianne to thank for that, and she knew it.

"Did Walter leave us any gas?" Except for a fine layer of dust on the dash, Walter's truck was as clean as the day he bought it. Liars and cheaters did that, Lois thought, they kept up appearances. But his air-conditioning felt good, and Susan was driving, squinting out at the sun and looking small behind the wheel.

"It's half full."

"Cheapskate."

Susan glanced over at her. She wasn't wearing any makeup, and her hair looked as if she'd slept on it on one side. She was still pretty but looked older than she needed to, and she was also smiling like a wiseass.

"What?"

"Nothing. You just can't tolerate people tripping up in life, can you?"

"What, did he just trip and fall between another woman's *legs*?"

Susan let out a deep laugh, different from the ones that had come from her last night when she was being all charming; this one seemed to come more from the real her, though she also looked pale and a little distracted, and she accelerated past a farm truck, its bumper crusted with dried mud, five or six Mexicans sitting in the back. Their hair was whipping around their dark, lined faces, and one of them was smiling at another. Lois could see his lips moving in the wind. Suzie said, "'Member the last time we drove to Punta Gorda together?"

"Nope. Can't say I do."

"Yes, you do."

Then she did. Lois hadn't thought about this in years. It was a school day, but that was beside the point. The night before, once again, Susan had completely ignored her curfew, and Lois was driving too fast around Arcadia after midnight in her nightgown and slippers, looking for that Mexican boy's El Camino. It wasn't in front of the one-story house where he rented a room from a family of pickers, and it wasn't in a strip mall or barroom parking lot, either. She tried not to drive as fast as she was, but it was as if Lois's own heart had a fever and its voice was screaming through her veins: *I'm not losing you too. I am not losing you too. I am not going to lose **you**.*

Twice Lois saw an Arcadia police cruiser idling at a curb. Part of her wanted to pull over and tell the cop who she was looking for, and part of her didn't. If they found that Mexican boy and he wasn't legal, then Suzie would lose him because of her and then Lois would most certainly lose Suzie.

And it was only as Lois turned back onto the north county road, her headlights lighting up the concrete bridge over the river, that she thought to steer down into the campground, and that's when her lights brought his red taillights to life, his El Camino parked deep there under the oaks. The rest was a smear of naked skin and shrieks and shouting, of that Soto boy jerking up his jeans and Lois jerking her granddaughter out of his car. There were scratches and blood, and there was sleeping that night in the hallway in a chair outside Susan's room. There was that early morning call to Lois's doctor down in Punta Gorda, and then that long quiet drive, Suzie's arms crossed in front of her, her refusal to wear her seat belt.

"I was surprised I didn't have to wrestle you into the damn car."

"I think you told me where we were going. That made me feel like a grown-up."

"You were something, all right. I've never seen anybody want to get rid of their childhood so fast." Though Lois had, and her cheeks heated and Susan glanced over at her.

"Noni?"

"I need to eat something."

"I owe you an apology. Many, really." Her eyes were dark and sincere, her lips parted like she wanted to say more.

"Oh, please."

"No, I put you through a lot."

Lois's throat seemed to close up, and she wanted to tell her granddaughter that she could have been so much worse, but she didn't think she could get the words out, and besides, up ahead was a break in the fields, a corrugated roof flashing under the sun. It was a three-pump gas station with an outdoor ice machine, and it looked like it might have a convenience store in there too. "Pull in here, honey. I'll pass out if I don't eat."

THE AUCTION was in Punta Gorda Isles, a neighborhood of big homes on saltwater canals Lois had heard about but never seen. As Susan drove slowly down West Marina Avenue, Lois took in the homes on both sides of the street, cream-colored stucco monsters with terra-cotta-tiled roofs in the shade of palm or banyan trees. Some had Cuban or Mexican landscapers tending to their flower gardens, and each home had a walkway down to their own dock and slip. There were small motorboats and large ones, many of them suspended over the water in their own private winch cradles. The driveways were laid stone or crushed oyster shells, and seeing all this luxury always put Lois in a lousy mood. Who *were* these people? Because unless you lived among them, you never saw them. Even their cars were shut safely away in the closed bays of their three-car garages, and Lois remembered Hurricane Charley in 2004, or was it 2005? How it ripped through all this comfort and showed these people just what was what. Lois knew she should never celebrate the suffering of others, but she did. She sure as hell did.

In front of the seventh or eighth house down on the right, a small white tent was set up, its ridgepole a pointed flag hanging in the heat. Beyond it the street ended in a cul-de-sac in front of the largest home around, a four-story house of glass behind a high stucco wall surrounded by palm trees. Its driveway entrance had to be eighty feet across, and Lois would be damned if she was going to walk farther than she had to. "Park in front of that castle."

"We'll block their driveway."

"Just a piece of it. So what?"

The inside of the estate sale house was so crowded with potential bidders the air-conditioning didn't seem to be working. The foyer's floor was some kind of white Italian porcelain, and walking over it to get into the front rooms on either side were men and women with greed written all over their faces. Lois recognized some but not others. Rising above them all was a staircase with no risers, only treads, and they were made of shiny steel, the balusters too, running horizontally like what you'd find on a yacht. There was real money here, and Lois began to sense she wouldn't be adding much to her inventory today after all.

Susan stood close beside her. She was staring at a painting on the wall above the stairs. It was of some man about Walter's age, handsome and well-off-looking, the way Walter was, his navy blue tie in a Windsor knot at his wrinkleless throat.

Lois said: "That's probably the dead owner himself."

"I didn't think we'd be in someone's *house*."

"Absolutely, honey. His wife just died, too. It's the kids who sell off what's left. C'mon, let's check out the goods."

The first room was darker and cooler. Small palm trees sat in ornate pots in front of the windows and worked as well as half-drawn shades, which was good because up against the wall was not a Duncan Phyfe–*style* drop-leaf, but an actual Duncan Phyfe, Lois was pretty sure. She didn't know much, but she knew old mahogany when she saw it. Phyfe, some little Scotsman who worked out of New York City in the late 1700s, was known to pay $1,000 for just one mahogany log he'd have shipped up from Cuba. A picker Lois recognized, Carl Something, was kneeling on the floor beside it, looking underneath for a signature, though Don had told Lois that Phyfe rarely signed a damn thing. She nudged Susan's arm. "See that? That could go for over fifty K."

"Thousand?"

"I think it's an original."

The surviving kids must have already taken what they wanted. The floor—some kind of teak or bamboo—had a big footprint of what had probably been a real Persian, too. The walls were bare and thin steel wires lay flat against it, hooked into the crown molding above. In the center of the room was a gilt wood settee, and two women were studying it hard. One of them leaned over it, one finger pressed over her glasses so they wouldn't fall off her face, another finger rubbing the settee's arm.

"If that's real gold leaf, we should just leave now, Suzie."

"It's real, all right." It was Carl Something, breezing past holding a Pepsi bottle and a big fat checkbook. "So's the Phyfe."

The woman straightened and the other ran her hand over the seat and what looked like teal satin, though Lois knew it had to be something older and more durable. Damask or something like that. The word was just out of her reach. Don would know in an instant what it was, and he'd tell her in a way that didn't make her feel stupid.

From the back of the house, a man's voice was announcing the start of the auction. Bird wings seemed to flutter in Lois's chest, and she almost turned to leave, but there was Susan leaning over a pair of the loveliest Dresden lamps Lois had ever seen. The bases were white porcelain and molded into two lovers entwined at the foot of a tree, the woman's long dress covering both their legs. The folds of it were covered with a fine, intricate lace, and the man was looking straight ahead like his lover had just told him a secret he would never tell anyone else—it was safe with him, and she was safe with him, there at the bottom of that tree forever and ever.

"You like those?"

"I think I do."

Lois picked one up and turned it over. Fired into the bottom of the base was a faint blue crown with five points. It was the signature from one of the famous ceramic studios in Dresden in the late 1880s, or was it earlier? She didn't remember, but she knew this blue crown was the thing to look for, and she carefully set the lamp back down.

"Well, fork over two grand and they're yours. I can get more than that for them on eBay."

"You're joking." Susan looked over at her. Standing there with no makeup in her tight top and jeans and sandals, her hair too short and messy-looking to boot, Susan looked strangely at home in this kind of wealth. There had always been something high-class about her. Not just all her book reading and wanting to be an author and a professor. It was something else, something that made Lois feel far away from her, though today she did not. Today she was just having fun showing her Susan some of her life. The man out back was giving stragglers a last call, and Lois did something she often felt like doing but rarely did. She took her granddaughter's hand, then she led her from one shining empty room to the next.

22

WALTER WAS standing on his deck in the dappled shade of a hickory tree. Susan pulled his new truck alongside her Civic and switched off the engine and slid out into the heat. In front of her was a four-car garage, its doors open, and she could see a workbench and tools and a small sports car under a custom canvas tarp. She was thirsty and maybe even a little hungry, and as she got closer to the wooden steps of the deck, it was clear Walter was waiting for her. Behind him was a patio table under an open umbrella, a pitcher of iced tea, and two glasses. His silver hair was combed back wet and between his fingers was a thick paperback, his reading glasses hooked under his thumb.

"She buy anything?"

"Yeah." Susan laughed. "A pair of lamps we didn't even need a backseat for." She held up his truck keys. "Thank you anyway."

"No sweat." He took his keys and nodded at the table behind him. "Got time for a drink?"

There was her writing, the itch to get back to it. But that iced tea looked good, and she could see that Walter was holding the Penguin Classics edition of Chekhov's selected stories. Why not? A bit of caffeine and literary talk, it would help her get back to where she needed to be.

She thanked him and let him pull out a chair for her in the shade of the umbrella. A Mexican woman came out of the house and set a platter of deviled eggs, black olives, and wheat crackers on the table.

"I didn't know if you'd eaten or not."

"No, this is lovely." Though she could not look at those eggs.

The woman disappeared inside the house, and Walter took the pitcher and filled Susan's glass. He had to lean close to her to do it. She could smell cologne and the faintly sweet scent of old booze sweating out of his pores. Beyond him and the deck, the yellow pastures stretched to deep stands of flatwood pines that looked blue under the sun.

"I don't know how you do it," he said.

"What?"

"Read all this literature." He smiled sadly and tapped the Chekhov with his finger. "I just read 'The Bishop,' and I feel like slitting my throat."

She hadn't read that one in a while, and she'd never taught it, but she could still feel the close airless room the old bishop lay dying in, his feeling he'd lived the wrong life and would quickly be forgotten, and he was.

She took a long drink of her tea. It was cold and sour with lemon, and she felt grateful for it, though she preferred Bobby's, which he made with agave. She missed him. She did. "But don't you find it beautiful?"

Walter nodded. On his lower left jaw was a nick from shaving. He was looking at her the hungry way men always had, though there was something disarmed about him. It had been there when she'd borrowed his truck a few hours earlier, too, like a lion who was done hunting but still gazed at the gazelles.

"I used to read thrillers." He smiled. Susan put one cracker and an olive on her plate. "Did you enjoy them?"

"I thought I did. They made me feel like some hero in my own exciting little movie. But this—" He nudged the book with two fingers, around one of them a turquoise and silver ring larger than any class ring Susan had ever seen. It was like being with Saul Fedelstein again but without the unapologetic pleasure Saul took in his many spoils.

"That damn bishop. Chekhov makes *me* feel like the bishop and who the hell needs that?"

"You think you'll be forgotten?" It was a question she didn't mean to sound so personal, but it was, and now he looked at her as if she'd just opened some door he was welcome to walk through. He glanced down at her lips and throat and lifted his glass. "I just feel like the good Russian doctor made me sit down in front of a mirror and stare at it awhile."

"Some say that's what art's supposed to do." She could hear Bobby's voice, feel his big hand on her bare hip. *Life's one big fucking mess, Susan. To shape it too much is a lie.* "My husband would disagree, however."

"Would he? Why?" Walter looked at her hand around her glass. His tone had an edge she now recognized. Even lions who were done hunting pricked their ears when another male came prowling near the gazelles.

"He thinks life is one big shitstorm and to fashion it into neat, clear stories is dishonest."

"What does he do?"

Funny how this never came up last night, not with Walter anyway. Marianne had asked her what her husband taught, but Walter, sipping his tequila and staring at her, seemed to be listening to music from another time. Now he looked slightly put out, his eyes back on her face as if he were quietly preparing himself to be betrayed.

"He's a musicologist."

"A musician?"

"No, he's a scholar. He studies musicians and their music."

Walter nodded once. It was a dismissive gesture, and she didn't like it. She lifted her glass and sipped her tea, swallowing twice.

"But doesn't music do the same thing literature does?"

"Not the kind he listens to."

"And what's that?"

"Just this obscure avant-garde jazz. I don't really know if anyone listens to it but him." She laughed, but she was beginning to feel she was opening her husband's underwear drawer and pointing out to Walter the ones with holes in them and those with urine stains that had never come completely out. This little move was not new to her, though, was it? It was part of the fuel she'd always needed to walk away from one man to another, an amplification of the previous one's flaws and a myopic staring at the new one's attributes. When she went from Brian Heney to Edward LeBlanc, it was that one drank and the other did not. With Marty Finn and Saul Fedelstein, it was that one was bisexual and would always be poor and the other wanted only her and had something she'd never even been close to—deep, seemingly endless wealth and the freedom from work that went with it. When she left Louis for Alan Chenier, she actually told Alan she thought Louis was the most unattractive man she'd ever been with, and Louis knew it and that's why he was so bent on fucking all the time.

These betrayals came as naturally to her as slipping off one coat to try on another, but she was not going to do that now. Bobby was more of a friend to her than any man had ever been before. He had taken very little from her and asked for less. That email from him: *Play that plastic sax and then come home.*

And what *was* she doing? She was beginning to write honestly for maybe the first time is what. And she was doing something she hadn't even known she needed or wanted to do; she was making things right with the woman who'd raised her; she was, perhaps for the first time since she was very young, actually loving Lois.

"I've never really understood academic people." Walter's chin was down, his eyes on hers as they'd been the night before. It was like he was appraising her and considered her of very high value but was not yet sure how to incorporate her into his holdings. "Do you know what a remora is?"

"No."

"It's a sucker fish. They spend their entire lives swimming beside marlin or sharks sucking bits of food and feces off the bigger fish."

"You're saying scholars are parasites?"

"I'm saying they make a living off other people's work."

"I'd say bankers do that more than scholars, wouldn't you? And besides, scholars create their own work. My husband's written a beautiful book about the music he loves."

"I'm sorry. I didn't mean to offend you."

"I need to get going."

"Eat something first."

That black olive now looked grotesque to her, though she should eat the cracker, but to reach for it now would feel like she was signing some kind of contract she was not prepared to honor. She stayed a few more minutes so as not to be rude. She talked about his view from the porch, and he nodded and kept glancing back at her as if he knew he'd stepped over the line and wasn't quite sure what to do about it. She stood and thanked him for the tea and his truck, then she was behind the wheel of her old Honda, which, after Walter's pickup, felt like a go-cart, the air inside it hot enough to bake something on her dashboard. She broke into an instant sweat and pressed her window buttons, rolling down all four as she accelerated under the oak arches of Marianne and Walter's ranch onto the asphalt of I-17 heading north. She switched on her AC too, the hot wind from outside blowing back her hair, but now her nipples felt tender again, and she tried to ignore this, for there was the cleansing sense that she had just behaved herself, and she didn't want to feel too virtuous about this, but she did. Instead of betraying Bobby, she had stood by him and as soon as she got back to Lois's she would write back to him. She might even call him, just to hear his voice, the sounds of Ornette Coleman's happy madness filling the house without her.

PART

THREE

23

MIDAFTERNOON JUST north of Baltimore, Daniel gets tired of his book on tape and shuts it off. No, it isn't that he's tired of it, it's more that he isn't listening to it and he has to keep pressing the button to make it go back and when it begins to play again, he still doesn't listen much.

It's called *A People's History of the United States*, a title that intrigued him because of the word *People's*. The actor reading it has a deep voice with some loose stones in it, and the book begins with Columbus arriving at the shores of what he thinks is the Indies and Asia. But it's the Bahamas and the people living there are Arawak, and soon enough Columbus kills or enslaves them all, just another con from the yard taking territory the only way it's ever been done.

The Ping On boys from Chinatown were some of the worst, though none of them had ever gotten cleared to come down to Norfolk. Danny had seen a few of them up to Walpole, though. Little Chinese fuckers tatted up more than anyone else. One of them was trying to move in on one of the Winter Hill micks and things got hot for a while, though Danny was down at Norfolk then and only heard about it, one dead from each crew, both shanked two days apart, and then things were square.

Chinatown. He was still going on his long walks after work, and he'd stick close to the water, light a Winston, and smoke it slowly along Atlantic past the harbor hotels. They were built of iron and glossy granite and tinted glass and they had doormen with gold tassels on their shoulders, men who when he strolled by their grand entrances looked through him as if he were dirty steam in the air from under a manhole cover. He would never be a man with money. He'd never thought to want it then. But at least when he was inside the screws saw him. At least there he had existed.

But what was this sudden desire for respect? That was wrong, too. Who did he think he was? He was lucky to be walking free at all, and he should remember that. He should never forget that. But *was* he lucky? Yes, he'd done his time but he had not paid his "debt" because he never could, not for what he'd done, and so it seemed almost cruel that he'd gotten out at all.

He discovered Chinatown when the weather turned cold. By then he'd bought a lined denim jacket and cut his hair and shaved off his sideburns. He'd lost some weight, too, and he still preferred walking along the harbor and seeing water, the gulls gliding overhead, the smell of barnacles and rust and seawater. After everything, he'd never stopped loving that smell of the strip. Across Fort Point Channel were acres of brick mills and warehouses being turned into office buildings and restaurants. One night in November, a light snow falling, Danny could see three white circus tents set up over there too, a spinning Ferris wheel all lit up with red and white bulbs, him and Linda and Suzie on one at night just like that so long ago, their baby daughter between them and Linda holding on to her with both hands, his wife's long hair sifting away from her face as their car rose up and up till they could see out into the black ocean just before sinking down, down to the sweeping, curving bottom, and Danny turned and ran across Atlantic Avenue, a truck's horn booming, snow falling under streetlights he hurried under, his head down and his hands in his pockets. Up ahead were the skyscrapers of the banking district, so many of their windows a fluorescent glow, men and women working overtime doing who knows what. Off to his left was South Station, and he ran across Summer Street and considered walking into the terminal and catching a train somewhere, anywhere, though his PO would call it in and then Danny'd be back behind the walls where at night he wouldn't be able to walk anywhere.

Up against the concrete wall of the terminal three men sat huddled under a tarp and blankets and newspapers, their faces in shadow, then Danny was across the street, cars moving by him slickly on the asphalt, and he cut right up a street called Kneeland and soon he was in the neon-lit barrooms and brightly lighted laundries and teahouses of Chinatown.

There was the skin-tender feeling he was fleeing something while being pulled toward something else, and that something turned out to be standing next to a barroom called Pinky's Lounge. In its small front window was a neon-tubed *Miller High Life* sign, the first *l* in *Miller* out so that it read *Mi ler High Life*. And there, in the darker shadows of a Chinese dry-cleaning store, a woman was smoking a cigarette. On her feet were white platform shoes with six-inch heels, her legs bare, her miniskirt white too. Her fake fur coat was buttoned all the way up, and black hair hung loose around her shoulders, big hoop earrings hanging from her ears, but it was the way she stood, one arm folded under her breasts as she drew deeply on the butt, its tip glowing bright.

It was Linda. *His* Linda, alive again in front of a closed Chinese laundry.

And she was looking right at him. The way she used to, like she'd been waiting for him and now he'd finally come, and two hands took hold of Danny's guts and squeezed and he turned and retched against a shuttered window. He wiped his mouth and looked back across the street just as a sedan pulled up and dead Linda leaned into the open passenger-side window, climbed in, and was gone.

The hand had let go, but Daniel's heart was pounding on a door bolted shut.

The next night, even though he told himself not to, Daniel walked right back to Chinatown. The snow had stopped. It was colder and his lined denim jacket and wool cap did not feel like quite enough. And the

thing is, as he came around that corner for Pinky's Lounge, his hands
in his coat pockets, his shoulders hunched in the cold, he told himself
to turn back and just go walking along the channel, go smell seawater
and rusty freighter and put your mind on anything but this woman.
But there in front of the closed laundry, the fluttering neon light of the
barroom on the sidewalk, a man was holding her up against the wall.
His hands were around her throat and her stilettos were kicking in the
air, and her night bag was flopping against his back. They were both
so quiet and Daniel was already moving, the man's hair blond bris-
tles, his neck wide, and all Daniel could see of the woman was the top
of her head, just a glimpse of her hair and her hanging stilettos and
night bag which dropped to her side and Daniel's first punch was on
a run into the side of the man's face. The man's arms dropped and the
woman dropped and the man spun out and away, giving the Reactor
an open target, this face Daniel can still see as clearly as that moment
over twenty years ago. This man had the small eyes and fleshy face of
a screw, his mouth open for air and an answer to what was happening,
his right arm flapping out beside him, and in the quarter breath of the
Reactor's next punch Daniel could see who this son of a bitch looked
like—Polaski, Polaski the bully and the sadist, and even though he'd
gotten his years ago from Willie Teague, Daniel never got to give it to
him himself, but he did now, the second punch an overhand right that
shot the man straight back and down, his skull slapping concrete, then
Daniel was on him, swinging at his unprotected face, swinging and
swinging, and it was strange how the man became Chucky Finn and
Chico Perez and all the rest. It was like dancing to a very old song in
very old shoes in a room you've never really left, and maybe the Reactor would not have quit at all were it not for the crying behind him. The
gasps for air and the crying; they were the openhearted cries of a girl
who was truly hurt, and that stopped him. The Reactor had spewed
what he spewed and the vault was already closing and Danny—yes, it
was Danny who'd done that—rose to his feet and glanced back once at
what lay there and did not move.

Then he was Daniel squatting beside this woman. Up close he could see that she was Chinese. Her black hair hung loose around her shoulders the way Linda's had, and her long throat, though whiter, was Linda's too, but her face was a mess, and the Reactor's door paused ajar, belching white heat, and he wanted to go back and kick that sonofabitch in the head until it was soft and wet under his shoe. But there was his parole to think of, and anyway this woman was gasping and coughing, her nose gushing blood over her split lips and teeth and fake fur jacket.

Daniel helped her up. From inside Pinky's came the thump of the jukebox, the drone of a game on one of the TVs, a cackle and a laugh. She stood and jerked away from him. "*Fuck* off!" She started walking, swaying like she was drunk, then her right foot buckled and she bent down and uncinched her stilettos and carried them dangling in one hand as she walked barefoot and crying past Pinky's Lounge then through a low dirty snowbank into the side street.

Her night bag lay open on the sidewalk. Daniel squatted and brushed into it a pepper spray canister and four wrapped condoms, two vodka nips, a Bic lighter, and some loose bills, then he was walking by her side, and she said nothing more, just kept crying and bleeding and sniffling to her building. Its front door was dented and covered with hot paint graffiti, its stairwell dusty concrete. She turned to him, and he could smell booze. "I said fuck *off*." But as she began to climb the stairs to the second floor, he followed her anyway. Twice she almost fell backward, and he put his hand out for her and then he was at her door, and she yanked her night bag from him and found her key. She was crying again and had to wipe her blood off on the back of her arm and she couldn't get the key into her lock. Daniel took it from her and she told him to fuck off again, but she didn't try to push him away or resist when he followed her inside and she sat at her small kitchen table and he went looking for a towel and hot water and soap.

Her place was even smaller than his, just one open room with a kitchenette and a bathroom you couldn't enter without the door knocking into the toilet. Her nose wouldn't stop bleeding and both lips were split and already her left eye was closing up. She kept crying in Chinese and English, pushing his hand away when he pressed a warm wet towel to her lips and eye. His knuckles were bleeding. She jerked away from him and swore in Chinese and lay on her bed under the window.

But she didn't fight him when he put a cool wet cloth over her eye. She didn't fight him when he pulled her out of her bloody fake fur coat or when he pulled a blanket up over her or sat at her small kitchen table till she stopped crying and sniffling and then was asleep.

He sat there a long while. She was snoring lightly, and her face was turned to the wall. He could see only her jawbone and her black hair. Something bad had just happened to her, but he could not deny that something very good had just happened to him. What he felt sitting in that metal chair at that fold-out table in that beat-up hooker's one-room walk-up was *needed*. It was like being a husband again. The joy of getting paid after forty, fifty hours of scraping dried paint chips and caulking open joints between clapboards and hauling and raising ladders and dipping his brush into wet paint and brushing it on back and forth, back and forth, the sun on him, his shoulders a burning ache he took pride in because it had to be taken and then the check and the cash and setting it on the counter for Linda to spend any way she needed to. It was the way she looked up at him, like he was something she knew would always be there the way an oak tree is there or a stone in the corner of the foundation of your house. She'd take their truck and go food shopping, and she'd leave baby Susan behind and he'd play with her and make her laugh and change her diaper when it needed changing and hold her against his shoulder and bounce-walk through the rooms of their cottage, humming to her till she was asleep and he'd lay her down in her crib and feel the way he felt then with this woman but without the love.

She hadn't moved or even turned her face away from the wall. Daniel walked over to her bed and leaned down and held his breath to listen for hers. It came as a light rattle between her split lips, and her eye was swollen shut, dried blood caked beneath both nostrils. The damp cloth he'd laid over her eye lay on the mattress in a wet spot near the radiator. He picked it up and dropped it in her kitchen sink. Taped to the fridge was a Polaroid of the woman and a young waitress in a teahouse. They both had their arms around each other laughing, and they looked like kids, their bare shoulders white and bony, their necks thin stalks, a gold chain around the sleeping hooker's. Both of them wore dark lipstick and the waitress's teeth were stained with it.

Daniel let himself out and down into the street. The sky was lightening up between the buildings, and it was colder than it had been all winter, Daniel's nose and ears burning from it. He needed to sleep a few hours then go to his barber's chair and get to work. But in the air was also the sweet yeast smell of baking bread, a bakery and coffee shop half a block east. And the thing is he wanted to go into that shop for a coffee and something soft and warm to bring back to that hurt woman that *he* had helped, no one else. Just Danny Ahearn.

That night, lying in his bed in his one-room across from North Station, the elevated train rumbling by every few minutes, he pictured the Chinese whore who wasn't Linda but stood just like her when she smoked, he pictured her holding his hand as they walked down the strip, the hot sun on them, the thumping of the Himalaya's amps ahead, the smells of fried dough and pizza cheese and menthol cigarettes, the whore's hand turning into Linda's, the whore gone, Linda flesh again, her bare bottom in both hands, her legs around him as he sank into her for the first time, above them the clackety-clackety jerk of the Himalaya cars and the screaming of girls who were only happy.

To feel that again.

Happiness.

It was a reflection in a broken mirror from old photographs he'd lost and could not find, but seeing this woman was at least that. A sliver of what once was. And so he went back again. Even though he told himself not to, Daniel walked right back to Chinatown. The snow had stopped. It was colder and his lined denim jacket and wool cap did not feel like quite enough. But the hooker standing against the laundry wall beside Pinky's Lounge wore less. Her legs were covered with torn fishnet stockings, and this wasn't the girl who looked like Linda. This one was round with a blond wig and a yellow leather jacket unbuttoned halfway down to show her cleavage. She saw him standing there across the street.

"Hey, *you*. Wanna party?" She started crossing without waiting for his answer. Daniel stepped back and turned and walked away.

"Faggot!"

He walked faster, moving west, passing a store for sewing supplies, a poster board duct-taped to the inside of the glass and covered with dollar signs and Chinese characters, down a side street of closed offices and a tailor and beauty shop, their doorways shuttered and padlocked to the concrete. At Kneeland, a Boston Police cruiser was parked at the curb of a strip club, and one of the cops was sipping a coffee behind the wheel, the other standing at the doorway to the club laughing with the bouncer. His big head was shaved and it took Daniel back to Chucky Finn, and there was the gut-dropping sense that he was going straight back to bad things. Then the cop at the wheel stared at him, and Daniel put his hands in his pockets and he walked out of Chinatown.

He stayed away after that. He still wanted to go back, but he did not, for he and women just do not mix. End of story.

But as Daniel flicks on his indicator and checks his rearview and pulls into the exit lane, that phrase feels wrong to him because stories never end. Even after we're gone, what we've left behind lives on in some way. All those chairs he's caned over the years. People will be sitting in them long after he's in the ground. And if they have them re-caned, some man or woman will punch through the rail holes bits of old cane that he put there.

And his own flesh and blood. She probably has no memory of him whatsoever. Whatever she knows about him is as bad as it gets. But that doesn't have to be the end of the story. His letter to her, his trying to see her, that'll be part of their story now.

There's a burning and a heaviness in Daniel's abdomen and groin, the sun in his eyes as he takes the ramp and slows for the turn to a Mobil station and a piss and a pair of cheap sunglasses he's going to buy if they have them. For he has kept his needs small for so long, and surely he can do that for himself, that, and maybe he'll go looking for a fresh peach somewhere, too. A fresh juicy peach.

24

SUSAN STOOD on the front porch with her cell phone pressed to her ear. She was listening to her own voice on her and Bobby's answering machine, and she didn't like it. It struck her as a cold greeting. And her voice sounded tired, and yes, depressed. "You've reached the Dunns. Leave a message. Thanks."

It left her not wanting to leave a message at all. "Bobby, it's me. We need to change our recording. I sound like a bitch. You must think that anyway, I don't know. I don't blame you if you do. I just called to say I miss you. My work seems to be going well."

She wished she hadn't said that. Saying things like that could be a jinx. "Anyway, call back. Love you."

Why no *I*? Because she did feel love for him, didn't she? In just these few days away from their small red kitchen and big bed and Ornette Coleman's words painted on Bobby's study wall? Her plants and books and writing room where she'd tried to become Corina Soto but was faking it?

She needed to get back to work, but where did she leave off this morning? She was a little girl standing in the dim light of their kitchen.

A man's voice and a hairy arm and a yellow telephone cord. The word *hurt*.

Susan pushed her cell phone into her back pocket and stepped inside the house, but once she got to the kitchen her heart was fluttering and she had to sit down. She was aware of her nipples again, how sensitive they were against the inside of her shirt, and she knew she could close her eyes and lay her head on the table and fall asleep right in this chair. No, this was no bug. It just wasn't.

She stood and grabbed her keys and then was pulling into the lot of a Walgreens that had not been there when she was young. Inside the bright and air-conditioned cool Susan bought a pregnancy kit from a teenage girl who wore glasses with red rims. Susan asked her where the restrooms were, and the girl looked at her like she was being asked to do something she shouldn't, but she pointed to the back of the store and said, "Down aisle eleven." Susan thanked her, and now she sat on a toilet in a stall of the ladies' room, squinting at the kit's tiny screen. She imagined her ankles in steel stirrups, that cold white light above for a third fucking time and, goddammit, how could she have let this happen again?

The first time, she didn't know whose it was. It could have been Peter Wilke's or Chad's or that boy from Miami before Peter or Sanjit's or—she'd stopped thinking about that part of it. But she'd told her roommate Andrea, and then the procedure was over and Andrea was handing her two Tylenol and a glass of water, pulling the blanket up to her chin and making her brownies. The second time it happened it was Brian Heney's, but she did not tell him because she knew he would want to keep it because that would mean getting to keep her.

The ladies' room door opened, and then a woman was peeing in a nearby stall. Susan peered down at the dispenser. The screen was still blank. She was forty-three, and Bobby was ten years older than that. They had their work. Well, *he* had his work. No, she did too. She had this new thing she was writing. She had her commitment to Phil Bradford and her second graduate degree. She had—what? The woman flushed her toilet and moved quickly to the sinks. Susan could hear the faucet running then the hand dryer, its blower loud and unrelenting, and here came one red line then two and oh wonderful, just fucking *wonderful*, the dryer turning off as the bathroom door opened then closed, and the room went quiet.

ON THE slow drive home, the sun seemed too bright, the orange trees too orange, the sky too blue. Susan's windows were open half-way, but the road wind sounded muffled somehow, and as the asphalt curved past the road prison she stared at the concrete tables in the outdoor visiting area behind chain link and razor wire, and what else could she do right now but get back to work? It was as if she'd just opened a bill so large she knew she would never be able to pay it, but she still had time before it was due and so she would stuff it into a drawer for now.

Back in Noni's kitchen Susan brewed coffee. While it dripped, she dumped Lois's ashtray into the trash then wiped it clean. She washed out Noni's coffee cup and scrubbed her lipstick off the rim, and Susan thought it touching that Lois had put some on today but nothing else. No eyeliner or blush. Nothing. And she used to really cake it on.

Susan took a banana from the counter and made herself eat it slowly. Then the phone rang and it was Lois, and Susan did want to cook dinner for them both, but just the thought of those raw chicken breasts sitting in olive oil made her queasy, and now the coffee didn't smell so good, either, but she poured some into her mug and as she walked up the stairs to her room, she wondered where Bobby could be on a weekday afternoon before classes started, and she felt small and self-absorbed that she did not wonder about her husband's days nearly often enough.

Her room was cool, the new air conditioner moaning softly in the window. She sat at her old desk and opened her laptop and file to where she'd left off.

It could have been life.

Then she was slipping into the skin of her younger self, staring at the twenty-two-foot walls of Norfolk Prison in early September 1991. The sky was a pure blue above the razor wire coiled along the top, and Susan had gazed at it from behind the wheel of the used Corolla Don had bought her as a graduation present. She'd driven over fourteen hundred miles in less than twenty hours, stopping only once in Virginia after nearly dozing off and sideswiping a guardrail. In her purse was just under two thousand dollars, tips she'd earned all summer working at a sports bar in Gainesville, drinking too much, smoking too much, sharing an apartment with a quiet Chinese woman who studied computer science and kept her milk and eggs in one of their kitchen cabinets. Two of the bartenders had hit on Susan all summer, and her last night working there, closing up with one of them, she got drunk on Patrón shots and fucked him in the bed of his pickup parked out behind the dumpsters. He was short and had thick shoulders and arms and a shaved head. He'd smelled like sweat and limes, and right after he came he began to cry, telling her he was engaged and if he was already cheating on his fiancée then how would he ever not cheat on his wife?

Ever since Lois had told her about her father, Susan knew she would go looking for him. It was the main reason she'd stayed and earned money in Gainesville after graduation; to go back to Arcadia would be going back to Noni's hatred of him and her fear and her gun and her claustrophobic fucking antiques store, which was nothing more than a shrine to the dead and gone.

When Susan could drive no longer, she'd pulled into a rest stop just south of Maryland and parked in front of the bathrooms building under a flickering exterior light. She climbed into the backseat and locked all four doors and lay down with a T-shirt over her face. Fifty yards away, seven or eight hulking eighteen-wheelers were parked in parallel spaces one after the other, and she imagined the drivers as men her father's age, lying awake in their sleeping compartments, thinking of their wives and children back home. This was a sentimental thought, she knew, and she was sleeping where she was was not safe, but her eyes burned and she was too tired to care and it might take her a long time to find her father, and she wasn't going to start blowing her money on a room she did not need. Not till she had to, anyway.

In my room at the Holiday Inn I'd dressed in charcoal rayon slacks and a gray blouse and light sweater. I wore my black shoes with low heels and no necklace or bracelets, just silver studs in my ears and some eyeliner.

It was a weekday, and the prison's parking lot was crumbling asphalt. Weeds poked up through some of the cracks, and most of the cars were dark sedans with blue Massachusetts license plates. It was hard not to feel guilty of something as I walked under the granite archway into a small courtyard. On both sides of the sidewalk was patchy grass under the sun. It was littered with cigarette butts and maybe I imagined my father smoking one, though he was no longer in this place and besides this was on the free side of the concrete walls that rose high above the building I walked up the steps and into.

Susan stopped. She sipped her coffee. It was cooling and bitter, but it was going down okay. Her eyes were on the wall above her bed but not on the wall above her bed. There must have been a uniformed officer she had to confront first. Maybe a metal detector or some kind of pat-down. A waiting room. But all that came to her now—and had never really left her—was the woman sitting across from her at her cluttered desk with the brass nameplate: *Asst. Supt. Murphy.*

"He's no longer in our custody." Her eyes were flat, and she wore a light blue business jacket bunched up in the shoulders. She was ten or fifteen years older than I was and heavy and had the colorless skin of a smoker, so many of those butts out in the courtyard probably hers. On the wall above her hung a framed portrait of the governor of Massachusetts, his thick red hair parted on the side, smiling down at me in his business suit like every frat boy I'd ever met: it's good being me because being me is being on top and very soon I'll be on top of *you*.

"But where is he? Can't you tell me that?"

"He's no longer in our custody." Asst. Supt. Murphy was enjoying this, and I regretted dressing like I was interviewing for a job. I also regretted being young and thin and showing up with a deep tan I got from lying in the sun between shifts at the sports bar.

"Is he on parole?"

She just stared at me. Or maybe she didn't. Maybe she picked up papers on her desk and ignored me. Both memories feel accurate. But I knew I had to say the word I did not want to say and did not know I did not want to say until I said it. "I'm his daughter."

I'd already told her that I was looking for my father, but this new word may have helped even though I felt like a liar saying it.

She handed me a business card. "Like I said, he's no longer in our custody."

I drove out of that parking lot slowly, looking in my rearview mirror at those thick, high walls, at a guard tower I could no longer see as the road curved through woods and I drove west for the highway and my room at the Holiday Inn.

My father's parole officer's name was Nicholas Xenakis, and his office was in Lawrence. It was one of those mill towns on the Merrimack River I'd known about but never visited, and the fact he was Greek did something to me. It was like I was on some fateful odyssey now, except as I was getting closer to where I was going I could already feel that I did not want to go at all.

I just wanted to see this man who was my father. Noni owned no pictures of him, and the Internet was still a few years away. The only photo I carried of my young mother was that Polaroid of her on the strip looking so young and pretty but cheap and insecure.

At the Holiday Inn I changed into a sleeveless top, shorts, and flip-flops then checked out and hit the highway, driving north. This was so long ago. I may have found a room in Lawrence first, then gone to the beach. Or I may have gone to the beach first, I'm not sure, but I knew I wanted to see the strip again before I did anything else. On the seat beside me was my Rand McNally map, and after almost an hour I left the highway and drove past malls and fast-food drive-throughs, past truck and car dealer-ships and a marina supply yard, then I was on back roads that cut through pine trees and trailer camps and one-story houses that used to be trailers.

I rolled down my windows and smelled pine needles. At a boarded-up gas station I turned north and got lost and ended up crossing the border into New Hampshire. It was a two-lane road of convenience and liquor stores, a tobacco shop and gun outlet, a tattoo parlor beside a Mexican restaurant built of yellow plywood with one lone pickup truck in the lot at noon. I was hungry but wanted to eat at the beach. I turned around and found a road heading east past motel cabins and a mini-golf park, a tow-ering orange bear standing in its center. Just beyond that was a tire depot. My friend Kimberly Mitchell's house used to be in the woods behind that, and I wondered if she still lived around there, though I did not want to see her. I didn't want to see anyone.

Then the woods opened onto the marsh, and I could see the strip less than a mile to the east. Under that deep September sky, it looked dirty and insignificant, and it's only now, as I write this, that I know why I wanted to go back there at all. Before Noni had told me the truth a year earlier, I'd remembered living behind the arcade after my grandfather and Paul were gone. I remembered how small and dark our apartment was, and I remem-bered the heat outside, or the cold. There was the constant breaking of the surf onto wet sand, the smells of fried clams and cotton candy during the season, the pinball machines' pops and pings, electronic explosions, pool balls breaking. There was Noni's cigarette smoke and sometimes a drunk outside yelling or laughing. There were both TV's going all day and night. There was Noni's perfume and hair spray, the whirring lights of the kiddie rides, kids screaming.

There was all that cheap glee amid all that deep grief that I'd thought came from a car and a bridge and a river at night, but ever since Noni had told me the truth, I had begun to remember a different night and all my memories of that place felt like a trick of the mind.

What I wanted to see more than anything was the house I'd lived in before I'd lived with Lois.

A cheerful buzzing. Susan glanced at her phone and saw it was Bobby and turned it off. Part of her was glad he was calling, but not now. He was always so good at reading her moods and what she might be thinking. She drank from her cup and closed her eyes and swallowed. There was the dank taste of coffee, then the feel of a slice of pizza in her hand. It was from Tripoli's on the Midway. The same sweet red sauce and greasy cheese and the napkins she held under it as she chewed. The memory began to turn her stomach.

I hadn't been to that place since I was twelve, and now I was twenty-one. It looked small and seedy and like its time had come and gone so long ago that it was as obscene as seeing an old man in a Speedo. I ate a slice of pizza and went walking.

Most of the shops along the Midway were closed, their windows boarded up. When I was a girl, there had been a gateway to a kiddie park full of rides and the bumper cars tent, but in that space now was a dumpster under a ripped blue tarp seagulls were picking trash from.

It was a weekday in September, so I knew there wouldn't be a crowd there, but I didn't expect it to be as deserted as it was, either. At the end of the Midway I walked around the guardrails onto the beach and looked out at the water awhile. In the sand were a few empty Coke and beer cans, the broken tip of a Styrofoam surfboard, a bottle rolling back and forth in the waves. Off to my left there was a building I remembered that was built on wooden piers, and at the base of one a red T-shirt was snagged on a rusted nail and I turned and walked south for the Penny Arcade and my and Noni's old place.

The arcade was still there. Its doors were wide open the way they used to be, but inside were only a handful of machines, no Skee-Ball or pool table or even pinball. Two or three teenage boys skipping school stood or sat at a few games with lit names like Smash TV, Area 51, and Lethal Enforcers, their faces in a trance as they jerked on controls and shot down men and blew up armored vehicles. They reminded me so much of Paul I may have felt a pang to call him later, though I don't believe I ever did.

My uncle-brother. I only lived with him for three years. I was three and he was fifteen, then I was six and he was eighteen and gone to the Air Force. If I had any images of Paul from that time, I held only a few: Paul sitting on the black sofa in front of the TV beside me shoveling potato chips or Cracker Jacks into his mouth; Paul's back under the blinking lights of the arcade; Paul leaning against the hood of his first car in the lot behind our apartment. It was a four-door sedan, and it was long and blue with white-walled tires. He was in a red-and-white-striped shirt, a beer can in his hand, and he was smiling down at me like he'd just learned an important secret about life, but he wasn't telling me.

C'mere, Suzie. Get lost. Half of me a reminder of his big sister, the other half of the one who took her away.

At the back wall where the door to our apartment used to be were cinder blocks mortared together. I rushed outside and around to the lot where Noni used to park our car right near our front door. It had been metal, the windows on either side covered with bars so I'd always felt locked in. But there was no apartment. In its place were thick wooden posts leading to a second story that had been built over the arcade. Where our kitchen and living room had been, there was a motorcycle and a gas grill, a hammock hanging between two posts. Where Noni's bedroom had been, there was an empty paved parking space. Where my mother's and Paul's bedroom had been, there was a poured concrete patio, a round table and four chairs chained together and fastened with a padlock. In the center of the table was a plastic Wiffle ball bat and a faded tube of suntan lotion.

That may not have been what was on that table, but it's what I see there now. And that's when the anger started, and I began to walk fast down the beach road, looking for the house of my birth, and things got worse.

A whole block of cottages had been torn down. In their place was a three-story complex of condos covered with vinyl siding. Each unit had a small deck, and I knew those on the third floor probably had a view of the ocean above the roofs of the cottages on the beach side. I remembered some of these. They had the same wide clapboards and shuttered windows. Their roofs had tar patches here and there, and if they had gutters at all they were bent and rusted and led to drainpipes buried in the sand. If they had steps to their front doors, they were crumbling concrete or wood that was so warped from the sun the heads of the nails had risen up out of the planks.

I remembered that my cottage had concrete steps and that it was two or three blocks from the beach with a view of only more low-rent cottages across the street. A dog was barking. Somewhere back there an engine kept revving. A breeze blew in from the ocean and the temperature dropped and I was sorry I'd left my sweater back in my car. Or maybe the temperature didn't drop. Maybe I'm just writing this because I'm sitting in an overly air-conditioned room in Arcadia, Florida, twenty-two years later. But I remember finding our old house, though it was like seeing an old friend who's just had a haircut or lost a lot of weight.

The cottage's name was still Ocean Mist, but the sign looked new, its edge beveled and painted dark green. The siding was vinyl like the condos but so very white, and the concrete steps to the door were gone and in their place was a deck built out of fake boards, the kind that's made to look like wood but is really some kind of poured plastic. The posts were fake, too. Strung from one to the next was real rope, and on the wall near the door was one of those orange Coast Guard life rings.

A radio was playing. Or maybe it was a TV. But I remember voices coming in from the airwaves, and I remember the sun on me but feeling cold anyway and staring at that door that used to open right into our kitchen with the yellow linoleum. And that's when the new owner walked out of it.

She was probably the age I am now. She wore a sun hat and white sunblock on her nose and lips. She held a plastic tumbler of what looked like Coke or iced tea and on the small table beside her chaise lounge was an upside-down paperback. I wondered what she was reading. She stood there staring down at me.

"Can I help you?"

"I used to live here."

"Who hasn't? It's a rental."

We may not have said these things, but I remember not liking her, especially when she sat down and picked up her paperback like I was now dismissed. She was reading shit, too. One of those cheap thrillers written by a staff under one name.

"My mother died in this house."

"Excuse me?"

"When I was a kid. She was stabbed to death."

The woman seemed to go very still, though she was sitting in her chaise lounge with the book in her lap. I might not have looked so good, either.

"I think you need to leave."

I know she said that because it matched the voice in my own head nearly word for word. *I need to leave.*

But there was something about her I detested. It wasn't that she'd been rude to me. It's because of what she or the new owner had done to our cottage. They'd made it cute and benign-looking, and it was like seeing in three dimensions the lie I'd been fed since I was three, and this woman with the sun hat and sunblocked nose and lips and shitty paperback, she may as well have been a gargoyle at the gates to the black pit my mother had been thrown into and forgotten.

"I need to see the inside."

I don't recall when the yelling started. I just know I wanted to see the kitchen, but then there was how she yelled the word *cops*. That accent I'd heard only from Lois the last nine or ten years. Cawps.

"I will call them right fuckin' now." She was out of her chaise by then, holding the kitchen's screen door open with her hip, reaching her hand around the corner and pulling out the receiver of her wall phone. It was white, too, when I know our phone had been the color of mustard, my father's hairy forearm holding it to his ear. Why go inside and see more whitewashed bullshit anyway?

I turned and started walking straight back to the Midway and my car. My face burned and my throat ached and I may have yelled something back at the woman, I'm not sure. Maybe something about the piece-of-shit paperback she was reading. Maybe something about lies.

Then I was driving too fast along the highway wishing I'd walked up onto that fake deck and into that house. Wishing I'd walked from room to fucking room.

I drove south. I passed cars from the left and from the right. The flash of a woman's face in her driver's window yelling at me, her eyes dark, her teeth white. I followed signs for Lawrence, and when I hit the bridge over the river I looked off to the west at long mill buildings that lined both dirty banks, at the brick smokestacks rising in the air, and there was that poem about the shirtwaist fire I'd read in school. Dozens of immigrant women having to jump to their deaths from buildings just like those, their escape doors locked.

I took the exit ramp too fast and my left tires bumped over the curb, and I slowed down and I hated Lois then. Why tell me?

Halfway through My Year of Two Dannys, I sent Noni a list of questions.

Did my father's father drink?

Did he get mean when he drank?

Did people like my father?

Did he have friends?

Did his parents call him names?

Did his father hit him?

Did his father beat him with anything?

Did his mother hurt him somehow?

And there was this question the others led to like lemmings off a cliff: What did my mother do to—

The rest of this question was an obscenity, and I knew it. But I kept the first part and crossed out the word *to* and mailed my list to Lois.

Noni's letter came back in days.

Your father is a criminal and your mother loved you. What did she do? She was a mother to you. The best.

Please be careful up there.

Susan stopped. She'd already written about what came next. That's where she'd started. There was her motel room in Lawrence overlooking a park. From her second-story window she'd watched two men and a woman her age pass around a bottle in the shade of a sickly elm tree, and there was a dog chasing a tennis ball a fat man in shorts kept tossing. There were empty beer cans at the base of some kind of bronze monument to the war dead. But this wasn't important. What was important was when she'd asked a cop where Canal Street was and finding the office of Nicholas Xenakis.

Susan scrolled down to the end of this section. She stared at that last line. And so what was Susan Lori to him? What was she to anyone? She sipped her cold coffee and swallowed.

It wasn't long after this that Susan Lori drove back south, stopping in Statesboro, Georgia, where she stayed because it was a campus town with a lot of bookstores. And then she found herself living with Delaney. They worked in the same restaurant, a cool dark place that served fresh produce and organic chicken to professors and students who'd walk in from campus down the street. Susan Lori's sports bar money got her a small studio apartment in the rear of a house owned by a gay couple, two men who drank and fought a lot. The younger of the two would smoke cig-arettes under the pecan tree in the backyard, and sometimes she'd watch him from her window as he stood there, one hip cocked like a woman's, inhaling deeply and staring at the ground like he was working up the nerve to apologize.

Watching others was what she seemed to do now. Since her trip north, it was as if she'd stepped into the in-between of all things. She had zero interest in ever meeting her father, and she was through with school. All she was working for was earning enough money to house and feed her-self, to buy used or new books at the store two blocks from the restaurant, to lie on her bed in her small room and slip inside the lives of others over and over again. It was like being fifteen, sitting on the floor of the Arcadia High School library, her face in book after book, ignoring living people for the imaginary spirits on the page.

Except she began to ignore herself too. She was smoking too much and eating only when she felt like it, and it'd be a bowl of cereal or a limp carrot she'd dip into a jar of peanut butter, if she thought to go buy some. Her days off were the worst because even with a book in her lap, the air in her apartment seemed to buzz with invisible voices: *Zit face! Spoiled little bitch! He's no longer in our custody. He's no longer in our custody. He's no longer in our custody.*

And she drank too much. At first it was only wine, two or three glasses. But then she started drinking bourbon, and so many mornings she woke on her sofa or across her bed, still dressed, her face a dry riverbed, her mouth the stones, her small quiet room feeling like a tomb.

Late in the afternoon she'd go to work hungover, and it was always a surprise that people smiled up at her from their tables as if she were nor-mal, as if she had not begun to appear like some useless night creature who had no business serving the public.

But she still looked the way she did. Her male customers flirted with her, and one of them told her he had never seen anyone as captivating as she was. That was his word, too. He was sitting at the corner table, and when he said it, he'd looked up at her and smiled behind thick-framed glasses, his eyes slightly magnified above a scruffy beard. He was probably a teaching assistant in graduate school, an art historian or political scientist, and standing there with her empty serving tray looking down at him, part of Susan Lori could feel herself reaching for the old pleasure of being desired, but what had it ever gotten her but the feeling she'd been lessened somehow? Not by the sex itself but by having been wanted so much. What did that have to do with what she wanted?

"That's nice. Go fuck yourself."

The man looked as if he'd been slapped with rotting fruit, and when he began to fumble for new words she turned and hurried back into the kitchen. There was the feeling she might be driving too fast in the dark with no headlights, but Susan Lori was also beginning to believe that she could live happily without a man for the rest of her time. She had always relied on that invisible account of hers that always seemed to be full, though something new was happening; it had never occurred to her before that she did not have to spend any of it.

At the end of her shift, she'd sit at the bar and order a bourbon from Delaney. She was a cliché of feminist beauty with large breasts and boxy hips, and she kept her hair cut short and dyed black, the roots rust-colored. She had high cheekbones and thin lips, six piercings in one ear all the way up the lobe, and each one was a tiny silver animal of some kind—a fox, a turtle, a leopard, a snake, an eagle, a porcupine, though Susan Lori would not see these clearly just yet. What she saw was that Delaney seemed to see *her*.

Not whatever men did that got them to say words like *captivating*, but something other than that, deeper maybe.

"You look stranded. Anyone ever tell you that?" Delaney was leaning close, washing dishes in the bar sink.

"No."

"Well, you do." Delaney smiled. Her work was nearly done, and she poured herself a soda water on ice.

Susan Lori nodded at Delaney's glass. "No bourbon?"

"Bourbon doesn't like me."

"Wine?"

"Hates me."

"Beer?"

"Can't fucking stand me. I don't drink."

"Then why're you a bartender?"

Delaney stuck a straw into her soda and sucked on it, her eyes on Susan Lori like she was weighing something important. She swallowed and said, "It's good hours for a poet."

"Yeah? I write."

"Poems?"

"I lied. I don't write. I start things, but—all I do is read."

"'A writer is a reader moved to emulation.'"

"'Scuse me?"

"Saul Bellow."

"I haven't read him."

"I don't read men, period. Not anymore, anyway."

It seemed a stupid thing to say, though Susan Lori, at least that fall, was drawn to it. "Why not?"

Delaney stared at her. "Because there are other voices out there, that's why."

"Like yours?"

"Yes, like mine."

Things got hazy here. Susan knew she liked the first poem of Delaney's she'd read, and she knew she was sitting on the porch of Delaney's rented clapboard when she'd read it. She remembered that Delaney wore shorts and was barefoot, her toenails unpainted and clipped, her knees drawn up to her chest as Susan finished reading a poem about an old woman's love of motorcycles, though the old lady had never been on one and probably never would. The last line of the poem had the rattling idle of an engine in it, then the quiet of a graveyard, and to Susan's ear Delaney was hitting a sentimental gong a little too hard, but it was affecting, and knowing that this woman she knew and worked with had written it made Susan want to write something as well.

They started meeting a few mornings a week in a coffee shop three blocks from campus. They would share a small table against a wall covered with old posters of rock bands going back to the seventies—Golden Earring, Grand Funk Railroad, Black Oak Arkansas—and they'd write. Then they'd share with each other what they wrote.

Susan Lori wrote her first story then. No, it was really just a few scenes, and it was told from the point of view of a young woman who comes back to her apartment from class to find her dead roommate's naked torso, her head sitting on their turntable with its mouth half open like she wanted to finish saying something, though Susan's protagonist somehow missed this.

Delaney didn't believe it.

"C'mon, she'd see the head right off. You're just writing in slow-motion here. It's like blood-porn for you."

Blood-porn. That stayed with Susan Lori awhile. The truth was, Delaney did not like her writing. No, she admired some of Susan Lori's sentences but not what she was writing about.

"I mean, I know you were there then and all, sweetie, but don't you want to write about something less sensational?"

Like what? Susan Lori wanted to say. *Your polemical pussy poetry? Every single poem celebrating the feminine over the masculine? As if one could exist without the other?* Susan Lori meant this literally, as in sperm and egg, but she heard it in that other way, and she was beginning to feel that she could, in fact, live without any boy or man ever again.

Then Delaney invited Susan Lori to move in with her, which Susan Lori did on a warm and windy afternoon, the smell of rain in the air, and

that's when her in-betweenness began to feel less like a floating stasis
and more like a warm, dry place of refuge.

Refuge. She'd forgotten that part of it. But how could she have forgotten *that*? That was central, wasn't it? How could she have forgotten that that fall, winter, and spring with Delaney, she had felt oddly
protected?

We had no air conditioner and slept together naked in front of a fan.
One morning she woke me with her tongue and it felt as natural as floating
on water, though it's not what I prefer.

I learned how to do it to her too. I did not not like it. Her taste and smell
began to pull me to her, and because I had the same parts I knew so quickly
what to do that it was like speaking a foreign language in your dreams.

Delaney gave me Rilke, and Rilke gave me this: "Beauty is the beginning of terror which we are only just able to bear."

But being wanted by Delaney was like a drunk getting used to drinking
iced tea.

An engine downshifted outside. Lois and her VW. Shit. Susan
should have put on the rice by now. Her cheeks heated and she swallowed, and she felt caught doing something perverse. She was seeing
Delaney's vagina again. Just inches from her face.

It was neither beautiful nor ugly, but its smell and taste, Susan Lori
had come to want them in a way that surprised her. There was satisfaction, too, in using her fingers and tongue to make Delaney come. It was
not unlike the pride Susan Lori took in doing anything well: serving a four-
top with warmth and efficiency; having written papers till dawn that sang
right to their final sentences and periods. But when Delaney did it to her,
the pleasure Susan Lori took felt tinged with the hollow gratitude you give
to someone for a gift you never asked for or wanted in the first place. A
sweater you know you'll never wear, a scarf you know you'll give away.

"Suzie?" Lois was calling from downstairs.

"I'm *coming*." A snort came out of her, a truncated laugh of self-loathing. Was she really writing about this, for Christ's sake?

But living in heterosexual abstinence had brought a lovely stillness and clarity then. And because Delaney did not drink, Susan did not, either, or not much anyway, and when she sat down at that coffee shop table and wrote across from her friend and sometime lover, what kept coming was the pull of that other Danny, the one in Gainesville.

"You identify too much with these girls." Delaney handed her back her notebook. She had a cold, and the skin beneath her nose was chapped, her eyes slightly clouded. "God, it's like you're jealous he never killed *you*."

She was wrong. There was no jealousy, but there was something else, the belief that if that other Danny was going to kill anyone it shouldn't be the nice girls. It should be girls who needed to be punished.

It should have been girls like her.

Yes, it should have been me.

"Want me to start the *rice*?"
"Fine. I'll be right *down*."
Fuck.

It should have been me.

Susan deleted that last sentence.

. . . girls like her.

She could hear Lois down in the kitchen moving things. Probably pulling out a pot for the rice. Probably pissed off that her little Suzie was still the same unreliable bitch she'd always been. "*Talk is cheap, young lady.*" How many times had she said that to her? How many times had she used the word *cheap*?

What changed in those in-between months with Delaney in her rented clapboard house in the shade of live oaks a mile from a campus full of young women and men, was that Susan Lori stopped feeling cheap. There was still shame. There was still that factory town on that dirty river and its grassless wino park, its street of half-open shops and a cop in his cruiser across from the building that housed the man who kept his thumb on the one who helped to give her life but had taken her mother. There was still that trashy strip on the beach. But some of us will always come from the dark undersides of things, like turned-over mushrooms in the woods, like squirming maggots in a dead dog on the side of the road, like a young woman curled on yellow linoleum while Susan Lori stood there calling and calling her.

But for a few months, at least, Susan Lori did nothing that took from her more than it added. Then Delaney told her it was time for her to go, that she carried too much "baggage" and it was starting to feel like work just being around her.

"Suzie? Are you coming *down*? What do you want to do with this *chicken*?"

It might have been Brian Heney after that. It didn't matter who it was, only that Susan Lori would soon go back to the push and pull of a man as he withdrew funds from an account he had never earned, and neither did she, this falling, reckless sense that she was spending some dark inheritance she could not get rid of fast enough.

25

IN HIS room at the Econo Lodge ten miles south of Richmond, Daniel lies on his bed with his shoes on. His eyes ache, and there's a pulsing in his back that isn't going away. When he'd checked in, he'd pulled down the shades, but outside there are voices, a woman calling a man's name, Bob or Rob, and the man calling back, "*You* have that!"

The chances of Susan wanting to see him are low, and there was what that young woman said to him in the motel's restaurant less than an hour ago. Daniel had eaten only two bites of his steak, but what he'd swallowed felt like warm stones in his gut, and he wanted to leave. A woman was sitting at the bar. She was wearing a black skirt and a white blouse, a thin leather briefcase at her feet. At her elbow was her glowing telephone and she was tapping it with her fingers. She looked to be forty, forty-five years old, his Susan's age.

Daniel waved over his waiter and told him to bring his check over to the bar. Then he made his way between empty tables to this woman he did not want to scare off, though he knew what this looked like, what he looked like.

The woman bartender gave him the once-over. She was pouring white wine into a glass. She slid it on a coaster toward the business-woman. "Menu?"

"Yes, please." She glanced up and smiled at the bartender, and that's when the young woman saw him standing there a stool away. She kept her smile nailed to her face, and she slid her finger along the screen of her phone.

"I don't want to bother you, miss."

She didn't say anything, or look up from her phone. What was he *doing* anyway?

The bartender set a menu to the side of the businesswoman's glass, and she was eyeing Daniel like he was her first bit of trouble in an oth-erwise easy shift. "Would you like something?"

"Just want to see the news." On the TV now was footage from a baseball game, some pitcher's wincing face as he watched a ball sail high over his head. The young businesswoman had a shiny diamond on her ring finger, a silver bracelet on her wrist. She tapped her phone and the screen went blank and she picked up her menu and sipped her wine.

"Your check, sir." Daniel's bill was on the bar. He pulled his cash from his front pants pocket and picked out one of the C-notes and dropped it onto his check. The young businesswoman pretended she hadn't seen his wad, but she was sitting more erectly on her stool, and Daniel could feel things had just changed between them, that that four grand in his pocket had made him less dangerous or more so, but either way he had her attention and now was the time to move.

"I just want to ask you a question. Then I'm on my way."

She looked up from the menu, then at him, taking him in for the first time. He was aware of his khaki work pants that might have a splash or two of varnish on them, of his yellow shirt with the frayed collar, his smudged work glasses hanging down against his chest, those white hairs of his sticking out above the top button.

"Look, I really have a lot of work to do."

His face was on fire, and he may as well have been the boy he was before he became "The Sound," every girl looking at him like he was some distant neighbor's pit bull to be ignored or put down.

"Thank you, sir." The waiter left his receipt and change, and Daniel's eyes were on this girl who could have been his daughter's sister. Her hair was dark, her eyes brown, but her nose was a bit more like his own and had robbed her of the beauty that might have been hers, though she didn't carry herself like a homely girl but more like one of the smart ones used to leading a roomful of other smart ones.

"My daughter's a professor."

"Good for her." Her voice was neither warm nor cold. She pressed the button on her phone, the screen lighting up. "I'm sorry, I have a meeting soon."

"I haven't seen her since she was a little kid. I'm driving down to Florida to visit her."

Now the woman stared at him as if she was not sure how to take any of this.

Again, that heat in his face. A burn and an ache in his lower back, his legs tubes of smoke. He rested his hand on the bar to steady himself. "If that was your father, would you want to see him after those many years?"

"That's up to her, isn't it?"

"Yeah, but you're her age and—"

"It would depend on why he's been gone so long." She reached down for her briefcase and pulled out a computer she opened on the bar. She turned it on and sipped her wine, the screen opening up into a pale glow on her face, that light on her cheek and throat. After Suzie was in bed, Linda liked to watch TV with the lights off, and he'd sit beside her on the sofa, his legs and arms heavy from another day of climbing and descending ladders, from hauling cans of paint and dipping his brush and brushing it along clapboards and the casings of doors and windows, the skin of his hands dry, his fingers slightly swollen, and he loved to look at the side of his wife's face in that light when she laughed, when some pretty actor on some stupid show made her laugh. Even for that, Captain Suspicion would take notice, and Danny tried to ignore him because she was sitting there on their couch in their house *with him*, wasn't she? That soft TV light flickering across her face?

"Is this one bothering you, ma'am?" The bartender set down the young woman's silverware wrapped in a napkin.

"No, it's just—I have a meeting now."

"You heard her, sir."

Those stones in his gut. His face in front of some invisible fire. That ache in his back and hips and that young lady's words like kicks into his head. *It would depend on why he's been gone so long.*

He gathered up his change, leaving the coins and a ten for the waiter. The young woman tapped keys on her computer, and her screen became a video of a man in a tie smiling at her, behind him other men in ties, and Daniel wanted to thank her but did not, and as he walked back toward the exit and the elevators and his room on the second floor, he saw himself starting up his truck first thing in the morning and heading back north, back to his trailer and shop and small fenced-in yard in the shade of the pines, though lying on his bed now, he knows he won't.

He wishes he made a copy of his letter on the library's xerox machine. He remembers most of what he wrote, but not enough, and why did he put in all of that shit about the Reactor and Captain Suspicion? She's going to think he's nuts.

On the desk is the printout for how to write your own will. He'll just rest a bit, then he'll go sit at that desk and get to work. But he needs to find a typewriter or a computer and a printing machine somewhere. His professor daughter would have one, and he pictures some university office like he's seen in the movies, shelves filled with books, a big desk in front of high windows overlooking the trees and grass of the campus, her college degrees framed and hanging on the wall. Maybe next to them are photographs of her husband and kids. Maybe one of their crayon drawings, too.

Linda liked to draw. She'd buy Susan coloring books and they'd color together. But then Linda got tired of the coloring books and she bought blank paper, and she and Suzie Woo Woo would color whatever the hell they wanted. Linda's weren't very good, but they weren't bad, either. There were a lot of daisies and shining suns, and once a little brown dog. Things like that.

Every picture Suzie drew, even if it was purple lines across the page, Linda kept. The best ones she thumbtacked to the window casings above the kitchen sink. Orange squiggles and red circles and one that looked like a heap of black branches.

A sick roiling through Daniel's gut, a band of sweat along his scalp. That night, standing there, Linda on the floor at his feet, the sounds she made, then how quiet she was. In his head and veins, the Reactor was standing there breathing hard, mute and deaf and dumb, this piece of shit who could only come out swinging, and Captain Suspicion may as well have been smiling. It was not anything Danny could see, just feel, his dark satisfaction that all movements had finally led to this one: Linda smiling up at Squeeze's brother Bill, her hips pointed at him; Linda smoking out front of the arcade like signage, one arm crossed under her breasts; Linda's tongue in his mouth, the easy way she let him lead her under the Himalaya, her shorts off, his down around his ankles, the way she gave herself to him so easily. Too easily.

What she'd been screaming at him in that small kitchen of the Ocean Mist was that she'd had enough. She was leaving and she was taking Suzie with her and, "You can't do shit about it!"

That one word *can't*, it was the button that had always switched on the Reactor: you *can't* be one of us; you *can't* talk to that pretty one; you *can't* walk with the basketball players and the smooth talkers and the boys who drive to school in Mustangs and Chargers; you *can't* change that hooked nose you got or all those zits or your eyes that are so close together you look stupid. You *can't change* anything.

All you can do is shut them up.

All you can do is stop them from laughing in your face.

All you can do is stop her from leaving and taking your daughter, too.

But that's where he was full of shit. It was his wife leaving that did it. He knew if she left then she could go fuck whoever she wanted to. He loved his little girl, he did, though maybe he should've given some thought to her standing just six feet away.

A low burning behind his ribs. Daniel has to sit up. His mouth begins to fill with saliva, and he knows what's coming and he stands and hurries to the open door of the bathroom, the wine and the chewed meat rising and retching out of him onto the sink, then he's on his knees over the toilet, his pink piss there from before dinner, an upward heaving, then a sloshing and a half heave and a string of bile and air. He rests his forehead on his arms. There are the smells of what's come from him, the nearly sweet rot of the dead and the living side by side.

Daniel's work glasses are pressing against his chest. He stands and flushes the toilet and sees his glasses are bent and the sink is splattered with what needs to be cleaned. He feels better, though his legs may as well be walking through high mud. He needs to lie down again.

He rinses out his mouth and takes a dampened washcloth to the sink. He hangs it to dry on the shower curtain and walks back to his bed and sits on the edge of the mattress. He pulls his glasses from around his neck, squinting at them and bending them back straight. He folds them and sets them on the bedside table. He wants to lie down again, but that ache in his back remains, and he stands on legs he's grateful he can still count on. At his desk he gathers up the printed-out pages on "How to Write Your Own Will." He takes them back to his bed where he puts on his work glasses and lies back against the pillow. He wonders how many heads have lain on it. How many men? How many women? How many of them were alone, like him, and how many were in bed with someone else?

Daniel props the second pillow behind his head and reads the first sentence of what he'd printed out.

Create a list of personal information that you will need for your will. The listing should include your full legal name, birth date and address; your marital status and if married, your spouse's full name; the names, birth dates and addresses of your children, even if you do not intend to leave anything to one or more of them; the names, birth dates and addresses of every other person who you intend to name in your will; and the name, birth date and address of the person who will act on your behalf when you die to execute your will.

His daughter's real address. Daniel pictures himself in a day or two on her university campus. If she doesn't want to see him, if she won't come near him, how will he find out where she lives? He'll just have to put down her work address, that's all. And who the hell will "act on his behalf"? He thinks of his parole officer years ago, that nicotine gum he was always chewing—though he'd still sometimes go smoke out on the street—those circles under his eyes. But he was stand-up. He laid down the law without ever looking at Daniel like he was a nobody. Nor as a somebody, either, simply a necessary part in the big punishment machine that churned out the PO's check every week. If he's still alive, he might do this for Daniel.

There's the lady at the Council on Aging too, Marnie or Marjorie. She's a big girl just a bit younger than he is, and she smiles at him whenever he comes in to find out who he'll be driving around that day. She has blue eyes and a pale double chin, and he bet she likes her wine at night. She might do it for him.

Create an inventory of your belongings. This includes all your possessions and property—for example, stocks, bonds, cash, real property and promissory notes—and their estimated values.

This one's easy; everything's going to his daughter: his truck and his lot, his shed and trailer. All of it. That and whatever cash he has in the bank, which after the four thousand he'd withdrawn is now eight thousand and change. He'd paid $97,000 for the lot and his trailer, all from Liam's life insurance policy his mother had kept for years and years. His new shed and fence would increase the value, too. Susan should be able to get over a hundred thousand for it all. But then Daniel pictures her keeping it. Wouldn't that be something? A place for her and her family to use for a vacation now and then? Why not? It's two miles from the beach. But why would she want to go back there? Did he really think she'd want her *kids* there?

Standing in that dim yellow kitchen. The echo of what Linda had screamed at him—*you can't can't can't!* At his feet, she lay still and he needed to get help. He was telling the woman on the phone that his wife was hurt, and for a long while, it seemed, his street address was not coming to him, only the name of their cottage, the Ocean Mist. He may have told her that, too. *We live in the Ocean Mist.* And that's when he saw Suzie standing down there to his left, three years old, her dark hair all curly. Around her lips was a ring of chocolate ice cream, and she was staring at her mother and then she began to call for her and this called their address back to him and he told the dispatcher woman and hung up the phone. He unlocked the kitchen door and opened it wide, then he picked up his daughter and carried her back to his and Linda's bedroom.

On the lamp table on Linda's side of the bed was a stack of children's books she'd read to Suzie. Now that she was bigger, many nights they'd let her fall asleep between them and stay there till morning, and nothing was better than drifting off to Linda's voice reading to their Suzie, their daughter's tiny voice asking a question about a rhyme she didn't understand because she loved rhymes.

Wonder and think. How much water can fifty-five elephants drink?

The book was by that doctor who drew his own pictures, too. Goofy creatures with big noses and floppy ears and big feet. One night, Suzie had pointed to one of those books that was her favorite, though she shortened the title to *Rink Fink* and called it the one about the elephants. This was from a book called *Oh, the Things You Can Think*—no, it was *Oh, The **Thinks** You Can Think*, and that night, lying back on the pillows and pulling Suzie up beside him, her head against his shoulder, he opened that book and began to read.

"But I want to see *Mommy*."

And why is it
So many things
Go to the Right?
You can think about THAT
Until Saturday night.

That's a line that's never left Daniel. Later, in the Hole, it rose up in the wind of all those other voices. That line, and Suzie's voice: "Is Mommy okay?"

His upper arm pulled Suzie in close, and he held the book with both hands above his chest and their two faces, and then something happened that surprised him, though it shouldn't have: "The Sound" began to take over. "Rink Rinker Fink." He could see himself up in the DJ booth of the Himalaya, the microphone at his lips, that dirty plexiglass between him and the lighted strip, and he took his time with each word, giving each one enough air so he could float to the next and the next and it would become a song you couldn't help but fall into, Linda looking up at him like he was holy, like he had come into her life only to bring her to somewhere better.

But Suzie wasn't listening, and her body still hadn't relaxed into the side of his. She said again that she wanted to see her mommy, and so what could he do but pull her in tight and hold her and not let go? He could smell the ocean in her hair because bath time did not come till after supper. He could smell that and the coconut lotion Linda had rubbed on her earlier. He could smell the dried sweetness of the chocolate ice cream he had not wiped from his daughter's face, and there was that other smell, too, nearly sweet as well but ancient, now drying on the skin of his right hand and forearm where it had splattered and where it remained just inches from their daughter's face, and she should not see this, but Danny kept reading—no, the Sound did—one goofy rhyme at a time. Under one of them was a drawing of a kid diving off a wooden springboard into an inflated pool of water, his arms and legs spread wide, his face grinning like he just didn't give a shit about anything anymore.

The Sound read on and on, slowly turning one page after another. There was a picture of a mother creature holding its baby creature, some rhyme about sticks, and Suzie began to squirm and say she wanted to go see her mother, but the Sound told her no, Mommy wants to be alone right now. "Sometimes when you're sick, you want to be alone."

And that drawing of the kid belly-flopping off that board, that smiling kid's closed eyes, his ponytail curled in the air, Danny wanted to fall right into that—no, he was already in that picture, hanging in midair, waiting for what would happen next to hurry up and happen. There was the thought, as insistent as a lit cigarette to his own skin, that he should get up and run out to the kitchen and do what he could for Linda. Take a dishrag and press it to what he'd done. Try to slow or stop it. But he knew better. He knew where the Reactor had gone with what had clattered in the sink. The Reactor always went for the white-hot center of things—a sneering boy's sneer, a laughing man's teeth, a disloyal heart's—Danny couldn't even think the word, just felt the echoes of its soft pierce and thud up his arm, just saw how his wife had looked at him then, the knowing in her face that was the same knowing she'd shown him in her raised eyes when he was The Sound up above them all, as he was now, reading to Susan, her small torso pulled into his, her bare foot on his knee.

The first to arrive were two EMTs. Over The Sound's voice, there was a knocking then a rapping. A man calling out words like "911 call." Like "emergency." Like "hurt." Suzie knew that one, and she lifted her head and said, "Daddy?" but The Sound read on, and Danny pulled her back to his chest and the open book in his hand, these goofy creatures with their silly rhymes, as if all of life was supposed to be one big adventure of funny times with friendly creatures and why did we always have to take everything so damn seriously? Why did Danny have to give that serious man in the doorway any attention at all? Can't he see I'm reading a book to my girl? Can't he see that she's three and everything will be all right? And wasn't it funny that he was the same one who'd tended to Squeeze's brother Bill? Danny knew this because the man had a crew cut that nobody had then, and he was fat and there was a dark mole on his throat, though Danny hadn't noticed that the last time. In the air, there were questions. But they were floating debris in the wake The Sound was plowing through, taking his time, in no hurry whatsoever. Then Suzie's voice was in the air, and her question was not about a rhyme or a picture but about her mother, and Danny patted his little girl's back and said, "Mommy's getting help now. She's okay. It's okay." *Okay* a good word, a perfectly fine word that did not feel like a lie at all, not until the doorway filled with one cop's face then another's, then four of them were in his and Linda's bedroom and everything was just fine till one of them tried to pick up Suzie and take her away, and the Reactor came out like he'd never come out before, and even weeks later Danny had nightstick bruises on his skull, an itch from nine stitches along his chin, a burn in his shoulders and elbows from getting chained and yanked, but nothing was as bad as the cool lightness of Suzie's body gone from the side of his. Nothing was worse than that.

It was the last time he ever touched her, and it was one of the only times he'd read to her. That was Linda's job, not his. But he wonders now if Susan remembers him doing that. She was three. She might.

But does he really believe that's all she's going to remember about that night?

A woman's laughter out in the hallway, then a man's voice. A nearby door opening and closing. Daniel's eyes are on the paper in his hand, but he's not reading it. His tongue is thick, and his mouth tastes like dried bile, and he's listening for more sound out there. That man and woman in their room next to his or across the hall, their voices sound young, in their thirties or forties still, and that woman's laugh. In it is—what?—trust. Like she's been with him awhile, and she knows he'll look out for her. She knows he wants only good things for her. That he isn't with her just because of what she might let him do to her in that room. That he holds her in a high place in his heart. All of this is in her laugh, and it's hard to take.

Daniel's bladder burns. The bones in his back feel like they're being squeezed.

He held his wife in a high place, he did. But she acted like she was in a cage, which—he won't deny it—was true. Those last weeks, the snake slithered through each and every tunnel of Danny's brain, and the voice that came out of him in his own house only asked questions or gave orders. "You go straight to the arcade and come right back. And don't talk to anyone but customers. If you know anybody, you ignore them, you hear me? How come you're wearing lipstick? You never wear lipstick. No, we'll go food shopping *together*. Why did you look at him? Do you *know* him? How come you don't talk to me anymore? You used to talk to me. Those jeans are too tight. Put on something else. Who was at the beach? Did you sit alone? I don't want you talking to anyone on the strip, you hear me? Nobody. They're not your friends. You don't need friends. You have me."

But he thought he loved her. He wanted to love her.

A moan. At first Daniel thinks this has risen up from forty years ago, how when things were still good Linda would hold his face in her hands, her own face jerking slightly with each of his thrusts, her eyes on his, and she made the sound that's coming from the room next door. It's the woman making that sound, and Daniel hears only pleasure in it. He almost gets up to press his ear to the wall and hear it more clearly, but he doesn't move.

The thing is, he was happiest with Linda not during all that but after, when they lay side by side, drifting off to sleep. Her bare back was warm against his chest, and it was those times when he knew he would never be alone again, and he could not believe his good fortune. He had been The Sound, and now he had this, and he would do anything to protect it.

The moans are more muffled now, and there is the rocking of the bed, the occasional tap of the headboard against Daniel's wall. He picks up the TV's remote, but he's not sure which button turns it on, and he never liked television. For a few years, he owned one, but each and every show was full of people living with other people: handsome husbands and pretty, funny wives; smart, good-looking kids and their smart, good-looking friends. In each episode someone would be in some kind of trouble—an angry boss, a college friend standing at their door and never leaving, a letter left in the wrong drawer and found by the wrong person—and within thirty minutes all would be resolved, each episode ending with hugs and laughter. Watching this, Daniel felt like he was a lone visitor from a cold planet far away where he'd never been welcome in the first place, and he'd turn the channels as fast as he could, but even the crime shows were too neat and tidy, all the bad people caught and locked away by the story's end, the cops healthy and in good shape, strong and moral and cheerfully ready for the next bad thing to come down the pike.

What else was there but sports and game shows and the news? But those were bottled up and delivered the same way, like life was a staircase you climb every day in a massive store of shiny products that, if you're good enough and lucky enough and if you climb straight enough, will all be yours and you'll never have a reason to be unhappy.

The room next door is quiet. Daniel wonders if the sounds he heard were real or not. Then more steady tapping against his wall. He stands and carries his instructions to the desk and picks up the pen on the pad beneath the lamp. The last three tell him to type his will, then sign and date it in front of two witnesses. The final piece of advice reads:

Make at least two copies of the will. Give the original to the person who will execute the will on your behalf, give one copy to your spouse, and keep one copy for yourself in a safe place in your home.

Daniel sees his kitchen drawer where he keeps his calculator and notepad for figuring his caning prices. He could put it there. But what if there's a fire, or his roof leaks? Maybe he should buy one of those small safes at Home Depot. But no, some punk could break into the trailer one day and think there's something valuable in there. Better not to draw attention to it whatsoever.

Against his wall come five or six rapid taps then quiet, then soft voices, then that woman's laugh again. Quieter now, thick with love.

Then they're both in the bathroom. Water in the pipes. Does he hear that, or just think it? He puts on his glasses, turns over the instruction sheet to its blank side, and writes:

Daniel Patrick Ahearn, November 28, 1949, 26 Butler Place, Salisbury, MA

Single.

He stares at that only a second before crossing it out. He writes:

Widowed.

A heated tingling through his face and on his neck, though the word is accurate, no matter how you look at it. He flips the paper over, reads the rest of the first item, and turns the page back to where he was writing.

Susan Lori Ahearn Dunn, Eckerd College, Florida

He'll have to make that more accurate later. He writes:

Person who will execute me— He stops. He crosses out the word *me* and he writes *my.*

A door closing then muffled laughter. It's the man's this time, and hearing it, Daniel feels it as a sign of hope that he's heading in the right direction— with this will, with this trip south, with the letter he sent his daughter that she's probably already read at least once. And how did he end it? He wishes he could remember that, but he can't. But he better have written *love*. He sure hopes that he wrote the word *love*.

26

Susan's cell phone rang, and now she was talking to her husband, and that gave Lois the chance to go outside to her car for the bag of Dresden lamps. The sun was low to the west, and it made the dead pine needles in her gravel driveway look golden, and Lois was breathing hard from her slow climb up the stairs with those lamps. From down in the kitchen came the smell of chicken broiling. Suzie had found a Cuban or Mexican station on the radio and men were singing in Spanish above strumming guitars and high-flying horns and all of life seemed to be a raucous party under the sun. It was hard to miss the change in her granddaughter. Even though she came into the kitchen apologizing for being late in starting their dinner, she looked . . . *happy* wasn't the word. She still wore no makeup and her short chopped hair was a mess. She looked too thin too, but she seemed lit up from somewhere inside herself, if that made any sense. At first this ticked Lois off, and she wasn't sure why. She wasn't really hungry and didn't care that their dinner hadn't been started. Maybe it was that Suzie had found something to do in this house that made her feel good for once. Why couldn't she have been that way as a kid? It would have made things a hell of a lot easier. Though her reading used to do something like that to her as well. Susan would be in her room for hours then come down in a spell from some faraway world that Lois was never invited into herself. Then the boy years began, along with their fights upon fights upon endless damn fights.

But tonight Suzie seemed to read all this in Lois's face, and she said, "I wrote a lot today, Noni."

"I thought you said you weren't any good at writing."

"I'm not. I'm just beginning not to care anymore."

Lois could do without the Spanish music. There was too much of it in town as it was, but there was a festive lightness in the air that she and Suzie were making together in this dark old house, and Lois was glad Susan was still on the phone with Bobby because now she could wrap these two lamps she'd decided to give them both.

Well, Marianne had helped with that. Just before they closed the shop for lunch, Lois told her how much Suzie had liked those Dresdens, and Marianne turned to her and said, "You should give them to her and her husband."

Perhaps if she hadn't said *husband*, Lois knew she might not be doing this at all. Her business was doing well enough, but these two lamps were a good acquisition and eleven hundred bucks was eleven hundred bucks. But still, all through lunch the idea hung inside her like the vanishing fragment of a good dream, and now, sitting on the edge of her bed with a roll of wrapping paper and reaching into her bedside table drawer for the Scotch tape she knew was in there, she felt that old excited anticipation she used to get the night before her children's birthdays and Christmas, even Easter when she'd leave out baskets for Linda and Paul she'd stuffed with chocolates and jelly beans and wrapped yellow and pink candies shaped like bunnies. As they got older, she put money in that fake green grass, silver dollars she made Gerry get from the bank, though he rarely helped out with any of this, and that was all right too, this feeling of being alone while she celebrated the love she felt and maybe, okay, fine, was never really very good at showing when it was not a special day. Each December or April or October, for Linda's birthday, and August, for Paul's, and later, May for Suzie's, it was Lois's chance to show them just how much she loved them, and often, while wrapping their gifts, sometimes sipping a glass of wine or something stronger, her eyes would well up and she could only hope that whatever she was wrapping would be good enough. Would say everything she never really seemed to say herself.

But where was that goddamn Scotch *tape*? Lois lifted out three or four furniture and toy catalogues, eBay printouts, two empty prescription bottles for pills she could not remember having to take. There was the broken case for her drugstore readers that were nowhere in sight, an unopened package of mini–tissue packs, her loaded pistol she no longer kept in its case. She lifted it out by its handle and set it on the mattress beside her. And there it was, in a nest of pennies and paper clips and hairpins, a brand-new double pack of tape she bought who the hell knows when or why.

Marianne had wrapped both lamps in bubble wrap, then laid them side by side in a large ivory cardboard box they ordered in bulk from New Jersey. She covered it with its top and taped its sides, and she helped Lois find two better shades for them out back. They had an entire shelf of lampshades, glass and fabric—ovals, bells, and drums, rectangles and squares, Empire, Victorian, and Arts and Crafts. In the dusty sunlight, between two sconce half shades, Lois saw three bells in oyster silk. They were just right, and two of them were in good shape and close to the same color as the porcelain figurines of the two lovers, the bell-shape in proportion to it all, the silk a nice complement to the poured lace of the woman's dress.

Marianne seemed a bit cheerier after lunch, too. They'd eaten at the Sawgrass, and over steak salads and iced teas, Lois went on and on about Gerry's galavanting around, about his giving her VD, about his drinking and spending money they didn't have then leaving her high and dry, though she did get to keep the arcade. Marianne kept shaking her head, chewing and shaking her head and dabbing at her lips with a napkin. And Lois could see her doing what she'd hoped Marianne would do, which was to compare her lot with Lois's, and they hadn't even mentioned the infinite black hole in the dead center of that lot.

On their short walk back to the shop, Marianne gripped Lois's hand and said, "I know how blessed I am, Lois. I do." And Lois could not deny the joy she felt tending to her, but again, Marianne's pitying sincerity irked her, and Lois had said: "Hey, none of us get out of here alive, honey." It might not have been the right thing to say, but when *didn't* Lois utter the wrong thing? But that lunch talk had put Marianne back on an even keel, and after they'd picked the right shades, Marianne had driven over to the drugstore for a big gift bag the shades sat in now in the parlor, and Lois's fingers felt too thick for the scissors as she snipped and snipped at the wrapping paper she'd pulled from her closet. It was a Christmas wrapping—repeating gold ornaments hanging from a spruce branch—but that's all she had and anyway it was the thought that counted.

Downstairs Susan had turned the music down a bit, and Lois could hear her voice. At first it'd been chatty, but now it was underscored with some kind of alarm or higher level of attention. *Jesus Christ*, she thought. *He better not be leaving her while I'm doing all this.* Lois paused and straightened up. After what Suzie had said to her about her not knowing if she loved her husband or not, how would she take this gift to the two of them? Would she accuse her of not listening to her again? How many times, when she was young, had Susan screamed that into her face? You don't fucking *understand* me, Lois! Or maybe she'd done it only once, but it had hurt, had brought Lois back to Linda, who'd never screamed a word at her, just slipped away without once asking for guidance about anything.

But downstairs Susan was laughing and Lois could only take that as a good sign, though maybe she should just give these lover lamps to *her.* Why not? The way she stood there in that castle in Punta Gorda staring and staring at them. Just give them to *her,* you old bat.

The music volume went back up downstairs, a Spanish DJ's phony voice talking fast and gabby about who knows what, then Lois heard in plain English, "Ernie's Dodge Trucks," and then it was Spanish again, and Suzie was calling up the stairs. *"Noni?"*

"Don't come up!"

"Are you all right?"

"I'm *fine*."

"Bobby's coming. Is that okay?"

"Tonight?"

"Yes, *tonight*."

"That's A-okay with me, Suzie Q."

Susan laughed. Lois hadn't called her that in years. So many of them. And wasn't that something, that Bobby was coming? Maybe this was all that couple needed. Or maybe that's all Susan had needed. Just a little distance for her to see more clearly. Lois folded the wrapping longways over the box then ripped tape from its dispenser and taped the paper's edge to the cardboard. It would be good to have a man in the house again. How long had it been? Susan had brought Bobby a year or two ago, but they'd only stayed for the afternoon. Paul never brought his family here. Lois always had to drive to Miami. Walter and Marianne had come over for dinner once, but not in a long while. Before that, it was Don, and going back, it was one of Susan's many boyfriends, Brian Something, that redheaded fisherman who smoked hand-rolled cigarettes and didn't talk much and kept staring at Suzie like she was a meal he would not be denied much longer.

Lois finished wrapping the box of Dresdens and carefully turned it over and reached into the corner of her closet for her bag of ribbons and bows. But the room shifted and her torso and legs felt like stone, then heated bird bones, and she knew she shouldn't try to carry this box down those stairs herself. It'd been dicey enough carrying them up in a paper bag with handles, so no, she'd just have to bring Susan up here, and so what?

Time for a glass of wine and a nice dinner before her sweet grandson-in-law came along, though she did not think of him that way as she stuck a big gold bow over a gold ornament in the center of the box. What she thought of him as was her friend, a friendship that had really only just begun this past Christmas at Susan and Bobby's little house in St. Pete, that strange jazz music playing, tall kind Bobby smiling down at her as they both diced vegetables for the meal the three of them would then share, the kitchen's light reflecting softly on his bald head, Susan somewhere else in the house like she was giving the two of them to one another as a gift.

SUSAN WAS standing at the sink washing lettuce, and Lois poured herself a glass of Merlot and sat heavily in her chair at the table. She generally did not smoke right before eating, but one with this wine would do nicely, and she opened a fresh pack and tapped one out and lit up with the lighter she always kept on the windowsill. Outside, a peach light lay on the oaks and pines, and Lois could not remember the last time she felt this good. The nicotine was kicking into her veins like a reliable friend, this wine-warmth in her chest and face, her lovely Susan fixing them dinner, her devoted husband on the way. And there was that very expensive gift waiting for them upstairs—yes, them, that had been her original plan so why not stick to it?

The faucet shut off. Susan laid the wet lettuce on paper towels on the counter.

"It'll be nice to see, Bobby. Is everything all right?"

Susan turned around to face her. Low across her top was a streak of water, and she *had* gotten too thin lately, her hair a mess. She should look better for when her husband came, and Lois could feel words of advice begin to rise up her throat, but she drank and swallowed instead. They'd been down that road enough.

"Everything's fine. He says he has some important mail for me."

"Like what?"

"Well, I think I may have sold something."

"On eBay?"

Susan smiled and shrugged. "It's a short story. I wrote it a long time ago, but Bobby talked me into finishing it and sending it out, so I did."

"When do I get to read it?"

"You really want to?"

"*Yes.* How many times do I have to tell you that? What's it about?"

"You wouldn't like it."

"Listen, missy, how would you know what *I* like?" She inhaled on her cigarette and squinted at Susan through the exhale. "Well?"

"The Gainesville murders."

"Oh, wonderful."

"I told you."

"I didn't say I wasn't interested. It's—can you imagine how hard it was for me to have you up there then?"

"I think so."

"Well, I don't." Lois stopped herself, or the words coming out of her stopped on their own. Susan didn't seem to notice. Lois shook her head. "Well, I want to read it."

"That's fine with me." Susan put on an oven mitt and opened the door and pulled out the steaming chicken. There were the smells of rosemary and burnt lemon. She stuck a fork into the breasts and turned them over, then pushed the tray back in and shut the door.

"Well, we should celebrate when he comes, honey."

Susan smiled, but she looked pale, and she set the oven mitt on the counter and walked down the hall and into the downstairs bathroom, closing the door behind her. "You all *right*?" Lois coughed, then inhaled on her Carlton. The room was a bit too quiet now. "Suzie?"

The toilet flushed, and Lois could hear the muffled voice of her granddaughter saying that she'd be right out. Lois sat back with her wine. She tried to picture where she and Bobby would put those lamps back in their home in St. Pete. Maybe their living room, which was also Bobby's office, one lamp on each side of their comfy sofa. She hoped Bobby would like them as much as Susan seemed to, and it was funny when Lois thought about it. Those two intertwined lovebirds at the base of a tree, it was a little romantic for Susan, wasn't it? But maybe that's just what she needed, a little romance.

The bathroom door opened, and Susan was stepping back into the kitchen. With the back of her hand, she brushed a strand of hair away from her forehead, and her eyes seemed dark with some kind of emotion Lois hadn't seen coming.

"You okay?"

"I was such a selfish bitch then."

"What? When?"

"When I went back to Gainesville. I should have known what that would do to you, of all people."

Lois waved at the air as if what Susan was talking about were as unimportant as having forgotten to check the mail, but her eyes began to burn and she couldn't look directly at her and she reached for her cigarette, but then Susan was walking across the floor, and now her bare arms were around Lois's shoulders, her granddaughter's turned cheek pressed to the top of Lois's head. "I'm sorry, Noni. I'm so sorry."

Lois nodded, and nodded again. She patted her granddaughter's back, could smell the skin of her warm shoulder, and Lois felt grateful and embarrassed and she wanted Susan to pull away and she wanted her to stay. Right here. Like this. For as long as it took to make everything right again, which it would never, ever be. *So be thankful for this*, she told herself, *be thankful for this moment*, because she'd needed to hear those words, hadn't she? Not from Susan about young Suzie, but for what had happened to her and her family that should never happen to any family anywhere at any time.

"Okay, honey. Okay. You're gonna burn your chicken. You need to check that chicken."

But Susan held on, and Lois was no longer certain if she was doing this for her or for herself, but did it matter? *Just enjoy this*, she told herself, just, *for one damn time, enjoy the damned good.*

27

DANIEL'S PENIS burns and he needs to piss. He begins to swing his legs to the left, but there's more bed there than there should be. And to his right, where's the wall and his trailer window? And where's the pilot light of his water burner he can always see straight ahead in the doorless closet of his kitchenette?

A hotel.

In Virginia. That young businesswoman at the bar. He turns and squints his eyes at the glowing orange numbers of the clock: 4:46 a.m.

His hip burns, and he gets up and stands and makes his way around the bed in the dark. There's a line of light beneath the door up ahead. He fumbles for the switch in the hallway, and the light coming on is flat and too bright. A peephole in the door in front of him. On the carpet is a folded piece of paper. A razored heat flashes through his chest and face—*What? Who?*—and he can only think it's his Susan. A letter back to him. But how would she know how to find him? And so soon?

He leans down and picks it up, his knees stiff, that hip burn moving into his back and groin. He opens it, and it's his bill. Like they can't wait for him to get of here fast enough.

He steps into the dim bathroom and leaves the light off and drops his bill onto the counter and tries to piss. From his lower back comes a gathering burn then a short release into the water, then the gathering again that feels like the passing of time no one can feel but him, and for the first time in a very long time he feels not merely alone but afraid in the endless silence of being alone. Like he never left the Hole at all. Like these twenty-three years on the outside have just been the voices pushing him out to his yard to cane chairs under the sun, into Port City to walk the street like a ghost, into the library and its shelves of books on tape and its computer table and that tall older one who probably remembers his face from faded newspapers and his mother lying in her hospital bed with so much love in her eyes for him, her boy, the artist's boy, The Sound, who could never control himself, this old man who is now pissing blood and feels the way he did after fourteen years and eight months on the inside, that his time is short and he is ready to leave where he's been, but he is afraid of where he is going.

Of what will come. All of it.

There's a whimper in the air, and he longs to see his mother again. Not when she was old and sick, but when she was still young, sitting beside him on the sofa in her housecoat while he read to her from his comic books. Kicked out of school again, and she treated him like he'd just done something special or soon would one day.

He needs to leave this hotel, and he can feel the highway out there in the dark waiting for him.

He shakes himself off and flushes the toilet and washes his hands. The water is warm and he splashes his face three times. He should clean his entire body, too, then he needs to shave and comb his hair and put on a change of clothes. He still has nine hundred to a thousand miles to go, another eighteen to twenty hours of driving. He won't get there tonight, but he should the next day, and he wants to look presentable for the entire trip. And no more staring at or even talking to strangers. No more wine.

He turns off the faucet and flicks on the overhead light. Again, it's too bright, the man in the glass old and ugly, his face wet, this shining, squinting mug that only a mother could love.

DANIEL IS driving in silence in the dark, his headlights on the oncoming asphalt of 95 south. Just before turning onto the highway, he'd pulled into a Jiffy Mart and filled the tank of his Tacoma and bought a large coffee and a tin of aspirin. He took four before getting behind the wheel, dry-swallowing them, and he can still feel their dusty trails in his throat, even when he swallows hot coffee that he wishes were stronger.

He doesn't remember if it's a Wednesday or a Thursday, but it's still too early for traffic, just a few eighteen-wheelers behind him and up ahead. Off to his left, above the dark shadows of what seem to be woods and a housing complex, there's an occasional lamplit window here and there, or an outdoor bulb flickering through the trees. The sky is a pale lip of gray out to the east, and he thinks of the ocean and how he has been to the strip only twice since moving back, when he circled the Midway and never even once stopped or stepped out of his truck.

Three years before his release date he'd been eligible for furloughs. But his mother was still living on the beach then, and he didn't want to go back to that. He couldn't. And no one else would have him, so he stayed behind the walls and when his mother met him at processing three years later, holding her was like holding a sweater full of bones. There were the smells of talcum and dry skin and wool, and she made crying sounds, though when she let go of him her small eyes were dry and her hooked nose was his hooked nose and she said something about God and home and if there were more hugs after that he does not recall them now.

The sky begins to lighten now, its dark curtain getting slowly pulled to the west. The guardrail is easier to see, and down on the other side a ribbon of water cuts through a grassy bottomland. There are a few cars on the road, their taillights red in front of him, their headlights insistent as bees behind. He knows he's driving too slow again, and he doesn't care. He sips his weak, cooling coffee and thinks about turning on his book on tape. But no, it's good just driving in the quiet like this.

Lying in bed with Suzie, reading to her. There was—he had to say it—a certain peace. Like a hot blowing rain that had finally ceased, then comes the calm. Then comes the quiet sun.

PART

FOUR

28

SUSAN LAY naked under her sheet, one leg over Bobby's hip. Her childhood bed was too small for them both, but she didn't care. It was good lying beside her husband again. He was naked too, and there came the memory of his weight on her then in her, his hungry darting tongue. Lois's shadowed face out on the screened porch, Bobby's too, both of them laughing like two old friends who'd picked right up where they'd left off. Bobby had brought red wine, and they opened a bottle and finished it off then opened another, though Susan had only had half a glass, something neither of them seemed to notice. She'd told herself she wasn't drinking because it wasn't going down well, but that wasn't true. It went down just fine, too fine, better than the chicken she'd had only two bites of, but when she swallowed that wine there came the reckless feeling that she was rushing into revealing a decision she had not yet made, and so she stopped. Lois smoked a lot, too, way over her limit, and she'd turned the kitchen radio back on so there were Mexican love ballads playing, and it was hard not to see just how much Noni liked Bobby and wanted the two of them to make it.

But Susan *had* been happy to see him, hadn't she? His cheerfully tentative hello at the door, then Lois calling him into the kitchen and his tall gentleness stepping into the light, his bald head and sweet smile at them both, though when Susan rose to hug him he looked into her face as if he were searching for something.

Noni asked him if he'd eaten and he said he had.

"Then let's drink," Lois said. "Now, where's that important mail?"

Susan poured him a glass of wine and handed it to her husband, but Bobby stood there quiet, glancing from Lois to her then back at Lois. Susan had never seen him quite like this before. He looked caught in some kind of test he hadn't prepared himself for, and she said, "I told her you had some mail for me."

"Oh, shit." He lifted his hand and dropped it. "I'm sorry. I left it back at the house." He turned to Noni and said something about stress and the start of the semester and losing his mind, but there were splotches of red blooming on his throat and Susan knew he was lying. It was not something she believed he'd ever done to her before, and there opened up in her the dark certainty that of course she hadn't sold any of her writing. She wasn't any damn good at it. And then she felt sorry for him for lying just to have an excuse to come see her. It ticked her off and made her feel far away from him. It reminded her why she'd needed the time away. He simply needed her more than she needed him.

But this low mood didn't last long. Lois started talking about all the things she forgot every single day, like that she had a business to go to, and Bobby said: "Think you'll ever sell it, Lois?"

"Nope. I'll probably drop dead selling some rich bitch a German mirror."

"She's really good at it, Bobby. You should've seen her at this auction we went to. She kicked ass."

Bobby glanced over at Susan. The red splotches on his throat had faded, though he looked like he needed to explain himself to her. He also looked relieved at how quickly the conversation had turned, and that's when Lois had said, "Suzie, there's something on my bed for you two. Can you go get it?"

Susan's mouth was dry, and she wanted cool water. She stared at the white Dresden lamps on her bureau. Their silk shades were more ivory than white, their bell shapes too much of a thematic exclamation mark to the entwined lovers at the bases of the lamps. They were saccharine and tacky, yet somehow beautiful too. Like the lights of a Ferris wheel a mile away at night, and Susan knew how much Lois had spent on these and she lay there feeling moved and grateful. She needed to pee.

She lifted her leg off her husband's hip. Bobby was snoring lightly, and there came the image of Lois's revolver on her bed. It had lain there beside catalogues and prescription bottles and a dispenser of Scotch tape. Beside it was the big box wrapped in Christmas colors, and before picking it up Susan put the gun back inside Noni's drawer and pushed it shut. She hadn't seen that gun in over twenty years, and she didn't quite know what to think of it now. It was probably good for Lois to have it, out here living alone, though it made Susan feel uneasy, and as she peed then brushed her teeth, she could see the last line she'd written yesterday. Something about fucking boys again and spending a dark inheritance.

A pale gray light came through the window above the shower. It was early. Her legs felt heavy and her stomach too empty, but she couldn't imagine eating anything. She wanted to get back to work. Her reaction last night to there being no acceptance letter felt like a setback, like the old Susan who still needed her writing to give her some kind of reward and glory. But what she needed was to get writing again, right now, for *it* and nothing else.

She stood naked in the dim hallway and glanced down at Lois's closed bedroom door. There was the muffled hum of the air conditioner, and Susan hoped her grandmother would sleep another hour or so, Bobby too. She thought she might be able to drink some coffee, but that could wait. In her bedroom she pulled on some fresh underwear and the shorts and top that lay on the floor beside Bobby's clothes and sandals. She opened her laptop and file and read the last few words of yesterday's last line: this falling, reckless sense that she was spending some dark inheritance she could not get rid of fast enough.

From here she could see Bobby's long bare foot hanging off the bed. His toes were bent and callused. She wrote: When I first met Saul I was teaching as an adjunct at Miami Dade Community College and living with Marty Finn. Marty had a performance at a black box theater in Coconut Grove and because I'd seen it already, I waited for him at a bar near the beach. My hair was long then, and I wore big hoop earrings and knew what I looked like, the way I've known ever since I was sixteen and drunk Gustavo peered into the window of Noni's shop and saw me reading behind the register.

Am I this shallow? I don't know. I'm not sure. When Saul Fedelstein appeared beside me I had been there for nearly an hour, and he smelled of gin and baby oil, his white hair combed back, his shirt collar open. He leaned one elbow on the bar and looked at me. Behind us, men and women talked and laughed over the notes of the piano the player played. Jazz, maybe. I'm not sure of that. Only Saul raising two fingers to the bartender and ordering a Blue Glacier.

"A what?"

"You can taste mine."

He didn't offer to buy me one, and when his drink came in a martini glass, light blue as a swimming pool and up with a twist, he gestured for me to taste it and I did. It was strong. I could taste vodka and gin and something sweet. Then he turned the glass and raised it to his lips and put them right where mine had been.

I'd been sipping a Pinot Grigio. It's the kind of thing one drinks when waiting for something to happen, but now something was happening, its heat spreading out through my sternum. "What is that?"

"I don't see a ring on your finger."

"I asked you a question."

That's when Marty breezed in with Troy and three others I knew but did not know. Marty's smile at me was wide, sweet, and sincere, his thick red hair sticking up in three or four places the way I liked it, and as they made their way to the bar Saul reached into the front pocket of his silk pants and slid his card just under the base of my glass. "When that's over, call me. We could have some fun."

Fun? As in playing some kind of *game?* Even when Susan was a girl, she rarely went looking for that. How many times had her best friend up north, Kimberly Mitchell, told her, "All you want to do is read. You're no *fun.*" And she wasn't. Not for anyone, really. Not for Marty, or before him Brian Heney with his long hair and thick back and fingers scarred from fishhooks and anchor chains. Susan could still see one of his hand-rolled cigarettes between two of those fingers as he raised it to his lips and squinted out at the sun on the water, one of his hands on her ass, even in public. That's what he and the others got from her. Her body, their simple belief that that meant they got *her.*

"You don't let in the joy, baby." It's the last thing Marty said to me before he left. He ran his finger over my eyebrow, something I used to like, though standing beside his packed yellow Cooper on a Wednesday after-noon, it felt like a curse, and I stepped away and watched him drive off. I went back inside and lay down on my bed. I stared at Marty's half of the closet, the bifold doors still open and the light on over an empty pole and a few hangers, one of my silk scarfs draped over it. He'd borrowed it from me for a dance piece, and when I'd given it to him there was the sense that I gave very little. I wished he'd taken it with him, for Marty was warm and kind, and another woman would have loved him but I did not, and now I was alone in this quiet apartment. It was too quiet. Too empty. The two things that my darkness loved.

Less than a week after Marty left, I found Saul's card and I called him. *We could have some fun.*

She had not had fun. But Saul was the first man—the only man— who wanted no more from her than she'd wanted from him, which was to be left alone but not so alone that she'd end up in bed for days feeling nothing, this nothingness that years later her husband would call her enemy.

The bedsprings squeaked. Bobby turned over onto his back, his arm splayed out where she'd lain.

Is it an accident that I've married only one man, and that man has devoted his intellectual life to a musician whose work celebrates chaos?

Yes, but this direction felt only partially true.

The poet Jack Gilbert: "Teach me mortality, frighten me into the present." I married Bobby because I was afraid not to marry him.

I sat on a concrete bench under the sun outside the Student Union. I was between classes and eating a salad off my lap, and a group of boys sat in the shade of the pines twenty yards away. They were laughing and talking too loudly the way young men do. They looked as if they'd just come from the gym, their tank tops spotted with sweat, their shoulder and arm muscles swollen and pronounced. It was not a look that had ever excited me, but it was hard to ignore their glowing masculine health. Then one of them glanced over at me on the bench and nodded at the others, and there was a quieting and a focusing that both flattered and assaulted me. I turned my body as if wanting a different angle of the sun and there, on a bench beside mine, sat a young woman in shorts and a bikini top, her honeyed hair long and curly, a sheen of sweat along her shoulders and clavicle and between her breasts.

My invisible years are beginning. I'll be walking across the quad between two female students in their tight tops and jeans and boots, chatting about whatever comes up, maybe scheduling a conference or answering a question about an assignment, and I'll notice a young or not so young man walking in the opposite direction glancing from one student to the next, their eyes passing over me in the center as if I were air.

This is new, and it is not unlike going from healthy to sick, or how I might imagine what losing a limb is like; what you formerly relied upon you can't anymore, and there's very little you can do about it.

Then I found myself sitting in Bobby Dunn's small red kitchen while he sautéed spinach and seemed to look right past any beauty of mine that remained, and he was speaking to that part of me I tried to show in the classroom, my love for stories that brought me into the dark, bottomless hearts of others.

Maybe Bobby's passion spoke to my own, which felt endless when our bodies are not, and so I married him.

So you don't love him at all? It was a voice inside Susan's head she did not write, for her face was warm with the kind of shame that comes from monopolizing a conversation. It was Corina Soto she should be turning her attention to. Not this solipsistic anti-memoir. Not this.

Saul Fedelstein standing on the balcony of their suite overlooking the Tyrrhenian Sea. It was late June and he was in a white linen suit, his silk shirt unbuttoned to his deeply tanned sternum. What little hair he had left on his head he'd combed back with Parisian hair gel, and the sun was low over Capri Island, and Saul had just told her that Rudolf Nureyev had once owned that island, that it was known for its "hedonistic weekends and Roman orgies." He said this with a slight nod before he sipped from his Negroni. It was a typical Saul gesture. Like he'd been there and done that himself. Behind him the balcony's wall was a white stone, but in that light it was the color of nectarines, as was Saul's suit, his back slightly stooped with the age he could no longer deny. They had just made love, but he'd had to take two pills first and it took longer for him to get it up and even longer for him to come, and she'd begun to chafe and now she lay on the chaise lounge with her own Negroni, wanting to leave this place and go home.

But where was that? Saul's yacht in Naples, Florida? Her and Lois's house off the county road in Arcadia?

He was looking north at the yellow villas built into the hills among the pine and chestnut and olive trees. Beneath an arbor to her right was a bowl of lemons, and she could smell them and she almost said to Saul, *Like you've ever been in an orgy.* But she kept quiet. There was the tinny acceleration of a motorcycle somewhere, a man's laughter carrying up from one of the open-air restaurants on the beach. Her vagina burned, and her lover looked grotesque to her then, and she felt like getting drunk.

Saul looked down at her. In his left breast pocket was the triangle of a blue silk kerchief. He was smiling at her, but it felt less like warmth and more like an appraisal. "You're not so much fun anymore, Susan."

Her face grew hot.

"We eat, we drink, we fuck, but you're elsewhere, my dear." He made a slight circular motion with his drink, the cubes clinking lightly in his glass. "I think we should call it quits." He said this in the same tone he'd used over a year earlier when he'd slid his card under her wine glass. *We could have some fun.* And Susan Lori could see, yet again, one reason why he'd been so successful in business: he simply ran the actual numbers—not the ones he hoped for, but the ones he truly saw—and he made his decision quickly and cleanly.

"Don't look so hurt."

"I'm not hurt." But she was. Except for Marty Finn (and yes, Gustavo) she did the leaving. What was this?

That night he took her to dinner at a place on the highest peak over Positano. It was one of the only modern buildings on the Amalfi Coast, and one-quarter of its main floor seemed to float out into the air over a drop to the rocks and sea hundreds of feet below. Saul had reserved them a table in the center window at the very edge of the candlelit room, and he started by ordering them champagne, tomato bruschetta, and fried ravioli.

For the chauffeured drive up the hill, he'd been as quiet as if she were a subordinate who'd just been demoted and he was being respectful of her newly changed status. But now he was expansive. He drank deeply and pointed out their view of the sun setting over the sea. It made the water a flat and shadowed maroon that to Susan Lori was the color of melancholy itself, and while he went on about the private ships moored out there and who owned them and other pleasures to be found along the coast, some he'd experienced as a very young man before his second wife, she kept her eyes on his aging face, and it was hard to swallow and her eyes stung and she shook her head once to keep from crying.

The creaking roll of the bedsprings, Bobby sitting up on one elbow. His face looked slightly swollen, and he was smiling at her, and it was as if he were lying naked on the floor of that restaurant in Positano. She wanted him to go back to sleep.

"I'm just getting in some work."

He nodded. She looked back down at the screen. Her fingers began to move again.

Then Saul was talking about his middle daughter, Rachel, who was six years older than Susan. "You're like her."

"What do you mean?'

"I used to think she had no ambition, but now I know better."

If Susan had said something then, she did not remember it now. Bobby rose out of her old bed, and she ignored him.

"I've told you about her."

"Not much, no."

In the candlelight he was staring at her. Somewhere in the ceiling above them Italian accordion music emitted from hidden speakers. The room was air-conditioned and smelled like melting wax and the olive-oil-fried ravioli the waiter was setting before them. Then came the stewed tomato of the bruschetta, and Saul said, "I didn't see it right away, but—"

"What?"

"All that reading you do."

"People read, Saul."

"Meh. Rachel read a lot too, and then she killed herself."

It was a piece of news that only diminished his mood for half a breath. He was leaning forward. He grasped her wrist and held it. "You're a bright girl. Go do something with your life."

It was such a cliché. And on another night, she might have pushed his hand away. She might've told him to go fuck himself or maybe some other woman younger than his youngest daughter. But that night her eyes welled up and she nodded and said, "Thank you."

He'd never quite held her hand like this before. There was no need in it. No sexual adoration, just an older man wanting to pull up a young woman, that's all, and she did not want him to let go.

The toilet flushed. Noni was up. Bobby began to get dressed, and Susan stared at his bare buttocks as he stepped into his underwear. He pulled on his shorts and shirt and picked up his sandals. In the hallway, Noni half yelled, "I made coffee."

He winked and raised his chin at her to continue. "I'll get it."

She heard herself say thank you. She should stop soon, but why?

When they got back to the States, Saul gave her a check for $10,000 to get started. This had made her feel like a call girl, but how else could she have described those months with Saul Fedelstein?

No, it was more than that. Yes, it was transactional for them both, but there were other moments between them, too. They'd be sitting together in the deep cushions of the stern, sipping wine and looking out at the sun setting into the water, and he'd rest his hand on her knee and wink over at her like she was the best thing that had happened to him in a long time, and he just knew she was going to accomplish something one day. And so often she would wake before he would, their cabin smelling like warm teak and the sea, the sky a blue promise outside the port windows, and she'd lie there awhile staring at him while he slept. There was the slight drift and sway of the water beneath them, which felt to her like real life. Nothing nailed down or fixed or permanent in any way, and she'd take in the lines in his forehead, his slack mouth and white stubble, the dry skin of his throat, and she'd feel a strange gratitude toward him. Like he was doing his best to solve a problem she did not even know she had.

And now he'd sent her packing, and she found a small place to rent that was too empty, too quiet, and the grief she felt was like a weight pressing her head against the floor. She cried a lot. And slept too much. She tried to read but then bought a small TV she'd watch for hours, taking in very little of it, smoking one cigarette after another, drinking an entire bottle of wine so cheap Saul would not have allowed it on his boat. She kept seeing his lined and almost comically tanned face inches from the candle in the center of their table. She kept feeling his hand in hers.

And then she killed herself.

That was not something Susan Lori had even considered before, but hearing those words high above the sea from Saul about his middle daughter, it was like being guided to some fateful door she somehow needed to know about.

That August, her bank account getting low, Susan Lori signed on to teach three courses at a community college just north of Miami. But it had been a year since she'd taught, and, standing in front of a roomful of students, some young, others her age or older, she felt like an impostor about to get caught at any moment. These were composition courses, and she assigned a lot of papers so she would have a lot of homework to do herself.

That was a bad fall. It was the first and only time she'd slept with a student, and his name was Gary. He was twenty-four and had gone back to school after serving in the Army in Iraq. He still kept his hair military-short, and he wore a faded baseball cap at all times, and he had a wide waist and short arms and legs that bulged every time he moved. His first paper had been a reflection on "something significant that had happened" to him, and while many of the other students wrote about dying grandparents or divorce or a bad car accident, his paper was one long unedited description of watching the sun rise over the desert. It was written a bit abstractly and had no punctuation whatsoever, but what struck Susan Lori as she sat in the living room of her rented apartment reading it over a glass of red wine was its subtle structure. Because the reflection wasn't about the sunrise or the desert at all. It was really about what Gary alluded to only once, the van of dead "hajis" in the foreground. He goes on to describe the colors of the sun and the flatness of the landscape and it's only toward the end of the essay that we learn where the narrator has been the whole time, on the flat roof of the building he was on watch to protect. And it's only in the final lines that we learn of his fingers on the trigger of the M16 he'd emptied into the oncoming headlights of that van hours earlier. It's the kind of van entire families travel in, and now the sun's coming up and he watches it "spread its light over the dirty land."

"Coffee." Bobby set the mug on the desk beside her open laptop.

"Thank you." Writing about Saul and all the rest, Susan felt disloyal. He leaned down and kissed the top of her head, and she felt like a fraud because she knew that this wasn't *writing*. This was some self-conscious journal of her sputtering little life, that's all. But she could not deny that it was coming for her in a way no writing quite had before.

She knew Phil Bradford was going to hate it, but she didn't care. Maybe she'd send it to Diana Clark. But why? Susan liked and respected her, but she didn't really care what she thought, either.

. . . watches it "spread its light over the dirty land."

There was simply this dark quiet tug to pull it out and get it down, and it did not even matter whether or not anyone would read it at all.

Adjuncts shared an office. The afternoon she met with Gary to discuss his paper, Susan Lori had it to herself.

Susan remembered his ball cap pulled low over his eyes. She remembered that his T-shirt was yellow and that made his arms look dark, and she remembered how directly he looked at her as she praised his essay. It seemed as if he were listening and not listening. Or that, sitting there so still and quiet, he was honoring another conversation going on in his head at the same time, and it was telling him what he wanted and what he wanted was her.

Susan Lori was wrong to think that she was the one in charge of that moment. She sat across from him at the worktable that passed for a desk, and when she began to point out his errors in grammar and mechanics and punctuation, he said, "I have a lot of stories." His voice was as low as Brian's, but it had sand and smoke in it, too, and he smiled at her and she found herself agreeing to meet him for a beer.

"Suzie?" Noni's voice calling up the stairwell. There was the steady low hum of the air conditioner, then Bobby walking down the stairs, his voice in the foyer. Susan was just about to call back to her, but she could hear the front door shut, then the VW start up, her good husband protecting her solitude so she could follow herself back to herself.

Gary scared her. When they had sex he put his hand around her throat. He didn't squeeze hard at first, but when she twisted her face away he grabbed her chin and grunted, "Look at me. Look at me." Her hair had been long then, and he flipped her over and entered her from behind and wrapped her hair in his fist and pulled on it. She told him to stop, but he pulled harder and she had to arch her neck back and all he said was, "You sure? You sure about that?"

She was, but she still let him into her apartment three or four nights in two weeks and slept with him every time. His hands were big, his fingers thick. On that last night he squeezed her throat till darkness began to fill her eyes and she was floating above a maroon sea with Saul and they were both knocking on an iron door and he kept whispering, "Rachel, Rachel," and then Gary let go and Susan Lori gasped and screamed at him to get the fuck out of her house.

It was after midnight. She lived on the first floor of a complex in the rear of the building. The yard was a strip of grass with a chain-link fence along-side a concrete culvert, a streetlamp shining over it and into her bedroom window. Gary sat naked in a chair smoking a cigarette.

"I said get out." She was kneeling on her mattress, the sheet around her. She seemed to be waiting for something, and she knew it could not be good and there was nothing she could do about it.

"You act like you're better than everyone else in the room."

"Leave, Gary."

"You think you teach people, but you're really just showing off how many fuckin' books you've read."

"I'll call the cops."

"But I can see through your bullshit. You're a fuckin' misfit and you know it."

Misfit. It was a word she had not seen or heard in a very long time. She could feel something inside her prick its ears like a dog being called by its master, and she said nothing.

"But that's cool. I'm a misfit, too. That's why we're together."

She sipped her coffee. It was hot and a little too strong, and her empty stomach seemed to receive it carefully. Her top sheet was hanging off the bed where Bobby had left it.

"Please leave."

Gary took his time. He stubbed his cigarette out on the arm of the chair. He stood and slowly pulled on his clothes.

"And we're not together."

He leaned close to her. He tucked one strand of hair behind her ear. "That's what you think." He picked up his work boots and walked barefoot through the living room and out the door. He left it open and unlocked and she still had the sheet wrapped around her when she pulled her door shut and dead-bolted it.

The next class, Gary's seat was empty. Susan Lori could only see this as a good thing, and she hoped he'd dropped her course. But when she started her car in the faculty lot, there was his brown Jeep across the street, Gary flicking his cigarette away and climbing in behind the wheel and following her home. She pulled into her parking space. She thought about using her cell phone to call the police. But then Gary's Jeep pulled up beside her, and he was smiling and holding up two or three sheets of paper. His cap was tilted back a bit. He was clean-shaven and looked like he'd just showered.

"I wrote something new."

"You could've given it to me in class."

"Yeah, I'm taking a break."

"From school?"

"You."

"Then why'd you follow me home?"

"No, the fake you. Professor Bitch you."

She should have told him to leave at that very moment. He handed her his paper—"Misfits I Have Known"—and she paused too long and he put his arm around her and walked her to the door of her apartment complex as if they were a couple, as if they'd been one for a very long time.

She sipped more coffee. She had to pee again. But she was back in that living room sitting on that rented couch—coarse plaid with wooden arms scarred with the black worms of cigarette burns.

Gary sat across from her, watching her and waiting.

This was nearly ten years ago, and she couldn't bring it all back, especially after what came next, but once again Gary's writing was focused on images and many had stayed with her.

His mother standing drunk and naked at the top of the stairs. He was twelve and he'd brought his friend home from school, and she was accusing her son of being a "fairy."

His older brother's collection of magazines he kept on the floor of their closet. More naked women, but they were tied up or chained and they clearly didn't like it.

His father's hands. How his disease made them curl into "baby's fists." The way his muscles shrank to bones under clothes that used to be "too tight on him."

Gary's girlfriend Jessica. When he thought of her he could only see her tits and teeth and the restraining order she pulled on him.

Susan Lori glanced across the room at him. He'd crossed his bare legs, and she saw for the first time a long pink scar from his ankle to his knee.

There was this little "haji girl" walking away from a blasted marketplace. Stone dust covered her face and shoulders, and her hair was sticking wetly to the side of her head. "And the thing is" she had a sad little smile on her face. Like she was about to cry but could not.

When Gary was a boy, there was this drunk he would see riding his power mower in the breakdown lane of the highway to go get his daily bottle.

There was this neighbor's cat who thought he was the "bee's fuckin' knees."

Susan stopped. That's when she began to know she was in real trouble, and she didn't want to call up those images now, Gary back stateside and luring the cat to his patio with an open can of sardines just before he "stomped its head." He went on to describe driving to a neighborhood with his .45 and shooting two dogs three streets apart. One was leashed to a post on its front porch, the other was barking at him from the front yard and sidewalk, and Gary shot it from his slow-rolling Jeep.

That old lady in her wheelchair at "Mama's home." Her hair was gone and she had to be over ninety, and she wore smeared red lipstick and smiled up at him "like an old whore." The last page was all about one whore after another. His mother again. Past girlfriends. His brother's ex-wife, who left with their son and never came back. There were airport whores and barroom whores. Military wives, who were "base whores." There were hair salon whores and bank teller whores. Waitress whores and street whores and tattoo parlor whores. There were nurse whores and doctor whores and rehab therapy whores. Those were the worst, the bitches who were supposed to be helping you. "Like the Teacher Whore reading this right fucking now."

That was his exact line word for word. It had floated darkly inside her since, but she'd never written it down before and now that she had, there was no stopping what came next. Her tongue felt thick in her mouth, and she was typing fast.

She lowered his last page and perhaps it was the way she looked at him. Or perhaps he was going to do this no matter what because he was on her before she could even speak. A jolting shock of white, a thudding bloom of green and red, her shirt bunched in one fist while he kept shooting burning colors into her brain with the other. There was his screaming and her head knocking back against the wall. There was the splintering of her cheek, the strangely far-off thought, like a small voice in a black well, that she would die now.

"You fuckin' use people! You hear me? You *use*!"

He was so much stronger than she was, and her shirt was ripping, her arms flopping on either side of her. It seemed he was just getting started, but then she was lying on her side on the carpet and the door slammed and she was alone.

Susan stopped. Her fingers hummed just above the keyboard. The room was cool, but she could feel the sweat on the back of her neck. She sipped her coffee, and it was nearly the temperature of the room.

As soon as she could stand, Susan Lori locked her door and sat back against it and cried. Her head throbbed like it was giving oxygen to an accidental fire, and one of her eyes began to close up, her nose bleeding into her mouth. She spat it into her hand and stared at it. All those years reading and wanting to write, she fancied herself a seeker of the truth, and now her young war veteran student she never should have fucked had delivered it to her, hadn't he?

You *use* people.

She did. Men anyway. But no more than they used her. And how did he know this? Did he see immediately why she'd slept with him in the first place?

Why?

Because Saul dumping her made her question whether she still possessed what had always come so easily. And this one had seen that she was working her levers and he was simply the machine. But did he also see how afraid she'd always been of being alone?

Did he see *anything* but what he wanted to fucking see? Susan Lori wished for her grandmother's silver pistol then, and she imagined raising it and pointing it at Gary just before he got to her with those impossibly heavy fists, her finger pulling the trigger again and again.

She stood and made her way to the bathroom. Her face was not her face. She ran warm water over a washcloth and dabbed at her nose and lips. Her left cheek was swollen up under her eye. She should have driven to the emergency room or called an ambulance, but instead she took three aspirin and broke ice into a plastic baggie and lay down on her bed with the ice over half her face.

The way Gary pulled on her hair and thrust himself inside her. "You sure? You sure about that?" As if he could see clearly what the others never could—the soft black guts of her shame, that she could not love anyone who would love her. What Gary had felt was her resolve not to love anyone.

Bobby. Susan stared at the empty bed. She stared at the cup he'd brought her. There was his trusting smile. His good cooking and open door. There were those two red lines in that kit she'd dropped into the trash container of the Walgreens ladies' room. She should stop soon. She should go spend some time with him, and they should talk. Because she could not say she did not love him.

She was a misfit like Gary. Susan Lori reached for the phone and she called the police.

A car engine starts up outside. Bobby's Kia. The last time they were here two falls ago, he'd found a rare Coltrane album in a shop on Oak Street, and he was probably going off to explore again, but as she listened to his car driving away she sat there feeling disappointed and just a little relieved. She walked across the hall into the bathroom and peed. Without looking into the mirror, she washed her hands quickly. In the kitchen she poured more coffee into a new cup, but now it didn't smell so good to her and she dumped it in the sink and filled the cup with water. She grabbed a banana from the counter and carried it and the water back up the stairs. It was as if she'd been in a deep mine for a very long time digging on her hands and knees. But in the past, there had been mirrors on either side of her, a bank of bright lights at her back, a stand of bleacher seats filled with men and women who read books, all of them watching her and waiting. But now it was just her kneeling in the dirt, her and this one stranger and no one else, and perhaps for the first time, she was beginning to glimpse something real just inches and feet ahead her, something she could only find with words, words that were not lies.

It was a time for aired ugliness. Gary was arrested and there was a police report in the newspaper then an uncomfortable phone call with Susan Lori's department chair, her "inappropriate involvement" with a student. There was resigning before she could be fired, and there were charges to be filed against Gary, and there was a judge who denied him bail and locked him up to wait for his hearing.

No, this was too distant. She was writing this like a journalist. *"Just let the shit hit the fan, honey."* Diana Clark. Susan wanted to talk to her about all this, about what she was writing and how, but not now.

Me:

He sits across the courtroom from me in a pea-green jumpsuit. He's grown a beard and let his hair grow longer. This makes him look softer and a bit bewildered, and I fight the urge to revise in my head what he did to me.

Six weeks have passed. My face has healed though my left eye seems a bit narrower than before. Sometimes it twitches and tears up. My cheeks used to be high and pronounced, but now they look asymmetrical, my left a bit wide and flat. In the dead center of my upper lip is the thin line of a scar.

He denies nothing. Then he is sentenced and escorted handcuffed out of the courtroom and he looks back at me as if I've done precisely what he'd always known I would and he doesn't care either way, the sun spreading over the dirty land.

Susan Lori:

What remains about this fall and winter just north of Miami is not Gary being sentenced to two years. It was not moving to an apartment closer to the water and living off the very last of Saul's money while she looked for work. It was not the way she began to check the locks of her doors and windows each night in a way she never had before.

Wasn't it? When did she ever do that before? Lois was the frightened one. Lois was the one who had bars bolted over their windows in their old apartment behind the arcade. Lois was the one who had two dead bolts installed on the front and back doors of this house off the county road. Her grandmother was the one who had all the downstairs windows replaced with new ones that locked and that she never opened and covered with dark drapes and kept the house in an air-conditioned cocoon. Noni was the one who owned a gun.

No, it was the way Susan Lori began to check the locks. She kept imagining Gary getting released and coming for her. She imagined other men coming for her, too, men she did not know, though why would they? She rarely left the house at all. But this new gesture of checking locks in the middle of the night, it was like hearing the faint strains of music from a horizon you've been driving away from for years then finally beginning to dance to it. Susan Lori never had the dread that moved through her grandmother, but it was like growing up with someone who'd survived Auschwitz then seeing a swastika and starting to run.

The light in the room was different, her unmade sheets bright with the sun. Outside the window the oak leaves were almost too green, the sky beyond bits of blue that could shatter.

But more than this, it was her face in the days and short weeks after her beating. It was how people looked at her new face.

Susan Lori went out only when she had to, mainly to the grocery store a mile down the street. Women, old or young, would look at her with pity, some with knowing expressions, and one or two older ones looked like they wanted to come over and talk to her. But boys and men were different. They looked at her as if they'd just opened a surprise package in the mail and found something broken that needed to be sent back. One boy, seventeen or eighteen, leaned against the wall outside the Kroger's smoking a cigarette, a skateboard at his feet, and he glanced up at her from his cell phone and actually shook his head as if she'd disappointed him.

She felt utterly exposed. Not her face, but that her outsides were now as plainly ugly as her insides. She may as well have been walking up and down the aisles with no skin at all, her entrails shining and stinking like dried blood.

It's afternoon and almost winter. All the cottages have padlocks on the doors and the rides are closed and some of the places that sell cotton candy and pizza and fried dough have boards where open windows and busy people used to cook.

Paul wants to show me something. I'm six, and he's eighteen. It's cold. The sun is out, but it's cold. He has on a new Army jacket. It's green and too big for him and he thinks he looks like a soldier but he looks to me like my uncle who just wants to be a soldier because he likes to kill fake soldiers in the arcade.

"C'mere, I want to show you something."

He's smiling at me. I don't like his smile. It always brings a pinch or a slap or a kick and mean laughing. I turn to start running, but he grabs my arm and pulls me onto the sand. It's hard to walk. I'm yelling at him to let me go. We're between two big buildings, and the ocean is behind him, the waves small and quiet. Then he pulls me under the building where loud music plays in the summer. There are thick wet posts and a wooden floor way above us, and it's dark under here and smells like wet seaweed and I want to leave but I want to know what he wants to show me too.

"See?" He's pointing to something on a gray brick. It's rusty and a little sandy. He picks it up. It's a gun.

"Is it real?"

"Yeah. I found it, and I'm gonna kill your father with it."

"My daddy's dead."

Killyourfatherwithit

It's just a remembered sound in her head. Like Grandpa Gerry's laugh in front of the TV, like a scratch on a record to a song she'd forgotten—killyourfatherwithit, killyourfatherwithit, killyourfatherwithit.

Then Paul points the gun at me, and I run back out into the light and he's laughing like he'll never stop.

Her fat uncle Paul who hated his air-freight job and who over the years had become a brooding collector of nearly thirty handguns and rifles and even an AK-47. Three or four summers ago, standing in his backyard while hot dogs and hamburgers flamed on the grill, he'd held it out to her, and she was surprised at how light it was.

"But why do you need this, Paul?"

His face was sweating and flushed, his thinning hair short above his ears. He was squinting at her as if she were an absolute moron. "Why *wouldn't* I need it, you mean."

He'd taken it back from her and then shook his head. "Just turn over the burgers, all right?"

He disappeared into the house with his new gun, and there was that familiar dance between them. Her uncle-brother who—so much like his mother Lois—would invite her in then push her away.

The phone was ringing. Had been ringing.

Killyourfatherwithit

She stood and walked down the dark hallway to Lois's even darker room. It was too cold, the air conditioner on high. She picked up the phone. "Yeah?" Strange how she felt, like she was still six and rising up through year after year to her forty-three-year-old self hearing the voice of her husband. "Sound good?"

"I'm sorry, what?"

"Take a break. I'll buy you lunch." He asked if she wanted to meet him downtown or should he come pick her up?

"And I do have some important mail for you, Susan."

"Then why'd you say you left it at home?"

"I'll explain over lunch. Should I come get you?"

She said yes and hung up, though just the word *lunch* made her want to stay right where she was. And what did he mean by *important mail*? Would there be no course offerings for her in the spring? It was a little early to hear about this, but adjuncts were always the first to go, especially if they hadn't worked for a semester. That had to be it. And Bobby was being careful with her. He loved her, and so he was being careful.

Lois's room was like a crypt. The shades were halfway up, but the windows were covered all the way with lace curtains and lined with heavy drapes. Noni's comforter was pulled back just enough to have allowed her out of bed early this morning, and her bedside table was coated with dust. On a stack of toy catalogues and *People* magazines there was her digital alarm clock, an empty reading glasses case, three prescription bottles. Susan read the labels: warfarin, Lipitor, Cymbalta. She knew the first two were to control her high blood pressure and cholesterol, but what was Cymbalta? She'd seen TV commercials for this. A middle-aged woman looking worried in her kitchen, then thirty seconds later smiling in the sunshine. Anxiety? Still?

Susan walked down the hall to the bathroom, where she was going to shower and cleanse herself of where she'd been all morning, this little girl running away from her family on the beach, this little girl running away from her brother-uncle and his rusty gun and his mean laughing. This little girl running and running and running. *You use people. You use.* And she was going to prepare herself for where she was headed next, to yet one more reminder that her life was probably more than halfway over and she was being set adrift yet again, her husband the only steady thing she had and now she was pregnant too and all she really wanted to tell him was: *C'mere, get lost.*

29

IT'S PAST noon, the sun high over fields of cotton and corn and maybe soybeans, Daniel isn't sure, but on both sides of the highway are acres and acres of it, this part of North Carolina flat, something he does not recall from his bus trip south so long ago. Soon comes a bridge over the Roanoke River, and he glances down over the zipping steel railing to the muddy water and the sun glinting back at him.

There's a narrow island there too, just a spit of maples and pines and a bare patch strewn with white rocks and a tractor tire lying on its side.

At his last stop he pulled into the lot of a Big Boy's 66, and it was a slow walk from his Tacoma past all the eighteen-wheelers to the men's room door. His back was stiff and there was an ache that seemed to come from beyond muscle and bone and is still with him no matter how he shifts in his seat. Before leaving the truck stop, he topped off the tank and bought a cold Coke and a bag of potato chips, though he has not opened them, nor has he eaten anything since that steak last night, but his body seems to be going along all right without it. He can't say he feels strong, but there's some kind of fire lit inside him and he's being pulled toward whatever's feeding it.

He keeps glancing down at Susan's photo taped to the dash. For a moment, in the dull glare of the sun, it looks like a mug shot, and again comes the knowing that whatever is beautiful and good about her can only come from her mother. So why would she want to see *him*?

The river and the bridge are behind him now. The fields give way to asphalt parking lots and cars and trucks glinting under the sun. There's a Walmart Supercenter, an auto body joint, a white Baptist church. Daniel's book on tape has been playing a while, but the narrator's voice is a rainfall of one word after another and only a few drops have gotten in—*women, Plains Indians, holy people advice.*

Daniel leans forward and turns it up.

When bands lost their male leaders, women would become chieftains. Women learned to shoot small bows, and they carried knives, because among the Sioux a woman was supposed to be able to defend herself against attack. The puberty ceremony of the Sioux was such as to give pride to a young Sioux maiden:

Walk the good road, my daughter, and the buffalo herds wide and dark as cloud shadows moving over the prairie will follow you . . . Be dutiful, respectful, gentle and modest, my daughter. And proud walking. If the pride and the virtue of the women are lost, the spring will come but the buffalo trails will turn to grass. Be strong, with the warm, strong heart of the earth. No people goes down until their women are weak and dishonored . . .

The blare of a car horn behind him, then a white flash in his rearview, a new pickup accelerating past him on his left. He glances over in time to see a young man behind the wheel flipping him off. Then it's just North Carolina plates and a white tailgate growing smaller and smaller. He's driving just under fifty miles an hour. For a long while now cars and pickups and eighteen-wheelers have been passing him one after another, but until that kid took Daniel's pace personally, he hadn't noticed it at all. It felt familiar too. People barreling past him to go do important things. But now there's someone waiting for him, or at least she knows he's coming, and he has always driven slow, but today he knows he's driving even slower.

The narrator has moved on to other things. He's talking about 1756 and a girl named Elizabeth Sprigs writing to her father about her servitude. Daniel wants to hear this, but those words about a woman defending herself are snagged inside the current of his head and he presses the button to make the story go backward.

Another horn. He steps on the gas.

In the Zuni tribes to the southwest, for instance, extended families—large clans—were based on the woman, whose husband came to live with her family.

That morning a few weeks after Labor Day, the Midway was empty of cars and strolling people and Danny was doing touch-up with Liam on the Broadway Flying Horses. Liam had a leather case of fine brushes, and he wouldn't let Danny do any of the brushwork himself, but Liam needed every horse cleaned and prepped before he got to it, and that's what Danny was doing when Linda walked up to the carousel and said, "Hey."

It was a warm morning, the sun out, and she wore a halter top. Her thin gold chain was bright against her brown skin. She wasn't smiling, but she wasn't not smiling. She looked scared or pissed off or like she didn't understand something or all three. Back then, Danny would start to get hard just seeing her, and he glanced back to where Liam was painting on his knees on the other side of the carousel, and said, "Hey."

"C'mere."

She didn't have to ask. He dropped his rag and bucket and got close enough to kiss her lips. But she turned her head and pushed three fingers into his shoulder and said, "I'm gonna have a baby."

Almost like it had nothing to do with him. Like it was something she had to do by herself. Other guys would have run from that kind of news. Other guys would have seen it as some big heavy chain around their necks and now they had to walk alone into icy water. But Danny didn't. For Danny it was the world locking him into the first real luck he'd ever had so only more good luck could keep coming.

Whatever horrors can be imagined in the transport of black slaves to America must be multiplied for black women, who were often one-third of the cargo. Slave traders reported:

"I saw pregnant women give birth to babies while chained to corpses which our drunken overseers had not removed . . . packed spoon-fashion they often gave birth to children in the scalding per-spiration from the human cargo . . . On board the ship was a young negro woman chained to the deck, who had lost her senses soon after she was purchased and taken on board."

Daniel lets it play, though he does not listen. He keeps thinking of those young Indian women carrying knives to defend themselves. And he sees Linda getting to him first. He sees her eyes widen as he and Captain Suspicion make their sick little move, and he sees her beat him to it, pulling her blade from her belt or whatever a Sioux girl would wear and then driving it into his chest and stopping his snake-filled heart cold.

This is something he has never considered before. Ten thousand times he has pictured anything but what happened, but it always ends with him not doing what he did. There were dreams of Linda running past him and out the kitchen door. There were plenty of those wishful pictures, but never her turning on him first.

A camp bus passes him on the left. Each window is filled with teenage boys and girls in red T-shirts, and they're a hive of talk and laughter and clowning around. If Danny had been on that bus, he'd have been the quiet kid keeping to himself and staring out the window. And if Will Price had never heard his voice on the ladder that morning, Danny would still be that kid. But if Will Price hadn't heard his voice, Linda Dubie would never have looked up and seen him behind fake cloudy glass in his red blazer with that mic to his lips. She never would've waited for him under the orange lights of Joe's Playland, and she never would've told him he was the best one, and he never would've walked her home, and who knows if anything bad would have ever happened at all?

But he wouldn't have his daughter, would he?

Daniel glances at Susan's photo taped to the dash. She has her mother's looks and that same almost reckless light in her dark eyes. Like she'll do anything she damn well pleases when she pleases and there's nothing you can do about it. How much better it would've been for this woman to have grown up with her mother who would've gone on to marry someone good.

Daniel reaches for his can of Coke, cracks it open, and takes a long sweet drink of it. It's no longer cold, but it's going down well and maybe he'll be able to eat something soon too. He's deep in farm country again. On both sides of the highway are thin stands of pine, the fields beyond them thick with low green plants in brown furrows under the sun. Maybe Linda wouldn't've married anyone good. Maybe she would've just found another boy to wave in Gerry's and Lois's faces. It did feel that way sometimes. Like she'd chosen the one kid neither of them, especially Lois, was ever going to like, and that was another reason, maybe the main reason, why she never even brought up ending that baby growing inside her.

"You gonna raise it with me, or not?"

These may not be her words, but Daniel can still see the way her chin was raised up like she was going to do it with or without him, and maybe that's when he began to know too that she did not love him all the way yet, and so everything he did after that moment he did like a man trying to catch and keep a dove flying through his house.

Even free white women, not brought as students or slaves but as wives of the early settlers, faced special hardships. Eighteen married women came over on the Mayflower. *Three were pregnant, and one of them gave birth to a dead child before they landed. Childbirth and sickness plagued the women; by the spring, only four of those eighteen women were still alive.*

Daniel switches it off. He's had it with this book. It seems like the only thing we all have in common is that we fight our way to life only to suffer deeply once we get here. But what about the good things?

Like the smells of the ocean and wet paint.

Like lying naked on his side up against his naked wife, the way the sea air blew into their room and lifted their white curtains and she said, "That's so pretty."

Eating a slice of pizza under the sun.

Suzie pressing her small ear to his chest, her high sweet voice. "It's so loud, Daddy."

Pee Wee Jones and him quietly playing checkers.

A light rain on the flat roof of his trailer.

Sipping instant coffee alone on his bunk, the blue light of dawn opening up in his cell.

Walking through Port City one spring afternoon, his hands in his jacket pockets, his thin hair combed back, and a passing woman smiling at him.

The way this late summer sun lies on that green highway sign a hundred yards up ahead, the newness of the towns written there: *Smithfield, Benson, Dunn.*

Dunn. Forty-one miles. Daniel can only see this coincidence of names as a good thing. A tiny thing, but good, and that's where he will stop and find another toilet. That's where he'll stop and make himself eat something before he hits the road once more, heading south.

30

THE SAWGRASS was dimly lit and air-conditioned cool, ceiling fan blades revolving slowly from oak trusses high above. At the bar a heavy couple in their sixties or seventies drank beer and picked from a basket of french fries, and a few feet away a shaded lamp hung low over the center of a pool table covered with blue felt. A rack of only three cue sticks was screwed to the wall, which was made of vertical planks of tongue-and-groove pine, and it was patchy with old posters of bands that had played on the black plywood stage in the corner, this place a night joint for ranchers and ranch hands and local businesspeople, and it struck Susan as funny that she had never once stepped into this place on a Friday or Saturday night, that she'd fled for Gainesville and then she'd just kept fleeing.

The bartender seemed to be the waitress, and Bobby stood at the bar ordering them iced teas and fish tacos even though Susan had told him she wasn't hungry. He'd just smiled at her and said, "You should eat, babe." As if he knew something when he did not. Though he had a right to, didn't he? Susan wasn't so sure. Nor could she remember the last time she'd ever written so deeply for so long, and she was thinking about getting back to work later this afternoon too. This wasn't because she thought she was writing anything special, either. It was because of where it had pulled her. To Saul and Gary. To Paul and his rusty gun.

Bobby was smiling at her as he walked back to the table holding their iced teas in two big beer mugs. He was wearing the same clothes he'd worn last night—his faded Hawaiian shirt and loose shorts and sandals—and she'd almost forgotten how thin and hairy his calves were. Hooked over the back of his chair was the leather satchel he carried all his schoolwork in. It was wide and deep enough to also carry full-sized albums, and he had one in there now he said he'd found in a shop off Oak Street that he was going to show her once he got their drinks.

"This place is a trip." He set her iced tea down in front of her. It had no lemon, and its straw was too short, and on another day she might've sent it back, but not today. On the ride into town, her hair wet, her makeup minimal, she'd felt both emptied out yet filled and she was sweetly tired but ready to work some more, and for the first time in a long while there was the nearly virtuous sense that she was earning her keep somehow. And even the knowledge of what she was carrying didn't take away from this, for there was still the sense that there was time stretched out ahead and she didn't have to say or do anything just yet, that unpaid bill pushed into the back of a closed drawer.

"You look good, Susan. Your work must be going well."

She nodded, though the word *work* didn't seem right. "Except I'm writing the kind of shit I hate."

"You just don't like nonfiction."

"I don't like memoirs."

"But you're writing one."

"Not if I don't show anyone."

"But what if it's good?"

Hope sparked and flared inside her. She wanted it to be good. She wanted it to be something worth reading. But she'd stopped imagining someone actually reading it. Even Phil Bradford, who was being paid to read what was coming out of her. Especially him.

"It's a fucking mess, Bobby. I'm writing it in just about every point of view there is."

"Sounds like free jazz to me, baby. No tonal center." He smiled at her and reached into his satchel and pulled out the album. On the front cover was a photograph in profile of a black man with a thick mustache. He wore a knit cap and aviator sunglasses, and his legs were crossed, his lips parted like he was captivated by something far away. *Cecil Taylor—Live in the Black Forest.*

"I can't believe what you can find in this fucking town, Susan. Ornette came from R&B, but this guy was classically trained. He studied theory and played the piano, but he broke all the rules just as much as Coleman did. His sidemen had to follow whatever he did on the piano, and he never wrote a single note. At least Ornette did notations, but not Taylor. Man, he was *out* there." Bobby was shaking his head and staring at the album's cover, at the handsome musician he'd probably written all about as well, and Susan was back on Walter's deck under that wide umbrella. *Do you know what a remora is? It's a sucker fish.*

Bobby was saying more about Taylor and his music, but she wasn't listening. She was watching him. He had slipped on his glasses and was reading something to her from the back cover, and there was such passion in his face and voice. With other men, all that had been directed at her and her only, and it was like being pinned underwater by a ton of roses. Paul pulling her into the shadows where he'd found a rusty gun.

"I've been writing things I never remembered before."

Bobby lowered the album. "You have?" He slid it back into the satchel.

She shrugged. "Yeah. It's weird, that's all."

"What kinds of things?"

"Just, you know, childhood shit."

He studied her a moment. A light sheen of sweat lay along the top of his bald head. He drank long from his iced tea, then set it down and reached into a pocket of his satchel and pulled out a stamped letter.

"This came over from the English Department. They put it in my mailbox." He slid it over to her, and she knew right away it had nothing to do with the college because it was too thick and had been sent overnight. It was addressed to Professor Susan Dunn. The handwriting looked childlike and labored. *No, the fake Professor Bitch you.* Gary. A hot fork began to turn inside her and then her eyes shot to the words in the upper left corner of the envelope. They were printed less neatly, like they were written in a hurry, and what they were saying brought a heated stillness to the air, a muffled hum, Bobby sitting across from her just an oval of flesh over a faded Hawaiian shirt— *Daniel Patrick Ahearn.*

Bobby was saying something. His words were bubbles rising up from deep waters. Then came the slamming of her heart like a small fist against a locked door, and she was taking in air and saying, "What the fuck, Bobby? What the *fuck?*"

"Open it."

She tossed it at him. "No, you."

"You sure?"

"How'd he *find* me? How'd he know I *teach?*"

"Google?"

"But how's he know my last name? What the *fuck*, Bobby?"

The man at the bar turned his gray head and stared at her and she wanted to punch him in the face. He turned back to his wife and fries. Susan needed to stand so she did. "This is fucked up, Bobby. This is so fucked."

Bobby slipped his glasses back on. He tore open the envelope and pulled out what looked like twelve to fifteen pages. Susan could see they were handwritten in the same careful scrawl as her name on the envelope. And she was not a "Professor." What the fuck did he know? What gave him the fucking right?

"Sit down, baby. This is something you should read, not me."

"I don't want to read it." But she sat down and he handed it to her and she read the first line, and it was like sipping something poisonous that its maker had tried to make sweet:

My dear daughter Susan,
Ive got no right to call you these things. But even with every-
thing that happened

"Here's your lunch, folks. Enjoy." The waitress set down a plate of bright colors that smelled like lettuce and steamed fish, and there was Bobby's voice thanking her, the muffled clink of silverware wrapped in a paper napkin, and Susan dropped the letter and rushed past the bar down a wide hallway, the walls a smear of posters, the bathroom dark and cool as she retched into one of the sinks. My dear daughter? Jesus *Christ*. She retched again then ran cold water and cupped some into her mouth and spat. She rinsed the sink and shook her head at the three words pressing into her brain: *Daniel Patrick Ahearn.*

Back at the table, Bobby was waiting for her, his food untouched. "You okay, baby?" She shook her head and told him to eat then sat down and picked up what she'd dropped. *But even with everything that happened you* **are** *my daughter. Our daughter.*

Your mother was a very good mother. I hope you remember that about her. She did not deserve

Dark pinpoints of heat seemed to be holding the pages in Susan's hands. She began to read faster.

Susan, I used to be Danny.

You're a grown woman now so maybe I can tell you this. Danny was all blood and body. Danny didn't know how to think or sit back. Danny was a reactor. When he was a kid he used to read comic books but he could of been a hero of one himself and you could call it "The Reactor."

He described being a new kid, implying that he was teased but that Danny would "only take it for a half-minute or two maybe less."

White heat gushing. Susan's grandmother trying to keep him cooled down with her love. *But then I—but then Danny found another kind of love and everything got messed up.*

There were crossed-out words, but Susan could make out the word *Your* then the word *mother.* Her mouth was dust and ash, and she could feel her heart beating in it, and she kept reading this long story about men on the beach making him feel like he didn't deserve his wife *who didn't talk much but when she did it was all about you. Suzie Woo Woo.*

Suzie Woo Woo, an echo inside an echo inside her.

He went on to say that Linda quit school at sixteen and she loved the beach and the strip and she read books and kept to herself. He said: *Don't forget Linda was quiet and if you're beautiful and quiet other girls that age think you're stuck up and then your on the outs.*

Yes, Susan thought. *Yes.* She glanced over at Bobby. He was watching her and slowly chewing his food. He looked like he wanted to ask her something, but he kept quiet.

She kept reading, her father telling her all about beating up a man for just looking at Linda, for giving him a "sneer," and how he didn't trust her because when he got hauled off to jail she didn't follow him.

He had never trusted the strip rats but it never came to him not to trust <u>her</u>. She had chosen him. She and Danny and how from day one they could never hold back from each other. Susan. Danny lost his way. That's not the right way to put it really because it looks like I'm making excuses for him. I'm not. He deserved everything he got and more. But he went crazy for a while. That's what I'm trying to say. And when people are crazy it's like being around a drunk or somebody so high on something your conversation with them is from another planet. You can't talk to them. Linda couldn't—

He went on to say that he went crazier "behind the walls," that he was on Suicide Watch. But he wasn't strong enough to take his own life. *A better man would of thought of you first anyways. A half orphan becoming a full orphan. But Danny was no man. He was nothing.*

"You should eat." Bobby was holding his mug of iced tea. Behind him the bar was empty, and the woman bartender was flipping through channels on a TV Susan had not noticed earlier. "He's fucking explaining himself to me."

"As in, justifying?"

"This is so—" What? This long letter from this man she did not know, the one who had forever taken her mother from her, who the fuck did he think he was, telling her all this shit? Like she fucking *cared* about his time in *prison*? "I'm just so fucking angry right now, Bobby."

"Maybe you should read it later."

I see you're a professor and I'm very proud of you for that. "I can't read this." She flicked the pages in Bobby's direction. They skittered against his plate, the upper third of her father's pages folding into themselves. "He's telling me he's *proud* of me. Who the hell is he to *tell* me that?"

"You should eat something." Bobby picked up the letter. He reached for the envelope beside her plate.

"And he has no idea what a fucking comma is or grammar or— I can't eat." She stood. "I need a drink."

She walked fast to the bar. Their waitress/bartender had settled on a cooking channel, a pretty brunette smiling into the camera above a stove of sautéing mushrooms and onions. The sound was on low, and the TV chef's voice was like one that hangs on in daylight after a night dream you don't remember. The woman bartender was talking now, and Susan could see that she'd never really looked at this woman once. She wore a western button-down shirt with blue pearl buttons, and she was somewhere in her sixties, her hair a dried-out blond with gray roots, her face thin and lined, her lipstick faded but still bright in the corners of her lips. She was the age her own mother would have been, and she was saying something about the food.

"I'm sorry?"

"Is it all right? Would you like something else?"

"Yeah, a vodka on the rocks."

But as the woman filled a glass with ice, Susan did not want that drink. She did not know *what* she wanted. *I see you're a professor and I'm very proud of you for that.* That hot day in May in Gainesville. Climbing those metal stairs to that bunting-draped temporary stage. The bright sun and sweating under her robe and mortarboard, how she took her degree from the smiling dean, and from the crowd came Paul's "Yo, Susan!" and it was pathetic how she squinted out at the crowd looking for him.

Susan. Danny lost his way. What did that fucking mean? People lost their way all the goddamn time and they didn't hurt anybody.

But that one word *Susan*. That stopped her. The directness of it. The sincerity, maybe. She didn't know. The woman bartender was talking again, and Bobby was handing her a ten. Susan looked up at him. He was giving her that same careful expression he'd had last night when he first walked into their kitchen. "Want me to read it to you?"

"No. Yeah, I don't fucking know." She picked up the cool, beaded glass then put it back down. "Let's go someplace else."

"Fine." Bobby asked the woman if they could get Susan's untouched lunch to go, and the woman put an empty Styrofoam container on the bar then disappeared into the kitchen, Bobby walking back to their table for her lunch and his leather satchel and Black Forest jazz and this letter from a man who said he was proud of her, this Daniel Patrick Ahearn who used to fucking call himself Danny.

31

LOIS SAT cross-legged in her front window display spraying her chamois cloth with vinegar and water. She was cleaning yet another mirror she did not recall buying, this one a nineteenth-century Italian rococo, and she was sweating from having already cleaned three others—two Victorian dresser mirrors and an English bull's-eye with a chipped gilt frame. Now Marianne was in the back looking for more, and Lois began wiping the glass free of dust and smudges when she saw Susan and her husband stepping out of the Sawgrass Saloon. Bobby had his leather bag over one shoulder like a woman or an aristocrat, and he wore small round sunglasses, his bald head glistening with sweat. He seemed to be guiding Susan to his Kia, and she didn't look so good. Her short hair was still a mess, and she was too thin and looked shaken, too.

Oh, Lord, what now? They'd had such a good time last night, the three of them, and when Susan and Bobby opened their gift right there in the bright kitchen, they seemed to be very happy with those Dresden lamps, especially Bobby, who kept glancing over at his wife as if those lovers at the base of those two lamps might seal something that had become unglued.

Before he'd met Suzie for lunch, Bobby had come into the shop and shown Lois the album he bought over at Midge Perkins's store. She was a birdlike little bitch, who sold anything older than 1975, and Lois didn't like her, and she almost told Bobby that, but he was so excited about his purchase that she'd kept her mouth shut.

Last night Suzie kept saying, "You shouldn't have, Noni. You really shouldn't have," but she'd kept running her fingers over the porcelain lace of the woman's dress, and Lois knew she'd done the right thing. But now they both looked so damn serious as they disappeared into Bobby's little car then drove west down Oak Street. Was that girl *ever* going to stay with a man?

"Would you like me to take over?" Marianne was holding a square mirror with a black and gold frame. A strand of hair hung over her left eye, and there were tiny beads of sweat above her upper lip, though her lipstick still looked fresh. Lois was thirsty, and her shoulders burned. She could feel her sundress sticking to her upper back. "Please. I'm getting too old for this, honey."

She extended her legs, and Marianne set down the mirror and offered her hand, which Lois took. She needed water, and she needed a cigarette, but as she walked back through the shadows of her cluttered shop, through the smells of oiled hardwoods and the vinegar on her fingers, the low gurgling of the dehumidifiers, her own words hung there inside her. *Too old for this.* Not wiping down mirrors for a window display she'd probably replace in a week, but worrying about that girl ever being happy, that girl who was forty-three years old, for Christ's sake.

32

JUST BEFORE the Dunn exit the sky darkens and it begins to rain. Daniel still has no appetite, but he needs a toilet and so he takes the off-ramp and is soon driving slowly through a town of two-story brick and concrete buildings, their glass fronts beaded with water. There's a luncheonette up ahead, and he pulls into a small lot and parks beside a sedan, its wheel wells splattered with mud.

The pain in his lower back has become like a fever in his legs now, and he pats his front pocket for his wad of cash and rises slowly out of his Tacoma and locks it. The rain is warm and soft. He stands there a moment with his eyes closed and raises his face to it. Something heavy rumbles by in the wet street behind him, and he opens his eyes and makes his way over the sidewalk and into the luncheonette. It's bright and loud with talking people. There are the smells of coffee and hamburger grease, and a young girl in an apron and tight jeans is holding a coffeepot and calling him sir. She's smiling and calling him sir, "And please sit wherever you like."

He asks for the bathroom, and she tells him where it is, raising her coffeepot and pointing with it to the back of the place past a table of old men and women, one of the women delicate and classy-looking. As he passes she smiles up at him, and he steps into the men's room and there comes the feeling he's been here before, in Dunn, North Carolina, though he never has, and as he walks into the stall and lashes the door shut, he feels more alone than he did early this morning. Just some dried leaf blowing across an empty field, and now there is very little waiting to be done. What comes out of him seems to have no urine in it whatsoever. He watches the toilet bowl darken with it, and there's the urge to call for help. But to who? And for what?

Linda's eyes. The dark shock in them then the knowing then the gathering herself to face what she knew was coming and could do nothing about, all in a few beats of his poisoned and poisonous heart. She was more stand-up than he'll ever be.

He flushes the toilet and washes his hands at one of three sinks. The mirror is long and scratched, and in the upper left corner is a faded decal in the shape of a fish: *Jesus Loves You.*

Just outside the door is laughter, talking voices, all the happy, busy noise of the living, and he thinks of his will. He needs to finish writing it out, and then he needs to find a typewriter.

He avoids the mirror and turns the water to cold. He cups his hands under it and splashes his face three times, chills rolling down his back and into his legs. He pictures them as bones. When he got paroled he worked up his nerve and asked his mother where his wife was buried.

"The ocean, honey."

He wished they hadn't done that. There should have been a place for Linda's loved ones to visit. He taps the hand dryer button, the blasting hot air on his big hands. It's wrong to even think it, but that's where he would've wanted to go. In that same box in that same hole in the ground, him and Linda curled side by side, the smell of the ocean outside their window, a light wind lifting their curtains in a soft, white wave.

33

T HEY WERE parked in the lot of Susan's old high school under a sable palm that offered little shade, and Bobby had kept the engine running for the AC. Both sun visors were down. He had his glasses on and was reading the letter to himself, but she was waiting for him to get to where she'd left off back at the Sawgrass. *It's where he says he's fucking proud of me.* In the nearly empty lot were a white painter's van and a pickup truck with a rack and two long ladders strapped to it.

"Jesus, baby." Bobby was looking at her. His eyes looked big behind his glasses, her father's pages resting on his leg. "He sounds kind of—"

"What?"

"Well, sincere." He touched her shoulder. "Sorry."

"Just—just read it. But skip that shit about him being—" She couldn't say the word. It was a thickening mass in her throat. Bobby lowered his head and read: " 'That worm I talked to you about? Well it became a black snake and it filled Danny's veins so he was scared all the time. But what could he do with this? He was The Reactor.' "

"The fucking *Reactor*?"

"He may not be right in the head, baby. You sure you want to hear the rest?"

"No."

Bobby rested his hand on her knee. One of the painters was smoking a cigarette under the portico of the school. He was small and from here his arms looked brown and thin. "Don't stop anymore, Bobby. Just get this over with, all right?"

"Sure thing." His hand slipped off her, and she looked at him as he began to read again, this first true friend she'd ever had.

He went on to read her father's detailed story of spying on his own wife, of leaving work in the middle of the day to catch her but never catching her doing anything " 'but working the arcade or taking care of you.'

" 'Everything I'm writing to you now Susan is the story of a changed man.' "

"Jesus Christ."

Bobby looks over at her then keeps reading.

Dear Susan,

The sickness I had has been gone a long time now, that's all I'm trying to tell you. Captain Suspicion. That snake in my guts. All that—none of it had anything to do with <u>you</u>.

You should know that I tried to find you too.

Through the windshield the high school had soft corners, the front glass doors foggy, Bobby's face as well. His hand was back on her knee. "Almost done."

After five years on parole I was cleared to go out of state and I quit my barbering job and took a bus as far as Georgia. But I changed my mind and went back home Susan. I didn't want to bother you and I don't want to bother you now but I'm coming to see—

Bobby stared at the page, his lips pursed.

"What? Fucking read it. *What?*"

"I'm coming to see you in a few days just this one time and I hope that's all right with you.

Love,
Your Father
Daniel Patrick Ahearn

"That's *it*? When? When the fuck is a *few* days?"

"He doesn't say."

She grabbed the letter. "When'd you get this?"

"Yesterday."

She read the last line to herself. *I didn't want to bother you and I don't want to bother you now but I'm coming to see you in a few days just this one time and I hope that's all right with you.*

LOVE,
Your ~~Dad~~ Father
Daniel Patrick Ahearn

"*Love?* Jesus." She jerked on the door handle and stepped out into the heat. There were the smells of dried palm bark and the exhaust from Bobby's car, her heart punching her sternum, sweat breaking out on her face and neck. One of the other painters was walking under the portico then out into the sun for his truck. A dust mask hung just under his chin. He was staring at her as he walked around to the rear of his pickup and lowered the tailgate and pulled out an empty plastic bucket. She thought of her father, the painter. She pictured him wrapping his paint roller in cellophane and driving back to the beach to catch her mother cheating on him. That fucking snake inside him he called "Captain Suspicion." The painter lifted the tailgate back into place and glanced at her face and breasts and legs.

"What're you looking at, *motherfucker*?"

The painter kept walking, raising his hand in the air the way people do to homeless men or women who yell at voices in their heads, Bobby rising out of his car and saying, "Let's go, baby. Let's get out of here."

34

THE SUN was still out, but just beyond the citrus fields the sky looked low and heavy, a long yellow cloud hanging above the pine woods. It was the color the air gets in hurricane season, which they were in now though they'd been spared so far, and Lois downshifted for the turn on the county road then accelerated past the road prison, its outdoor visitors' tables empty behind the chain link, and she drove faster toward home. She was tired, and she was thirsty, but she had no appetite, and she was going to tell Susan and Bobby to cook something up for themselves.

After leaving Marianne to finish up their window display of mirrors, Lois had settled in her easy chair for a while, resting and fighting the urge for a cigarette. She'd had too many the night before, at least two days' worth, and she'd sat there staring at her Sue Herschel doll collection on the shelves across from her desk, each one staring back at her like they were waiting for her to feed them or take them someplace more fun. On the shelves beside them was a plaited skip rope from 1912, its wood handles dark from so many young hands. There was an 1830s stagecoach drawn by two white stallions, and a German Noah's ark. On its gabled roof was painted a dove with an olive leaf in its beak, and under that was a Schoenhut toy piano, its tiny keys yellowed, and a 1920s Mickey Mouse organ grinder next to a dinky Heinz tomato ketchup van. Bobby loved that one, and he loved being in her shop, and why wouldn't he? He'd written a book about what someone else had created. Why wouldn't he be the kind of man to appreciate what the makers of fine toys and furniture could do, too?

Over the dehumidifiers, she could hear Marianne humming a tune up front. Lois began to doze and what came to her was Susan's tall, friendly husband selling that bitch from Ohio that Biedermeier mirror but with a big smile on his face, Suzie sixteen again and sitting in this very chair, a paperback open on her lap.

When Lois woke, Marianne was talking to a couple in front of the walnut plantation desk. They were young and both wore glasses, and Lois pegged them right away as office workers from Tampa or St. Pete. They probably worked with computers all day but wanted only antiques in their new childless home, and she pushed herself out of her chair and made her way out back for a smoke. She sat in her lawn chair beneath the fire escape and stared out at what was still inside her head, Bobby and Susan owning this place, the emphasis being on Bobby.

Maybe Lois should feel bad about seeing it this way, but she didn't. He clearly valued old things, and he was good with people, and he was the only man Suzie'd ever had who was good with her, too. He seemed to take her as she was and he gave her free rein, which she needed, but was she good with *him*? Her whole life she'd left one for the next, the way some people trade in cars once they hit a certain mileage. But maybe Bobby knew this and wasn't going to put up with it. Maybe at lunch today he'd laid down the law.

Lois hoped so. Her granddaughter had always been too involved with herself, as far as she was concerned. All that reading and writing and thinking. Maybe owning a business together would be just the thing they needed. It had been good for Lois and Gerry, at least until it went bad. The day they'd closed on the arcade, it was early spring, cold and gray, but they'd driven out to the beach and Gerry had a key to the padlock at the base of the roll-down doors and he'd squatted in his winter coat and tie, his hair greased back, a smoking Chesterfield between his lips, then he pulled up that big door, creaking in its steel tracks above, and they walked in together holding hands. There were only a few games in there then, two Ping-Pong tables and a pool table and the Skee-Ball that took up the whole south wall. There were none of the pinball or vending machines that would bring trouble years later, and Gerry had big plans. Standing there in the shadows of what they would build, he looked so young and handsome and happy that she'd never loved him more than she did at that moment, her French pipe-fitter husband who'd borrowed every bit of their down payment from uncles and friends and after two years had paid it all back. He was a good man then, that's how she'd seen him anyway, as good, and when they let themselves into the back apartment, Lois still did not want to live there. She didn't like how small and dark that place was, and besides, they were renting a nice ranch in the woods two miles from the beach. It had a lawn and a back patio, and she liked to sit out there in the summer in the inflatable kiddie pool with little Linda, and now they had baby Paul, too, both of them at Gio's place that afternoon so that Lois and Gerry could take a stroll through their new lives.

"Think of the money, Sweet." That's what he called her, and she knew it'd be foolish not to live in that apartment themselves. They'd save more by living there than renting it out. Besides, they owned it along with the business and when they walked into what would become Linda and baby Paul's room, there was a mattress and box spring on the floor from the previous owner—an Irish/Italian who was barely sixty and retiring "with a pot of gold," Gerry had said—and her happy, happy husband had pulled off his winter coat and laid it on that mattress then made her sit, calling her, *Sweet, my Sweet, Sweet, Sweet*, and he tugged off her rubber boots and nylons and underwear, and pulled her dress up, then he was pushing himself inside her and there was only his breath against her throat, *My Sweet, my Sweet, oh, my Sweet*, the far-off but close smashing of waves on the beach, this feeling that they were both climbing some shimmering rainbow together and neither one would ever let the other fall.

Lois slowed for the turn down her two-track. It had been so long since she'd thought of Gerry in this way. She'd nearly forgotten it had ever been good once, but it had, and anyway Bobby was nothing like Gerry. Bobby *was* a good man. Though as she got closer to her house his car was gone and there was only Susan's, and there she was, sitting on the front steps. She had her elbows propped on her bare knees, and beside her was her cell phone and a glass of water. She looked like she'd been sitting there a long time.

Wonderful. Here we go again.

Lois killed the engine and gathered up her pocketbook and rose out of her VW, her heart pounding faster the way it did now whenever she stood. The air was hot and still and smelled like dead pine needles and the tar from her roof shingles she'd have to replace before too long. She called over the roof of the car, "Everything all right?"

Susan just looked at her, then half shrugged. "I have to tell you something."

"Don't tell me you two broke up."

"No."

"No, you're not going to tell me, or no, you didn't break up?" She hooked her purse strap over her shoulder and made her way to the front steps. She was breathing harder than she should. Her granddaughter's legs were slightly parted, and she could see the color of her underwear, pale blue.

"Will I need a drink for this?"

"Do you want to sit down?"

"No, but give me a sip of that water, please."

Susan handed her the glass, and Lois drank down half of it and handed it back. She was sweating. "All right, then tell me. What's wrong?"

"I did get important mail yesterday."

"Bobby went home for it?"

"No, he had it already."

Susan must've seen something change in Lois's face because she said, "He didn't think it was the right time."

"So you didn't sell that story, honey. So what?"

"No—"

"What, Suzie?"

"I got a letter from my father."

At first Lois saw Gerry and his greased-back hair, his ready-for-the-world smile. *Oh, my Sweet. My Sweet. My Sweet Sweet Sweet.* But then a trapdoor flopped open inside Lois's very organs, and there was her Linda in the arms of big hook-nosed Ahearn, his eyes too close together, that red suit jacket he wore like he was some royal prince and not just another barking carnie, her Linda in her coin apron swallowed up forever in his big freckled arms.

The step tread slapped Lois's rear, and she had to lean forward and breathe into her own heartbeats, but they were like whirling bats in her head. Susan's hand was on her arm.

"You okay?"

Lois nodded, though she was *not* okay.

"I don't know how he found me, Noni."

His mother. That simpleton calling late on a Sunday afternoon. Two years ago, maybe more. She said she was dying, and she just wanted to say goodbye to her granddaughter, that's all.

How'd you get this number, Mary?

Your brother give it to me, Lois. He's in the book.

Gio would do that. He never met one woman he ever said no to about anything. Lois had been sitting at her kitchen table, a smoking Carlton in her ashtray. It was late fall, close to a Thanksgiving she'd be spending with Paul and his family in Miami. The light coming through her windows was golden, and maybe she felt just a bit sorry for this woman who'd lost her granddaughter to the Dubie family. Just enough anyway to give her a morsel but not the whole meal.

She's married now. Her last name's Dunn. That's all I'm telling you, Mary, and I'll thank you not to call me again.

"Are you all right?"

"I did it, Suzie. I gave his mother your married name. Your grandmother. Tell me the truth, did she ever find you?"

"No."

Lois could see her now, wearing those housecoats and long dresses even in the summer. This woman who had a plain face and talked to herself all the time and married "the Magic Mick" Ahearn. She was like some peasant from the old country, and Lois would be surprised if she could even read or write. Hearing her voice after so many years was like the doctor telling you your tumor was back, and for weeks after talking to her on the phone Lois regretted giving her that name. She wanted to call Susan about it, but it'd be like grabbing a shovel and digging up something better left buried. "Where's this *letter*?"

"My room." Susan seemed to sit straighter. "Noni?"

"What?"

"He says he wants to come see me."

Danny Ahearn towering over her Linda as he hugged her too tight, the lights of the arcade making them both look blue. Lois sitting in the back of that cruiser trying not to scream and run inside that house to her child, but she was holding crying Suzie to her, and Ahearn was being carried out that kitchen door by four or five cops, his hands cuffed behind him, his legs trying to kick, his face bleeding. The way he stood in court in his jumpsuit and turned to her and Gerry and Paul, his mouth saying words that were like a drill now in Lois's stomach.

"You can't see him. I won't allow it. I'll call the friggin' *cops*."

"I don't think he's breaking any laws, Noni."

Lois turned to her. Susan had never sat so erectly in her life. Her hands were folded in her lap, and her chin was tilted up, and Lois could see she'd clearly been working up her nerve for—for *what*? "Don't tell me you *want* to see him."

"I don't know if I do or not. I just thought you should know."

"*Why?* Susan, he's a—" Her throat felt squeezed in an iron vise, her breathing one shallow wave after another.

"I almost didn't tell you, but Bobby thought you had a right to know."

"He's damn right I have a right to know. Where *is* he?"

"On the way home."

"Why?"

"Because the letter was sent overnight mail."

Lois's porch steps may as well have been a boat, her gravel drive a shifting sea. "You mean he might be there *now*?"

Susan fingered her cell phone. "Not yet. And he doesn't know where we live, as far as we know."

"I forbid you to see this man, Susan. I *forbid* it."

"I'm not sixteen anymore, Noni."

"But why would you *want* to?"

"I'm not sure I do. It just seemed disrespectful not to at least tell you."

In the fading light of the afternoon, Susan looked middle-aged and beautiful, even with her thin arms and legs, her chopped hair and very little makeup. Her mother would be in her sixties now, but she wasn't, was she? Nor did she get to be Susan's age or even ten years younger than that. Her life was forever stolen from her by that sick ugly Danny Ahearn, and what gave him the *right* to think he could come *visit* Susan now? *Now?* Lois's face was hot and wet and the words coming out of her seemed to help her stand. "I'll kill him. So help me God, I will kill him."

"Lois."

Lois stood and began to make her way to the front door. "And I'm coming with you, too."

"No, you're not."

Lois had reached the deck, but the house was being lifted and tilted sideways, her arm swinging out to right herself, her hand reaching for the screen door's black handle, but its blackness crowded the corners of her eyes then shifted to the center till that's all she saw, the porch treads whacking her shoulder and the side of her head, Susan calling and calling her name.

35

HALFWAY THROUGH South Carolina, the radio is one Christian station after another and Daniel switches it off. An hour ago it stopped raining and he kept watching the late-day sun as it sank into soybean fields to the west. Now a strip of light is holding up a bank of dark clouds above the highway, and the taillights ahead of him are bright and too red. His back and hips ache. He's passed through towns with names like Turbeville, Manning, and Summerton. Santee, Branchville, Smoaks, and Yemassee. They make him think of the Civil War and long-ago times and he's not sure why except with each passing mile there's the feeling he's descending somewhere foreign and dangerous, and there's nothing he can do about it.

According to his map he's around three hundred miles from St. Petersburg, about six hours of driving if he doesn't stop. That bowl of chili he'd eaten half of in North Carolina is a warm lump in his gut, but at a gas station in a town called St. George he bought a twenty-four-ounce bottle of Coke he sips from now, wedging it back between his seat and the console. The Coke seems to settle his stomach, and he can feel the caffeine moving through his sluggish blood like some screw kicking cons out of their bunks right after lights-up. He's been going since before dawn, but why stop?

He keeps thinking about that young waitress back in Dunn, how pretty and warm she was. She'd seated him at a table in the corner near a window, and she'd brought him a menu right away, that coffeepot still in her hand. After he'd ordered his chili, it was hard not to take in how tightly her jeans fit her and how lovely her behind was, though he'd looked away quickly, for it was like passing a fenced-in yard just as the owner steps through the gate and you see a garden of flowers. If he had a granddaughter, which he might, she could be the age of this young woman who'd served him chili and crackers and later smiled at him with all her face as he left her a twenty for an eight-dollar meal.

He hopes he does have grandchildren. That'd be something anyway. And maybe they don't know anything. Maybe they're still little kids.

But he's getting greedy. He is. If Susan does have kids, or even one, why would she let him meet them? He'll be lucky to even lay his eyes on her.

He glances down at his daughter's picture taped to the dash. Its bottom has started to curl, and she's shifted slightly to the side. He reaches over and presses his thumb to the Scotch tape, pressing it hard, leaving it there longer than he knows will do any good whatsoever. There's the blare of a car horn, and he looks back at the road, brightly lit and unwinding.

Maybe driving straight through isn't such a good idea. Daniel's eyes burn, and his lower half feels sewn into his seat, and he's driving slower than even his slow pace. Three times since crossing over into Georgia, cars or pickups have come up fast on his rear and flashed their lights then laid on their horn as they passed him, two on the left, one on the right. He's driven by signs for Pooler and Garden City and Savannah, Tybee Island, Pembroke, and Richmond Hill. Once more they pull him back to the war between the states, and again there comes that rising dread that he's driving back through time itself. But he's been doing this his whole damn life, ever since he first went down.

It's true, but so did ten thousand other men. Him and Pee Wee Jones. That one afternoon he and Daniel were playing checkers on Jones's bunk, Pee Wee had just taken one of his kings and said, "You wanna take that move back, Danny A, but you cain't."

"Nope."

"Uh-uh, what's done is done."

"Yep."

They were quiet awhile, studying the board. Pee Wee's hair had started to go gray at the sides, and behind him, taped to his wall, was one of his pencil sketches, this one of a naked woman with an Afro and her hands on her hips and her legs spread like she was daring anyone not to look.

"If I could go back I just never would've drank that gin. I didn't even like gin, but I drank it. Next thing I know I'm waving heat in my daddy's face. Twenty years of getting beat down and beat down and beat down and no more, I suppose."

"You shot him?"

"I shot 'em both."

Danny didn't ask who he meant. You didn't do that. And now Pee Wee's eyes seemed to be miles and miles from somewhere else, and Danny double-hopped two of Pee Wee's homemade men.

"All I can think about is going back and emptying that bottle before I ever touch it. I must've played that over ten million times. I still buy the bottle, but then I dump it out into the street and I walk home and that is that."

Danny didn't say anything. Or maybe he did, but Daniel doesn't remember that now, only that he'd missed Pee Wee when he was bundled back up to Walpole for going after Polaski for calling him stupid nigger one time too many. And then Danny was stuck with the rest of them, with cons like McGonigle, who if he ever went back in time only went there to feel that thrill again or whatever the hell it was he felt when he'd—what? Did Daniel really think he was better than him? Yes, because McGonigle only regretted getting caught.

Up ahead, past a sign for Fort Morris Historic Site, there's another sign—gas, food, and lodging. Daniel checks his rearview, but there's only a lone pair of headlights a quarter mile back. It must be close to ten o'clock and it's a weeknight, most of the good citizens probably in bed right now. He misses his trailer, the fan blowing warm air over him, a light rain on the tin roof. And what's his daughter doing right now? It's a question that for many years he stopped having in his head. He'd like to say that never happened, but it did. He just stopped thinking of her. In many ways she became like the characters in his books on tape when he was done listening to them. It was like they left inside him only the dried husk of what they'd been, a locust's shell stuck on tree bark.

Except all those other husks were truly empty and hers never was.

Did she read his letter alone? Did she wait till her kids were in bed first? Or did she open it right there in her professor's office? And how did he start it? He remembered the first part, but what came after?

> *My dear daughter Susan,*
> *Ive got no right to call you these things.*

That was the way to start, wasn't it? Wouldn't she want to keep reading, knowing right off that he knew that? But what came next? And why did he have to go into all that shit about him and the Reactor and Captain Suspicion and all that other shit? Did he want her to feel sorry for him? No, but she needs to know how he was, that he was— what? A boy? Just a jealous little boy? A boy who now wants *her* to take care of him.

Did he? *Does* he?

The exit's coming up on him, and he steers into the right lane, his headlights on a torn trash bag on the side of the road. Clothes have spilled out, a purple sweatshirt and a white pair of pants, and it brings him back to trash left on the beach. The court paroled cons to where they committed their crimes, and Daniel hadn't minded living with his mother, but it was bad being back on the strip. She'd sold the Sea Spray and bought another cottage on the north side of the Midway three blocks from the water. His first day out, it was early spring, and he'd gone for a long walk. There were patches of snow on the asphalt and the sand, the strip boarded up for the season, though by the looks of the place there was no real season anymore. His father's masterpiece, the Broadway Flying Horses, was gone, sold to someone, Daniel later learned, who packed it all up and shipped it to the West Coast. The arcade was half empty and half gone, too, a condo built on stilts where the Dubies used to live. That first afternoon, that's as far as he'd walked. He could feel his and Linda's old cottage four blocks south like a vibrating sac of poison inside him and if he walked there it would have split open and moved through his veins to his head and heart.

And the strip looked smaller somehow, the buildings shorter, the beach sand shallower, the water dirtier-looking than he'd remembered. But the worst of it all was walking toward the Himalaya and not seeing the Himalaya. Instead, there was a new building there on iron piers. It had long, high windows and a wraparound deck with shiny steel railings. On the side of the building was a faded banner from the season before, *The Outlaws, August 10th–September 13th*. Daniel stared at that a long while, then he turned and walked fast back to his mother's cottage where she stood at the stove in her buttoned-up cardigan talking to herself while she stirred the Irish stew she knew he loved.

"Yes, I washed them, don't tell me I didn't." Between these words to no one, she hummed a tune he didn't recognize and she did it in the high, wavering voice of a woman older than she was, only sixty then, though her back and shoulders had already begun to slump and he stood there thinking that he had done that to her, this piece of shit whose one bright and shining moment had been in a plywood and plexiglass booth eight feet above the asphalt, hovering there like the moon itself, like it would always be there the way the moon would always be there and he'd be remembered as one of the kings in red who had risen to it with his voice, the one good thing he'd ever been given. And now some backhoe had crushed it down in a day.

Soon he found work with a painting company up in Portsmouth. He was thirty-nine years old then, and his boss was ten years younger, a big friendly kid who'd dropped out of college to make money. He'd gotten a contract for thirty new condo units on the Piscataqua River, and he had a crew of six, most of them loud boys in their twenties Daniel ignored as he worked. At lunch, they would gather in what would soon be the lobby of the building, and they'd sit on the floor and eat. At dawn every day, Daniel's mother would pack him a meal of two baloney sandwiches, a bag of potato chips, and two or three chocolate chip cookies she baked from store-bought dough. But the boys he painted with talked too much about the good times they'd just had or the good times they were about to have, all of it having to do with booze and bars or the new ride they were about to buy, or some ball game he didn't even know about, and at every lunch break they always got around to talking about women, the ones they'd fucked or would like to, and it was like being back in school again, on the outside looking in, except these boys didn't seem to know one thing about anything, especially about how wrong and hard things could get, so at lunch Daniel stopped eating with them and instead would stay in the room he was painting, eating his mother's sandwiches in new paint fumes that made everything taste like that too.

Those boys didn't like him for that. One night, standing out on the sidewalk at the end of their hours, Ricky, a skinny kid with an entire arm tatted over with green dragons, said, "What's the matter, Ahearn? You too good for us?"

Daniel had turned to him. The kid was smiling, but his eyes were not, and the others, including his boss, were watching. Daniel could feel the Reactor's heat drop to his hands, Danny happy to end this before it began, but he was a parolee now, and besides, Danny was dead and gone. Daniel was about to say that he just liked being alone.

"Knock it off, Rick," their boss said. "He's a better fuckin' painter than you'll ever be."

"Hey, I'm just busting his balls." Rick lit a cigarette then turned and walked down the sidewalk, smoke drifting over his shoulder. A few of the others were talking about where to go for a few beers and some important basketball game, and Daniel could see his boss wanted to do that himself.

"Sound good to you, Daniel? We'll grab some wings."

But those early months out, Xenakis had laid an eight p.m. curfew on him. He had to get back. "No, my mother's sick."

His young boss looked only mildly pissed off and put out. He told the others to order him some wings, he'd be there in an hour, and he and Daniel drove quietly down the highway in the work van that smelled like dried caulking and dusty canvas tarps. It was what Danny's life had smelled like, too, that and the ocean and the damp sand of the beach, and here he was fifteen years later right back again in the dark heart of where it had all gone wrong. He needed to leave, and leave soon.

"Your old lady's not really sick, is she?"

One of the van's headlights wobbled slightly, its shaky light on the highway ahead. Daniel stared at it. "No."

"That's cool, you got other plans."

"I got a curfew from my PO."

"You do time?" The kid's tone was as upbeat as ever, but Daniel could feel a thickening of the air between them, and he wasn't sure why he'd told him. Maybe because he was lonesome. Maybe he thought he could be a friend.

"Yeah, I did time."

"Drugs?"

Daniel stayed quiet. If he told this kid the truth, he'd probably lose his job. If he told this kid the truth, he'd never be his friend.

Things changed after that ride. Daniel's boss was still respectful to him and often praised his brush and roller work, how clean and efficient his lines were, but he did it too carefully, like he was afraid to rub Daniel the wrong way. And he probably told one or two of the others on the crew too, because they started looking at him like he might be a scorpion not far from their feet. This was no good. At least when he had his own painting business he mostly worked alone, and he was better alone. He'd always been better alone.

At night he and his mother would sit in her small living room and watch TV. She liked the old shows with the old actors in them like Jackie Gleason and Lucille Ball and her husband with the Spanish accent. For every stupid thing Lucy did, Daniel's mother would laugh. But it was hard to watch a happy couple doing happy goofy things together, and Daniel would stand and go to his bedroom, which was also his mother's sewing room. After Liam died, she took up making things, mainly dresses for young girls she gave away or sold to a shop owner up in Seabrook. Hanging on hangers on the back of the closet door were over a dozen little dresses, and Daniel would lie back on his bed, tired from the day's work, his bedside lamp on, his mother laughing in the other room, and he'd stare at those dresses. *Daddy, I'm here. See? I'm* **here.** He put in for a transfer as soon as he could.

And he needed a job where he didn't have to talk to people. That barbershop in Boston wasn't the best place for that. He'd work his eight hours, cutting hair and shaving faces while trying to make small talk, but he had a rep as the quiet one and his regulars would tease him about not having an asshole because he had no opinions, either, even on the Celtics or the Bruins or who he wanted to be our new president.

Daniel slows his Tacoma and peers at the possibilities. To his right is a lighted gas station island, a Holiday Inn just beyond it, a Fairfield Inn just beyond that. But to his left is the dark rise of a hill and at the top there are two more motels, a Marriott and a Hampton Inn. The second one is the name of the beach just north of Salisbury back home, and he likes that it's on a hill where he might find a room overlooking whatever there is to see. He accelerates up the hill, still thinking about telling his PO how he wanted to work someplace else doing something different. Xenakis stared at the unlit cigarette he was always holding between two fingers.

"What else can you do? Furniture, right?"

"Yeah, caning."

Then came those good years in that shiny little town he never should have left.

Andover had a central square and all its buildings were made of repointed brick with granite lintels over plate-glass windows that never seemed to be dirty, new dresses or suit jackets or skiwear hanging on the other side. There were fine restaurants that posted their menus in lighted glass boxes near their front entrances, and only late-model cars were parked at the curbs, the men and women who drove them looking like they'd gone to college and gotten good jobs in tall buildings down in Boston or else worked in banks or law offices or car dealerships here in town. After his PO okayed it, he got work refinishing furniture in a warehouse just across the town line in Lawrence, and he rented a room off Andover's central square in the back of a house full of small rented rooms like his. It had a kitchenette and a bathroom and small table and bed, and it looked out at a narrow lawn that sloped down to thick hedges ten feet high. There was a two-car garage and a concrete driveway, and after only three months of refinishing tables and chairs and old desks and nightstands, Daniel's boss, a warm Dominican named Hector, gave him a raise and Daniel told him he was even better at caning. Hector started telling customers and soon Daniel had his own work space near one of the cracked windows overlooking the river. There he weaved damp strips of cane under and over themselves while Spanish music played on a boom box out on the floor behind him, the other guys shouting out in Spanish to each other while he worked, and he'd look out at the sun on the brown river, and it was good being alone again.

One night he dreamed about his father. In the dream Liam was standing on the strip in his white painter coveralls smiling at him, waiting for his son to catch up because Danny had the tools and Liam couldn't do anything without them. Except Liam wasn't angry and impatient the way he would've been in life. He was warm and calm, like the two of them had all the time in the world. And Daniel woke to the first light of dawn seeping from the sides of his pulled shades, his father's long, silent absence feeling like a broken bone he'd never set.

He should've gone to his funeral. Except everybody knew him. They knew what he'd done. And he should've stayed in Andover, where he got treated with nothing but respect, where he was Ahearn the Caner, or just Daniel, and when anybody who knew his work said his name it sounded solid to his own ears, like tapping the walnut leg of an old Victorian and feeling no rot whatsoever.

All those years down in Andover his mother had never seen his place. One or two Sundays a month he'd take a cab up to see her after she went to church, and the two of them would sit in front of her TV and eat the dinner she had to've gotten up before the sun to cook. Usually pork roast and canned gravy and bottled applesauce and frozen peas she boiled till they were nearly mush. She'd always been better at breakfasts. Sitting in front of whatever was on, probably an old movie on the old movies channel in the old times when it seemed that every man wore a suit and a hat and every woman wore a dress and pearls, it was hard not to feel like Danny expelled from school again, Liam off at work, just the two of them, Danny the troublemaker and his mother who loved him no matter what he'd done.

One afternoon, his plate empty, he looked over at his mother as she watched what she watched. She still wore her apron over her church clothes, and her thin hair was matted in the back. In the soft warmth of that sofa with his full belly and slowing breaths, he could feel how he was as much a part of her as if he were one of her arms or legs or kidneys and liver, that she could no more push him away than she could cut off her own head.

And he never got that from his own wife. He didn't. And so it was his mother's fault.

That's what he was thinking then. He was. That her devotion to him ruined him for any other woman. That he'd expected his Linda to put him first too. That maybe his mother shouldn't've been so good to him all the time.

Then the Andover years had slipped down the drain out to sea and she was eighty-three and then she was gone. His parole years were behind him then. He could come and go as he pleased, but for three months he lived in his mother's cottage off the strip, though he never walked around there again. With some of the money she'd left him, he bought the Tacoma, and he started driving down to Port City just to go walking. But it was different there. No one knew him. He wasn't Ahearn the Caner, he was no one.

The courthouse just south of downtown. It was a red-brick three-story box overlooking a sunken pond where ducks lived and where Canadian geese stopped and rested every fall on their way south. There were tall maples and oaks, and around the water were benches bolted into concrete pads with the brass plaques of donors sunk into them. It was a place he'd only glimpsed from inside the courtroom forty years before, but now he'd walk down there and feed the ducks and try not to feel as if he were floating naked in deep space, his dear mother his last living cord to anything good or familiar, cut and withered and buried in Long Hill Cemetery three miles from the beach and within earshot of the highway. It's where Liam was buried too, his granite stone low and stubby with just barely enough room for his name.

That's why he bought the trailer. To be close to his folks.

And now here he is, standing in his fourth-floor hotel room looking out over Georgia's darkness. Here and there is a faint glittering of light from a house window, maybe, or a far-off streetlamp on some residential road through the pines. Out on the black horizon a radio tower blinks its tiny red lights at him, and he can only see this as some kind of nagging reminder. He's been on the road for over sixteen hours. The bones of his lower back feel dipped in some cruel fire that has not yet reached the rest of him but will, and in the bathroom behind him he's turned the toilet water as red as that blinking light, yet he still feels the pressure to go, his mouth gummy, his eyes sending an ache back through his brain where there are only these words:

Rest, Ahearn. Sleep. Sleep till you open your eyes, then write out that will and type it and get the hell down to St. Petersburg. Get the hell down to Suzie.

36

I
T WAS after nine when Susan pulled back up to the house, her head-lights sweeping over Noni's red VW still parked in front of the porch where she'd left it. The house was dark, and as Susan fumbled for the light switch there were the smells of dusty drapes and old ciga-rette smoke and last night's chicken. She could feel the too-quickly-approaching time when this old place in the woods would probably be half hers, and she didn't want it.

She was actually hungry but couldn't take the time to eat anything. In the kitchen she flicked on the overhead light and opened the fridge and pulled out a foil-wrapped piece of chicken, but when she parted the foil its smell seemed to lift and tilt her organs and she shoved the chicken back onto its shelf and made her way up the dark stairwell, turning on her bedroom light and stepping into this place that had seemed to bring about all that was happening. At her feet was the empty gift bag that had held the shades for the two Dresden lamps sit-ting on her bureau, this entwined pair of porcelain lovers with electric cords wrapped around them like snakes. Should she take these now? No, she was only going back home until— Jesus. Until what? Was she really going to go *meet* her "father"? The way he'd first signed his let-ter as *Dad* then crossed that word out and wrote *Father*, like he knew how much she'd hate him if he wrote *Dad*.

"You need to see him." Bobby's arm around her as they sat side by side on her bed after the high school parking lot. His knee against hers. His ease with the rage that she hadn't felt coming.

"No, I *don't* need to see him. He's a piece of fucking *shit*." She couldn't sit any longer and she'd stood and paced the bedroom of her girlhood and she went off about what this man had taken. She said the word *mother* more than once, and she yelled about the grandparents she never knew, maybe cousins on that side as well. She yelled about there being no justice, and how she couldn't believe you could do that to another human being then one day walk free. She yelled how she would never have had to move to this stinking little cow town in Florida, and that she wouldn't've had to live with her depressed and controlling fucking grandmother her entire life, either. But as she'd yelled all these things in her calm husband's whiskered presence, her throat sore, what kept coming, like a fever she could no longer deny, was the word LOVE, how her father had written it in capital letters and underlined it over the word *Father* and his name and how this opened a burning room inside her, and not just because it was cruel for him to have written it, but because, yes, oh, yes, she needed that word. And more, she needed to feel whatever was behind it, and so yes, she needed to see and maybe even meet the man who had written them, never mind what she'd written about that Susan Lori in Lawrence, Massachusetts, not needing to ever see him again. That was twenty years ago. Twenty *years*. And that's when the tears came and she wouldn't let Bobby hold her, but she said, "You have to be with me."

"That's fine, baby. That's fine."

On her made bed was her duffel bag she'd packed earlier, her closed laptop sitting on her desk like some portal that had conjured the very letter sitting in its envelope beside it, had conjured the man coming to see her "in a few days." *Killyourfatherwithit.* Paul laughing at her as she ran out from under the Frolics into the cold sun. But all that she'd begun to write in this room felt thin now, like an instruction manual to a big necessary engine that had started on its own and now was taking her where she had to go whether she wanted to or not because blood-pumping life was always more real and insistent than mere words.

She sat at her desk and opened the letter and stared at his handwriting. It was the careful scrawl of a man who'd rarely been called to write anything in his life.

My dear daughter Susan,
   Ive got no right to call you any of these things.

She folded the pages and stuffed them back into the envelope. Lois in her hospital bed. How she'd turned her face away and refused to talk to her anymore. It was the old Lois, the woman who when she looked at Susan seemed to see only bad things or bad things coming. The doctor was handsome and black. He said Noni had merely fainted, but she was dehydrated and her blood pressure was "alarmingly high," her oxygen levels low, and they'd wanted to keep her overnight for observation.

When the ambulance had arrived, Noni was already coming to on the floor of their porch. "No way. I'm not going anywhere." But her voice was weak, her face gray, and she let a big EMT press an oxygen mask to her mouth and nose then strap her onto a board that another EMT helped lift onto a gurney. And as Susan had followed the ambulance in her car she thought of her father beating up a man just for smiling at her mother, and it was probably a mistake to have told Lois. But when Bobby said she had a right to know, there came the smell of Noni's hair as Susan had leaned down and hugged her at the kitchen table—like Carltons and old skin and dehumidified air from the store—as she apologized for having been a selfish little shit for going to murderous Gainesville without a thought about the pain that would've opened up inside Lois. No, it had been right to tell her about this letter, though Susan should've known what that would've done to Lois, what that would've done to the two of them.

"You're going whether I like it or not, aren't you?" Noni's voice was reedy and came from high in her chest, but it had the same hot edge to it it'd always had. Her IV arm looked splotchy. Susan was sitting in the chair near Lois's raised bed tray, and whatever stream of consistent peace that had begun to flow between them this past week now felt dammed up and Susan was Suzie all over again, staring into the hard eyes of her grandmother with nothing to say that she wanted to hear.

"I don't know, Noni."

"Oh, you know, all right."

That's when Lois turned away and that's when Marianne walked in, her newly made-up face bright with concern. Susan thanked her, and she couldn't leave that room fast enough.

Now she picked up the envelope and pushed it and her laptop into its case. She hooked the strap over her shoulder, grabbing her duffel bag off the mattress and switching off the light, but in the darkness of the hall she stopped and made her way down to the cool tomb of Lois's bedroom. She found the overhead light and opened the drawer of the bedside table and pulled out the gun. It was heavy in her hand, its grip hard and checkered against her palm. She did not want it, but she could not leave it where Noni could get at it, either. She was old and she was weak, and Susan would probably be back here before she was even out of the hospital, but still.

She shoved it into the side pocket of her duffel bag and left her grandmother's cold, cold room, the light flicking off under her hand.

37

LOIS LAY alone in her room waiting for the nurse she'd just buzzed for the second time, but everyone had become strangers to her: Susan and this calm distance in her Lois had never seen before; Marianne and her sudden lack of anything to say except, "Rest, dear. You really need to rest." Even Walter had come by, and he stood there in his finery like he'd come straight from a dinner with bankers or other ranchers. His face was flushed from martinis and cognacs, and his turquoise bolo tie hung heavy around his lined neck.

They were all acting like *she* had a problem. Like there was something wrong with *her*. Her doctor had already come and gone, too. He was some young black kid with thick glasses, and he spoke in a low, careful voice, already an expert at giving bad news. So her blood pressure was up and her oxygen levels were down, so what? She was big and she'd been smoking too much and she was *old*, for Christ's sake. She'd only fainted.

"We'd like to keep you for observation."

"Nope. No way."

"But why not, Lois?" Marianne was sitting in the chair beside the bed. Even for this, she'd worn a fresh outfit, a cream shift over navy blue slacks, her makeup reapplied, her hands folded primly in her lap.

"Stay out of it, Marianne. Please."

The doctor—the name on his tag was Dr. M. Johnson—reached over Lois and checked her IV bag, then he looked back down at her as if she were a chore he didn't have time for just now. "If you leave, Mrs. Dubie, it will be against my best medical advice. You'll have to sign a form."

"Fine. Bring it."

But he left without another word, and Marianne sat there staring at her. "Lois."

"Go home, Marianne. You, too, Walter. Jesus *Christ*."

"C'mon, darlin'." Walter had rested his hand on Marianne's shoulder and he'd winked down at Lois and she'd looked away, but there was only the thin blue curtain separating her bed from her roommate's, whoever the hell that was. Then Marianne's cool hand had squeezed hers, and Lois jerked it out of its well-meaning but ignorant-as-hell grip because, once again, she did not know *anything*.

Imagine, dear Marianne, that one of your grown sons living his happy life down in Miami or out in Los Angeles actually never got to grow old enough to do that because someone who was supposed to love him, had signed on to live with him, in sickness and in health, in good times and bad, on and on, had *killed* him instead? And then imagine,

Marianne—whose biggest problem is your rich husband's roving fucking eye—then imagine that the person who did this to your baby is not
executed like should have happened. No, instead he spends only fifteen
years in a prison where they get to take classes and learn a trade. He's
even allowed to leave the place on weekends as long as he behaves
himself and comes back home in time. And then imagine, Marianne
dearest, that after those fifteen years, which was not even the age of the
child he stole from you, they let him out and wished him good luck?

And now, twenty some-odd years later, he wants to come and see
the child you'd raised for him, a child that was no cakewalk to bring
up, either. She was beautiful the way her mother had been beautiful,
but she kept to herself and she buried her head in books, and she
started sleeping around just as soon as the first boy looked at her, and
whose job was it to protect her from these boys, Marianne?

Lois's heart monitor was beeping faster, the bright green lines on
the screen more jagged than before. Around her upper arm was the
squeeze and release of the blood pressure cuff, and her mouth and
throat were a dried-up streambed. She sat up and pressed the call button beside her and kept it pressed. "I need a *nurse*, damn it!" She fell
back to the pillow just as a doctor walked in, though he was wearing
the same light blue the nurses wore. He had a doughy face, and his
hair was graying, and she pegged him right away as a man who had
done one thing his whole life only to quit and start something new and
this was it. "You a doctor or a nurse?"

"I'm your nurse. What can I do for you, Mrs. Dubie?"

"You can unhook me off all this shit and give me that form to sign
so I can leave. How many times do I have to say it?"

"You wish to leave?"

"Yes, I told the doctor that hours ago."

The nurse was studying the monitor. "Your BP is still awfully
high, Mrs. Dubie."

"You just bring me that form or I will rip these things off myself,
do you understand me?"

He stood there and looked down at her with eyes Lois hadn't seen coming, like he could see someone suffering and he was sorry for it. This made the room blur, for she did not know what she was going to do except go home and sit her Susan down and talk to her, to try and keep her from going out that door yet one more time to be with whoever the hell she pleased. Like no time had passed whatsoever. All those years of screaming and Suzie running out that door anyway, but now her granddaughter wanted to see the man who had made Lois the vigilant and frightened woman she'd become, the man who had taken everything and who, yes, would take Suzie, too.

The nurse's hand was on her shoulder. She reached up and squeezed his hairy wrist, a watch there, its band soft leather. "Please, I just need to go *home*."

38

BOBBY WAS unloading Lois's gun. He and Susan were sitting side by side on their couch in his study, and it was just after eleven o'clock, the only light coming in from the kitchen and from Bobby's desk lamp over a stack of books and papers. This entire room was nothing but stacks of books and papers. Packed into shelves on the other side of the room were the spines of books Susan had seen many times before but whose titles she'd never really taken in fully: *Jazzology, The Jazz Theory Book, The Realm of Musical Sound, The Chord Scale Theory & Jazz Harmony, After Modern Jazz: The Avant-Garde and Jazz Historiography, My Life in E-Flat.* No novels or short story collections, which were the only books in her writing room off the bathroom where at two in the morning she'd lopped off her hair. On the wall above Bobby's shelves were Ornette Coleman's words painted in black by Bobby one night when he was half drunk on a bottle of red and close to burning his dissertation. *That's how I have always wanted musicians to play with me: on a multiple level. I don't want them to follow me. I want them to follow themself, but to be with me.*

She thought about her father's fucked-up jealousy snaking through his veins. "Captain Suspicion." What the fuck was that? By giving his pathology the name of a comic book hero, he'd romanticized it and made it palatable, acceptable even. Jesus.

It was quiet for once, just the low rush of air from the AC vents. Bobby rarely tolerated quiet. Even when he was writing or grading papers he played his jazz. When she had to do her own work she asked him to put on headphones, but he needed to pace the room so she'd gotten into the habit of closing her writing room door and pushing little pink foam buds into her ears, and for what? Corina Soto who'd led her to Susan Lori who'd led her to *killyourfatherwithit*? And somewhere along the way she'd gotten pregnant, too. Lovely.

"This is a dirty gun, baby."

"Aren't they all?"

"No, it needs some serious cleaning." He'd flipped the cylinder out and now he squinted into each of its six holes, their bullets on his side table on a *JazzTimes* magazine. The cover photo was of a man named Freddie Hubbard singing with a trumpet in his hands. Two of the bullets lay across his open mouth.

"What do you know about guns, Bobby?"

"Shit, I'm from Texas. My daddy owned six or seven of these at least."

She stared at him. And why couldn't she draw up even one detail about his father other than that he sold insurance? "Did you shoot any of them?"

"Didn't have to. I had some too." Bobby set Lois's pistol on Freddie Hubbard's face. Surely he'd told her this before. Surely she'd asked him about his life and he'd told her this.

"You had guns?"

He looked over at her. "Still do."

"You *do*? Why don't I know this?"

He shrugged. "It never came up." He rested his big hand on her knee, his desk lamp behind him silhouetting his head and face. She could be sitting here with a stranger, given all that she had never asked about all he'd done and been before she'd come along.

You use people. You use.

"It's probably too late for him to come tonight, but I do wish we had his ETA, baby."

"Bobby?" Her voice shot up her thickening throat like an arrow.

"Don't worry."

"I'm sorry I'm a bad wife."

Bobby put his arm on the back of the couch and leaned in close. He ran his finger along her cheek. "Where's this shit coming from?"

"I'm cold, Bobby. I've always been cold."

He kissed her temple and smelled her hair. "What if I don't agree with you?"

"I don't even know what your father did for a living. Did I even ask?"

"He's dead." He kissed her temple again, and she wanted to push him away.

"Do you know why I cut my hair?"

"No."

"Because I don't—" Was she going to hurt him too? *Bobby?*

"What, baby?"

"Because I don't *feel* things, Bobby. I don't—"

"Bullshit, I think you feel so damn much you get bottlenecked then don't feel a thing."

"Love even?"

"For me, you mean?" His voice was calm and steady and so free of fear and need that she turned to him. His eyes were two shadows. She could smell his sweat. "Yes."

"What if I don't need that?"

"That's fucked up, Bobby. I'm your *wife.*"

"Yeah, well, what's fucked up is half of us racing up some dark canal to the other half of us waiting there for the fastest fucker to make us *one*, that's what's fucked up." He looked at the study wall and nodded. "Then after nine months of this multiplying oneness we get squeezed out into this loud bright shitstorm where our first hello is a hard slap to get us to breathe and then for the rest of our lives we're trying to get back to that damn growing oneness we felt for nine months in that warm dark beautiful place." He turned to her. "That's why we make love, baby, that's why you read all those stories and try to get your students to read them too, that oneness. It doesn't matter to me whether you think you love me or not. I know you love what we have here. And I know you feel that, too. Don't you?" His finger grazed her jaw.

When he'd asked her to marry him, they were sitting side by side on this very couch. It was late morning on a Sunday, and they'd both drunk too much coffee and she'd let him read the first few pages of Corina Soto and he told her it was genius. Not ingenious, but genius. He told her she was going to write a great novel and that she should go back to school and study with a master. Sitting there in her underwear and the oversized T-shirt she'd slept in, her mouth dry from coffee, she'd believed him because he wasn't a bullshitter. The weekend before, she'd read his entire dissertation and was surprised by how much she'd enjoyed it, how well written it was for an academic book. It wasn't at all like so much of the theoretical reading she'd had to do in graduate school, the prose so dense with abstractions she'd had to reread nearly every sentence just to get through them. Bobby's sentences were as generous as he was, one eye, it seemed, always on the engagement of the reader. Somehow, in his every word choice, there was warmth too, or at least the hint of it, of tall Bobby Dunn standing to the side and smiling down at you, trusting you to get it without his having to suffocate you into submission with vaguely worded platitudes and endless footnotes.

That was the thing. Bobby *trusted*. He trusted that one true note would lead to another then another without having to think too much about it, that if something was working now it would keep working later and that life was one big messy improvisation and you couldn't do any of it without stepping into what you did not yet know, and the worst thing you could do was to just sit there and try to shape it too much. But you could and should seize the next note, and he said, "Let's get married tomorrow. Right after class."

"Okay." It came out of her just like that. Because there *was* a oneness between them, and it began to multiply into her writing again then getting into her second graduate school up in Vermont, this high that led to the low she had come to know so well, her feeling nothing about anything, her wanting to lie down and sleep for days. And now, sitting beside this man she felt she did not deserve, she could almost sense that other multiplying going on inside her, and she'd never told the other two boys but she needed to tell her husband. She could at least do that.

"Bobby?"

"Let's go to bed, baby." He stood and took her hand. Susan felt relieved and let him pull her up. There was Lois's unloaded gun sitting on its own spilled bullets like a mother on her eggs, the other half coming fast to see Susan whether she wanted him to or not, and she told herself she would tell Bobby in the morning. That's when she would do it. Then Bobby turned off the desk light, and she followed her husband into the dark.

39

THE GREEN and purple lights of the arcade, Linda in Danny Ahearn's arms. His red blazer and big hands and hooked nose. The way Linda had let him hold her like that. Then in Lois's head Linda became Susan, Susan at forty-three, her thin body and chopped-off hair, and Suzie was letting him hold her the way he'd held her mother, and Lois was going to be sick. Her taxicab was pulling away on the county road, and the three steps up onto her porch may as well have been three hundred. Her heart was a bird flinging itself against the bars of its cage, and she had to rest and lean against the railing and get her breath before she could continue. She could smell pine needles, and she could hear the river through the trees, and the space that no longer held Susan's car may as well be a smudge of red lipstick on the shoulder of one of Gerry's shirts because, yes, she had been betrayed like this before. How could Susan be *doing* this? How was it possible that her granddaughter had driven off to wait for *that* man?

The way he'd turned to them in court and said, "I'm sorry." His face and throat were flushed and his hands were cuffed together in front of him, but it was as if he'd just borrowed their car and totaled it, that's all. Like he hadn't meant to pick up that kitchen—oh, God, no, no, she was not going to let herself fall back into that black fire. She would not allow herself to see her Linda go through what she did in that moment, over and over and over again, night after night after night after night after night. No, not that. Not that.

I'm going to kill him. These words in Lois's head were like a calming melody to the flinging bird in her chest, and her heart seemed to straighten out and slow itself to a clear flight that carried her up into her house, the front door unlocked, for Christ's sake, Suzie always so bent on what *she* needed that everything else fell away. Well, not tonight. Nope. Not now. How many *years* of Lois's life had she spent thinking about that man walking free? How many years did she lie awake at night picturing him drinking a glass of milk or a cup of coffee? How many years did she imagine him waking well rested in his bed and eating eggs and bacon while the morning sun streamed through his windows? How many times did she think of him walking down a street and breathing fresh air deep into his lungs? How many times did she see him buying a newspaper and sitting on a park bench just to read it? Or to listen to music on his radio? To watch a TV show and laugh? How many times did she think of him drinking a cold beer in some barroom with a roomful of men swapping jokes and telling their happy lies? How many times did she picture him with a woman? Making love with a woman between clean white sheets when he should have been dead? When he should've been slowly tortured to death then killed. Yes, tortured. She'd seen this too. And she had no shame about it whatsoever. She pictured her and Paul doing it. They'd drive all the way back to Massachusetts and find Ahearn in whatever hole he was living in. Her son would hit him over the head then dump him in their trunk and they'd drive to some woods somewhere and they'd tie big ugly Danny Ahearn to a tree and then, yes, start in on him with razor blades and a knife, with pliers and an ice pick, with a blowtorch and a length of rope and whatever she and her son could find to make that man cry out for the one who would never come to help. Fifteen years. My God, *fifteen* lousy years. She was halfway up the stairs to her second floor, but she had to rest. The top of her head felt like trapped air, her throat wet on the outside but dry on the inside. Her son had eaten his rage. Her Paul whose dream to be a soldier then a fighter pilot got lost under rolls of fat and an endless collection of guns. Gerry's fault. The names he would call that boy— fatso, fuckwad, lazy piece of shit. And he'd called Linda names too. Stupid. He'd called her stupid. And so what was left for her to do but prove him right? Then Lois had Suzie, her granddaughter who unlike anybody in her family had gone to college. Her Suzie who loved the boys, yes, but who also loved to read and write and would make something of herself. *Did* make something of herself. A college professor. Her Linda's little Susan. Imagine that. And she was writing a book, too. And she had a husband who loved her and treated her better than any man Lois had ever known.

Lois was moving again, the railing hard and worn under her hand. She saw Danny Ahearn's flushed face and neck, his too-close-together eyes as he stared at her over his shoulder in that courtroom. Paul was a teenager, and he'd lifted his finger and pointed it at Ahearn like a gun. She'd been proud of him for that. How many times after Ahearn got out did she sit by the phone and almost call her son? Three? Four? Once with her loaded gun in her lap. But Paul was married and had his own child and a good job in the air freight business, and no, she would not lose him too. Nor did she want to lose herself more than she already had. To drive even one mile north would be letting Ahearn continue to steal from her whatever he could. Her attention. Her constant, vigilant attention to him and him only. And then what? She finds him and shoots him down then finds herself behind the same walls he never should have left?

No. She put her gun away, and she worked longer hours at the store. She went to auctions and estate sales with Don, and she found excuses to go back to the store at night, to sit among all the furniture and toys made by the loving dead. Here her constant dread slipped out of her and she began to pray for Ahearn to suffer in any way a man could suffer. She wished upon him cancer, arthritis, blindness, deafness. She prayed he would get run over and paralyzed and confined to a home where the help was cruel and he had to sit in his own shit and get bed sores that burned him to his bones. She prayed—as she did nightly when he was in prison—that he would get stabbed, that he would get stabbed over and over and over again, but slowly, so slowly. And when computers came along, she fought the urge to type in his name, though she did it once very late at night when she'd had too much wine. She typed: *Daniel Ahearn*. She stared at that name the way one would stare at a raised scar in a lover's skin, and she deleted every letter and stood and walked as quickly away from that machine as she could.

But life had bloomed around all this. Susan had bloomed. Her breasts and hips, her acne fading like a bad memory. Her hair was thick and brown, and she had the wild look her mother had, though Suzie's beauty seemed to go deeper than Linda's. Linda never seemed to know or believe she was beautiful. Gerry's fault again. And hers, Lois's, for not standing up for her, for letting Gerry say or do whatever he wanted just so he'd *stay*.

The "I'm Sorry" prayer. After Linda—after she was gone—it was one Lois recited daily and nightly and she'd close her eyes and see her daughter staring at her. Sometimes she'd be small again, a streak of pizza sauce on her cheek. Or she'd be older, seventeen or eighteen, standing in the doorway to the arcade with her arms crossed and her coin apron at her hips. She'd be looking at Lois with that same look she'd given her so often in life, that she felt sorry for her. That she couldn't wait to live on her own and not be anything like this woman who let her husband say or do whatever he wanted.

How many times had Lois blamed herself for that? All her horribly short life, Linda had watched a man completely ignore a woman. If Gerry had gone away to buy new machines or to look into a new arcade, when he came back he never asked Lois any questions about her life, about what she'd thought about and what she'd done while he was gone. If she went walking out on the strip with the kids, he was more than happy to let her go do that by herself. He rarely touched her unless he wanted sex. He never told Lois what to do or how to do it, but if she mouthed off she got a slap, and otherwise he hardly seemed to *see* her at all. Then in no time Linda was married to the first boy who gave her every bit of his attention, a boy who made her a puppet to his hand.

I'm sorry, Linda. I am so very, very sorry, baby. Please. Please forgive me. Please, honey, please. I am so so sorry.

And then she'd been given a second chance with Suzie, and it had not been easy, but she had kept that girl as safe and watched-over as any one woman possibly could. Suzie hadn't cared for that, but so what? This time around Lois had done her job, and she'd be damned now, tonight, really *damned*, if she were to let those too-close-together eyes see Suzie at all. To see her husband and home. Lois would be damned if she allowed Ahearn to breathe the same air.

To breathe.

Her time here was nearly over, and this was a debt she had owed her daughter for forty years, and, well, it looked like it was high time that her mother finally paid it and paid it in full.

She switched on her bedroom light. She was breathing harder than she should be. At the corners of her eyes was a flurry of white bees, and her mouth tasted like her own tongue, and as she sat heavily on the bed she could see the drawer of her bedside table was already open. On top of her catalogues was the double roll of Scotch tape, the broken case for her reading glasses, the unopened package of mini-tissues, and the expired prescription bottle on its side. The bird in her chest was perched as still as a tombstone; she did not even have to lift the catalogues and look underneath, for they were level and flat as could be, but she dug under them anyway and lifted them up and out, a bed of pennies and paper clips and hairpins staring back at her like the sting after a slap. How stupid could she have been? Susan sitting so straight and still on the porch steps and later in the hospital. Like she'd made up her mind about something big, and there was nothing Lois could do about it. Not one solitary thing.

40

HER HANDS were pressed against Bobby's warm, damp chest beneath her. She seemed to be straddling high above him, so far away from his face in the darkness, and she could smell her own wetness as he filled her and emptied her, filled and emptied, and it was every boy and man coming and going again since Gustavo. There was the darkness of their bedroom and its familiar shadows—the upholstered head-board Bobby had inherited from a blind aunt, their matching reading lamps, off now, their shades like dim centurions in shadow. She didn't know where she would put Lois's Dresden lamps, but what had pulled Susan to them was not their fine porcelain lace but the way the woman's head lay on the man's chest, the way her dress covered his lower legs. There came Bobby's small sounds of pleasure. And now she was making her own sounds, and she hoped they sounded to him like an apology. Because he was right; what she married when she married him was not him but that oneness he'd talked about. But couldn't that be enough? To love the life you'd made with someone else even more than you loved the one with whom you'd made it?

Bobby was moving faster now, and she folded forward to receive it, her cheek pressed against his, her phone buzzing inches from her head on the side table. She sat up.

"Ignore it, baby. Ignore it."

But she could see Noni's name, which meant she was calling from her house, which meant she'd left the hospital. "Shit."

Bobby's fingers were digging into her hips and then he filled her all the way and made that sound he makes, like a man falling back to being a boy who can't wait to be a man who gets to do this.

"It's Lois. She's calling from her house."

Bobby let out a long breath and dropped his arms to his sides. She lifted herself off him and stood and grabbed her phone and walked naked into their bathroom and sat on the toilet. She squinted at the glowing screen of her phone: 12:41 am. She imagined Lois standing in her bright kitchen, a Carlton between her fingers, worried about her granddaughter yet one more time when she should be in bed, a hospital bed, at that. Susan almost pressed the buttons to call her, but not while she was still waiting for what Bobby'd left inside her to drain out.

She wiped herself and flushed. She set her phone on the toilet tank and washed her hands in hot water. The phone buzzed again, its blue glow on the toilet like the answer to a question Susan had not even thought to ask. She wiped her wet hands on her thighs and picked it up and tapped the screen. "Noni?"

"Where's my gun, Suzie? Why did you take my *gun*?"

41

THE MORNING sky is a bright gray haze, and Daniel has been behind the wheel just under one hour when he drives over St. Marys River into Florida. Hanging over the halfway point of the bridge is a large rectangular sign: *Welcome to Florida, the Sunshine State,* the o in *Florida* a juicy-looking orange. He'd slept well, though whatever he dreamed hangs on to him like a list of important things to do he now can't find. His trailer was in it, Pee Wee Jones sitting at his table in front of his checkers set like he'd been waiting a long time for him to come play. In the yard were young girls laughing, though as Daniel slips on his gas-station sunglasses now, he does not know who they were or why they were laughing.

It's the longest he's slept in quite a while, over nine hours, and he took a hot shower and washed his hair twice and then shaved his face slowly in the hotel mirror. If the map is right, St. Petersburg is less than five hours south, which will get him into his daughter's city around four o'clock. He still does not know where she lives. On his way out of the elevator this morning he passed a small glassed-in room called the Business Office. There were computers in there and a printing machine and he'd thought about going in and typing up his will. But he needs her street address, and he still doesn't know who will execute his will when he's gone.

And how's he going to find her? Go to her school? What if she doesn't want to see him?

But he just wants to see *her.* And he wants her to see him seeing her. Just that. If he can just look into her eyes, even from across a room or a field of grass and palm trees, then she'll know. She'll know what he feels for her.

At least he hopes so.

He passes signs for Yulee, Fernandina Beach, and Jacksonville. Cars pass him on the left and on the right, and he moves to the exit lane and veers onto the rumble strip along the breakdown lane, the thump-thump-thumping of his tires before he pulls the Tacoma back straight. He's rested but as tired as if he's worked a ten-hour shift caning or cutting hair or both. For breakfast he drank half a vending machine Coke, and now he needs more aspirin for the hot iron fist his back and hips are sitting in. Beyond the guardrail rises a high concrete sound wall, a single pine poking over the highest edge, and he feels like he's back inside. Like he has never truly been free, even when he was done with Xenakis and reporting in, even when he bought his own place and set up his own shop. Even driving these fifteen hundred miles without having to tell or ask anyone. Who's he shitting? There's only one way he'll ever be free.

Daniel glances down at his daughter's photo on the dash. It's his Linda who got to live, his Linda who stood in the sun at the Broadway Flying Horses, the way she held her head just like that. "I'm gonna have a baby." And that baby looking just like her mother, her eyes pulling you in only to push you away.

There comes again the thumping of the rumble strip, and it may as well be a CO kicking his bunk to rise and fucking shine.

Shine, Ahearn. Fucking *shine*.

42

LOIS DROVE down Susan's and Bobby's street and parked one block away on the opposite side from where they lived. From here she could see both their cars still in the driveway, Bobby's black Kia looking small beside Susan's. Lois had started out just before dawn, the day breaking slowly over fields of St. Augustine grass and palmetto scrub that looked blue then sage as the sun rose above the pines and its color faded into a gray light that aggravated her already aggravating headache. It had come on after she'd hung up on Susan at nearly one this morning when her granddaughter told her, "We have it here, Noni. I don't think you need that right now."

"That is *my* property, missy, not yours. What gives you the *right?*"

"I think you know."

"You're protecting him. Jesus, Mary, and Joseph, you're *protecting* that man."

"No, I'm protecting you."

That's when Lois had hung up. Or maybe she didn't then. Maybe she'd yelled a few choice words first. "Who are *you* to protect me? When have you ever cared about *me?*"

But no, that may have been her dream when she'd finally fallen asleep hours later. For a long while after she'd hung up, she kept thinking about driving up here right then, but she was so tired, so very tired, and then Don was there. He was standing in her shop wearing his red plaid shirt he wore nearly every day in the winter. Its elbows were frayed so thin Lois had told him many times to throw it out, but he wouldn't. His gray hair was pulled back into that stubby ponytail, and his reading glasses hung from his neck, and he was smiling at her while Susan stood in front of Lois's desk speaking as calmly as she had on the phone and yesterday afternoon sitting on the porch, except in the dream Susan was a teenager again, her shorts too short, a paperback in her hand. No screaming. No throwing things. Just a calm explanation to Lois as to why she should never be permitted to own firearms. That's the word she'd used, and it was one Lois had never heard Susan use in life. Don seemed to be on Suzie's side, too. His smile said that he was proud of her and that you, Lois, would be wise to listen. Then he was gone and that Mexican boy Soto, who'd been no boy at all, took Susan's hand and they walked out the back of the shop, not into the parking lot, but into the arcade, where Ahearn stood in his Himalaya blazer, his hands cuffed in front of him, looking over his shoulder and telling Lois, "I'm sorry."

It was so early that cars and SUVs still filled the driveways of Susan's neighbors' houses. It was a good neighborhood of stucco homes and clipped lawns, and many of them had bush daisies and vinca planted along their walkways to the porticoes over their front doors. The owners of the house to Lois's right had laid a bed of rocks and seashells at the base of a thick palm tree, and they'd set two wrought-iron benches on either side of the trunk like anybody walking by was invited to sit and take a load off. Across the street the front door of a blue house opened and a man in a tie walked out sipping from one of those coffee driving cups. He lifted his car keys and pressed a button and the lights of his sedan flashed and he climbed in and drove off without looking over at Lois. Her head pulsed flames behind her eyes. She needed coffee and she needed food, though she wasn't hungry, nor did she know how she was going to do what she had to do.

Sometimes she left a half-empty water bottle or Pepsi on her backseat. She could've used either now, and she turned and looked and just that movement made her car list a bit to the side. Catalogues were spread about, and there was the blue sweater that'd been there since last winter, pinned now under the shotgun's stock, but no water or cola.

She could leave her car and go knock on Susan's door, but what would she get besides breakfast and a lecture about checking out of the hospital? What would she get other than that high-and-mighty stone wall Suzie had put up around herself ever since she'd read that letter?

Lois needed to read that letter. She *had* to read that letter. What could he possibly have said to Susan to get her to want to see him? My God, he was evil itself. All those letters from him before they moved to Florida, DOC #53345, she still sees that number written in his own hand, she still sees Susan's name written in that hand, and she sees her own hand stuffing those sealed letters deep into the trash.

Directly across from Susan's house a new pickup pulled out of its driveway then accelerated to the main road, the traffic thicker there. On the other side oak trees and yellow pines bordered the grounds of Susan's college, the campus buildings beyond. Last Christmas Bobby and Susan had driven her slowly through it all, pointing out the building where Bobby had his office. It was bright white and nearly all glass, and it looked out over a man-made pond where a great blue heron stood in the shallows under a palm tree. Lois had felt for that entire holiday visit that Suzie had finally landed somewhere good. Now all Susan had to do was accept it and not do what she always did, which was to drive away and leave it all behind in the dust.

There's something wrong with me, Noni. The two of them sitting out on the porch with their wine earlier this week. Maybe Lois had been wrong not to take her to a head doctor when she was still young. One of the "officers of the court," a warm woman in a navy blue pants suit, had given her the names of doctors who "specialized in trauma." But that just wasn't Lois's way. She'd never trusted doctors, especially psychiatrists. They were for crazy people, and her granddaughter was far from crazy. She'd seen the worst thing a child could see and so Lois had her marching orders. She'd just show that child a million things that were bright and safe and happy. She would do that over an entire childhood. She would bury those horrible moments under an avalanche of love.

But the way Susan was acting now, leaving her to come here to wait for *him*, that quiet wall she was sitting so straight behind, my God, it was as if the last forty years had never happened at all. It was as if her Suzie had been chained to that night in that kitchen the entire time, and now the one who'd locked her up was coming down to squeeze those chains so tightly around Susan's heart that it would just stop altogether.

No, I'm going to kill him. I am going to kill him. So help me God I will do it.

Lois reached into her pocketbook, a tremor in both hands. She lit up a Carlton and turned the ignition key and opened her windows. The shotgun had been in one of the rear closets since Don was alive and well. He'd bought it and four others at an estate sale along with the chestnut and glass armoire that had held them. He'd also scored a saddle and five or six cowboy hats, and Lois had made a window dis-play out of them that had sold within a month. Suzie was a teenager then. Lois remembered that because her granddaughter, in a playful mood that was rare indeed, put the black one on her head and posed as if for a photograph against the brass register, her bare arms and legs crossed, a knowing smirk on her face like she was telling Lois, *Oh, this is me, by the way, your little outlaw renegade.*

Lois had no license to sell guns, so Don sold the shotguns pri-vately on the side, all of them except the one in her backseat, which for nearly thirty years had been leaning in a corner of the shop closet behind rolls of thick brocade fabric Don had bought on a whim. He told her it was historically authentic and two hundred dollars a yard but that he'd gotten it for next to nothing. "Who knows, Lo? Maybe we can upholster some furniture ourselves."

She missed that about him the most. His belief that anybody could teach themselves to do anything and that whatever good came your way you had to create yourself. No handouts. No favors. Just on-the-job training. Just start doing and the doing would teach you how to do better.

Except what did she know about shotguns? Not one thing. She barely knew anything about her pistol Susan had stolen. Lois had only shot it once, that afternoon when Don insisted she learn how, and the two of them had stood together on the banks of Bone River. The kick in her hand and the ringing in her ears and the smell of burnt gunpow-der then that small hole in a tree root that hadn't been there before she'd pulled that trigger. There'd been such power in that shiny steel object in her hand and it scared her and it thrilled her and it made her want to make hole after hole after hole in the body of one man only.

Lois inhaled deeply on her cigarette and blew smoke out her win-dow. Another neighbor backed out of a driveway, a young woman behind the wheel with those white earbuds in her ears for her music. How would she hear a siren coming up on her? Or a horn honking? Or a child's screams?

But Lois was calm thinking these things. She needed an Advil for her headache, yes, but ever since she'd pulled that shotgun out from behind those rolls of fabric she'd never use, the overhead bulb bright and dusty, the window dark with the predawn she'd driven through, there came a certain stillness and a clarity and a falling away of a clutching, grasping darkness that had been with her ever since those whirling blue lights flashed by the windows of her arcade apartment so long ago. No sirens. Just those lights. Once. Twice. Three times, the third cop car's engine louder than the first two. And Lois's body knew before she did, and she was up and out that door and running to her married daughter's cottage.

But now she had no bullets or shells or whatever they're called. Back in the shop it had taken her only a moment to find the latch that opened the shotgun, but both the barrels were empty and she began looking through all the closet shelves. They were filled with broken bric-a-brac she'd never been able to move: a chipped autogiro from the 1930s, a tinplate horse-drawn carriage with no horse or driver, three miniature Alfa Romeo racing cars without one wheel, Don's collection of square-cut nails from before the Civil War, but no box of bullets. Nothing.

A child's laughter. Or was it crying? No, it was laughter and it was coming from the house to Lois's right, the one with the wrought-iron benches beside the palm tree. It was muffled and from behind a closed window, but it sounded like a young girl being tickled. Then there was a woman's voice, and that's when Lois noticed the chalk drawings on the sidewalk, squiggly orange and green lines that ran off into the bush daisies. Linda, the joy she took in being a mother, the way her face lit up whenever she looked at her daughter, tickling her and calling her Suzie Woo Woo.

Lois stubbed her cigarette out in the full ashtray and started her VW and turned on the AC. She'd broken out in a sticky sweat, and now a minivan pulled away from the curb two houses down from Susan's and it was time for Lois to get out of here. She needed a drugstore for Advil and then she needed a gun supply shop. She hoped her flip phone was charged so she could call information, and she hoped it was somewhere in her pocketbook, where she would leave it for weeks at a time. She put the VW in reverse and used only her mirrors to back away. To turn around would make her dizzy again, to turn her head would make her calm morning start to spin.

43

OUTSIDE THE kitchen window a car drove by and Susan stood then sat back down, her heart slapping against her sternum. Bobby had been gone for just over an hour, and she hadn't told him yet. She'd been planning to once they sat down with their coffee, but he had an early committee meeting she hadn't known about, and when he told her this as he hooked his leather satchel over his shoulder, relief began to open inside her that this, too, was not the time to tell him. Then he was standing at the door, looking back at her. "Should I skip this meeting?"

"No, you go, I'll be fine."

"If he comes, though, you call me, okay?"

Susan smiled and said she would. Then he was gone, and she couldn't touch her coffee or even look at it. Also, she was worried about Lois. After Noni had hung up on her last night, Susan had called right back but got no answer. As soon as she woke this morning, she'd called Lois's house again but still got no answer. Then she called Lois's old flip phone and got a computerized voice mail. It had been early, though, and Noni was probably still asleep, but Susan kept seeing how gray her grandmother's skin had looked last night at the hospital. She kept seeing the loose splotchy flesh of her arms. Or maybe Lois had been awake and she was refusing to pick up. Susan hoped that's what it was, just Lois being the old Lois. In a few minutes she and Marianne would open the shop and Susan would call then.

She opened her file and scrolled down to where she'd left off.

. . . and I run back out into the light and he's laughing like he'll never stop.

Did that even happen? Yes, because she can still feel the soft sand under her shoes, how hard it was to run fast in it, how she kept slipping and the air was so cold on her face and Paul's laughing was so mean, so very mean.

Grandpa Gerry walking into low waves in a dark suit. His shirt was white and his tie was black, and his belly pushed against the lower buttons. She was seeing him from someplace off the ground. Noni's breasts pushing against her. Noni's hair smelling sticky with spray. Noni's smeared eye makeup, and Noni crying and having to put her down.

This was new.

There was the earth-yanking lurch that Susan was running down a hill she hadn't known about. She began tapping the keys to keep falling into it.

I was in a dress. It was blue and had ruffles along the hem. I kept staring at Grandpa Gerry all dressed up and getting wet. He held something in front of him I couldn't see. A seagull shrieked. Noni was crying. Brown seaweed lay in the sand in front of me. I never liked it because it looked like dead snakes, and I stepped back in my party shoes. They were black and pretty and I wore short white socks with lace.

Noni reached down and took my hand. There were other people on the beach. Grown-ups dressed in dark clothes. My auntie Gina was in a long black dress that looked like it would rip because there was a baby in her. My uncle Gio wore a suit the color of my dress and his hair was combed back and he had on sunglasses though it was cloudy. There were my big cousins. Mike in a white shirt with short sleeves that showed his skinny arms. He was wearing a striped tie.

Tina holding one of the baby cousins. Mr. Price, the man who owned everything, standing in seaweed with his arms crossed in front of his shiny brown suit. One of the little cousins was laughing and one of the aunts or uncles got mad and the little cousin went quiet, and Grandpa Gerry's suit was getting all wet. The water was up to his belly now, though all I could see was his back, his black suit back, and now his arms were doing something. He lifted something over his head and turned it upside down and white and gray powder fell out onto the water. It floated in a clump then broke apart and sank. Noni's crying was a burn in my ear and she was squeezing my hand too hard and it hurt and I wanted her to let go and I was crying and Noni let go and I was running. I was running away.

Susan stood. This girl. This girl who had been her. She had never gone this deeply before. She sat back down.

I ran away.

She hadn't even noticed she'd slipped to first person again. She did not care.

A party after, though nobody was laughing, and it was too quiet. It was in a restaurant. Grandpa Gerry was still all wet, and he sat in a chair by a window in his wet clothes. His pants were sticking to his legs. His shoes left spots on the red rug, and out the window was a Ferris wheel and a clown's face on the sign over the Kiddie Park.

I wanted to go there. I wanted to go on the kiddie rides. Grandpa Gerry was sitting next to Mr. Price, and they were drinking brown juice in little glasses and Grandpa Gerry was talking quietly and he was shaking his head and kept saying bad words and Mr. Price was saying things too, but even quieter, and he kept patting Grandpa Gerry's arm over and over again.

Aunts in black. They buzzed around Noni like bees. A sting in my shoulder. Uncle Paul was smiling down at me, his face all tight, his fingers still pinching, and I pulled away and said, "Ow!"

He had pimples on his cheeks. He had a double chin, and he was wearing a white shirt like Mike, but it wasn't tucked in and he pushed at me a piece of chocolate cake on a napkin. I knew Noni told him to give it to me and I didn't want it.

I wanted to go home.

Home.

I was standing in front of the tub and I was wet and she was rubbing my hair with a thick white towel. I was laughing and she was laughing and she kept calling me "Suzie Woo Woo, my Suzie Woo Woo!" I smelled like soap and shampoo and there was the cleanness of the towel and every time she pulled it off my head there were her brown shoulders and her pretty face and her laugh and her smile and she kept saying, "My little Suzie Woo Woo!" before she did it again and again, and I kept laughing and she lifted me up and I wanted to keep going up and up.

There were my daddy's shoulders and his big sweaty head, his hands around my ankles as I rode high above the carnival sounds and carnival smells, the sweet cotton candy and the cinnamon dough and all the kids who had to walk or run by themselves to the noisy lights of rides, but I was already getting my own ride and now it was over. Now it was gone.

Uncle Paul was always taller than me. He would pinch me and call me spoiled. He would kick me when Noni wasn't looking. Grandpa Gerry was gone, too. It was like he just walked away in his wet clothes.

Being with Noni was like living inside a sad whale. It was dark and it was hard to breathe and she hugged me without letting go, but I wasn't Suzie Woo Woo anymore. Noni never smiled.

Her face looking at me. We were in the kitchen. I was sitting at the table and my feet didn't reach the floor. The TV was on. People were laughing, though it sounded fake. The back of Paul's fat head from the couch. Spaghetti on my plate. Noni looking at me. She looked scared and she looked mad, then she started to cry and she came over and hugged me too hard and said, "I'm sorry. I'm sorry. I'm sorry, honey."

But it was like she had done something bad to me, and she wanted me to tell her it was all right, but all I wanted was to go home.

Susan stared at that last word. Home had always been Noni. It had been their apartment behind the arcade. It had been their house in the oaks and pines fifteen hundred miles south. But this home before home, if any of it had remained, it was that hot kitchen, that yellow floor, that telephone cord against her father's arm. His deep voice, a whale about to swim away.

Sitting naked in front of Macio's computer. She hadn't thought about this in years. She wrote: Then the Internet would get invented and that girl would be a young woman who would look up her father and find a picture of him. It would be from the front page of a small newspaper called the *Daily Gazette*, published in Port City, Massachusetts. It was that town on the river her grandmother would sometimes drive them to for an ice-cream cone, or to just walk and look in the windows of women's dress shops that were starting to open their doors then. Half the town was blooming and half looked abandoned. The headline above the photo read: "Ahearn Sentenced for Wife's Slaying."

There was something biblical about that word choice, and the young woman did not like it; it was the word used for cutting down dragons and many-headed serpents, not a wife and mother who did nothing to deserve what she got. Looking all this up for the first time, the young woman sat at the bedroom computer of a bass player she was living with named Macio. It was after midnight and hot and the young woman was naked and sweating and it was the worst way possible to see her father for the first time; in the newspaper photograph he was looking directly into the camera, so now he was looking directly at her. His wrists were handcuffed to a chain around his waist, and he was dressed in a corrections jumpsuit of some kind, and he was being led through a courthouse door. At his sides were uniformed cops. Her father's eyes were too close together, his nose hooked, his hair so short that his ears stuck out. There were the young woman's grandmother's words in her head. "He was a big ugly prick and he knew it and your poor mother couldn't take a breath without him okay-ing it first."

Her father's letter on the table. She needed to see that picture again. Twenty years ago, she hadn't even printed it out, and if she ever thought of it over the years it was the way you recall a detail from when you were drunk—the bulb burns in a lampshade from a bed that isn't yours.

Susan opened Google and typed: *Ahearn Sentenced for Wife's Slaying.* When it did not come up right away, when other Ahearns came instead, one a judge who'd imposed a harsh sentence on the wife of a town selectman, she typed: *Port City Daily Gazette.* Then there it was, the same photograph. Her father was handcuffed and looking right at her. Except in this one he's dressed not in a jumpsuit but in a coat and tie. His hands are still cuffed in front of him, and there are uniformed cops on either side of him in the courthouse doorway, but he's wearing a suit when all these years she'd remembered something else. It made her wonder about the accuracy of other memories she'd been recording.

But the headline was the same, and so was his homely face. His prominent nose and his ears sticking out, and the thing was he looked brutish and not very bright. But his letter, these weren't the thoughts of a stupid man. They just weren't.

Oh, Jesus Christ, was she just going to sit around for the next "few days" and *wait* for him? He'd sent it overnight mail two days ago. What if he'd flown down right after mailing it? What if he'd rented a car and Googled their names? Could he even *find* her address that way?

She tapped back to the empty Google bar and typed: *Susan Dunn, St. Petersburg, Florida.* Within a second came: *Susan Dunn in St.*

Petersburg, Florida—Whitepages. She tapped it open: *One White-pages profile found for "Susan Dunn in Saint Petersburg FL," and 35 possible matches.*

"Thirty-*five*." She read down the screen.

1) *Susan Dunn*
   Age: 54–60
   Current: Saint Petersburg, FL
   Prior: Unknown
   Knows: No Known Associations

2) *Susan Dunn*
   Age: 40–44
   Current: Saint Petersburg, FL
   Prior: Hallandale Beach, FL
   Knows: Robert Dunn

Hallandale? Her last apartment three blocks from the water. *Knows: Robert Dunn?* Jesus. It even had the range of her age, and to the right of these intrusions was *View Profile*, which she opened, and there, for anyone and everyone to see, was not just her and Bobby's street address but a map of their neighborhood with a red arrow marking their house. In the upper right corner were two boxes: *Neighbors* and *Directions*.

Something dry and black roiled through her. She looked out the kitchen window then stood and walked fast into her bedroom. She opened her bureau drawer and jerked out jeans and pulled them on. She yanked off her nightgown and grabbed a purple top off the closet shelf and slipped it over her head. She considered a bra, but there was no time for that, and she brushed her hair back with both hands and snatched her purse off the floor.

In the kitchen she pushed her laptop into its case then hooked the strap of her purse over one shoulder, the strap of her computer case over the other. She picked her keys out of the ceramic bowl near the stove and at the door she stopped. She peered out the window. There was her Civic sitting in the driveway. There was that old dark spot on the concrete beside it. The sky above their neighbors' houses was bright gray, the fronds of their sable palms still as bones. There were no cars parked anywhere. None of any kind. And just who the fuck was *he* to come to her house? Who in the hell did he think he *was* anyway?

She pushed open the door. She turned and locked it, her head and neck and back feeling exposed as the bolt slid into place. She walked quickly to her car and dumped her computer and purse into the backseat, then she started up the engine and backed out without putting on her seat belt, without thinking about where she was going, without thinking anything but this: *I will **not** wait for him. I will not be the one sitting around to wait for **him**.*

44

BETWEEN FLAT green fields and strip malls come Lawtey, Starke, Waldo, and Hawthorne. Soon enough there's Lochloosa Lake, Island Grove, and Citra, then a sprawling housing complex as Daniel heads west then south on I-75, Ocala coming and Marion Oaks coming and not long after that there are signs for Tampa and St. Petersburg, and Daniel's having third, fourth, and fifth thoughts about it all. He never should've written that damn letter. And he sure as hell never should've said he's coming to see her.

Not one letter from her when he was inside. After five years in, she was eight. After ten years in, she was thirteen, fourteen, fifteen. Eighteen when he got out. She could've written to him then, but she didn't, and why would she want to see him now?

She won't. She doesn't.

His gas needle is just about on *E*, and he should take the next exit and gas up and point his truck north.

But then what? Tell her he's coming and then don't do it? What if she *does* want to see him again?

"See how you are?" Sills's voice in his head. He used to say that all the time. Danny would be late for the barbershop or the caning room, walking fast behind two cons in the yard, and he'd step off onto the grass of the quad to pass them, and Sills would be standing at the shop doorway with his arms crossed, shaking his head at Danny and saying, "See how you are? I could write you up, Ahearn." But he wouldn't, and there'd be a smile in his eyes Danny knew he never deserved but took anyway, and that's what he feels as he takes the Ocala exit, that he wants something he has no right to, that he's asking for something he should never ever get.

Sills getting shot, that bothered Danny for a long time. There were a lot of COs Willie Teague could've plugged that nobody would've missed, but not Sills. He was rock-solid stand-up. Some screws were too friendly and didn't last long. They made the mistake of making friends with guys on the inside and then one day they're getting busted for smuggling in a dime bag, skin magazines, nips of real booze. One screw, Kenny Yameen, gave one of the Winter Hill guys a conjugal with his girlfriend in the assistant superintendent's office just before visiting hours closed. But Yameen also videotaped it on the sly, and he made the mistake, drunk one night, of playing it at his house to a roomful of other drunk screws. After he was busted, he moved and changed his name, not because of the DOC but because of the Winter Hill con on parole who was no longer his good buddy.

But Sills was respectful without being a target to get played, hard without being a hard-ass, and he always looked Danny in the eye like Danny was a man. Then Sills was dropping to the ground with a hole in his chest, and Danny had stood in the doorway to the barbershop in the endless quiet and emptiness of where Sills used to be and he was Danny and the Reactor all over again standing in another doorway because yes, he too, had done to another what Willie Teague just did. Soon enough there came Willie's last shot, and it was like a call to Daniel from his dreams, that he was late in doing something that had to be done, but he just couldn't see it yet.

In front of him is an eighteen-wheeler of new cars. Their exhaust pipes are shiny, their tire treads deep, and as the rig steers off to the left there appears a gas station called RaceTrac. Under these words, over the pumps, are *Boiled P-nuts, Gift Shop, T-shirts*. He should eat something, maybe just a bag of nuts.

In the shade of the awning over the pumps he rises slowly out of his Tacoma into the heat. He pats his front pocket for his cash and smells gasoline on warm concrete. A radio is playing. It sounds like some kind of love song, a woman singing. One bay over a young black kid is washing his windshield and using the squeegee to do it. His driver's-side door is open, and Daniel can see a woman sitting there. She's much older than the boy, and she's in a dress and pearls and her hands are folded over a black purse in her lap. She's looking straight out the window and she's smiling at the boy and Daniel knows she's his mother. He pulls the handle of the glass door advertising chewing tobacco and Red Bull, a bell ringing above him, and Daniel misses his own mother. She was never quite right and she'd never had any lasting friends and she was always talking to that voice in her head, but she loved him the way that mother loves her son. And no matter what was going to happen down in his daughter's town, nobody could take that away from Daniel Ahearn. Not even Danny. Not even him.

45

LOIS STOOD in the Pharmacy section squinting at shelves of bottled painkillers and fever reducers. Her purse hung from the crook of her elbow, and the ache behind her eyes felt like an electronic pulse from some machine she just needed to unplug, yet she still felt strangely calm, even with a jittery thrumming through her legs, she did.

After leaving Suzie's street Lois had ended up on I-275 heading south. The first exit took her onto a bridge over water, dozens of white boats moored there under the bright gray sky, and then came a dirty clump of palm trees and a wide parking lot for this Walmart she was standing in now. A young salesgirl was squatting a few feet away, stocking a lower shelf from a plastic basket beside her. Lois said, "Where's your Advil?"

The girl looked up at her, her skin bad on both cheeks, and in that moment Lois could hear how bitchy her tone had been. But the girl smiled and stood. "Advil? It's right here, ma'am." The girl plucked a bottle from the shelf Lois had been staring at, handed it to Lois, and smiled once more. Lois could see how pretty the girl would be once her skin got better.

"Thank you, honey. Is there a gun store near here? My son's going hunting." That same calmness telling this lie. Such a calm. And again that warm smile pointed up at her. Lois could see acne on the poor girl's forehead too, and her eyebrows needed plucking.

"Yes, ma'am, Sporting Goods." The girl turned and pointed her arm down the aisle. "Just past Electronics and Home Furnishings. Would you like me to show you?"

"I can find it, honey, thank you. And listen . . ."

The girl looked up at her, her smile a bit unsure now. Lois was about to tell her to wash her face with cold water to close her pores. It was the same advice she'd given to Suzie and to her mother. But this girl didn't seem to know how bad her skin *was*—she wasn't trying to cover it up with anything whatsoever—and who was Lois to point that out to her? "You're a beautiful girl. I just wanted to say that, honey."

"Thank you." The girl looked quickly down at her work, her back straight, and as Lois turned and walked away with her Advil she could see how much that girl had needed to hear that. It made Lois feel good that she'd said it, but it also pulled her to an empty quiet room of no words like that ever coming out of her for Suzie. But how could they? If she'd told her beautiful Susan how beautiful she was, that's all she'd think she was good for. And how many times had Lois told *Linda* how pretty she was? One hundred? Five hundred? How many afternoons in her bedroom behind the arcade had she sat her daughter on the table of the makeup mirror and told her to point her face up at her mother and close her eyes so she could brush mascara onto her long lashes? Lois could still feel Linda's small jawbone against her fingertips. She could still feel her daughter's light hand resting on her knee. "You're so lucky, Linda Lou. You got my features, honey. You're going to be a beauty like your mama, honey, but even better. My, my, my, you'll be the belle of the ball."

Across from the registers was a glass cooler of bottled waters, and Lois pulled one out and twisted it open and took a long drink, swallowing three times. She set it on a shelf in front of cans of WD-40 and worked the cap of her Advil until she finally got it open, her purse swaying heavy from her forearm. She pushed her finger into the seal, shook out two pills, and popped them into her mouth, swallowing them down with more water. There was the chatter at the registers, cash drawers sliding open and shut, the squeak of shopping cart wheels, a country singer on the store's sound system whining about one thing or another. From deep in the back of the store a baby was throwing a tantrum, and Lois needed to get out of here. She screwed the Advil cap back on but didn't want to carry that and the water bottle and her purse, so she left the water where it was—*So what, I'll get it when I come back*—and she made her way down a central aisle past racks of T-shirts and shelves of plastic-wrapped underwear for kids, cartoon colors, blues and yellows and reds, Spider-Man on one of them, on ten of them.

The store was too cool, and she wanted her sweater back in her car. She should call Marianne. That woman would've called the hospital first thing this morning. Then she would've called her house. Once she got no answer she might even drive over there. And then she'd probably call Susan, if she had her number, which Lois didn't think she did. Inside the warm gelatin of calm Lois had found herself in, there came a low vibrating itch to get back to Susan's street. A young man was standing behind a glass countertop, the lighted shelves beneath filled with silver and black pistols, their barrels long and short, narrow and wide, all of them meaning business.

It was hard to get her breath. It would be nice if she could sit down. She set her purse loudly on the countertop.

"Yes, ma'am. Can I help you?"

Another polite one. Lois wanted that water she'd left back on that shelf. She looked around for a stool, but there was none.

"Are you interested in purchasing a firearm today?"

That word from her dream. The boy was leaning against the edge of the counter with both palms so his bare forearms were exposed. They were smooth and pale, and Lois could see a network of blue veins just beneath the skin. He was young and had a wispy mustache and goatee. His name tag said: *Clay Moore*. To his right was a white Styrofoam cup of coffee Lois could smell and wanted for herself. "No, just bullets, or whatever you put in a shotgun."

"Not a problem, ma'am. What gauge, shot, and length are we talking about?"

"Excuse me?"

"For your shotgun."

"I don't know. It's not mine. Just give me anything."

This Clay smiled, his teeth crooked but as white as if he'd used a whitener on them. "That'd be very dangerous, ma'am. You don't want your weapon blowing up in your face."

"It's not mine, it's my son's."

"Do you know the gauge?"

"No, I don't know anything about it. It has two barrels."

"Under-over or side-by-side?"

"The second one, I guess. It's in my car. Can you come look at it for me?"

Clay seemed to take her in for the first time. She'd left without putting on any makeup, and she wasn't even sure she'd brushed her hair or put on anything more than her underthings and this housedress she felt too chilly in now with this superstore's AC. This Clay glanced at her purse and her watch and her fingers that wore no wedding ring, just a single pearl in a silver band Don had sized for her not long before he died.

"My son's going hunting. He needs it."

"Well, the only game in season right now are hogs and rabbits."

"I don't know what he hunts. Can you come look at my gun?"

"Well, that's kind of an important thing to know."

"Hogs, then." Yes, hogs. A big, ugly, pink-faced hog.

Clay smiled again, then looked behind him where a curly-headed man in a tie and a Walmart vest was sitting at a computer. "I'll be right back, Robert. I need to take a look at this lady's shotgun."

IT WAS only as she stood at her VW under the gray sky, the air warmer now, the lot filled with more cars and pickups than just a few moments ago, that Lois remembered she hadn't paid for the bottle of Advil in her hand. But it felt good to be back out in the heat, and just as soon as she bought what was needed, she was going to find a coffee shop or a bakery or both, then she was going to drive back to Susan's street. And who knows? She might even knock on the door. Walk right in and see what was what.

"This is a fine old Mossberg, ma'am, but it's in very poor condition."

In the daylight it was clear this boy was older than he'd looked back inside under fluorescent lights. There were faint pockets under his eyes, and in his goatee sprouted a few gray whiskers. He was standing at the open door of her backseat, the shotgun open, staring once more into both barrels before snapping them back shut. "Does your son ever clean his guns?"

"I don't know. I'll tell him to do that."

"It's a safety issue, ma'am. Nobody should be hunting with a weapon in this condition."

"Will it work?"

"Yes, but not well, and it could—"

"Just give me the bullets for it, please, honey. I have things to do."

He stared at her a moment. He glanced at the loose flesh of her bare arms, his eyes passing quickly over her sagging breasts that had once commanded such attention, this rising feeling that there was so little to lose now, really, and hurry up. Just hurry the hell up.

He began reading something etched into the side of one of the barrels. "Twelve-gauge, two-and-three-quarter-inch." He looked down at her. "And you don't know what he's hunting?"

"I told you, hogs."

"Double-aughts should do it." He leaned back into her VW and set Don's gun on the seat. Lois reached into her purse and pulled out her credit card and a ten-dollar bill.

"Would you mind bringing them to me? I don't feel so good."

"Not a problem." He plucked the card from between her fingers. "Can I interest you in a cleaning kit, too?"

Lois shook her head. "Take the cash, honey. It's for you."

"I'm afraid I can't accept gratuities, ma'am. I'll be right back."

She was about to call to him to take her Advil and ring that up too, but he was already walking fast to the automatic doors of the entrance, and it wasn't like she'd meant to steal them anyway. Maybe later she'd pay for them. Maybe then.

She sat heavily back behind the wheel and started the engine and opened all the windows. She'd been cold only moments ago, but now she was hot and she put the AC on low and pointed one of the vents at her face. She wanted that water she'd left near the cans of WD-40, and she wanted that Clay Moore to get out here soon, for she could feel herself beginning to lose something she needed in order to do what had to be done. It was that damn bottle of water, and it was this damn Advil, the feeling she was breaking the law when all she'd ever done her whole life was follow the rules that other people felt free to break, but not her, not Lois Dubie. And now this shotgun lay across her backseat like some massive pen for a contract she wasn't sure she wanted to sign, not with *her* name or with her hand, though when Clay Moore walked back across the lot, his khaki pants loose around his skinny legs, her credit card in one hand and a white plastic bag hanging from the other, she noticed that she signed her slip and took her card and bag with a smile and a gratitude that came not from the last twenty minutes, but from the last twenty-three years of not being able to do the one thing that should've been done. And now she was moving, dropping that heavy bag beside her purse and pulling out of the lot, a lone gull gliding low in front of her, flapping its wings once before dipping over the bridge railing and out of sight.

46

AT A Starbucks just off Gulf Boulevard, Susan sat at the window and called Noni's shop, the phone beginning to ring in her ear. Outside on the patio a young couple sat at a small round table, and they were the age of her students, both of them in shorts and flip-flops, the girl laughing at something the boy just said. Lois's business phone rang and rang, then the answering machine picked up and Marianne's warm recorded voice informed whoever was calling that the store was open from eleven a.m. to seven p.m. Susan hung up and called Noni's house. But there was no answer there, either, and Susan could see her grandmother squinting at the caller ID on the kitchen phone and letting it ring. Susan was tempted to call Noni's flip phone again, too, but it was probably turned off and buried in Lois's purse anyway. Susan glanced at her laptop clock. She had an hour and a half before the shop opened, and she would call then. She could smell coffee and cinnamon, and she thought she might be able to eat something, maybe a scone.

She opened her file.

"He was a big ugly prick and he knew it and your poor mother couldn't take a breath without him okaying it first."

She tapped herself three of four lines down into the screen's bright blankness. Latin music was playing—an accordion and horns and drums that made her think of South America, then Mexico, then Gustavo. She began to see her and Gustavo lying together on his bed.

Gustavo couldn't read, and so I would read to him. His rented room was on the first floor, and he would pull out the window screen then help me climb in. After we made love, we smoked cigarettes and I'd lie back on his shoulder and read to him from whatever I was reading. *Jane Eyre*, I think, though it could have been *Wuthering Heights*. No, it was *Jane Eyre* because at the start of the novel Gustavo kept asking why Jane was sent to the Red Room.

"Because her aunt is mean."

"Like your abuela."

She could hear the smile in his voice but his sincerity too. A month or so earlier Gustavo had asked her why she lived with her grandmother and not her mother and father, and Susan Lori had told him her dark little fairy tale of loss and privation she still believed then, her parents' car sinking to the bottom of that cold, fast-moving water. Gustavo leaned over and kissed her forehead and eyebrows three times. He told her he loved her. And Susan Lori felt she'd opened a door she should not have just so she could hear those three words. He said he did not know that books had real lives in them, and he liked how this story of this girl so far away so long ago made him think of when he was a boy.

It was the first time I'd ever felt what it was like to give someone something useful. Those afternoons reading to Gustavo, I felt what a holy person must feel, that I was in possession of something deeply private and sustaining but available to anyone, and even though I had to stop often and explain words and English phrases to him, it was like I could feel I had this power and I was giving it to him so he could have it too.

Dear Stranger,

Susan Lori loved Gustavo most because he led her to what she could do, though it would be years before she would do it, and then he was gone.

No note. No phone call.

Just his unrelenting absence.

Susan stared at that line. She glanced out the window. Her fingers began to move again.

Afternoons, he would pick her up at the high school. He worked the second shift at the citrus plant and he'd pull up in his El Camino and they'd have just under an hour before he had to punch in. Usually she'd be hungry and he'd drive her through the Taco Bell drive-through for a burrito and a Coke. Or they'd get coffee somewhere. Sometimes, if they really needed it, he'd drive her to his place on Pinellas, his landlords at work in the fields or whatever it was they did, and Susan and Gustavo would make love so fast she only had time to take off her jeans and underwear. His walls were bare. His small dresser had nothing on it but a plastic Virgin Mary and a carton of cigarettes. She was on the pill then, Lois had made sure of that. That doctor in Punta Gorda had written Susan a prescription after asking her only two questions.

"How old are you?"

"Sixteen."

"Are you sexually active?"

"What do you think?"

He waited, his gray eyes on her over the rim of his glasses. He was looking at her like she was an imposition on his entire day, and she had about one more second before he moved on to more important things.

"Yes."

Right after Gustavo came, always inside her, he'd tell her he loved her in English and in Spanish. And she said those three words back. She said them back because she believed them when she said them, because on those nights and Sunday afternoons when he did not have to go to work, the smell of orange pulp coming from his clothes and hair and skin, he asked her to read to him from books she loved, and it was like she was letting him into parts of her that were far more personal than what was between her legs. She began to think of what would come next for them, that they would get their own place or she could move in with him, live with him in that small room in the back of that one-story house on Pinellas. Or they could move far away together.

And when he dropped me off at the county road hours later, even on those nights when I knew Lois would start screaming at me, I felt good inside and out. Not dirty. Not ashamed. Not like a misfit. But like someone with a higher calling that could only come to fruition if it was shared.

Then it was a Monday afternoon in April, and Susan Lori stood in the high school parking lot waiting. The buses had gone. The kids with cars had all driven off. She stood in the quarter shade of the palm tree on a strip of dirt between the teachers' parking lot and where the students parked. Her math teacher, Mrs. Schmidt, walked out into the sun for her car. She had her purse over her shoulder and her briefcase in her hand, and she was fiddling with her car keys and squinting at Susan leaning against the palm. Sweating there. Thirsty. Ready to leave.

"Do you need a lift?"

Susan thanked her and told her no. "My boyfriend's coming." She had never referred to him that way, even to herself, and she liked those words coming out of her.

"Well, wait inside, honey. You'll get heatstroke out here." And she climbed into her car and drove off and Susan Lori waited.

After an hour, she began walking. She walked right to his house on Pinellas. She knew he'd be at work by then, but she had to see it anyway. Maybe he was sick. Maybe he needed her. But the driveway was empty.

Beside the front stoop was a concrete planter she hadn't noticed before. It was cracked to its rim, and brown soil spilled out onto the dirt.

Gustavo didn't come the next afternoon, either, so Susan walked to the phone booth in front of the Taco Bell and called the citrus plant. It was hot in that booth. It smelled like dried piss, the glass cloudy and scratched. She was put on hold twice before a man got on and without a greeting said, "He don't work here no more."

"What? Who?"

"Soto. You're calling about Soto, right? He quit." The man hung up, and there was the drone of a dial tone, the passing cars, my heart beating through the trapped air in my mouth. I walked to his house on Pinellas and there was a rusted station wagon in the driveway and I knocked on the door. A woman answered. She was old and she was Mexican, and I asked her where I could find Gustavo.

"Stavo? He go back home."

"When?"

She shrugged. From inside the house came the smell of hot oil on a burner. There was a TV on, and Susan Lori could smell frying tortillas. "No lo sé. He go home for his family. I have cooking." She smiled and closed the door.

Out the window, past the empty patio, and down an embankment, was a man-made channel of still green water, a rise of condominiums on one bank, Gulf Boulevard on the other, cars passing by fast.

Susan Lori stood on that stoop as if she had not heard what she'd just heard. Go home for his family. His mother and sister. Susan knocked again on the door. She waited and knocked. When no one came she moved around the side of the house to Gustavo's room and she pushed the screen out of the window and climbed in. A floorboard squeaked under her weight. She crept over to his open door and closed it. His bed was made. His walls were still bare. She pulled open his bureau drawers, and they were empty and smelled like dried wood. There were no cigarettes. There was no Virgin Mary.

She sat on Gustavo's bed. Then she lay on it, then she curled up on it. His pillow smelled faintly of oranges and sweat and her.

In the days and nights after, all she did was cry and sleep. For almost a week she told Noni that she was sick, and when she finally had to go back to school she ignored every boy and girl there, she ignored her homework and even her own reading, and everything she looked at—the teachers' cars in the parking lot under the sun, a green lizard on the sidewalk, a smiley face inked into a bathroom-stall wall—all were signs of nothing but a loveless world. And the feeling that was moving through her blood was, *Of course.*

Like spending a long day under the sun and then comes the wind and the rain and you're never really surprised.

She needed to stop and call Noni. She hoped she hadn't gone into her shop this morning, but she probably had. She wanted to hear Lois's voice. She wanted to hear that slightly bitchy tone and that *Jesus, Mary, and Joseph* accent from up north. She wanted to apologize to her.

But for what?

Susan's face heated. She swallowed and shook her head. She wrote: I let in Gustavo far deeper than I ever let in the woman who raised me. Then, over a month after he disappeared, his letter came. Susan Lori pulled it out of the mailbox right after school. There were big stamps that read "AeroMexico," the letters printed over the profile of some ancient soldier. There was no return address, but in black pen was:

Suzin Dooby
Country Road
Arcadia, Florida USA

Maybe I tore that letter open and read it right there. Or maybe I ran with it into the house. I don't remember. But it was as if there was new air to breathe. As if that thick, desolate air had been pulled away by an all-loving hand because there had been a terrible mistake and everything that had gone wrong would now go right.

Suzindooby,
My boy is very sick. I lie to you. I am sorry for this. I never forget you.

                                                        Gustavo Soto

The paper was the color of sunsets, garlands of roses in the corners, and they burned my fingers. I read that letter so many times it became like a curse and like a prayer: *I lie to you. I never forget you. I lie to you. I never forget you.*

Many years later, sick in bed with a fever, living with one man or another, I typed Gustavo's name into the computer. But there were so many of them, most of them in Mexico, old ones and fat ones, gangsters with neck tattoos, a businessman in a tuxedo smiling under the sun. There was a withered fisherman and a young unsmiling boy with his arm around a girl in a white dress. And there was a priest. I stopped and stared at that priest's face. There was how straight he stood, the way he held his head, the way my Gustavo had, like he knew just where he stood but would never apologize for it. Of course it was not Gustavo, but I stared at that man a long time. Then I closed my computer and slept a sick sleep.

A priest? Yes, because my time with Gustavo had felt sacred. And it came to me, in those long broken months after, that only hurting this deeply could reveal the soul, that if there was a soul this must be it, some central eternal part of you in love with the world.

But the world has to love you, too, and it didn't.

My cheek on Gustavo's bare shoulder, my book resting inches above his rising and falling abdomen. I loved how smooth and hairless he was. I loved his smell and the slick of his sweat against my skin. I loved how his tongue moved inside me and inside my mouth, even when he tasted like cigarettes or me. And nobody would listen as intently to what I read to him ever again. It was like he was trying to learn not just the language itself, but how to enter the story with me so that he might enter himself, so that he might unlock some door that would lead him to who he was meant to be and how he was meant to live.

And then he left me, and when I learned that he had only shared some of himself with me when I'd shared everything with him, well, maybe that's what I learned to do too. Fucking those boys at Gainesville, it was like I'd invited them into one part of me while another part, the deeper part, the part that loved, went to a back room and shut the door till it was over. Then, when all the clumsy furious pumping was through, especially with pale Peter Wilke, I stepped out of that back room and opened my book and read to him, but he did not even begin to listen as deeply or as hungrily as Gustavo had. Instead, he stared at me like I was an actress delivering lines, and he'd get hard and want to do it again.

Then came Chad from New Jersey and all the rest and I didn't even try with them. They could have my body while the very center of me locked myself in that back room, or they could have me only when I'd come back out, but none of them could have both at once, the way Gustavo had when I was sixteen. Then came Delaney, and I gave her both at the same time, but Delaney's tongue and fingers and mouth were not enough, and then there was Bobby and his passion for Coleman's free jazz, the light in Bobby's eyes and the sweat breaking out on the top of his bald head as he sautéed spinach at the stove and showed me everything he loved.

It made me want to show him too, but I didn't. Instead I moved in with him. I opened my legs for him while what I loved went into the back room and closed the door. Except I didn't lock it. I kept it slightly ajar and listened to the dissonant chaos of what this Bobby Dunn loved. Over time, it made me want to love again what I used to love, and I picked up my Corina novel and started again. Then, a Sunday after too much coffee, what I loved sitting on the threshold of the open door now, I read what I had of Corina, and Bobby told me it was genius and he meant it, and I felt myself stand and walk away from that back room and the next day at the office of the justice of the peace across from a Staples parking lot on Seminole Drive, we got married.

Now when we made love I did not retreat to the back room, but nor did I slip into the legs and belly and chest of the woman I was. I seemed to be stuck halfway between, a stasis my enemy loved, and so I began to feel nothing. I felt nothing for Corina Soto, the poor Mexican girl in Culiacán. I felt nothing for my husband Bobby Dunn. And it wasn't because I'd fallen out of love, because I'd never fallen in love in the first place. There had been no falling at all, just a careful walk from the back room to—what? To that oneness. Which was—

Trust. Faith. Letting go into the belief that everything would be all right.

My face in the mirror, feeling nothing as I stared at it, feeling nothing as I took my hair in one hand and raised the scissors to it and started cutting.

The patter of rain on concrete. It was coming down on the patio and the man-made channel. Out on the boulevard the driver of a passing sedan put on his windshield wipers, and they slapped and slapped and slapped. Blues was playing now, a chugging harmonica being pierced by an electric guitar. Behind the counter a pretty black girl was laughing with someone Susan could not see. She needed to call Lois. She needed to hear her grandmother's strident voice.

Those times she would rest her cheek against Noni's big soft breasts. How she could hear the muffled rise of her grandmother's breathing. How she could hear her steady, faraway heart.

47

THE CITY of Tampa almost behind him, a dense cluster of concrete and glass and open parks, cars and buses moving through it, people on its sidewalks and boardwalks coming and going, some under umbrellas because it's raining, and Daniel glimpses a farmers' market under a long wet tent, crates of oranges and tomatoes and a man in a wet T-shirt smoking a cigarette as the unfolding interstate now takes Daniel onto a bridge over a bay that stretches for miles to the north and to the south. There are boats out there, even under this rain. This bridge goes on and on, and he's grateful for the wide-open view, though it brings him back to that Sunday morning when he'd stood on the water side of the railing of the Tobin Bridge ready to jump.

He glances down at his daughter's picture still taped to the dash. He feels like he might be able to eat something. That bag of nuts he'd bought at the gas station had gone down all right, and now he wants some eggs. Maybe he can find a joint somewhere that sells breakfast all day. But maybe he should wait for that. Maybe that's something he can do with—

But he's getting ahead of himself.

Daniel has both hands on the wheel. He can feel his heart beating in his palms and fingers. At the other end of this bridge over this bay lies St. Petersburg, and what then? Just go to her school? But what if she's not there today?

Then he'll have to ask around. Find out where she lives. Maybe she's in the phone book. He'll find a St. Petersburg phone book and look her up. Then he can call her house, and—what? His stomach burns. It matches the hot, jagged grip on his back and hips, and now fried eggs don't sound so good anymore. He flicks on the radio. He wants music or the news, something to take his mind somewhere else, but it's still his book on tape. The narrator's quoting some old English law from the 1600s, a bunch of *hath*s and *loseth*s, and Daniel turns it off. Through his rising and falling wipers he follows a Dodge Charger onto a wider interstate, the Dodge leaving him far behind, a white spray shooting out from under mag tires. Probably a young man behind the wheel. Just a young man doing what young men do.

The rain eases up, and Daniel needs a toilet. He needs to study his map, too. He should be only ten or so miles away from his daughter's college, but he's not sure. To his left and to his right, stretching out for miles among pine and palm trees, lie neighborhoods of mobile homes and low wood and brick houses, hundreds of them, all these lives being lived with others, and it makes him think of Suzie again, of how she used to sit in his lap and press her ear to his chest. *It's so loud, Daddy. It's so* **loud.**

48

LOIS TOOK an exit too soon and found herself driving through a low-rent neighborhood. She passed a house on her left that had a collapsed carport, and in the next driveway an old air-conditioning unit was stacked in a rusty wheelbarrow and an obese boy sat on his stoop in a T-shirt in the rain staring at her as she drove by. Her headache was back, Advils or not, and she was itching to get back to Susan's but dreading it too. She should ask somebody how to get to the college, and that would get her back to Suzie's street. And she should call Marianne.

Lois pulled over alongside an abandoned lot, kept the engine running, then fumbled through her purse until she found her flip phone and turned it on. The battery was low. She squinted at the buttons and called her shop.

"Lois's Fine Furniture and Toys?" Marianne's polite and peppy voice, it irked Lois, even though there was no better way to answer the phone than the way she just had. But why did she always have to sound like the shop was hers when Lois's name was on the marquee?

"Marianne, it's me."

"Lois, honey, where *are* you? Are you all *right*? I called the hospital and heard you'd left. I've been calling your house all morning. My God, I was just about to send Walter over."

"I'm fine, Marianne."

"Are you *home*?"

"Look, I won't be in today. I just wanted you to know."

"Lois—"

"I'll call you later, Marianne. Goodbye."

Lois pushed buttons till her phone was off. Then she closed it and dropped it into her pocketbook, and funny how her fingers trembled just a bit. Funny how she felt right then, like she'd just said something far more important than she had.

At a gas station with full service she rolled her window down all the way and asked the man pumping her gas where the college was.

"What college is that?" He had to be fifty, a white man chewing gum and needing a shave. His eyes were a lovely blue, and he knew it and smiled at her with the kind of ease with women only slick players had and that she'd never had any use for whatsoever.

"Eckerd. Is there another?"

"You need 275. Take the Twenty-second Avenue exit." He glanced in her backseat and had to've seen the shotgun but just winked at her and pulled his nozzle out of her VW, Lois's face flaming up as she handed him her credit card and couldn't get out of there fast enough.

The rain was really coming down on the highway, but it eased up once she was back in Suzie's neighborhood. She drove slowly up and down wet streets and mostly empty driveways and quiet-looking homes. Then she was back on Susan's street, and only Bobby's car was still parked in their driveway, and that same icy sweat broke out along Lois's forehead and the back of her neck. Had Suzie already gone to meet with him? Was she too *late*?

Lois kept her eye on Bobby's car through her arcing windshield wipers as she pulled into the spot where she'd been before. The child's chalk lines on the sidewalk were beginning to run in muted colors into the bush daisies, and Lois just sat there a moment. She took a long, deep breath but got little air for the effort. She looked over at that Walmart bag on her passenger's seat, staring at it as if it were a wild animal somebody had left there. Then she pulled it onto her lap and reached in for the box of shotgun shells. Winchester. Those damn westerns Gerry had liked so much, his stocking feet propped on the coffee table while he drank his 7&7s and watched men on horseback shooting other men down in the street. Oh, he loved that, but he was a coward himself. All his hard talk after Ahearn was arrested. How many nights did Lois have to listen to drunk Gerry go on and on about "people" he knew in the "system"? His "friends in Providence" who would have Danny killed "in no time"? But what happened? Nothing, that's what. Lois spent her days and nights wanting to die herself, to just walk out of their arcade apartment down to the beach and into the ocean. But there was Paul to think about and now there was little Suzie, who had seen it all and who did she have now but her?

"Nope. It was always up to me, wasn't it?" *Lois will do it. Lois will take care of that. Lois, Lois, Lois.* Raindrops pattered along her roof. She ripped up the flap of the box and nearly broke a nail doing it, though what was there to break? It had been years since she'd kept them long and manicured. And her hair. She used to have it styled once a week all year long, sometimes twice a week in the summer. When had she stopped giving two shits? After Don died? Or was it before, when Susan left for good?

The shells were made of green plastic. She pulled one out. It was heavy and smelled new, and the brass casing at its end was shiny and beautiful, but her hands were shaking when before she'd been so calm, and when she turned toward the backseat her VW listed again and a flurry of dark movement crowded her eyes. Was she going to have to step out into the rain then lean into her backseat to load that thing? And then what? Sit here and wait for Danny Ahearn, who for all she knew could be meeting with Suzie right this minute? And what if he didn't show till tonight or tomorrow? Was she really going to wait so she could cut him down in front of the same girl who'd seen what her mother had suffered?

A sound was coming out of Lois that was foreign to her own ears, her chest heaving for air and there would never be enough. It was like a twin of herself was crying, not her, but some younger Lois the older Lois had turned her back on years ago. It was the one who had held little Suzie in her blue dress at low tide on the beach. It was the one who had watched her Gerry walk out into that surf holding their daughter in a coffee can. It was the one watching those awful ashes, so little of them, so much lighter than they should be, fall into a clump into the ocean, quickly spreading out and dissolving as if Linda had never lived at all.

"Oh, honey. Oh, hon." The shell slipped from Lois's hand and rolled onto the floor at her feet. She wiped her nose and tried to breathe, but there wasn't enough air. There just wasn't. Her wipers were still moving. Her engine was still running. In the rain ahead of her, her granddaughter's husband's car sat in its driveway as solidly as a lighthouse before the rocks, and Lois pushed the box of shotgun shells onto her pocketbook and put her VW in gear and drove the short but long, so very long, distance to their house.

49

SUSAN STOOD outside under the eaves of the Starbucks with her phone pressed to her ear. It was still raining, but now the sun was out and a stippled puddle in the parking lot was the same pale lemon as the sky. Noni's phone rang and rang and Susan imagined her dead in her bed, her loose skin grayer than it had been in the hospital the night before.

"*Who are you to protect me? When have you ever cared about me?*"

"Answer the phone, Lois." Susan's voice seemed to rise up from some black promise of an earth-tilting grief. What was she *thinking*, leaving her in the hospital like that? Had she thought to even leave her a note? No, she hadn't, nor had she *ever* put herself fully in her grandmother's skin because never had there been a more self-absorbed and selfish bitch than Susan Ahearn Dubie Dunn. And Bobby was wrong. She shouldn't have told Lois about the letter. Doing that was so much worse than when she'd hopped that bus back to Gainesville where Danny Rolling still roamed freely, Susan too wrapped up in her own story to even begin to think of what her grandmother was having to suffer through.

And why *did* she tell her? Because Bobby said she had a right to know? That Susan would be disrespecting Lois's loss and treating her like a child if she withheld such news from her? No, this was all bull-shit. She'd told Noni about the letter because part of her wanted to hurt her with it. Because part of Susan was still angry at her grand-mother for ever telling her in the first place. Because, oh, how much easier it would have been to have lived all these years believing that her mother and father had died in each other's loving arms.

Susan punched in the speed-dial number for Lois's cell phone, though she knew Noni never used it. She waited five rings then called the shop. Marianne answered right away, her voice prim and a bit too composed, but there was a genuine warmth there, even answering the phone, and it was as if she were reaching through the phone and squeezing Susan's hand.

"Marianne, it's Susan. Did my crazy grandmother actually come in today?"

"No, honey, she didn't. But she called me, and she sounded strange. I'm worried about her."

"Is she at her house? She won't pick up."

"She didn't say. Susan, I don't mean to pry, but has something hap-pened that I might be able to help with?"

Susan stared at the puddle in the lot. A large businesswoman in a tan pants suit smiled at her as she pulled open the Starbucks door and walked in. Susan's eyes stung. Her throat was a thick mass of far too much to say, though she wanted to say all of it, beginning with what was growing inside her, beginning with that. "Yes, I don't know, I—"

Her phone buzzed against her ear. She pulled it away and saw "Home," her heart skidding along packed dirt, for Bobby could only be calling about one thing, the other Danny, her "father." My God, was he *here*?

"I have to go, Marianne. Thank you." Susan's fingertips were hot wax, and Bobby answered after the first ring.

"Hey, baby."

"Is he *there*?"

"No, but your grandmother is. And she's not doing so well. She's not doing well at all. Where are you?"

Slumping relief then cool disappointment, it was like being pulled in for a long, consoling hug then pushed far away. It was so familiar, really. So goddamned familiar.

"I couldn't stay there."

"I should've canceled my meeting."

"What's Lois doing?"

"She's using the bathroom. I'd like to feed her, but we're low on everything. Maybe you can pick something up?"

A Jeep pulled into the lot, a big man climbing out. His eyes walked all over Susan, and she turned her back on him and said to Bobby, "Okay. I can do that." She heard the big man open the Starbucks door behind her, and she kept her back to it and him and said, "I'll be home soon." Those last two words felt so natural, as natural as air and water and fire and sky, so why was she denying it? Wasn't it time to stop denying it?

50

THIS LIGHT is taking its own sweet time to change, and Daniel keeps staring out his passenger's window at his daughter's school, an electric current humming through his bones. From here it doesn't look like much. Beyond a scrappy stand of pine and oak, there's a scattering of buildings under the sun, the rain stopped for good now, though his windshield is still dripping and he flicks on the wipers one more time as a horn sounds behind him and he takes a slow left into the entrance of Eckerd College.

He should clean up first. The last few miles he's kept his printed-out directions pressed against his steering wheel, his reading glasses just under his new sunglasses, and if he hears another damn car horn go off on him he'll— What? He'll *what*?

He hadn't expected her school to be so close. He still needs to piss, and he wants to brush his teeth and wash his face and comb his hair, but now he's pulling up to a security guard's shack. It's painted white and is nearly all glass, and Daniel may as well be back inside, a screw eyeballing him as he steps into the mess hall or the barbershop or the school.

Except this guy's smiling and waving him on before Daniel can even pull to a full stop. The shack's door is slid wide open, and he's an older guy sitting on a stool, silver hair and an easy smile in a tanned face. No uniform, just a white shirt and khaki shorts and running shoes, an open newspaper on his lap. Daniel waves back and drives on.

This feels like a good sign. It does. So does the midafternoon sun shining brighter now, the way it makes the wet grass sparkle along a man-made pond, beyond it a modern building that's whiter than the security shack in Daniel's rearview mirror. Off to his left, through a line of planted palm trees, are more modern-looking buildings. They have concrete wheelchair ramps and tall glass windows and doors, and three young women are walking out of one into a parking lot. One is black, the other two white, and all three are wearing shorts and sleeveless shirts and flip-flops. The black girl is showing the other two something on her phone and the three of them laugh, then a bearded man in a tie walks ahead of them to his car, and he's got to be a professor, and Daniel is not ready to be here. Not yet. What if she just comes walking out of a building like that? What if her eyes lay on his red Tacoma with the Mass. plates and she sees his sixty-three-year-old mug staring out at her? Does she even remember what he used to look like? Would she have seen any picture of him at all?

He's driving down a narrow asphalt lane. Across it lie wet pine needles and a few flattened green leaves, and it must've rained harder here than out on the highway. He passes half-full parking lots. His back and hips burn. There's also a groin-heaviness he's been putting up with since way before Tampa. He needs to park and find a restroom. He needs to get himself cleaned up.

Two young men are walking on the other side of the road talking to one another. Their T-shirts are wet, and they've got the kind of muscles so many kids do today, everybody built like Jimmy Squeeze, who these days wouldn't even turn anybody's head. Daniel rolls down his window and slows to ask them where he can find a toilet, but they don't seem to notice and nothing comes out of his mouth and he drives ahead and pulls into the next parking lot he sees. In the car beside him a red-haired girl is talking fast into her phone she holds in front of her face. She looks pissed off, and even from where Daniel sits, rolling up his driver's-side window, he can hear the voice of the boy she's talking to. He sounds like he's defending himself, like she's all wrong about him, and *this* is wrong, Daniel being at this school before he's ready. He should just drive out of here and find a gas station where he can take a long slow piss then wash himself up again. Better yet, he should go book a room in a motel somewhere and take his time doing it right. He's wearing his best khaki pants, but they need ironing, this shirt too, and even though he showered and shaved early this morning he should do it again.

Daniel almost puts the Tacoma back in gear, but a hot point of pain is pressing against the tip of his penis, and he needs a toilet right now.

"I fucking *told* you that, Ethan! I *did* too!" The girl's voice is muffled now, but what she's spewing is in the air and it comes to Daniel that maybe that's the history of the world right there, people who can't get along spreading their hurt out to everybody else.

Daniel reaches back into his duffel bag for his shaving kit.

"Bull*shit*, you never *said* that! You're lying, Ethan."

Linda yelled at him more than he ever yelled at her. "You're sick, Danny! You're fucking sick in the *head*!"

Daniel touches the cash in his front pants pocket. He locks his truck and looks back at the girl behind the wheel of her car, but she's looking straight ahead through the windshield at the air itself, her pretty face ugly with bad feeling, and he walks across the road and through a bigger parking lot, his legs stiff, his feet like bear paws. Most of the cars have Florida plates, but there's one from Alabama, another from Illinois, and he thinks about young people packing up and going off to school somewhere. This was never even a thought for him growing up, not from his mother, not from Liam, and not from himself.

The closest building is coming up and Daniel steps over a curb onto short grass then a concrete sidewalk under a long canopy. There are floor-to-ceiling windows and inside is a gym under fluorescent lights, boys and girls lifting weights together, pedaling stationary bikes, one kid with a shaved head kicking a long black heavy bag with his bare feet. His hands are wrapped in bandages, and his T-shirt sticks to his chest and stomach, and Daniel knows there'll be a toilet in there somewhere for sure.

He steps to the side as an Asian girl in sweats walks out one of the side doors and he walks in. In front of him is a long desk, a kid sitting behind it staring at a computer screen. Against the wall is a glass cooler full of colored drinks in plastic bottles. The open gym door is next to it, a radio playing rap music in there—another pissed-off kid shouting his street meanness—the *thwump, thwump* of the heavy bag getting kicked, a girl's voice in there too, and Daniel needs to piss now and not one minute later. He steps up to the counter. The kid takes his time looking up, and again there comes that same old feeling, that Danny has to get permission before he can do anything, even take a piss, this time from a boy with big arm muscles busting out of his T-shirt.

"Faculty?"

It's like the kid just said something to him in a secret language. The boy's got black hair and he hasn't shaved his chin and cheeks, just his throat.

"No, I need to use the bathroom."

"There's one on the second floor. Down the hall on your left."

Daniel's groin is a cloud of stinging bees, and he knows he won't make it up the stairs. A sweating boy and girl walk out of the gym door and down a hall he hadn't seen. Screwed into the concrete wall is a sign: *Men's Locker Room—Women's Locker Room*, a single arrow pointing in the same direction. "Buddy, it's an emergency. Can I just use the locker room down there?"

"You a visiting parent?"

A wave of heat passes through Daniel's head. "I'm just visiting."

The kid looks him over, and Daniel's glad he shaved this morning. He's glad he wore his good polo shirt with only the slightly frayed collar. He's glad he's still got his work glasses hanging around his neck so he looks like the harmless old bastard he is, and the kid says, "Okay. Just sign in when you come back, sir."

Sir. Another good sign. And so is this buzzing that pops free the half door Daniel is hurrying through now with his shaving kit, the radio rap louder, the smells of damp rubber mats and disinfectant and sweat. A girl's voice again, and what if his Susan's in there? What if she's exercising in there right now? He moves quickly down the narrow hallway. The walls are covered with framed glass portraits of basketball players and baseball players and soccer players, all of them bunched up in organized rows smiling into the camera. Some of them have their arms around each other's shoulders, and there's a look in their eyes like they know they'll all remember this as a good time in their lives, a good time that they earned and that promises even more good times ahead, and it's funny what comes to him now, Pee Wee Jones and him standing side by side in a row of cons in front of the Threes, the Winter Hill gang behind them, the North End Italians on one end, the Charleston crews on the other. There'd be the Panthers and the misfit loners nobody bothered with. There'd even be the strangler-of-women McGonigle standing there with his sideburns and long black hair greased back, the screws standing behind them all, the bullies and sadists like Polaski, Sills alive again, the only stand-up CO in this framed photo of extortionists and junkies and rapists and thieves, of dealers and stickup artists and onetime murderers like him, Daniel Ahearn, who, as he walks into this college locker room for young men, feels that old angry sadness rise up in him like the ringing echo of a door slammed in his face.

The first stall is open, and Daniel is pissing blood before he can even latch the door behind him. It burns too. And the hot ache in his back and legs seems to be pulled into a funnel through what he holds in his hand. On the wall is an ink drawing of a hard cock shooting seed at a spread-open pussy, and it's forty years ago and he's staring at that wall drawing in his jail cell on the beach after going after Jimmy Squeeze's brother, the way Linda hadn't followed him as the two cops muscled him along, how she just stood there and raised two fingers to her parted lips and watched him go.

She didn't love him. She was afraid of him, and he should've left her right then, but he was weak. And now he's weaker. Not just his legs. Or this sick, gut-sucking release behind his navel. But that old need is back, that heart-clutching, air-stealing, skin-tightening pull to be with the one who will love him.

Before it's too late.

Before he's gone for good.

Susan. Suzie Woo Woo. Her high, concerned voice as he sat on the couch and pretended he was crying because he couldn't find her, his hands covering his face. "I'm here, Daddy. *See?*" Her fingers touching his over his eyes and nose and mouth. "I'm *here*."

51

BOBBY'S KITCHEN walls were red. This was something Lois must have noticed last Christmas, but she didn't remember that now as she tried to catch her breath at Susan and Bobby's small table as he filled her a glass of water from the sink. When she was in their bathroom, the sun came out, though it was still raining and her hair and dress were damp and she couldn't stop shaking. Bobby set the glass in front of her. "Just a sec." He stepped into his study and came back with a light wool blanket he draped over her shoulders. She thanked him. Or maybe she only thought it, because he didn't say anything, just sat down across from her, the sun coming through his front window and shining across the top of his bald head.

He was wearing a dark blue T-shirt, and he rested the elbows of his hairy arms on the table and looked at her like he was waiting for her to start talking. If anyone else was doing this—Marianne especially—Lois would stand and leave or tell them to look some-damn-where else. But she didn't feel this way with Susan's husband. She didn't feel that way at all. Turned down low in his workroom was that crazy, messy jazz he liked so much. It sounded so out of tune to her. It sounded like a bunch of drunks playing toy instruments on a sinking ship. She shouldn't trust a man who liked to listen to this, but she did. Not since her Don had she felt this way about a man, and now she was crying again, the same helpless blubbering that had carried her to his door. She lowered her face and shook her head, and Bobby got up and tore a paper towel from its dispenser and sat back down with it, one of his hands laying itself warmly over her own. She took the paper towel and blew her nose. "She has no damn idea. No kids of her own, so she hasn't got a *clue*, Bobby. Not one."

"You should drink some water, Lois."

"What it's like. To have someone do that to your own flesh and blood. She has no idea. If she did, she wouldn't even *think* of meeting with—Jesus, I can't even say his *name*."

"She hasn't met with him yet."

A white bird rose up into Lois's head, its wings flapping. "Then where is she?"

"Picking us up some food. I called her when you were in the bathroom."

Lois cupped both hands around the glass of water. "I need to see that letter, Bobby."

"I guess that's up to Susan."

"What has she told you?"

"Everything, I believe."

"When?"

Bobby shook his head once. From his workroom came the scream-ing of a saxophone and he seemed to be listening to it as if he couldn't help himself, its ugliness beautiful to him, and Lois felt ugly sitting there across from him. Not her damp hair and lack of makeup. Not her aging sagging everything, either. No, it was the naked ugliness of her own private story, of her history as a mother who had failed her one and only daughter. The tears came again, and she pressed the paper towel to her eyes until they ached and dark mushrooms bloomed behind her eyelids.

"That must've been hell for you all, Lois. I'm so sorry it happened."

Lois took in as much air as she could. She was too warm under this blanket, but she didn't want to take it off, either. She lowered the paper towel and drank some water and set the glass back on a table that seemed far away and too close.

"Did she tell you that she was *there*? Because we think she was. We think she saw it with her own eyes."

Bobby seemed to go quiet and still with concern, and it was plain to see how much he loved his wife. "I don't think she remembers much."

"Well, *I* remember. And if she had any feelings for me whatsoever she wouldn't even *think* of seeing that murderer."

"She loves you very much, Lois."

"Bullshit." Anger opened up inside her as suddenly as an old friend shoving a baseball bat into her hands. "All she's ever loved is books. Books, books, and more fucking *books*. She doesn't even love *herself*. All those—" One boy after another after another. In Lois's head there was a parade of them, their needy eyes fixed on her Susan, losers and degenerates all. "I hope you know what you've gotten into with her, is all I can say."

"I do. I think I do." Bobby half nodded and half smiled.

"You *think*? You'd better damn well *know*, Bobby, I'll tell you that. Jesus Christ, I gave that girl all I had. You think it was easy raising her? Well, it wasn't. It sure as hell wasn't. And I never wanted to move down here. I did it for *her*. To keep her *safe*. To start over so I wouldn't—" She was crying once more, covering her face with the damp paper towel, the blanket slipping off her shoulders. That music was all drums now, the sticks banging not on the skins but on the metal edges in a rhythm Lois knew all too well, fast and uneven and everything about to tip over the edge. It was the sound of her fear coming back in full force, of her bottomless jagged regret for not protecting her Linda, as if those shattered weeks after she was taken from her were not forty years ago, and Lois wished she were sitting in her shop right now, surrounded by antique furniture and toys stacked to the ceiling, surrounded by the smells of polished chestnut and old tin and vinegar-cleaned mirror glass, her dehumidifiers gurgling quietly in the corners, Marianne dusting all these lovely things made so well they had lasted and lasted and would continue to last.

Bobby pulled the blanket back up over her shoulders. Outside a car pulled into the driveway, and the sound of its engine shutting off rode right into Lois's heart like the echo of a cry she should have heard a long, long time ago but did not. Oh, Lord, she just did *not*.

52

Lois's VW was parked just inches alongside Bobby's car, but it was so good to see it here. Susan pulled up behind it and killed her engine then hooked her laptop strap over her shoulder and reached for the pizza and salads she'd picked up on the way home. In the bathroom of the pizza shop, she'd heaved three times, but nothing had come, and now the first thing she was going to do was apologize to Lois for leaving last night like that, and as she rose out of her car and pushed the door shut with her hip, she looked up and down her street. It was empty, the sun glistening on the wet grass. She could smell marinara sauce and damp concrete, and she began to feel a little queasy again, but there was a time-slowed holiday feeling to this day, like all things routine were being suspended so that something more important could take place, maybe even something good, and her father's letter began to feel like nothing but the shred of a dream she shouldn't have told anyone about because, Jesus Christ, maybe he wasn't even coming down here at all.

On her way up the driveway she glanced into her grandmother's car. On the backseat lay a shotgun. On Noni's pocketbook in the front was an opened box of Winchester shells. At first it was like looking at things as normal as a laundry basket and a bag of groceries, but now they were a cottonmouth coiled at Susan's bare feet, the hot tines of a fork pinning her heart to her spine. *Oh, no, you don't, missy. Nope. No way.* Years of Lois with her hands on the controls, and if she couldn't control something, then she would just try to stop it cold, wouldn't she? That night when she'd pulled open Gustavo's car door and jerked Susan out by her hair, all of Noni's transgressions over the years, large and small, how she'd just shrug and say, "So what?" never taking responsibility for anything, blaming everyone but herself.

Susan yanked her screen door open. Her computer bag swung, and the pizza and salads on top of it began to tilt, but then Bobby was in the doorway and he took them from her, smiling and winking down at her, though his face changed as he took in whatever was on her face. Bobby was saying something positive about the food, setting it on the counter and reaching for plates, but Susan stood in the middle of her kitchen looking down at her grandmother looking up at her.

"You brought a fucking *shotgun* to my house, Lois? Are you out of your *mind*?"

Lois was hunched over the table, one of Bobby's throw blankets draped over her shoulders. Her hair was thin and stringy, parts of her scalp showing, and she wore no makeup, so that her eyes had a loose, hound-dog look to them, her arms just withered tubes of flesh. In front of her was a glass of water, and Noni was clutching a crumpled paper towel in her liver-spotted hands, and it was clear she'd been crying, something Susan had not seen or heard since she was a little girl. Part of what had hurled her into this house receded like a wave pulled back out to sea, but she also stood there feeling tricked somehow. Controlled in a new, maybe desperate kind of way.

"I told you I was gonna kill him."

Bobby looked at Susan, then went out the front door. From his study came the erratic wailing of Coleman's plastic saxophone, and Lois's face seemed to suck into itself, her eyes filling and spilling. She squeezed them shut and shook her head. "I can't believe you want to *see* him. After what he did to your own *mother*. How could you, Suzie? Oh, how *could* you?"

There was the muffled slam of one car door then another, the kitchen door opening, and Bobby carrying the shotgun and box of shells right past them both into his office. Lois covered her face with her hands, her blanket sliding off her bare shoulders and loose sundress. Her back had a hump in it Susan had not quite taken in before, but the skin of her shoulders looked nearly as smooth as a woman's Susan's age, the age Noni was almost exactly when it all happened, and she'd been carrying it since, carrying it and carrying it, all while raising this girl who couldn't get away from her and her shop of "fine" things fast enough. Susan's face felt funny. She was about to move closer and put her hand on Lois's heaving shoulders, but Bobby was stepping back into the kitchen now. He'd turned the music off, and the only sounds were Noni sniffling and blowing her nose and saying, "I need a damn cigarette."

53

DANIEL HEARS a shower running nearby and then he's taking off his shoes and clothes behind a curtain with jumping dolphins on it. Voices now through the pounding spray. Young men. Just vibrations through the air as Daniel cleanses himself, rinsing all the soap down the drain at his feet and turning off the water. Steam rises off his skin. It feels tight and warm, and it matches the ache in his back and hips.

A towel. He didn't think of that. From the locker room come the voices of the young men, two or three of them, and one of them is laughing. "You are so fuckin' *gay*, Peterson."

"Yeah? That chick wants me bad."

There's more talk, and Daniel ignores it and jerks open the curtain and walks naked to the sinks. He's looking for paper towels to use, but there are none, just a bank of electric hand dryers set into the wall, and he presses the big button of the one closest to him and the machine starts up and he squats and leans back so the hot air blows across his chest and belly, his penis and upper legs. He turns and lets it hit his lower back and rear, and he feels like a fool. Like an unprepared and sick old fool.

One of the boys walks in. He's wearing only shorts, his stomach muscles showing, and he glances over at Daniel like he sees this kind of thing every day when he'd rather not. Then another boy walks in, and the machine shuts off and Daniel is crossing the floor half wet and the kid steps to the side like Daniel's the bull and he's the matador.

Back in his stall he pulls on his boxers and khakis, the material sticking to his damp legs. He pats his front pocket for his cash and pulls his shirt over his head, then grabs his shaving kit and heads for the sinks where the two boys are. The one closest to Daniel is running gel through his short hair and spiking it up in the front with two fingers. These young men are lean and have muscles, and it's hard not to think of what would happen to them both inside. Daniel pulls out his razor and shaving cream. Words come out of him he hadn't planned on. "You two know where I can find Professor Dunn?"

"What's he teach?"

It's the one closest to him, pulling his hair up into a point before he levels it off with his hand and tries again.

"She. English."

"I've never had her; you, Eric?"

"I'm an engineer. We don't do English."

"Sorry, man. That department's over in Seibert Hall, though."

"Where's that?" Daniel is combing back his hair. Standing in front of the mirror beside these two, he feels like a troll from some far-off woods and a time they've never even heard of.

"Just across the quad, man." The kid hooks his head to the right. "Fifty yards that way. You'll see it."

Daniel nods. He wants to say thank you, but it's like the kid just flicked his finger into Daniel's heart. Fifty yards. One hundred and fifty feet. It was the distance between the Norfolk auditorium and the shop. He can be over to that hall in minutes. Forty years, and now he can be there in minutes. But he's not ready. He needs to buy better clothes. He needs to—

What? Think of what to *say*?

Yes.

Daniel pats shaving cream onto his face. He runs the razor under the water, but his hand is shaking like some kid's, and what if he nicks himself? What if she sees him after all this time with blood on his face?

His hand and arm the last time he saw her, it was splattered with it. And she was three. Three years old. Lying beside him with her cheek to his chest. And now here he is, and he's not ready.

Daniel runs the water hot and cups it in his two hands and starts splashing the shaving cream off his face.

54

L OIS LAY on the love seat in her granddaughter's office covered by a light blanket, her shoes off, Susan and Bobby talking quietly out in the kitchen. From where she lay she could see the desk where Susan did her work, and it was surprisingly neat. There was a clear plastic box of paper clips, a jar of pens and pencils. There was a ripped-open package of printing paper next to a coffee mug next to a short stack of hardcover and paperback books. On top of them was a box of tissues, one sticking out of the slit like a white tongue, and on the wall hung a painting of nothing recognizable, just brushstrokes of red and black that Lois couldn't look at for too long because she began to feel she was falling somewhere dangerous. She closed her eyes and took a deep breath and tried to rest.

It had felt good to cry. Damn good. And now she felt the same kind of sweet-tired she'd feel after making love so very long ago, as if her heart and lungs and various organs had been gently cleaned with a warm, wet cloth by a caring hand. Why had she kept it so bottled up all this time? But that was a stupid question, she knew. Even when Don died, she hadn't shed but a few drops at his graveside up in Ocala. She missed him, yes, and she'd thought they'd have more time, but even for him she couldn't go down that road of tears again, for it was a road that went on and on and took you to nothing but burning eyes and a chapped nose and the endless echo of her pitiful sounds nobody seemed to hear or care about.

Except for little Suzie. She'd bring her grandmother tissues. She'd curl up next to her on the bed and lay her head on her chest. She'd say, "Don't be sad, Noni. It's okay. It's okay."

Lois wondered if Susan could recall any of that time. And when she thought of her childhood home, what did she see in her head? Their old apartment behind the arcade she'd lived in till she was twelve? Or was it the one before that? The Ocean Mist that her mother had worked so hard to make into a loving nest? Linda had her husband and new father-in-law, the wordless "Magic Mick," paint her walls white, and she sewed and hung white curtains from every window. She placed pretty objects on sills and shelves throughout the place, and she kept the windows open all summer long to let in the sea breeze.

Or when Suzie thought of home, did she think of their house in the woods near the river off the county road? Lois hoped that's what she thought of. It's the one where her grandmother had stopped her crying, after all. But that's when the yelling had started, too, though how could that be helped when Suzie began to buck her the way she did? *I was just trying to protect you!* Was that what Lois had yelled through her blubbering just thirty minutes ago?

"You can't control everything, Lois. You've always been like this."

The three of them were sitting at the table, Bobby eating his pizza slice while Susan picked at her salad and Lois sat back and smoked. It had calmed her for just a moment, but then Suzie began laying into her again about bringing a loaded shotgun to her house, and Lois had felt her outrage rise in her once more, though everything she said now felt old, old, old, and yet just as new as her next breath. "It isn't loaded, but it damn well will be."

"Great, Noni." Susan had stood. Her jeans were a bit too loose on her, and she wasn't wearing a bra, and her short dark hair stuck up in the back like she'd just fallen out of bed. She tossed her napkin onto her plate. "Then I lose you, too." She left the room then. Bobby smiled sadly at Lois and began to fork salad into his mouth. *Lose you, too.* This part hadn't even occurred to Lois, that Suzie would be thinking such a thing. She sat there feeling dim and a little selfish and, yes, grateful to hear it, but she almost started to blubber again, and she'd stood herself and said, "I need to lie down somewhere, Bobby. I need rest."

Out in the kitchen Susan and her husband were quietly talking. Every half minute or so Suzie's voice rose a bit and Lois could only make out a word or two. "*No, Bobby . . . she's **always** . . . so what am I supposed to . . . a fucking **gun**?*" And her tone was the same one she'd had as a teenager whenever Lois would lay down the law about a curfew and who she could or could not see, her granddaughter's voice high and pissed off just like now. It made Lois feel as if people never changed at all, and, well, that's because they don't.

Then came "*my father.*" It was like a hand closing around Lois's throat. It had been years and years since Susan had uttered those two words in front of her, and Lois sure as hell did not like the tone she heard now, like Danny Ahearn was somebody Lois had withheld from Susan and she had no right to do it and now Lois was jerking the blanket off her and sitting up, her head heavy, her legs swinging off the cushions. "I can *hear* you out there! If you have something to say, Susan, I'll thank you to say it to my *face.*"

She'd sat up too fast and Susan's office became cloudy, Lois's heart a fist punching her own ribs. Then Bobby was walking in. He was just a bald head and long arms before his face came into focus, warm and concerned, and he looked like he was about to say something when Susan stepped past him into the room. "Why can't you see this from *my* point of view, Lois?"

"That's all I've ever done your whole life, missy."

"What?"

"Yes. You bet I have. The whole damn time. You think a single *day* has gone by I haven't thought about it?"

"*It?* What about *me?* I might not even want to go see him at all, I don't know. I just want the right to fucking *think* about it without worrying about you aiming one of your fucking guns at somebody. Jesus *Christ.*" Susan turned and brushed by Bobby and disappeared down the hall. There was the slamming of her bedroom door, then Bobby pulling his wife's chair from under her desk and sitting in it so he faced Lois. He crossed his long legs and said, "I don't blame you for wanting to kill him, Lois."

Her headache was back. It was like a tight band being stretched across the front of her brain. And she was sitting on the edge of the love seat, but it was as if she were being pressed back into it, and when she took a deep breath, there was nothing deep about it.

55

FROM THE second-floor balcony of Daniel's room in La Habana Inn, he can see out over the street to the wet sand of St. Pete Beach and the Gulf of Mexico, the late afternoon sun shining so brightly off it he needs the sunglasses he'd left in his truck. He'd parked it up against the opposite sidewalk between a camper and an imported sedan, and beyond them are tall palm trees and an outdoor tiki bar, its thatched roof woven tightly and looking new. Out in front of it are tables under wide umbrellas he can see only the tops of, though he can hear the music playing out there, a man's voice singing over his guitar about his Chevy and a levee, and it's starting to bring Daniel back and he doesn't want to go back. There's a festive bite in the air, the feeling that where he's ended up is a place reserved for good times only, so he steps back into his room and pulls the slider shut, but now he's sun-blind, his small room floating shadows. On his way up the stairs with his key and duffel bag, he'd passed a mounted blue swordfish over a doorway that read *Business Office*, and after buying some new clothes, he's going to pick up the phone book in that office and start looking.

He isn't going back to her school. This was something he felt as he took a left at the main road just past the security shack. It was all wrong going there first. And not just for him because he hadn't been ready, but for her. What if he had walked into her building and knocked on her door and she didn't want to see him? She'd have to show that in front of the people she worked with. She'd have to be part of something ugly where she worked. And part of him feels like he came down here for him and him only. How is her seeing him going to be good for *her*?

He doesn't know.

And now he's out on the sidewalk and in the smells of the Gulf of Mexico—seabird shit and dried seaweed and oil from some far-off rig—and he doesn't remember walking past the little man behind the inn's desk, though his voice is in Daniel's head, "Enjoy your evening, sir." And the hazy sun is still three feet above the horizon, and Daniel's about to walk across the street to his Tacoma for his sunglasses, but they're cheap and don't do much good and at the corner, under a second-floor pub gallery where men and women are drinking and laughing and talking, there is a clothing boutique and the mannequin in the front window is wearing dark sunglasses and a straw hat, and Daniel heads in that direction, the musician near the beach singing how this will be the day that he'll die.

Daniel knows the song, but there's no sadness in him hearing those words, just a promise to himself to do it well when the time comes. For everybody's time comes, and yes, he feels light-limbed and weak as a boy and all he pisses now is blood, but he's beginning to make friends with the bone-ache in his back and hips and legs, and right now he has laughter above him and the hot sea air on his skin and a thick wad of cash still in his front pocket as he walks into a shop called Vintage Joe's.

Inside, a different music is playing. It's classical and it's the cello. The place smells like rolled cigars and washed linen, and there are racks of brightly colored Bermuda shirts, shelves of folded pants—brown, gray, blue—and there's a whole wall of suit jackets under a dim gold light so they seem like the finest a man could wear. And he's owned only one. The suit his mother and Liam bought for him for court. He wore it every day he needed it, and after he was sentenced and Linda's little brother pointed his finger at him like he was shooting him in the face, Daniel wore it straight to lockup, though fifteen years later, the day he was released from Norfolk, he did not want to be wearing that same suit when his mother picked him up. He called her and told her to bring him some of his old work clothes, and she did, and Daniel told one of the processing screws to give that suit to any con who might need it for a hearing. When his mother died all those years later it was a cold afternoon with patches of snow still on the ground, and for the service Daniel had ironed his best shirt and bought a black tie and a new wool sweater and wore those. But never a jacket again. Almost sixty-four, and he's never owned a jacket for the good times.

Over the cello a woman has been talking to him. And not from behind the glass counter where there are rows of sunglasses and other shiny things Daniel can't make out. She's standing three feet away, and she's lovely the way fifty-year-old women are lovely, like they know their beautiful time has come and gone and now they can just be who they really were all along. This one is warm and just a little heavy, her brown hair gray at the roots. Daniel wants to apologize for not hearing her, but he says, "I don't know."

"I do." She smiles. "Forty-two regular, I'd say. Here—" She reaches past him and holds a light green suit jacket up against his chest. "It's a Joseph Abboud. Summer-weight. Try it on." She holds it out for him to put his arms into, and he does, one arm at a time. She pulls up on his collar and pats his shoulders, smoothing her hand down along his back and away, and his eyes begin to fill, the cello rising and falling in the air like time bending here in front of him, this woman guiding him to a full-length mirror under a display of straw hats. Looking at himself in this new sports coat over his cleanest work shirt and khaki pants, it's like seeing an old house with half its siding torn off and only one section of new siding nailed up. But he likes how the jacket fits him, how it makes him look like he's maybe read a few books and has money in the bank, that he's a man of leisure, a hardworking citizen whose work is done.

The woman's hand is back on his shoulder. It's light, and it's heavy, and he doesn't want to move.

"That's a good color for you. Can I find you some pants to go with that?"

"Yes."

She steps back and looks down at his waist. "Thirty-six?"

"I don't know." But he does know. Once a year he drives up to the Walmart in Seabrook and buys what he needs, and the pants are always the same, 36–32. For years they've been that. His habits in concrete. His habits in steel. But why doesn't he tell her she's right?

Because he wants her to pull out that measuring ribbon she's pulling out now. He wants her to have to tell him to lift his arms up so she can step this close to him and get her tape around him and he can smell her hair—the warm skin of her scalp, the word *gardenias* in his head—then the ribbon falling away and she's saying she was right. "Thirty-two for the length?"

"Yes."

And as she flips through the folded pants on the shelf he sees her wedding ring, a dull old diamond, and he's Danny again driving down to Port City with five hundred dollars to spend and he spent all of it on the tiniest diamond in the shop, though when he slid it on Linda's finger in that office of the justice of the peace she smiled down at it like it was as good a ring as she'd ever seen, and when they got outside on those granite steps she turned it in the sunlight and said, "Look, it *sparkles*."

"These work." The woman holds a pair of lighter green pants to his waist. Her knuckles touch his belt and gut, and the cello swings lower now, dipping into notes that sound to him like a very old hunger that's never gone away. This woman. Her caring for him, like his mother making him a second breakfast after he'd gotten kicked out of school, his mother sitting close beside him in her housecoat while he read to her from *Enemy Ace* and Danny's favorite character, "The Hammer of Hell."

"Go try these on in the fitting room. I'll find you a shirt to go with it."

The fitting room is just a dark corner of the store behind one of those Japanese screens, each panel covered with pictures of women in geisha robes and men in cone-shaped hats. These new pants feel like light silk against his legs, the waist a bit loose, but he has his old belt, and now a shirt flops over the top of the screen. "Try this one." It's the color of cream with tiny palm trees the same color all over it, and it fits better than the pants, and when Daniel walks out from behind the screen wearing the jacket too, the woman smiles at him and says, "Very distinguished." And he can tell she means it, though her eyes have moved to his scuffed and untied work shoes, and she shakes her head. "Oh, dear, you'll need alligator-skin with that ensemble. Do you own any?"

"No."

"How about a belt? I have just the thing." She turns and leads him to the glass counter and pulls a shiny brown belt off a standing rack beside it. Daniel takes it from her and works it through the belt loops of his new pants. Doing this, he can see the scuffed toes of his work shoes, and he knows she's right about them, but again, there comes the feeling that he's overdoing it, that it's one thing to present himself well to his daughter, but it's another thing if he looks too good.

Like he's done just fine for himself without her.

Which he has not. No, he has not.

"No?"

Daniel's face warms and he pulls the new belt out of the loops and hands it back to her. "I'll just take the clothes."

"You sure?" She's smiling at him again, but it's a slightly teasing smile, as if she's known him longer than she has and she's earned to right to do this when she hasn't.

"Just the clothes." Daniel turns and walks back to the "fitting room." He didn't come in here for clothes like these. Just some new khakis and a polo. Maybe a new pair of work shoes.

The music is different now. When did that happen? It's some jazz singer, a black woman's voice singing slow and long about a gentleman she used to know. Behind her voice are the tinkling of bar glasses, a man coughing, Daniel probably a small boy when this woman sang this song. The war had been over for a few years, and Liam Ahearn had stayed in the Navy and was painting planes at the Lakehurst hangars in New Jersey, the same field where that massive blimp exploded before the war, Daniel's mother saying, "I was a little girl then, Danny, but I remember it. Nobody can tell me I don't. It lit up the whole sky. The whole sky, Danny."

Liam, the quiet sailor who'd maybe seen and done things in that war he'd never told his son. But the way he looked at Danny the last time Danny wore a suit, Liam was hunched in his courtroom seat beside Danny's mother, and he was dressed in a white shirt and a short black tie, and he was looking at Danny like he'd never seen him before but also like he reminded him of other men and they were no damned good.

Daniel carries the clothes over his arm to the woman. She's standing behind the counter now. The light from the display case puts her face in a strange shadow so that she doesn't seem so warm anymore. He sets the pants, shirt, and jacket onto the glass. Under it, lined up on a shiny white material, are pairs of gold-rimmed sunglasses, their leather cases open beside them, and he points to a dark pair of aviators, the kind Will Price used to wear. "I'll take those."

"The Ray-Bans?"

"Yeah."

Daniel will do that much, but not this suit. Did he forget who he *was*?

She hands him the new sunglasses, and she's smiling again. "Are you here for business?"

"No. Yeah."

She laughs. "You don't know which. That's a good sign. You must love what you do."

Soaking a coil of fresh cane in a bucket in his small yard under the sun. Working it through caning holes a dead man had hand-drilled over a hundred years ago. Weaving each strand with his needle-nose and fingers till the pattern looks like an artist had done it and it has just the right give and bounce. Yeah, he enjoys his work, he does, but now the woman puts on a pair of red reading glasses and is flipping over the tag on the jacket's sleeve and writing the price on a sales slip. He reaches over and touches her wrist. She jumps just a bit, and he pulls his hand back and wants to apologize. "Just the sunglasses."

"Really?" She looks at him through her reading glasses, and she's just used the surprised, slightly concerned tone one friend would with another. It's a tone Daniel has overheard in diners and restaurants for years but rarely, if ever, has had it directed at him.

"I just came in for these." He holds out the sunglasses he hasn't tried on yet.

"You do know that those cost more than your entire outfit." She smiles as she says this, and he just stares at her. Behind her reading glasses, her eyes look big and kind. "This is a consignment shop."

He looks down at that "summer-weight" jacket, the silk pants and shirt beneath it. "These're used?"

"We like to say pre-owned. But, you know, by the kind of men who can afford to wear them just once or twice before they toss them out like paper plates. I mean, look at this." She leans close to the price tag tied to the sleeve button of the jacket. "Seventy-five dollars. This would easily cost you four or five hundred new. You do what you want, of course. They just fit you so well, is all."

Again, that smile. Like they've both known each other for a very long time, like she knows all he's done but that was so long ago, and why not own some good clothes for good times?

"I'll take 'em."

"Oh, good. And do you still want the Ray-Bans?"

He nods and hands them back to her. On the shelf below the sunglasses are a row of money clips—some silver, one with a turquoise stone in the center, some gold, one black steel with tiny red stars glued around its edges. Will Price always carried a money clip too, and Daniel hasn't seen or thought of one since. Price paid them all in cash, and he'd pull it out of his front pants pocket, the bills folded and held together by a diamond-studded clip, and then Price would flick out the bills like perfectly placed words that never came easily to Danny, only the ones he was given to say up in the booth of the Himalaya when he was "The Sound." And if he could go to his daughter now wearing the red blazer and white shirt and pants that had made him somebody on the strip, he would. She'd see what her mother had seen. A man who had been going places. A man who, if things hadn't gone the way they had, might have become a Will Price himself.

"Would you like one of those, too?"

"Yeah. The silver one."

"With the turquoise?"

"Yes. Thank you."

"You're welcome . . ." She turns her head at him and draws that last word out, smiling, waiting to hear his name.

"Danny. I mean—Daniel."

"Karen. It's been a pleasure."

Daniel nods, his face a hot mask as she hands him the money clip and he reaches into his pants for his cash. But as he pulls it out it's clear the wad is too thick for that clip and now half his cash slips out from his hand onto the glass counter, over thirty hundreds, a few tens and ones, and there's the naked shamed feeling he just showed her something he shouldn't have.

"My, my, did you rob a bank?"

"No." Again the hot face.

"Of course not." She laughs lightly and begins to fold and bag his new old clothes. A lone trumpet is slicing through all the low bar noise from that club so long ago, and Daniel wants to tell this Karen that he'd earned each and every penny of every dollar on her counter, that he's never stolen from anyone. Not ever. And inside, all those falls and winters and springs and summers, over and over again for fifteen cycles of them, he'd never understood the cons who'd planned their wrongdoings—the Bunker Hill boys with their banks, the men from the North End and Winter Hill and Providence, guys who'd laid out in advance just who they were going to hurt and how and when.

But not Danny Ahearn. It was one reason he'd liked Pee Wee Jones so much, because they'd both gotten locked up from falling into one bad moment they never wanted to come in the first place. But it had. It sure as hell had.

Daniel gathers up a dozen of the hundreds and folds them into his new turquoise and silver money clip. He asks Karen if she's rung it up already, and she says she has, and he slips it into his pocket then picks up and straightens out the rest of the cash. The front door opens. Daniel turns and sees a man and woman, his age or older. The man's holding the door for his wife, two paper shopping bags hanging by their handles from his hand, and he's tanned and the little hair he has left is combed over his head sideways, his gut pushing against a maroon T-shirt with a setting sun in the center of his chest. His wife has let her hair go nearly white, but it's styled around her pretty round face, and her eyes take in the rack of Bermuda shirts. "Oh, honey, *look*. You'll find one here. You'll definitely find one *here*."

The man smiles, his eyes passing over the shirt rack and landing on Daniel, nodding at him like they're both in this together—wives and keeping them happy, even if it means buying and wearing a shirt you don't really want or need. You know, *wives*.

PART

FIVE

56

SUSAN SAT on the edge of her mattress, her fingers spread over a loosening knot of nausea she could no longer deny. Her mouth began to fill with saliva and there was an upward roiling and then she was rushing into the bathroom, the door slamming behind her as she dropped to her knees and hot shame heaved out of her into the toilet. The sperm and the egg. Her father and her mother. There was no cutting herself from either of them and she'd hardly even known them and now she was spitting into her toilet and why had she been so careless?

A knocking, Bobby's muffled voice. "You all right?" The door opened behind her, and Bobby's big hand cupped her forehead. She pulled away. "I'm all right."

"Think it was something you ate?"

"Maybe."

"Lois wants to leave, but I don't think she should drive."

Susan spat. The smell of her insides stung her nose, everything about her foul, really. Noni's pinched face in the kitchen looking up at her. *How could you, Susan? Oh, how **could** you?*

"I'll drive her."

"I can do that, baby."

"No, Bobby. I want to. Just follow us so I can come back *home*." Her throat closed up on that last word, though Bobby didn't seem to notice and he squeezed her shoulder and said, "I'll walk her out. You sure you're all right?"

"I'm fine, Bobby. Really, honey, I'm fine."

57

THE LITTLE man at the inn had helped, and it was good Daniel had come down the stairs in his new used suit and silk shirt because when he asked if the phone book was in the Business Office, the man behind the shiny oak counter took in Daniel with more respect than he had earlier, and he said, "We have no telephone book, Mr. Ahearn, but I'm more than happy to help you." He began tapping his keyboard and asked Daniel for the town and the name of the person he was looking for.

"St. Petersburg. Susan Dunn." Daniel felt as if he were telling a secret he should be keeping to himself.

"I see many possibilities. Do you know her age?"

"Forty-three."

Forty-three this past May 5. Daniel had the flu that day, and he spent it lying in bed in his trailer instead of working. Not a May 5 had come and gone without Daniel thinking about it, feeling her out there somewhere. And Linda liked to bake cakes. She liked to buy those tubes of frosting at the IGA. *Happy Birthday, my little Suzie Woo Woo!*

"Susan and Robert Dunn?"

"I don't know."

"This is the only listing with that age range for a Susan Dunn, Mr. Ahearn. Shall I print it out?"

"Is it in St. Petersburg?"

"Oh, yes. Do you know where Eckerd College is?"

DANIEL DRIVES slowly down his daughter's street, his old heart pumping an echo he can feel in his newly shaved face. His jacket's shoulders are bunched up at his collar, and he glances back down at the La Habana Inn slip of paper on his lap.

Susan and Robert Dunn,
137 Osprey Lane, St. Petersburg, Florida.

All the odd-numbered houses are on the left so that's where hers will be, too—133, 135. He's cruising as slowly as a cop, and he's afraid this will draw too much attention, but the next house has to be it. It's a one-story stucco the color of an artichoke, and his tongue and mouth turn to sawdust. There's a gray Honda parked in the driveway. *Hers?* For a heartbeat he sees her standing in the middle of their TV room in shorts with flowers on them, her shirt with a frilly lace hem. She's laughing at something he'd just said or done, and he would've taught her to drive. He would have done that. And then he's beginning to pass in front of that car and that house, and he eases off the gas and squints out at the black metal letters screwed in at an angle on the trim beside the front door: 137. The windows are small, most of them with light curtains, and his blood quickens and he accelerates to the stop sign at the end of her street.

The lanes in front of him are busy now with worker-bee traffic coming and going in both directions. There's a buzzing in his fingers and toes, and he can see her college campus right there on the other side, the pines and the oaks and the open guard shack he'd driven by twice. He looks in his side-view mirror but can only make out the end of her driveway and a patch of grass. *Is* that her Honda in the driveway? Her husband's?

A white SUV pulls up behind him. There's a blonde driving it. Her shoulders are bare, and she's tapping the wheel with two fingers and not like she's listening to music, and so he takes a right into a gap in the traffic and thinks of the married women of Port City, all those well-put-together lawyers and teachers and mothers and their busy,

busy lives. Susan's probably just like them, and he needs to call her first. He knows where she lives, but now he needs to call her.

Cars pass him on the left. He looks down at Susan's picture taped to the dash. He needs to find a phone. The sun is in a low haze, but his eyes don't hurt glancing directly at it, these sunglasses the finest things he's ever owned. On both sides of the road are golf courses in a blue-green light, men in white carts and white pants driving from one hole to the next, or standing on the grass with other men waiting for one of them to swing his club at the ball.

Back at St. Pete Beach, on his walk back to his room, he passed one couple after another, and then he watched five or six ladies leaving the outdoor tiki bar, laughing. One of them lit up a cigarette while another took their picture with her phone. They were all older than he was, or looked it, and he'd thought then that they were divorced or were widows, but now he thinks, no, they've played their own golf for the day and their men are still playing and, later, they're all going to get together for drinks and dinner, and what a strange and beautiful place this is. Like some heaven they'd earned for themselves, but they can feel the clock ticking so the plan is to squeeze as much pleasure from each minute as they can get away with.

Up ahead is the Pinellas Bayway tollbooth back to the beach. Daniel slows and hands the smiling operator a dollar. He's wearing a half-buttoned Hawaiian shirt, and he takes in Daniel with a warm nod, like he's seen him every day like this for many years. He slaps the dollar into his drawer then drops a quarter into Daniel's cupped hand. "You have yourself a fabulous night."

Now he feels foolish in this suit, and again, yet one more time, there comes the itch to just turn north and drive back home. He now knows where his daughter lives. He's seen where she works. And he has this printed-out photograph of her he can print out again new whenever he wants to. His little girl has done just fine—very fine, really—without him, and why mess with that now? What he should do is head back to his inn and use those Business Office computers to make out his own will. He can just put in her address and type up the rest then head home to find someone to execute it for him.

But he's here. He's *here*.

And so is the searing ache in his hips and legs that seems to be lodged in his lower gut now too. What he needs to do, more than anything, is find a toilet, and as the bridge slopes down to the intersection of what he's learned is Gulf Boulevard, he sees off to the left a towering grand hotel the color of pink roses, and what a look he gets from the young valet in white as Daniel pulls his old red pickup under the domed archway and steps out and hands him the keys. The kid is taking in Daniel in his new suit, but he's taking in his truck, too, his eyes dropping to Daniel's work boots.

"Are you a guest, sir?"

Ruthless gravity is weighing on Daniel's groin. "Nope. I won't be long." He turns and starts walking for the hotel's tall glass doors.

"Sir, I need to give you a ticket."

Daniel tells him he'll be right back, and then he steps into the hotel's lobby, and it's like stepping back into a time of high-class living that raged brightly years before he was born. Stretching out before him is a shining marble floor that catches the gold light of the crystal chandeliers hanging high above, the ceiling held up by columns all the way to windows looking out over the gray gulf. There's music playing, the soft rising and falling strings of a harp, and off to the right is a sitting area of deep sofas and chairs and a young woman in a black dress is sitting at that harp, her fingers moving along the strings like a butterfly flitting from one blade of grass to another. There's low talk and high laughter and a sharp pinch in his abdomen, and he sees a men's room between two palm trees in mahogany planters, then he's inside that men's room, standing at a urinal enclosed by slabs of polished gray marble.

He stares at a white vein in the stone and waits. He closes his eyes and hears whistling. It's the bathroom attendant, a black man in a white shirt and red bow tie he passed on the way in but ignored. The tune the man's whistling has to be his own. It's a cheerful one and Daniel shakes his head at any good cheer coming from a job like this. Even he has never worked at a job this low, and as a hot dribble comes out of him, then another, he feels bad about rushing right by that man without so much as a nod.

He pisses and waits. Pisses and waits. His limbs feel light and heavy, hollow and packed with dust. He should drink something. He should eat something.

But he should call her first, shouldn't he? "I don't know."

"Me, either, sir. Lord, I sure *don't*." The bathroom attendant laughs, and then Daniel is shaking himself off and stepping away without looking at what he's left behind, the urinal flushing on its own. The attendant turns on the sink faucet for him. A white towel is folded over his arm.

"And how are we today, sir?" He is bald, the brown skin of his head and face smooth, but the whites of his eyes have yellowed and Daniel can see he's an old man, a much older man than he is, and look how he's spending his last days.

"Good."

The attendant smiles as widely as if Daniel has just told him a long story that ends well for everybody. "That is fine, sir. That is fine indeed."

The man offers Daniel soap from a silver dispenser. Daniel holds out his two cupped hands and receives it then scrubs. In the mirror is a well-dressed man wearing dark sunglasses. In the mirror is Will Price, and Daniel says, "I need a phone."

"Yes, sir. They got one in the lobby bar. Been there since they built this palace."

"When was that?"

"Oh, 1925. When I was two years old." He smiles and shakes his head then reaches in front of Daniel to turn off the sink, placing the folded towel in his wet hands.

"So you're—what? Almost ninety?"

"Oh, no, sir. I'm still in my short pants." He laughs, this time harder. He pulls out a thin narrow comb and Daniel hands him back the towel then takes the comb and pulls it through whatever hair he has left. "You got kids?"

"Five that I know of." He shakes his head again and takes back the comb then holds out to Daniel a small glass spray bottle, the old attendant's index finger on the button. "Aftershave, sir?"

Daniel nods and offers his hands palms-up then slaps his face with a stinging liquid that smells like some garden at night in a faraway place. He wants to ask this old man about his kids. If they live nearby. If he sees them. He wants to ask what they think of him working all dressed up in a shitter. When at his age he should be—what?

"I'm just pulling your leg, sir. I been with the same woman for sixty-eight years. Imagine that. Sixty-eight years." He laughs and hands Daniel a wrapped breath mint. Daniel just looks at him, but it's like looking at something good and private he's got no right to look at, and he reaches into his left pocket and pulls out his money clip and takes out a C-note he drops onto the ones and fives in a glass jar beneath the mirror.

"No, sir. I can't take that. No, sir."

"Yes you can." Daniel unwraps the mint and places it onto his tongue, its sharp sweetness a scolding and a blessing as he walks back out into the grand lobby in search of the bar and its very old phone.

58

SITTING IN the passenger's seat of her own moving car, Lois stared out at fields of palmetto scrub under a sky the color of urine. Susan had tuned the radio to a news station, the kind at the lower end of

FM where all the broadcasters sounded like college professors, and Lois never listened to it because she felt talked down to, but it was better than sitting in this quiet car because neither of them had said one word to the other since St. Petersburg. It was Lois who got in the last one. "If you won't think of me, then think of your *mother*, Susan. Think about her."

No, it was Susan, because she said, "I can't believe you just said that." She shook her head, her eyes on the road, and she looked like she was going to say more, but she did not. Now the air had grown thick and still. In her side-view mirror, Lois could see Bobby's black Kia following them, Susan's husband sitting so tall behind the wheel. It was Lois's idea to go back home, but being driven and escorted like this made her feel like a child who'd broken the rules, and there was another feeling too, that what she'd worked so hard for since she was a young woman was slipping away, that Susan would do just what she wanted to whether Lois liked it or not, and you know what? So be it. Lois was too damned old and too damned tired to fight any longer. So damn be it.

"I give up."

"What?" The radio broadcaster was saying something about Syria. Susan turned him down. "What did you say, Lois?"

"So now I'm Lois. When I'm not trying to 'control' you, I'm Noni, but the rest of the time I'm Lois. Nice. I said I give up."

Susan glanced over at her. In the late afternoon light, after this day of rain and sun, Susan's skin looked sallow, and Lois almost wanted to take back what she just said. The man on the radio said *ISIS*, and Susan turned him off. "Give up *what*?"

"Worrying about you, that's what. What do you *think*?"

That came out harder than Lois meant it to. She looked straight ahead at the rushing hot-top road that led back to her old town and old shop full of old things. She hoped Marianne would still be there. She wanted to apologize to her for having been so short with her at the hospital, and she hoped Marianne would be up for a drink and a bite somewhere because Lois needed to talk. She needed to tell her that the murderer of her child had sent her granddaughter a letter. That he was coming to see her.

"It hasn't always felt like that, you know." Susan said this with her eyes on the road, both hands on the wheel. Lois was about to ask her how the hell she would know what *her* worrying felt like, but Susan said, "I've always felt like part of you hated me, Noni."

"Oh, Jesus, Mary, and Joseph—"

"No, it's true. And then when you told me about my parents everything started to make sense to me."

"How can you even say that?"

Susan looked over at her. Her eyes were dark, and her lips were parted like whatever she was about to say next was coming to her right now, and she was being made small and quiet in the face of it. "Because half of me came from him."

Lois's cheeks began to burn. She had to look back out at the fields. In the distance a lone white farmhouse was surrounded by five or six live oaks, Spanish moss hanging from their branches like a lingering sickness that would never go away. Lois made herself swallow. She made herself turn to her granddaughter and say, "If you don't know what I feel for you, then I don't even *know* what." But Lois felt like part of her was holding something back, that part of her was lying.

"See? You can't even say it, Noni. Because you know I'm right."

"Oh, yes, Suzie, you're always right, aren't you? Miss High-and-Mighty reading all her damn *books*. Miss College *Professor.* You're the smart one, aren't you? I'm just the old woman who gave you her entire *life*. Pull over, I want to drive with Bobby."

"What?"

"You heard me, Susan. Pull over right this damn *minute*."

Her granddaughter stared at her like she was a crazy woman, and maybe she was, but she was not going to sit in her own car any longer being told what she did and did not feel.

"Fine." Susan drove onto the gravel too fast, small rocks pinging under Lois's car like bullets.

59

"YOU'VE REACHED the Dunns. Leave a message. Thanks."

It is the voice of a woman Daniel does not know but does know, and it leaves him staring at the raised panel of polished walnut in front of his face. It took him a while to call that number, and he's sitting on a corner seat upholstered in red leather. He can't see through the frosted panes of the booth's bifold door but he can hear the bar voices out there, two men laughing, a woman trying to talk over it. There are no more harp strings here but jazz again, the kind that had been playing in the clothes shop where he'd bought this suit and these sunglasses sitting now on top of his head.

He's still holding the gold-plated receiver to his ear, and there comes a long high beep that leaves a ringing through his head he knows he's supposed to speak into. He hangs up. On the phone's shelf is a pad of hotel stationery beside an engraved pen in its black holder. He'd taken it out to write down the number the 411 operator had given him, and now he slips on his work glasses and reads it again, pushes in another quarter, and dials, no buttons, the rotary swinging back slowly after he pulls his thick finger from each of its old numbered holes. And it brings him back. It brings him back to standing in his own kitchen and dialing, his little daughter standing down there to his left. His head is air. His mouth tastes like something poisonous. This woman's voice on the machine, it cannot be his Linda but it is, and now here it comes again: "You've reached the Dunns. Leave a message. Thanks."

His breath sits still in his chest. It's that same take-me-or-leave-me, I-don't-care tone. Like when she told him under the sun at the Broadway Flying Horses that she was pregnant. "You gonna raise it with me or not?"

A long loud beep in Daniel's brain. And he didn't raise it with her. He did not, though he would have. This silence after the beep is a black pit of nothing he must step into or things will never be right. They can never— "This is, this is Daniel Ahearn, your—I'm here now. That's all. I'm here." He should say more. There is so much more he should say.

60

SUSAN FOLLOWED her husband's car into the small gravel parking lot behind Lois's shop. It had to be after five, and there Marianne stood under the fire escape locking up the back door. She wore a pressed blouse and skirt, and she turned at the sound of both cars and looked tired until she saw Lois's VW. She smiled and waved but appeared confused when Susan waved back. Then she seemed to see Lois sitting next to Bobby in his Kia, and Marianne stood there and waited, her purse and keys in one hand, her other smoothing her skirt.

Lois's door opened first. She grasped Bobby's roof and pulled herself up and out, her eyes on Susan for only a moment before she turned and jerked out her pocketbook and slammed the door and marched behind Bobby's car to her only friend and employee. Bobby was out now too. He glanced over at Susan and raised his eyebrows, smiling sideways at her the way he did in the face of the indecipherable, which was what he believed life was anyway and *baby, just accept it and ride it out and don't try to shape it too much.*

She felt queasy again. Following Bobby's car down Pinellas, she'd looked for Gustavo's old house, but it was gone. A swirl of ragged heat was gathering in her belly, and she needed a cold Coke.

*You're the smart one, aren't you? I'm just the old woman who gave you her entire **life**.*

And what did *he* do? Her "father"?

Did she really need to see him enough to hurt Noni this much?

Now Lois was whisking her hand at Marianne to unlock the shop's door, and Bobby was looking out over the lot to Susan. He winked at her like she should come inside for a minute, but she didn't want to go inside that dark morgue. She wanted to go back home and go to bed. She wanted to curl up and sleep. Sleep until everything had blown over. Lois's hurt and predictable rage. The echoes of her father's letter, the echo that he'd tried to find her, too. He said he'd taken a bus as far south as Georgia but then changed his mind because he didn't want to "bother" her. Well, he was sure bothering her now, wasn't he? And weren't these just *words*? And crazy words, at that? Comic-book-character references and third-person references to himself and never, it hit her now, never one word or phrase of atonement. The closest he came to this was his writing that he had no right to call her his dear daughter. And later in the letter was him saying that Danny got everything he deserved and more. But never, never one apology.

Bobby was following Marianne and Lois into the shop. It was like watching something essential slip away, and Susan climbed out of Lois's VW and yelled, "Bobby! We need to go! We need to go right now!" Her voice and tone was Lois's. Wasn't that funny? She sounded just like her grandmother.

61

H E SHOULD'VE left her his number at La Habana Inn. Why didn't he leave her his number?

Because he knew she might not call it, that's why. And he didn't want to give her that chance.

The bar is smooth gray marble, and Daniel keeps running his hand over it, his fingertips dipping into only one or two chipped veins. The room is loud with happy voices, the jazz music turned to rock and roll now, a song he doesn't know, nor does he know the man looking back at him in the mirror behind the bottles of rum and bourbon and scotch. He's dressed in a light green "summer-weight" jacket and open-collared silk shirt, and the expensive sunglasses sitting on top of his head make him look like the kind of guy who does all his wheeling and dealing on the golf course or some boat and he's just ducked inside to make a few calls. His eyes are still too close together, and he has his mother's long hooked nose, his father's jutting ears, and his work glasses hang from his neck, but he appears to be a man at the peak of his powers, all of his hard work paying off, and why not look like this when he finally sees her again? Why not look like the kind of guy who can take care of her now?

An ivory cocktail napkin is placed in front of him by a young hand. "Good evening, sir. What can I get you?"

The bartender's hair is dark and greased back like McGonigle used to wear his, though this kid's eyes have life in them.

"Just wine."

"Red or white, sir?"

"Red."

"I just poured a California Pinot. Would you care for a taste?"

"Yeah, sure."

He should call her back. He should ask if he can come to her house. But then what?

Daniel sits in the bar chair beside him. It's upholstered in a soft fabric and receives his weight as uncomplainingly as an old friend you can count on, though that's nothing he knows anything about. At the end of the bar, a black couple lean close to one another over a blue votive candle and a bottle of champagne in a silver ice bucket. She's all dolled up with red lipstick and styled hair, her gold earrings big circles that touch her brown throat. Her man is in a dark jacket and tie, his shirt a deep orange, his forehead nearly touching the woman's as they both laugh over something.

Pee Wee Jones could still be alive, he could. He also got second-degree, so he could be out now. Felons aren't supposed to be around other felons, but Daniel's parole's been over for years. He should look him up on the computer. Maybe he'll even do it at the one in that Business Office back at his inn. But what's Pee Wee's real name? Daniel never knew his real first name.

The bartender could be McGonigle's little brother. He sets an empty wine glass on Daniel's napkin then pours in a splash of red. Daniel waits for him to continue, but the young man just holds the bottle and looks at him and waits. Daniel looks back at him.

"Would you care to sample it first, sir?"

Daniel sips it, and the wine tastes like the sun on the torch pines over his trailer, its heat sifting down into him like good news he's forgotten to celebrate. He nods and the waiter fills Daniel's glass then asks something about dinner, and Daniel must have nodded or said something because there's a long black menu on the marble in front of him.

A woman laughs. Daniel turns toward her sound, but two chairs down a big man leans against the bar with his back to Daniel blocking his view, so Daniel looks at her reflection in the mirror between bottles of gin and vodka. She's a deeply tanned blonde, though her hair looks like a wig, and she's a large woman and he thinks of Lois. He wonders if she's still alive. She'd be in her eighties now, but she could be. She could.

It is a crime they're letting you out. I hope they hurt you in there. If you come looking for Susan you will be sorry.

The pain he caused that woman. Did she take it with her to the grave? Or is she still carrying it around the way he carries his?

But he's breathing, isn't he? Sitting here in his new suit drinking wine at a fancy bar. He's got a pocket full of cash, and he should go find his daughter and give her every penny of it right now.

"I will. I will."

The young bartender is passing by, two bottles of Heineken in one hand, two frosted glasses in the other. He stops and leans close to Daniel. "What's that, sir?"

Daniel shakes his head at him and says, "Nothing. I'm all set."

"No dinner?"

That's not what he means, but sure, no dinner. Who the hell is he to eat in a place like this? The bartender nods with a kind of automatic respect they must teach in bartending schools, and he heads to the end of the bar where the black couple sits. Daniel's lower back and hips may as well be sitting on a throne of heated razor blades. He takes a long drink of his wine. His stomach is as empty as it's ever been, and the wine has snaked into his head and lifted his brain and sent it floating. The big man to his right raises up off his elbow and lifts three fingers to McGonigle to bring them all another round.

But he should eat something. He needs to eat.

The woman laughs again, and Daniel stares at her in the mirror. Her plump shoulders are deep brown, and there are thin white lines in her upper throat where her double chin didn't allow in the sun. Daniel pictures her lying in some lawn chair with a book, her large breasts fanning out. Around her neck are three wide gold bands, and she lifts her martini glass and laughs again before she sips. She's like a lady from another time, the kind at the center of the room everybody relies on for good food and good cheer, and he thinks of one of those Sunday dinners at Lois's brother's house. Linda had had the baby, and she sat on the couch with her sleeping in her arms. For these dinners Uncle Gio and his wife would set up a long folding table in the living room because it was the biggest one in the house, and it had a bay window that looked out over the yard and the street. Lois sat at the end of the table telling a story. It must've been a funny one because her brothers and their wives were all laughing. Danny kept looking from Lois to his wife and baby on the sofa. It was dusk outside, and his little family sat up against that bay window in shadow. Linda smiled at him sleepily, and it was clear to Danny that whatever story Lois was telling, Linda had heard it many times before, but the thing is Lois looked so happy telling it again. This lady in this hotel bar is telling a story now too, her eyes lit up the way Lois's had been, like life is one big party full of one good story after another, and you shouldn't let anything keep you from telling them over and over again. Ever. Nothing should keep you from seeing life like that.

Daniel sips more wine. Shards of glass might as well be scraping his thighbones, and he shifts in his seat. He needs to get that tin of aspirin in his truck. And shit, he'd told that valet kid that he'd be right out. But he's thinking of how Lois looked in court at his sentencing. She went up to the stand and read a statement. Her words had stayed with him a long time because she talked about Linda as a little girl. She talked about what a worker she was. How she took care of her little brother Paul, how she was good with numbers and could read a whole book in one day. How beautiful she was, though she never "flaunted" it. *Flaunted*. That word hung in his head all the way from court to lockup to Walpole to Norfolk. It hung there a long time.

Lois wore a gray sweater over a black dress, and her hair was up high on her head like always, her makeup heavy, her lipstick dark, but even with all this it was like looking at a rosebush that had faded in the sun, and he kept thinking of how happy she could get at her brother Gio's table, like loud good-time joy was the only thing that could come out of her, and then along came Danny "The Sound" Ahearn.

The big man with his back to him laughs now, and Daniel raises a finger to McGonigle to bring him back the menu. He has no right to eat, but Daniel can feel his strength ebbing like a low tide that may never rise again, and he should've jumped off the Tobin Bridge that Sunday morning so long ago. He should have done at least that much for Lois and her family. And maybe he should've done it for Suzie, too. Suzie whose house he's going to drive to just as soon as he gets something inside of him, something he does not deserve but will take all the same.

62

J UST WEST of Pine Level, Susan asked Bobby to pull over so she could throw up.

"You serious?"

"Bobby, please." Before the car had rolled to a full stop, she opened the door and leaned her head out and it came heaving from her onto the moving ground. Bobby put his car in park and flicked on the hazard lights. Their ticking matched her heart's and she spat onto the loose gravel of the breakdown lane, a half-crushed Budweiser can sitting there beside a twisted white sock.

Bobby's hand was on her back. She shrugged away from it and unbuckled her seat belt and stepped out onto the shoulder of I-70. A semi blew past, its concussive wind rocking her. The sun was low along a stand of pond pines and turkey oaks, and stretched out before her was a sea of wire grass that was such a pale green she had to close her eyes to it. She leaned over, her palms pressed to her knees, her husband walking up beside her. "Here, baby."

She turned to see him holding half a bottle of water. She closed her eyes and shook her head.

"What'd you eat this morning?"

"It's nothing I ate, Bobby." She straightened and looked at him. Her tall, bald, kind husband from Texas. Her eccentric lover of insanely chaotic sound. "I'm fucking pregnant."

He just looked at her. "Really?"

"Yes."

He stared out at the wire grass and sipped from his bottle of water. He looked like he wanted to ask her something but didn't know how.

"I missed a few days. I don't know, I just—I forgot." She wanted to tell him that this had happened before.

"Well," Bobby turned to her. "This is a good thing, right?"

"Is it?"

"Isn't it?"

"I don't know." But she felt like running. She felt like running until she could run no more.

63

SHE COULD die here. That's what Lois was thinking as she leaned back in her deep desk chair and Marianne prattled on. There was the low gurgle of the dehumidifiers, the smells of polished walnut and musty upholstery and oiled dust. There was the last light of the day filtering off Oak Street and laying itself so softly onto their pedestal tables, trumeaus, and settees, a thin ray of it across the shelves of Lois's Sue Herschel dolls, their eyes open but oblivious, the toys beside them looking like little boys would be coming by very soon to pick them up once more—the Kilgore truck and Schoenhut horses and the *Greatest Show on Earth* wagon from the 1930s. That young huckster last week who tried to get it for a song, well, nobody was stealing anything from Lois, and how good it was to breathe again. She'd told Marianne all about that letter coming from the devil himself, and even though Lois was not listening to every word coming out of Marianne's tired but lovely face, it was so satisfying to hear the outrage in it. The moral, yes, the *moral* outrage that "that man" would "have the gall" to do "such a thing."

"And of course I don't blame you for wanting to shoot him, Lois. But I'm awfully relieved you didn't."

But something was off here. It made Lois lean forward and look more closely at Marianne. She was sitting on the other side of the desk in that cane chair from the 1800s, part of a set Lois had never found any matches for, so it had become Marianne's, and she was sitting so

straight and still it was clear she was holding something back. Lois
didn't like it. She didn't like it one little bit.

"Well." Marianne glanced down at her lap, then looked back at
Lois. "I suppose I can understand her wanting to at least lay her eyes
on him, honey. He is—"

"*What?* Her *father?* Don't tell me he's her *father,* Marianne. *I* was
her father *and* her mother. Jesus, Mary, and Jos—how would *you* like
it, Marianne? What if one of your precious sons was stabbed to death
by his own *wife?*"

"Oh, Lois—"

"Don't *Oh, Lois* me. Oh, I'm sure you'd be just thrilled about your
grandkids going off to see *that* woman." The next words, whatever
they were, stopped in her throat. Her heart was an old peasant in a
dark tent and just outside it was Susan, her small voice, *Because half
of me came from him.*

She was right about that. Loving and raising Susan was like loving a poisonous snake and calling it a kitten. But the kitten had been
Linda, Linda who nobody seemed to remember but *her.* Marianne
was uttering some kind of apology, but Lois was seeing her fifteen-
year-old daughter on her hands and knees painting a straight red line
onto the floor of her bedroom. She'd asked Lois first if she could do
it, and Lois must not have been listening when she said yes because
Linda was using real paint, bright red, but the floor was concrete anyway so why not? She'd rolled the throw rug and leaned it in the corner
and she made Paul—five? six?—stay on his bed while she dipped the
brush into the small paint can, then carefully drew the excess off on
the lid and brought the brush down in smooth, straight strokes. Her
hair was pulled back in a ponytail, and Lois could see her bra strap
behind her sleeveless top, her daughter in cutoff jeans, her legs pale so
it must've been winter because Linda lived in the sun all through the
season. Chubby little Paul sat on his bed in a near-trance watching his
big sister divide their room and doing it so calmly, telling him, "That

side is yours, Pauly, okay? It's like your own world. And this side is my world, okay? And I can't go into your world without asking you first and you have to ask me, too. Okay?"

Her Linda, who was always trying to head off trouble before it started, bringing Gerry a beer and watching TV beside him just so he wouldn't yell at her mother. Dropping out of school to help in the arcade. Not telling her one word about the kind of man she'd married.

Lois's eyes burned, and she shook her head in the face of whatever her friend was saying because she *was* her friend. She was, and, "Oh, Marianne, I'm sorry. I'm just so—*sorry*."

64

THROUGH THE smudged lenses of his work glasses, Daniel takes in words on his menu that make him feel like he's back on the outside again for the first time, everything too bright and loud and in a language he never really spoke in the first place: *baby kale, marcona almonds, and apple jus. Citrus soy gastrique and champagne mignonette and sherry maple gelée.* On every line there's a word he understands nailed to others he does not. Venison with a *butternut puree* and *currant jus.* There's caviar from Siberia for a hundred twenty-five bucks. There's lobster from Maine, a word that jumps out at him, but it's buried in other words like *pappardelle* and *leeks* and *truffle.*

"Anything look good, sir?" McGonigle's little brother leans closer than before because the place is louder now, all those beers and glasses of wine and martinis kicking in, the big man beside Daniel still blocking his view of the woman who's telling a story she keeps having to interrupt with her own laughter, and at the top of the menu are two words Daniel gets ahold of like a man being pulled along by stampeding strangers. He says, "Yeah, give me the crab cakes." And the young handsome bartender takes away the menu and is back in the movement behind the bar.

There's a barback working there now too. He's a skinny kid in a white shirt too big for him in the shoulders, and he has to work more than he should to lift a bucket of ice and dump it into the bin under the bar. *Jesus saves, brother.* Mike White, alive again, the kid's tongue flicking his lower lip as he lifts a second bucket into the bin and raps the bottom of the bucket twice with the palm of his hand. And Pee Wee Jones right there at the end of the bar with his woman. Daniel leans past the big man, and he watches Pee Wee kiss his woman's hand. She could be the one he drew naked, standing with her legs spread and her hands on her hips, this picture taped for years above Pee Wee's bunk, and it's good to see them together again.

And the other bartender could be a close cousin to Johnny Sills. Pouring a bourbon for the man on the other side of the laughing, storytelling blonde, he has the same face, a kind of warm sadness beaten into it, like every bad thing that he's seen has been the blacksmith's hammer that's made the face he now shows the world.

McGonigle places a rolled linen napkin in front of Daniel, a silver knife and fork tucked inside like smuggled contraband. Then comes a plate of crab cakes drizzled in some orange sauce, and the smell of it is the smell of the strip, Linda and him standing in the doorway to the arcade and his wife jerking her arm away from him, her face a girl's again, her eyes dark and narrow with fear, "You're *hurting* me." She touched her arm where he'd been holding her, and she turned and walked fast into the blue and red noise of video games and pinball machines, her coin apron tied in a neat bow above her rear. That carefully tied bow, that did something to him.

You're hurting me.

She'd said it in the bedroom, too. She was in her pink nightgown, her hair down, her bedside lamp on, and her arm knocked against the shade as she jerked away.

She said it on the beach in a black turtleneck sweater, again pulling herself from him, little Susan squatting in the low-tide sand in her winter coat looking for shells.

And Linda said it in the kitchen right after he'd tried to give her a ruby ring he'd found in front of the Frolics. "That's *enough*, Danny. Jesus, I can't fucking *breathe* around you." But why did she have to knock his hand away like that? Why wouldn't he grab her arm then? Why wouldn't he want her to feel how much she was hurting *him*?

The bar noise has gotten so loud and constant, it's like one long sound you get used to so much you hardly hear it at all. Like the Himalaya ride below him, those purple cars rattling along so fast on their greased tracks on worn plywood, all those screaming girls, their happy voices a steady, pounding rain.

65

SUSAN LAY on her husband's side of the bed, her face in his cool pillow. When they got home, he'd brewed her herbal tea, and it still sat untouched in its mug on the bedside table, but she felt better. She was glad he now knew, though what they were going to do about it hung over them both like some looming threat. "Baby?" Bobby stuck his head inside the door. "You need to come hear this. You need to come listen to this right now."

The floorboards creaked under his weight as he turned and walked back in the direction he'd come from, which was the kitchen then his office and there were only two things to listen to in there and one of them was not playing. Susan swung her legs off the mattress and stood too quickly, the room a moving thing she rushed out of and down the hallway to her husband's study. Bobby stood at his desk, his finger on the button of his voice machine. "It's him."

She nodded, though she only meant this as an acknowledgment, not for Bobby to press that button, but he did and now came her father's voice. He sounded younger than he should, and his accent was New England blue collar, his voice deep. *I'm here now. That's all. I'm here.* The *r* dulled and dragged into the air of the click that followed, Bobby looking down at her like he was studying someone who'd just been shot in the chest. But then his hand was on her shoulder, and for the first time all day she did not want to pull away.

Her husband picked up the phone beside the answering machine and pressed the star, the six, and the nine. Behind him, the shade was drawn, and on his desk under the glare of the lamp lay Lois's pistol and bullets and new-looking box of shotgun shells, her shotgun leaning against one of Bobby's stuffed shelves.

This is—this is Daniel Ahearn, your—

He couldn't say it. She was glad he couldn't say it. He should never be able to say it. Bobby wrote down a phone number. He hung up.

"Bobby."

"Should we call it?"

But she heard it like this: *Should we call it quits? Should we just call the whole thing off?* And there was a tilting, thickening flutter in her own blood that, yes, something was indeed growing inside her and it was her father. It was her own father. "Bobby."

"It's your call."

No, not this time. Not now.

He stood there taking her in a moment. His shoulders seemed more stooped than usual, and his small gut was more pronounced under his dark T-shirt. He looked like a middle-aged father to her. He looked like a man whose kids had already come and gone. She must've nodded because he punched in the number he seemed to have committed to memory. A woman answered. She could hear that, a woman. Was it his *wife*? Had he brought his fucking new *wife*?

"I'm sorry. I have the wrong number." Bobby poked the off button. He still held the phone at his shoulder. His face was shadowed but in the sideways tilt of his head she could feel his love of dark irony, of all disordered things making their own free sound. "He's at the Don CeSar, baby. He's staying at the Pink goddamn Palace."

SUSAN RESTED her knees against the glove compartment while Bobby drove. In their bathroom she'd brushed her teeth and rolled on some deodorant, and she'd been reaching for her blush and eyeliner when she pushed both away. *Are you fucking kidding me? You're going to make yourself look good for him?* But nor did she want to look as lousy as she felt. In her bedroom she pulled off her top and found a clean bra and a black sleeveless blouse she never had to iron. She brushed her short hair and looked in the mirror over her bureau. There were dark smudges under her eyes, and the word *wan* came to her. She looked wan.

Now Bobby was driving them over the bay, the water the color of cranberries, the darkening sky along the Gulf's horizon torn into strips of purple and orange. He looked over at her and nodded at her belly. "We gonna talk about that?"

He was staring at her, and she wanted to tell him to keep his eyes on the road. "Yes. But not right this minute, Bobby. Later, though, okay?"

His eyes stayed on her, his shadowed face showing nothing, and he half nodded and looked straight ahead.

"Thank you." Susan's mouth was dry. She crossed her arms under her breasts as if she were cold when she was not, and she was looking across the water at the sandstone mansions behind royal palm trees, the white motor yachts moored in front so much smaller than Saul's, and she was seeing her father as she'd last seen him. It was the way he stood on the sidewalk under the sun in front of his parole officer's building; it was like he didn't know what to do next until he was told to do it. And he had long sideburns and a hooked nose, everything about him big and thick, his hands and feet, his shoulders and forearms. There was how he'd glanced down the street in her direction, his twenty-one-year-old daughter sitting at that restaurant table watching him from her window, then how he stepped into the street and began to cross without moving his arms much. It was like part of him was tied up and locked away.

The road sloped down toward Gulf Boulevard, and off to the left the Don CeSar was an eight-story palace the color of Pepto-Bismol, its highest structure four bell towers under thick tile roofs, each window of its hundreds of rooms glowing. Susan had never stepped foot in there before because it was the kind of place Saul would've put them up in. It looked like the wet dream of a rum-running gangster from the 1920s, it looked like the last gasp of the Jazz Age, like a pink Christmas tree, and she felt sick again though there was nothing left to throw up. Folded in her lap was what she'd printed out just before she and Bobby left home, her young father in a suit and handcuffs, a cop on each side of him in the courthouse doorway.

The light, thank God, turned red, and Bobby pulled to a stop behind an old couple on a Honda motorcycle. "I don't think I can do this, Bobby. I really don't."

"You don't have to, baby."

"But, he's fucking *here*."

"Do you want me to go find him? You can wait in the car, and if you change your mind, we're gone."

The light switched to green, and the couple on the Honda turned left and Bobby followed them, slowing for the right turn into the entrance for the Don CeSar.

"Okay? You wait in the car?"

"Okay." Her voice sounded young to her own ears. The motorcycle couple accelerated past the hotel and Bobby turned into the softly lighted and arched porte cochere of the Don CeSar. Ahead of them a young valet in white held open the driver's door of a black sedan for a silver-haired man in sherbet-colored golf clothes. Susan stared at him.

His nose was straight, and he had the slender arms and legs of a natural athlete, and she swallowed and wanted water. Bobby was rolling down his window for that same valet, the black sedan pulling ahead.

"Are you checking in, sir?"

"No, I just need to run in for a minute. My wife's going to wait out here, if that's all right?"

"I think so, sir." The boy couldn't be older than nineteen or twenty, and he was deeply tanned, his teeth orthodontically perfect. He looked like he was trying to decide something important, and he stepped back and pointed to the far corner where a red pickup truck was parked beside a blue van, its roof rack filled with sea kayaks.

"Just pull over there for now, sir."

"You betcha."

It was not an expression she'd ever heard from Bobby before, and she could hear the charge in his voice, the adrenaline in it. He drove ahead and pulled in between the van and the truck.

"I'm going to be sick again."

"You want to come in?"

"*No.*"

He switched off the headlights and glanced over at her. The engine was still running, and he wore the shorts and dark blue T-shirt he'd been in all afternoon, and she despised herself for this but she wished he looked a little more respectable. She wished he'd at least thrown on a sports jacket.

"I'll leave the AC on for you, baby." He leaned over and kissed her forehead and took the printout from her lap. "I'm just going to see if he's actually here. Back in a sec."

He climbed out of the car, and she turned and looked over the rear of the pickup truck to see Bobby walk quickly past the valet, lifting his hand to him like he was a regular customer. Then he was inside, and she made herself look straight ahead and breathe through her nose.

I'm here now. That's all. I'm here.

Straight ahead was a row of potted palm trees up against a lat-ticed fence strung with white lights. Beyond this, just before a ten-foot stucco wall with a door in it, was a round patio table and four or five chairs. It looked like a smoking area for some of the hotel's employ-ees, and she wanted a cigarette right now. It had been years since she'd smoked, but she craved one, the way the nicotine calmed her down and woke her up all at once. And what was Bobby doing now? Asking for her father's *room* number? Would they even give it to him?

A foul taste flooded her mouth, and she needed to move. She switched off the ignition and climbed out of her husband's car and walked around the front of the red pickup to the smoking area behind the palms and lattice. In the center of the table a ceramic tray was stuffed with butts and ash. On the back of one of the chairs was a faded yellow sweatshirt, though it was warm now and she wanted a glass of water. Even a glass of wine. Two or three of them.

From the other side of the high wall came children's laughter, a splash in pool water. There was the low chatter of men and women, the tinkling of glass and silverware. There was music, too, a smooth jazz trumpet, its piercing notes the comprehensible kind her husband refused to listen to. Under the warm light of the porte cochere, another valet ran past with car keys in his hand, and she leaned against the wall and crossed her arms beneath her breasts. "Mommy! Mommy, *look*!" The child's voice was like needles in the soles of Susan's shoes. She turned and tried the knob of the door in the wall, but it was locked.

She kept her hand on that knob. *Mommy. Mommy.* A man was walking under the lighted archway in this direction. Through the diamond-shaped holes of the lattice she could see sunglasses on his head, a suit jacket, and a white shirt. Hanging around his neck were a pair of readers, and in his right hand hung his car keys glinting in the light. He moved slowly, heavily, his arms nearly still in his suit jacket, and her abdomen seized up and her throat narrowed and she went as still against that wall as if she were a shadow.

66

T HE VALET smiles at Daniel and pulls his truck keys from a pegboard in a case built into the wall. He glances to the far corner of the archway then back at Daniel. "Your vehicle's right there, sir. Would you like me to drive it around?"

"No, I'm all set."

Daniel reaches for his new money clip and flicks out a C-note. "Take a ten from this."

"Thank you, sir." The kid reaches into his front pants pocket and pulls out his own wad and counts out ninety dollars in tens and fives and ones. Daniel ate those crab cakes too fast, and he can feel them sitting in his gut, but they've also absorbed most of the wine and he's more clearheaded now but tired. Part of him is tempted to drive straight back to his inn and get a good night's sleep. Drive over to his daughter's place in the morning after another shower, after some eggs and coffee. But he left a message on her machine tonight, and he thinks of something Pee Wee used to say. He would make a good move on the board then slap his knee: "See how I roll, brother? You can't sit there when it's time to move. You got to *move*."

Then Daniel's walking to his truck, his keys in his hand, his legs heavy beneath him. The air smells like car exhaust and chlorine, and he hears again that message on his daughter's machine: *You've reached the Dunns. Leave a message. Thanks.*

And what did he say? He told them he's here. Like that's a good thing. And it might be. But for who?

His Tacoma is parked beside a small black car beside a blue van, its roof covered with canoes or kayaks. White Christmas lights hang from the top rail of a latticed fence behind a row of palm trees, and he hears a kid yelling and splashing in one of the outdoor pools. There's low jazz coming from speakers somewhere and as he opens the door to his truck he sees through palm leaves and pressure-treated lattice the torso of a woman leaning against the pink stucco wall, one arm under her breasts, the hand of her other holding the knob of an exterior door. Linda standing under the eaves of the arcade having a smoke. His wife he watched from the roof of the Frolics because he was no longer right in the head.

And that's what he needs to tell his daughter right now. He needs to leave this haunted place and drive to her house and tell her, *I was crazy, honey. I was sick.*

Daniel climbs behind the wheel of his truck and starts it up and puts it in reverse. From here he can only see the woman's legs and hips, her bare arm under her breasts, her hand on the doorknob like she's getting ready to run through that doorway or to let someone out. She stands as still as if she's a snapshot from another time, and he looks behind him and backs into the golden light of the domed archway, the valet in white waving at him as he drives away.

67

HE'D LOOKED at her. He'd stopped at his red truck, and he'd looked at her through the palm trees and the fence. She could only see part of his face, but he sure as hell was looking at *her*, and then he got into his shitty little pickup truck and drove away. It was like he'd grabbed her hair and held on to it and was dragging her down the street alongside him. How could he not know he was seeing her? She recognized *him*. How could he not recognize *her*? Or did he? Did he know it was her and then lose his nerve?

And that suit. Jesus Christ, he looked like a retiree on the prowl for a rich widow. He looked like a fucking player.

Then Bobby was walking under the light of the domed porte cochere and she let go of the doorknob and heaved air, her hands on her knees, a filtered cigarette butt between two paving stones at her feet. She spat onto those stones. Then she wiped her mouth and walked out to where her husband was calling her name.

THE SKY had darkened. On this side of the bridge over the bay there were smaller homes on the water, the lights on in only half of them because wealthy people used them for just a few weeks every winter. There were palm trees bottom-lit with security lamps, and the deepwater docks had green starboard lights and red portside lights, and Susan did not want to go where she and Bobby were going. She wanted to be back on Saul's yacht but without Saul. She wanted to be curled up alone in his stateroom bed with a book and a glass of wine—no lovers, no husbands, no fucking father.

Just the slow rocking of the boat. Like she was lying in the arms of a woman, a woman who loved her.

68

IT'S FULL night now, just a smudge of purple on the horizon in his rearview mirror. On both sides of the bridge the lighted homes of the lucky sit on the bay, and Daniel pulls his new sunglasses from the top of his head and lays them in his passenger's seat. The Isla del Sol Yacht & Country Club stretches off to his left, its large embossed sign lit from the top and the bottom, and he thinks of all those people back in that grand hotel built in another time—McGonigle and Johnny Sills and Mike White. Pee Wee Jones and Polaski and Lois, too. His mother-in-law Lois, his wife Linda behind the palm trees and fence and small white lights, her one arm under her breasts.

Linda jerking her arm away. *Let go. You're _hurting_ me!* Those three words echoing inside him all through the hours and days after she'd scream them. The last thing he ever wanted was to hurt her— was he sure about that? Didn't part of him want to hurt her?

No, he wanted her to feel what *he* felt, that's all.

Well then he should've stabbed himself.

The bay's behind him now and he passes a small plaza that looks soft under halogen lights. In red neon letters is *Tokyo Bay Japanese Restaurant & Sushi*, and Daniel glances at the front windows, sees an Asian woman at the register, her black hair pulled up in a bun on her head. He needs to tell Susan that he has lived alone, that he has tried to live right. He has. But this suit he's wearing, it's a mistake. He shouldn't be wearing it. He looks like a man who's doing well, has done well. And he hasn't. He's lived alone, and he's been so—

His hips seem to be pressing on his insides, on his liver and kidneys, on his bladder and lethal prostate, on the very time he has left. And he's already reached Susan's school. Up ahead on his right, through the pines and oaks, the guard shack is a box of light and the buildings beyond it glow tall among the palm trees like the old looking over the young. It looks like a place where only good things are supposed to happen, and it's where his daughter is a teacher, a professor, his Susan. Linda's Suzie Woo Woo. Who is he to dirty up this place now?

The traffic light goes from yellow to red, and he brakes and wants to turn around and drive back to his inn and change into his clean and wrinkled work clothes. He'll look more like himself then. He'll look like a man who has lived small and alone and learned to bear it the way he learned to bear those twenty-two-foot concrete walls and that one patch of sky. The way he learned to bear living in the skin of the man who did what he did.

There's the wet rattle of a diesel engine to his left, a white F-150 idling beside him. The windows are rolled up, and in the passenger's seat a woman is talking. Her hair is short and gray, and she wears glasses and seems upset about something, like she's telling whoever's in the driver's seat just what she thinks about what he or she said or did. Daniel leans forward and can make out a man in a baseball cap. His face is dimly lit from the dash lights below, and he's nodding his head like he's in full agreement with whatever the woman's saying. Either about him or someone else, it doesn't matter, he's agreeing with her. About everything.

Liam and Daniel's mother, that's what Daniel sees. Liam, who never raised a hand to his wife, but who treated her like she was a radio playing. And sometimes he'd nod his head at what came out of that radio and he'd wait for the radio to serve him a plate and take it away. Who knew what happened in their bedroom when Danny was asleep or reading his comic books under the light of his bedside lamp, but it was hard to picture them having what Danny had had with Linda, their eyes on each other the whole time, every word or sound that came from his Linda a small treasure to Danny.

He wasn't like his old man. He never ignored his wife.

No, he just watched her like a fucking eagle.

Heat from old rusty pipes moves into Daniel's hands on the wheel. Letting the Reactor out was always so easy, so simple and clean, bad feelings burned and beaten away with swift bad action. But it was like the tide, it kept coming back, one wave after another, and yes, the only reason he's been able to stay Daniel all these years is because he's put himself in his own solitary. And how he wishes to see his mother right now. To sit beside her in front of one of her shows that made her laugh. Her thinning hair and housecoat. How she'd talk to the TV characters like they were her friends in the living room with her and her grown son, the felon, the killer, The Hammer of Hell.

Daniel is at a full stop now, and he waits for a motorcycle to shoot past him on his left, then he turns into the neighborhood of well-kept yards and houses where his daughter lives with her family. Think of that. Her own *family*. Without him or her mother or any of the people she came from. On her own. By herself. He can only admire her for this. And can't he just tell her *that*?

His palms are damp on the wheel, his tongue thick and dry, that fine wine now a sour lining in his throat. Never before has he been this afraid. Not facing Chucky Finn and others like him up to Walpole. Not watching Mike White cut open for the balloons in his gut. Not even at his sentencing while he waited for the judge to tell him his fate, Danny's hands cuffed in front of him, Linda's family behind him, Liam and his mother too.

At the bottom of the street there is no stop sign and Daniel turns slowly to his left. He rolls his front windows down and smells damp asphalt and grass. In the low house at the corner, the picture window has no curtains and a wide-screen TV is on. It looks like a western from when he was a boy, a handsome man carrying a long rifle, but the couch in front of that TV is empty, and he thinks of helping Elaine Muir down from the seat of his truck, how she talks to him like he's a good man and always has been. When he gets back home, he will ask her to execute his will. She's the one he will ask.

His headlights flash on the corner sign for Osprey Lane, and as he takes the slow left onto it he can feel his arms trembling, a cool sweat beading in the center of his chest. He has never been brave. All those schoolyard fights then those on the inside, that was just Danny burning the fear before it ate him. But watching Johnny Sills walk out of the barbershop to calm armed Willie Teague, Polaski bleeding to death just yards away, that was brave. That's nothing Daniel has ever done. Danny and Daniel have never walked slowly toward what scares them.

The driveways of these places have cars in them now, and four or five houses up on the left Daniel can see that that Honda is still in his daughter's driveway. It's lit by a single flood over her front door, and in two of her back windows there's dim lamplight. Is she reading in there? He pictures her lying in bed with a book. Reading the way her mother used to read. Is she reading to one of her *kids*?

The last time he ever touched or saw her. Her little body jerked away from him.

He's getting closer and closer. He begins to ride the brake, waves of darkness passing through his head. Is he going to just pull into her driveway?

No, he's got no right.

None. But he's here, and fifty yards from his grown daughter's house Daniel pulls to the curb of the opposite sidewalk and he kills the engine and his lights, and he waits. He closes his eyes and waits to decide what he'll do next.

69

BOBBY WAS talking. There was acceleration and there was braking, there was the car turning left then left again, and there was his voice in the air like a bird flapping itself over the front and backseats. Like a fluttering madness. Like an unleashed sickness. But the madness and sickness were hers. Her husband was saying something about her father not being a registered guest, about how "wild" it was they'd parked right next to his "vehicle," another word she'd never heard him use before, his voice as impassioned now as when he'd first sautéed spinach for her in hot olive oil in his red kitchen, when he'd smiled sideways at her and told her all about the genius of Coleman dispensing with recurring chords altogether, that nothing has to have a shape and form, that nothing comes back to where it started.

Except he was wrong. She'd seen her father, and now, as she lay back in her seat, one arm across her forehead, she was small again, riding on his shoulders through all the loud bright magic that smelled like ketchup and cotton candy, like cigarette smoke and dead seaweed and fried dough. There was how she never wanted to let go of him.

Ever. And there was how she wanted to run. His screaming. His loud voice when he yelled at—who?

Mommy. Mommy, look!

Her mother's face. Her beautiful mother's face, her eyes narrowing into slits. "Get *away* from me!" And she picked Susan up and carried her fast down the street and Susan only wanted to go back because—

—because she'd loved him. She did. And he had not recognized her. He did not know her and he never would, and her mouth tasted like bitterness itself, the back of her teeth dry with bile, and Bobby's big hand was on her knee now, the bird and car slowing as he drove up their street. "That's the same truck, baby. That's his *truck*."

It was. Bobby's lights were on it, and Susan could see the rust on the rear bumper, the dusty letters and numbers of a Massachusetts license plate. And there was the back of his head and shoulders in the driver's seat, too. Jesus Christ, her father's shoulders. Her father's big hands and his fucking letter. *I don't want to bother you now but I'm coming to see you in a few days just this one time and I hope that's all right with you.*

*No! It is **not** all right. It is **not**.*

"Stop, Bobby. Stop."

"Baby—"

"I said fucking *stop*!"

Her husband began to pull over and she had her door open and her leg out before the road stopped moving beneath her foot. Then she was up and out and walking onto grass then back into the street, her father's small pickup truck in the bright lights of her husband's car.

"Susan, wait."

She kept her eyes on the back of her father's head through the truck cab's rear window, his big nearly bald head. Her legs and arms were water, her mouth ash, each step she took a wave rolling her into whatever was coming which was her father's truck door opening and him rising slowly and turning into the light. This old man. This old

man in a wrinkled suit and worn work boots, reading glasses hanging
from his neck, his eyes close together and his ears sticking out. He was
blinking into the glare of Bobby's headlights like some night animal
flushed out of the brush, and it was seeing the soft black guts of her
shame itself; her very shame was standing there and calling her name,
saying, "Susan? Suzie, is that you?"

70

DANIEL HAS to squint into the lights at the shadow walking toward
him. Her hair is short, her hips small, and it's seeing Linda walk
again, the light swaying of her hips so that she seemed to glide through
the strip on a current nobody else had. Nobody.

Except her daughter. Look at her. His daughter.

Here, just yards away from him, seeing him.

At long, long last. Seeing her father, Daniel Patrick Ahearn.

He has to steady himself on the armrest of his open truck door,
and his voice rises from the center of his sick, yearning bones.

"Susan? Suzie, is that you?"

"Don't call me that. You have no fucking right to call me that."
She stops. She stops and stands there. "Why are you here? Where do
you get off coming *here*?"

A man is walking up fast behind her. He's tall and thin in a dark
shirt and shorts, and he touches her shoulder then keeps coming. "Mr.
Ahearn? I'm Susan's husband. I'm Bobby Dunn."

His daughter's husband is bald. His daughter's husband stops just
feet away. "We're not sure what you want here, sir."

Daniel looks at the shadow that is Susan. Her arms are crossed
now, and she stands as still as if she's holding her breath. She stands
as still as if he scares her. *Scares* her?

But why wouldn't he?

No! Never. She should never be afraid of him. Ever. Not in a million lives. *Is* she? Is she *afraid* of him? The question itself is an iron hand squeezing then yanking his guts, his little Susan standing there as the knife clattered into the sink, her mother slumping to the yellow linoleum. Around their daughter's mouth was a ring of chocolate ice cream, and she was so small, standing as still as she is now. Looking straight at her father and not moving because if she moved she would make what was happening real. It would be so real then. "I'm sorry, I—"

"Oh God."

It's like his words are a lit cigarette he just pressed into her flesh and she's already across the street and walking fast up the sidewalk, crossing both her arms like she's freezing though the night is warm and smells like rain.

Her tall husband turns and watches her go. Daniel has to lean harder on his open door, his hips on fire, his legs gone.

He should go to her.

The husband steps closer. Daniel can see his shirt is a T-shirt, that his legs are skinny and he has sandals on his feet.

"Maybe I should talk to her, Mr. Ahearn."

"I don't—"

"Pardon me?"

"I don't want to cause trouble. I just—I'm sick, that's all."

Daniel's daughter's husband stands there and waits. He just stands there and looks down at him like he'll do this all night if he has to, and Daniel can see that he's stand-up, maybe even as stand-up as Johnny Sills, who always gave him just enough air to move through without feeling he had to beg for it. Though he should have been made to beg for it, Daniel knows that. He wants Susan to know that he knows that.

"I'm going to go talk to her. I'll be right back, Mr. Ahearn."

Mr. Ahearn. Such strange words. The respect in them. Like it's something he has a right to just because he's the man's wife's father.

But maybe he doesn't know. Maybe she never told him what he did.

Daniel squints into the headlights of the car her daughter's husband walks quickly back to. He watches him climb in then drive past him and into their driveway beside the Honda. *We're not sure what you want here, sir.* No, he knows. Daniel has a hard time swallowing, his eyes beginning to sting as his daughter's husband glances back at him once before he steps into the light of their front door and walks inside.

71

SUSAN KNELT on the floor of her writing room peering through a crack between the curtains. Her breath was high and shallow in her chest, and the lights of Bobby's car were still on him, this man who was her father leaning one hand on the armrest of his open door like he couldn't keep standing without it. His thick shoulders were slightly hunched in his suit jacket, and he turned and watched Bobby drive past him into their driveway. Behind her father's truck door, the interior light was dim and weak.

And his voice had been weak. *I'm sorry*— Like he'd forgotten to bring wine to dinner. Like he'd forgotten the fucking milk. *Susan? Suzie, is that you?* As if he'd been calling her that every day since she was three years old.

She watched him turn and carefully close the driver's door to his small truck. Then he stood there in his suit that looked too small in the shoulders and too large in the waist and legs, the hems covering the backs of his shoes and touching the asphalt. It came to her that he'd dressed up for her. That this was his idea of dressing up.

"Baby?"

She jerked at Bobby's voice. Her hand parted the curtain and her father looked this way and she jumped back as if the wall had just caught on fire.

"What do you want to do?"

"Nothing, I don't know, I want him to leave." And she wanted him to stay.

"I think he might be pretty sick."

Inside her a bright rising then a dark falling. "Did he say that?"

"Yeah, and he doesn't look too good." Bobby walked over to her. He pushed a short strand of hair off her forehead then cupped the back of her neck. He leaned close, and she could smell him—her husband's smell, something sweet about to turn though it never does, this smell that did not pull her to him nor push her away so that she was still standing right here, still here, not going anywhere.

"I think he just wants to say goodbye, baby."

"How nice."

Bobby nodded. "Can I invite him into the kitchen? For just a few minutes?"

Kitchen. Her mother curled on the linoleum against the cabinets. Her long hair fanned out. How quiet she was. How still, Susan's father standing there at the sink looking back at her.

Susan's stomach muscles clenched up, and she pushed past her husband into the bathroom and dropped to the open toilet and spat into the water. She could feel Bobby at her back, and he was all men at her back, all of them fallen away in the years behind her, wanting what they wanted when they wanted it, wanting *her*, they thought, though none of them had fully known her, for she had given them very little. Except Bobby. He knew. She had given it all to him, and he loved her anyway and now he wanted to invite into their home this other man waiting in the street. This first man and this last man, her very shame; Bobby wanted to invite it right into their home.

Nothing came. She lowered the toilet lid and sat on it. Bobby stood in the doorway blocking the light from the kitchen.

Susan? Suzie, is that you?

"Tell him he has ten minutes, Bobby. That's it. I'll give him ten fucking minutes."

72

THE CURTAIN moves, and Daniel wonders if it's their kids. It's not late. If they're not too young, they could still be up. Or maybe it's just one child. An only one like Susan.

Don't call me that. You have no fucking right to call me that.

He shouldn't have come. But seeing her. Hearing her voice. Watching how she walks, even after she said, "Oh God," and got away from him fast, it was worth it. Because she saw him. She laid her eyes on her father before he's gone.

So has he done this all for himself? No. He needs to tell her things. But what?

The front door opens and Daniel stands away from his Tacoma. He crosses his hands in front of him like he's before the judge or the parole board. Like he's waiting for that steel door to open after fifteen years and on the other side waits his mother.

This man Bobby Dunn walks through his lighted driveway into the darkness of the street. He's a tall man, and Daniel thinks about that, how his daughter chose someone so much taller than he is. Daniel's hips and back throb. Below his abdomen is a burning heaviness that feels close to breaking through, and he needs a toilet. He needs it now.

"Mr. Ahearn? Will you come inside for a minute?"

Again, these stinging eyes. "Thank you." And it's hard to breathe as he follows this Bobby Dunn across the street and into the driveway of his daughter's house, the ground shifting a bit as he moves between their two cars like a glass and steel gauntlet leading to the front door his daughter's husband holds open for him, Daniel stepping inside, the walls red.

At first it's too much to take, and Daniel almost backs out the door he's just stepped through. Is he really seeing what he's seeing? Yes, the walls are red and the light above is too bright but also not bright enough so that the air of the place seems smoky. On the counter and stove is an empty pizza box and three half-eaten salads in plastic take-out. So, one child. Maybe just one. Daniel wonders if they have a boy or a girl, his daughter's husband moving past him. "Would you care for something to drink, Mr. Ahearn? A glass of water?"

"Yeah, but I need a bathroom." Daniel wants to apologize for this, but nothing more comes out.

"No problem. Just a sec."

In this light Daniel sees that his daughter's husband is in his fifties maybe, his shoulders hunched a little the way tall men do. He half smiles at Daniel then disappears down a dark hallway, Susan down there somewhere, his Suzie in this same small house. Daniel has to steady himself against the counter. He hears rough whispers, then a door closing, then Bobby Dunn is back in his red kitchen. "It's at the end of the hall. Light's on."

"Thank you." Daniel moves past him and down the hall. On the walls are framed black-and-white photographs of musicians. One is a black man playing a saxophone, his cheeks full of air, his eyes closed, and another is of a white man in thick glasses playing the piano, his eyes closed too.

Just before the doorway to the lighted bathroom, there's a closed door to Daniel's right, and he can feel Susan behind it the way he can feel his own blood inside him. Again comes the black echo of a thought that she's afraid of him, that she fears her own father, and he raises his hand to knock on her door.

No, this is *her* house. She makes the rules, not him.

Daniel steps inside the bathroom and closes the door. For far too long he stands at his daughter's open toilet and waits. His legs are weak, a tremor behind his knees, and he leans one hand on the sink. This is not what he ever wanted, to have this be the first thing he does after all this time. On the wall is another framed picture, but this one's color and must've been taken from a boat because it's of a beach of gray sand, men and women lying on blankets in their bathing suits, a few little kids playing down near the water. Behind all this is an open-air restaurant, its tables shaded by yellow umbrellas, and rising above this are hills dotted with homes made of stone and painted white or tan or even red, and now the burning descends and leaves him and this time he looks, he looks down at the color he's leaving in his daughter's toilet, and he almost flushes before he's even finished. Out in the hallway a door opens and closes and there are footsteps that have to be hers. This beach, it looks like it's in another country, and he wonders how much she remembers of the strip. Does she have any good memories of it? Even one?

He needs to get out there. He's been in here too long.

When he's finally finished, he flushes then pulls free some paper and wipes down the toilet rim just in case. He lowers the lid and drops the tissue into the wastebasket and washes his hands. The soap is a green oval and smells like some kind of herb. Stuck to it is a single dark hair, his Susan's, her mother's little Suzie Woo Woo, and he wants to push that soap into his jacket pocket, but he doesn't. He puts it back in its dish. A short rose candle is beside it, its wick black and curled into hardened wax. In the mirror his suit jacket and silk shirt look like the clothes of another man, a better man, and the work glasses hanging around his neck are the only honest things he's carried in here, those and his worn belt and work shoes.

And the cash in his pocket. He can't forget that. Every bit of it earned honestly. Except for what his mother left him, it's the only way money has ever come his way, and he wants to give it all to his Susan. He wants to tell her that he's a short-timer now and that everything he owns is hers. He runs his damp hands through what little hair he has left, and he reaches for the towel folded on the rack, but he can't touch it. Instead he runs his hands over his pants and opens the door. Down the dark hallway is that red kitchen, a small table and three empty chairs, a clear glass of water set there for him.

73

S HE SHOULD have waited for him in the kitchen, but she couldn't. The light had always been too stark in there and she'd feel exposed. But this was worse because as Bobby stood there beside her, talking low in her ear, "Let's go sit at the table, baby. Or do you want to be alone with him?" her father came into view in the office doorway. He was looking in the direction of the table and the glass of water Bobby had put there for him, but now he turned and stared at the two of them huddled there in front of Bobby's cluttered desk, the lamplight on behind them. He was just a thick-limbed homely man in a rumpled suit, but she felt boxed in, the air in the room thin and about to get thinner.

Bobby said: "Have a seat, Mr. Ahearn." He meant right there at the kitchen table, she knew, but her father paused only a second then stepped into Bobby's office and sat at the end of the couch closest to the door. His eyes went from her to the shotgun leaning against the shelves near her hip to what was on the desk behind her under the light. Noni. Her crying face and humped shoulders, that look of betrayal on her face as she rushed into her shop of old objects made by the long-dead.

"I don't want to cause any—"

"Do you know whose guns those are?"

"No."

"Lois's. The woman who raised me, do you remember her? I told her you were coming and she came here to kill you."

"Baby."

"And your *letter*. Your *fucking* letter. What was *that*? Like your life was a comic book and my mother—" A hot stone in her throat, her voice squeezed off as her eyes filled and she shook her head and tried to swallow but couldn't. Bobby's hand was on her shoulder and she jerked away from it and stepped forward, but it was like stepping barefoot close to that cottonmouth on the bank of Bone River, and she wiped at her eyes and watched her father nod his head. He was nodding his big fucking head. He said, "I—"

"What?"

"I was a kid."

"Yeah, well, so was I."

"I know it."

"You don't know anything about me. Nothing. You didn't even recognize me at that fucking hotel. You were staring right *at* me."

In the light from the kitchen he sat there looking confused. His big hands rested on his legs like claws, and his pants had bunched up so that she could see his work boots and white socks and the pale hairless skin of his calf.

"Mr. Ahearn, what is it you came here to say?"

"Bobby—" But whatever words were coming seemed to get squeezed in her throat, for her husband's question felt like its own betrayal. Who gives a shit what her father has to say? What about her *mother*, who will never speak again? Her mother, who never even made it to twenty-five? Her mother, whom she could have known and loved and been loved by all these years? Her mother, the one person she'd needed more than any other.

But Susan stood there and said nothing. Instead, she waited. She crossed her arms in the airless quiet, and she waited for what her father was going to say.

74

BEHIND HIS hurt and angry daughter a revolver lies under the lamp among a handful of bullets, their brass casings bright and shiny. Next to these is a box of Winchester shells, and again Susan is a shadow, her arms crossed like her mother, her hip jutting out like her mother, her mouth like her mother when she got mad, and he made her mad all the time. He hurt her and he angered her and he did it again and again till he shut her up forever, and it was a crime he'd come down here. What did he think? That time moved forward? No, for the good times it slipped out of your hands like water, but when things went wrong time stopped. It stopped and stared at you and never took its eyes away from what you'd done. *I hope they hurt you in there. If you come looking for Susan, you will be sorry.*

"Is your grandmother here?"

"No."

His daughter spits that word out like a slap. Then her breath seems to cut off, and she looks like she wants to say more but doesn't. And when did he stare at her at that hotel? He'd seen nothing there but ghosts, and now the ragged heat in his hips and back has moved up to his face and he wants that water on the kitchen table. It's time to say something. Anything.

He makes himself look at her. Her hair is sticking up in a couple places like she just got up, and he sees her again when she was two or three, standing beside her unmade bed in her long white nightie, her bare feet small and pale, how she'd raise her arms and jump and he'd catch her. *Swing me, Daddy. Swing!*

"We used to have fun, you and me."

"I don't remember."

"I'm sorry, I—"

"Oh, *please.*" His Susan's voice is Linda's when she'd had it, when there was nothing left in her to give him. Not one more thing.

In both pockets under his hands is the cash he carried down here for her. He needs to tell her about his lot and trailer and shed back home. He needs to tell her how much he has in the bank. About his Tacoma and his CD player for his books on tape, his caning tools and two or three fresh hanks of cane, how they're all hers. Every bit of it.

A dark wave rolls behind his eyes and time slows or speeds up because his daughter's husband is handing him that glass of water.

"You all right, Mr. Ahearn?"

Daniel reaches into his right pocket, but his clipped C-notes are on his lap. "Thank you." He takes the glass and swallows cool water that tastes like metal and something sweet, and he wants to tell Susan that he loves her, that's all. *I never stopped. Every tick of a clock. Every patch of air I ever breathed in and breathed out, every beat in my chest, I could feel you out there, Suzie. And I don't pray, but if I did I'd pray that you'd always felt each one like the rings of a very old tree you could always count on to be there and nobody could ever cut it down because time would stop for that. It would stop and stare at whoever did that.*

"What's *that*?" She sounds afraid. *Is* she? Is that what she's been since he got here?

"Don't be afraid of me. You don't have to be afraid."

Did he say that or think it because she's looking at his cash and money clip like they're the bloody drug balloons of Mike White sitting in his cut-open stomach. In one hand is Daniel's glass of water, and the other is raising his clipped wad so he can start to tell her about his will, so he can—

"That better not be for me. Please don't tell me you're giving me *money*."

"I'm sick, Suzie. I want you to have it. I want you to—"

She moves without a word, stepping as widely around him as if he were a hole in the ground, a bottomless black hole. There are her footsteps down the hall, a door slamming shut. Daniel is still holding up the clipped cash, even more money in his other pocket, and his face has gone from hot to clammy, a cool sweat breaking out on the top of his stupid head.

Susan's husband is looking at him. He crosses his arms and leans back against shelves crammed with books. Daniel wants to explain things to him. He wants to tell him that he's not just this con in a new used suit who did the worst thing that can ever be done. He wants to tell him that he reads, that he listens to history books on tape. He wants to tell him that he drives old people to doctors' appointments and the food store. He wants to tell his daughter's husband how much he loves her. That he never wanted to bother her before so he stayed away, but maybe he shouldn't have. Maybe he should have tried harder.

"Do you want her to have that, Mr. Ahearn?"

"Yes." Daniel's arm has grown heavy and he drops it. He's tired, he's past tired. He looks straight ahead at one of the books on that shelf: *The Jazz Theory Book*. Those pictures in the hall. "You a musician?"

"I'm a musicologist."

Daniel stares at him.

"I study music."

Daniel nods. He drinks some of his water. "You two have a kid?"

"No."

This hits him like worse news behind bad news. Those three empty salad containers.

"Was her grandmother here?"

"Yes."

This Bobby Dunn walks over and sits at the other end of the couch. "How sick are you? If you don't mind me asking?"

Daniel shrugs. "I won't be here next year."

"I'm sorry."

Daniel looks over at his daughter's husband. Like him, he is not a handsome man, and his eyes are on Daniel almost like a scientist's would be, like he's ready to see or hear whatever comes and he won't judge it, he just wants to see it and understand it. *Musicologist*. Daniel has never heard of such a thing. "I was a DJ."

"Radio?"

"It was a ride on the beach. Where Susan—" An electric prod in his heart, a weight shifting on his chest. "I own a place up there. Near the ocean. It's nice. It's got pine trees and a new fence. A trailer. That's where I live. And I had a shed built for my caning shop."

"You're a caner?"

Daniel nods. "My truck only has ninety thousand miles on it. I've got some money in the bank, too."

Bobby Dunn nods slowly. "You have a will?"

"I started writing it out." Daniel sees Elaine Muir smiling down at him at the young doctor's office. He thinks of when he hands her his will and asks her to help him, how she'll see his daughter's name and address down here in Florida, and then will come the questions she'll have for him. All those damn questions—

That he's run from his whole life.

"Do you have any other children, Mr. Ahearn?"

"No. Just Susan. I was never with anybody but her mo—" Daniel exiles the word from his head. He swallows and looks at this man's stereo system surrounded by books, and then something makes him look higher, to words painted in black on the wall. *That's how I have always wanted musicians to play with me: on a multiple level. I don't want them to follow me. I want them to follow themself, but to be with me.*

"That's from a jazzman I'm into. Ornette Coleman."

Daniel reads that last line again. *Follow themself, but to be with me.*

A sharp but muffled sound comes through the wall, like a drawer slamming.

"I should probably go talk to her." Bobby Dunn moves to stand, but Daniel holds out his arm to stop him.

"Tell her everything I got, it's what my mother left me. Tell her it's from her grandmother."

But then comes the squeak of a door on hinges, then fast light footsteps, and now his daughter is standing in the kitchen under its dull light, his daughter in her black blouse and blue jeans—the woman on the other side of the palm leaves and lattice up against the wall, that torso behind tiny white lights—he *had* stared at her, but he'd never seen her face. He needs to tell her that, because only now, for the first time, her face is not in shadow and he can see her, his grown Susan, and she's even more beautiful than her picture. Her face is small, and her eyes are deep and dark, spots of gray under them, like she hasn't slept in a long while, and she's holding sheets of paper in one hand and reading glasses in the other. But she doesn't look angry anymore. That game they would play when he'd pretend he couldn't find her then pretend to cry, his hands over his face, Suzie running from behind the chair or out of their closet to stand in front of him. *But I'm here, Daddy. See? I'm here.* And through his fingers, her face was the face he's seeing now, the very same one. It was like she'd needed something that only he could give her right then. Only him. And so he would make that moment last longer than he knew he should. He would make it last until it was almost too late. And he wants to make *this* moment last. He wants it to last another forty years.

"Why did you do it?" Her voice is small. She holds up the pages of paper, and he can see the words and the crossed-out words of his own hand. "All this and—you never say why you did it, and—"

Her husband stands.

"You never say you're sorry." Her voice catches on that last word, and if she wasn't standing right there Daniel would walk over to that desk and load that pistol and shoot himself in the heart. He would. Right this very minute.

"I wasn't right in the head. It was like I—" He looks over at Bobby Dunn. He's looking down at him, his long arms hanging at his side. "I thought your mother belonged to me. I didn't let her—"

"What?"

Daniel shakes his head. He tries to swallow but can't.

—*follow herself. I just wanted her to be with me.*

"They never should've let me out, Susan. I wish they didn't." He makes himself look at her. He wants to stand, but he's afraid he'll spook her, that she'll run off and never come back.

He needs to tell her he loves her. He needs to just do that.

She's thinner than he'd thought she'd be, and darker, like she's spent as much time in the sun as her mother used to. And he's so grateful that she looks nothing like him. He's so grateful that she lives so far away and always has. He's so grateful that she never had to be close to Danny.

He clears his throat. He makes himself look right into her face, and please no, no, but it's Linda's face, it's her face right after he did it—so still, everything stopped, everything beginning to come so clear to her, and the thing is that that night he'd been trying to change himself. On the way home from work he'd told the voices in his head to shut their sick mouths. He told Captain Suspicion to leave him the hell alone: Linda Dubie was his. She had chosen him. She had given him little Susan. And when he walked into his house Linda was cooking fish. Haddock or cod, he doesn't remember, only that it was white and sitting in a pan with slices of butter laid on it, ready to go in the oven, and Linda had already peeled the potatoes she was going to fry up, and she was getting ready to slice them, and Danny said, "Want some help?" And he'd taken the knife from her before she could answer and he started slicing the first potato and that's when she said, "You're the one who needs help, Danny." Her voice was low, without enough air in it, and then she started saying other things to him and it was like a rock getting pushed off a hill, how it rolls slow then picks up speed, and he could see that everything she was saying to him she'd been rehearsing in her head for a long, long time. Long enough for the snake in his veins to know that every hissing word he'd been whispering in his blood was true because why would she be leaving him if she didn't have someone to leave him for? And then he was squeezing her arm and she was pulling back, screaming, "You *can't stop* me, Danny!" *You can't you can't you can't*—but he'd been trying to change, hadn't she seen that? Couldn't she see that it wasn't too late? He was trying to be a better man, and if he hadn't he never would have started slicing that potato, and he never would have held in his hand what he'd held, and he never—ever—it would never—

"I never loved anyone like her." These stinging eyes. His shaking hand still on his money. Linda gone, his little Susan gone—

"I never stopped thinking of you, Susan. All these years, I—"

"I need you to leave." She sets his letter and her glasses on the kitchen table. She stands there and crosses her arms under her breasts.

He needs to say the words.

He looks over at his daughter's tall bald husband. He's no longer looking at him like a scientist. His eyes are on his wife in the kitchen, and even in this dim room Daniel can see the love there. He can see that he loves her, that he cares for her.

He can see that he would never do anything like Danny did.

"Okay." Daniel sets his water glass on the coffee table. He leans forward and has to push on the arm of the sofa to stand, his new pants cuffs sliding to the tops of his work boots. His jacket feels bunched up around his shoulders, and a hot pain shoots through his abdomen, and he must look like a dressed-up clown. Like an old fool. He's still holding the clipped money in his hand, and he holds it out to this Bobby Dunn, and he takes it.

"We don't want that."

Daniel turns in the direction of his daughter's voice. He's about to tell her that it's from her grandmother, but that's a lie. The money is from him. Every cent earned weaving cane from one ancient hole to another. Under the hot sun or in his shed out of the rain, sometimes snow, the ticking of it against his window, an actor narrating history for him, telling him all about the lives of people who came long before him, of men who did good things and of men who did things as bad as he did, over and over again, so many of them so many times, and who got the worst of it? The women and the children. It was always the women and children. Like Susan stepping back and to the side, his path to her door clear now. He wants to tell her that she used to sit on his lap and listen to his heart. Does she remember that? Does she?

Then say it.

He glances back at her husband. Daniel takes a breath that does not enter his chest, and he walks into the light of his daughter's kitchen with the red walls. He's close enough now to touch her. If he stops here, he'll be able to reach out for her hand, or even her arm. Maybe he could just touch his fingers to her shoulder. Feel the warmth of her skin. But her arms are crossed, and she's looking at him the way she did the last night he ever saw her. Like nothing could be worse than what was happening now, and she has to stand as still and quiet as possible or she will die. And he has to move as slowly and light on his feet as he did then, as he made his way to their yellow telephone, stepping past his Suzie without touching her, without saying a word, not until after he dialed and asked for help and Suzie was saying, "Mommy? Mommy?" then he lifted his daughter and carried her away and laid her down and picked up a book and read her a story.

At the door he turns to her. This lovely woman. This woman in black in this red room. *You never say you're sorry.*

Say it. Say it now.

Her husband Bobby Dunn moves into the kitchen. He's still holding Daniel's cash in his hand, and Daniel wants to give him the rest in his other pocket too. He wants to finish his will and come back just long enough for her daughter's husband to take a copy because this man's wife is the best thing that ever came from Danny Ahearn. The only good thing. The one thing that will live on he won't want anybody to ever forget.

His hand is on the knob.

A cool trickle slips down his back. He says, "Thank you for—"

She's looking right at him. His breath snags in his throat. "I don't deserve you. I never did."

He steps outside and closes the door shut behind him. The floodlight lies across their two cars, his truck in shadows up the street, and it's as if he's pulled a blanket up to his daughter's chin and kissed her good night then stepped into his coffin and pulled down the lid. He stands there and smells rain-damp palm bark and concrete and grass. A car passes in the street, its headlights becoming taillights then nothing. And in that nothing he needs to go back inside and tell her three words. Just three. He turns and almost raises his hand to knock on the door, but he does not. He pulls his suit coat closed and he walks back to his old truck waiting for him in the near-dark, waiting for him like a mute but loyal friend.

PART

SIX

75

ONCE, WHEN Susan lived alone, her darkness coiled around her, she got very sick. It may have been the flu, she didn't remember, only that her bed had become a lone mattress on a hot endless sea and the days were long, the nights longer, and nobody even knew she was gone and who would miss her?

Noni would. Yes, her long-suffering grandmother would, though how could Lois also not be relieved? Oh, the shit she put that woman through.

Susan's father standing in the kitchen in his suit and work boots, his glasses hanging around his neck, his hand on the doorknob. *I don't deserve you. I never did.* And when the door pulled shut behind him, some tight cord that had been keeping Susan in place since she was a child snapped and she dropped to her knees and sounds came out of her that should never come from a living thing, Bobby trying to lift her up, his hands on her and Susan jerking away as if he were Gary because Bobby was full of *shit*: All chords recurred and when you tried to stop it, nothing was ever resolved and *this* would never be resolved because she did not want that man to leave, she didn't, and yet she would not rise and go to that door, and the sounds kept coming from her when none had come from her mother, her mother just lay there curled up and quiet and she never even said goodbye. No kiss. No smile. Not her fingers on Susan's cheek or in her hair. And then her father was carried away, screaming and screaming her name.

I never stopped thinking of you, Susan. All these years, I—

And she told him to get lost. *C'mere, get lost.* But she had to, for she could not bear to—

What?

Love him. Even after he'd done what he did. Because behind whatever she'd just yelled at him in her house, even behind what she'd asked him, her need for a clear answer so sharp it had pierced her, she could feel that old love for him lying inside her like some lake hidden deep in the woods.

And now the brush and high weeds had been pulled away, and she had not left her bed in two days, maybe three. For how could she love him and still love the woman he had forever taken from her? "My little Suzie Woo Woo." Her mother's tanned, beautiful face up close. Her fingertips rubbing a damp towel against Susan's head. And there was this: her mother's voice in two places at once, Susan laying her cheek against her breast as her mother read to her, and so her mother's voice was in the air where the picture book was, but it was also in her body where Susan could hear the beating of her heart.

Oh how could her mother have chosen someone who would do that to her? How could she have had a baby with a man who would do *that*?

Those two times before, Susan didn't allow herself to even think the word *baby*. Instead, what was growing inside her was the eternal fusing to a boy she no longer wanted anything to do with. Or at least that's what she'd told herself, that it was the *boy* she'd refused to love.

It was yesterday morning when Bobby finally brought it back up again. For a day and a half he'd been letting her sleep or just lie there, curled up under the sheets, her back to him, her back to the door that opened into the hall that led to the kitchen she'd only stepped into once or twice since her father left it. Bobby had just brought her a plate of sliced peaches and set it on the bedside table. He was dressed for work in sandals and khakis that needed ironing and one of his new Bermuda shirts under his gray sports coat. After he'd set down the peaches, he stood there staring down at her and she was staring at the tiny green parrots printed all over the yellow material of his shirt.

"I know you're working some shit out right now, but Susan—"

Something changed in his voice then. It made her look up at him. He'd just shaved, and his cheeks appeared smooth and clean, but his eyes were dark with something she'd never seen in him before.

"A woman I was with a long time ago—" He stood there quiet. He cleared his throat. "She got rid of ours without telling me. We weren't right for one another, but baby—" Bobby knelt down and rested both hands on the mattress, his face a foot away from hers. "I would've loved that child. Do you hear me, Susan? And I didn't get a chance to love it, and what's better than getting a chance to do *that*?"

He looked at her a full minute, maybe more, and it was as if he couldn't leave until his question was delivered as deeply inside her as his own seed.

When Bobby had been gone for hours, Susan pulled out her laptop and opened what she'd been writing and read it. It was sixty pages long, and it was nothing like what she'd been trying to write her entire adult life. It was not fiction, or literature of any kind, but it struck her as honest, at least. Because, reading it, what came clear to her was that she'd also been a girl lost in woods that held a lake she'd always sensed was there but could never step into.

But how had she gotten so lost? She still did not believe it was as simple as who her father was and what he had done. She needed to keep writing about this. She did, though she suspected there would be no answers in it for her.

These tender breasts, this fatigue, her nausea and not wanting to even eat a fresh slice of peach, it had to have happened before she went back to stay with Lois. It meant she'd skipped taking her pills in those horrible weeks when she'd felt nothing. The pregnancy had begun *then*, just before Susan cut her hair and wrote her first line about looking for her father. In the midst of her deadest time, she'd become pregnant with both at once.

Last night she emailed these pages to Diana Clark. She wrote no note to go with it, just this in the subject line: *Tell me what you really think—xo, Susan.* Then first thing this morning, right after she'd used the bathroom, she went into her red kitchen for a slice of bread and she glanced at the door the way the survivor of a car accident might glance at a stretch of highway covered with bits of broken glass. In her writing room she sat at her desk and opened her laptop. She only had one email, and it was from Diana Clark. There was a tremor in Susan's fingers. On the subject line were two words: *Your book!*

There were two full paragraphs, and she read them quickly, for there were far too many words of praise. It was like having someone analyze the way you breathed, or walked. Or died.

But on the last line came the Diana whom Susan had really sent this to. Not Diana the rigorous reader, but Diana the woman who was the age her mother would have been, the woman who wrote: *Honey, why didn't you tell me any of this?*

It was hard to swallow the bread. Susan read that line over two or three times, her eyes filling, for there was such love in that question, nothing but love.

She shut her laptop and lay on the sofa. Outside, the wind was picking up. She could hear it pushing against the windowpanes, and through the curtains the sky looked yellow. She closed her eyes. She did not want to sleep any more, but once again a heaviness settled into her legs and belly, and she curled onto her side and then she was waking up, her shirt sticking to her back. Outside, rain blew against her windows. She pressed her hand against her abdomen. On her desk the little green light of her laptop turned as steadily on and off as breathing. Bobby's face a foot from her own, his bald head and the deep need in his eyes that did not feel grasping; instead, it was like he was sharing with her a very important secret.

A car drove by. She could hear water sluicing out from under its tires, her father probably back north now. That worn red pickup truck. His sick body that wouldn't be here much longer. She closed her eyes and what came were her ankles in stirrups, that old fluorescent light above her so bright but far away. She stood and walked to the kitchen and opened the fridge. There was a bottle of white wine in there beside a yogurt, and for a long while she looked at both. The fridge's motor turned on with a low electric moan. Then she reached for the yogurt and, slowly, she ate that yogurt standing up, her eyes on her front door.

Epilogue

IT'S A Sunday in May, less than an hour past dawn, and through the trees the early morning sun glints off the river. It must have rained farther north because Lois can hear the water hissing past its banks. The fossil hunters will be out soon, and as much as they've irked her over the years—their damned excited voices over the old bones of dead animals—she will miss sitting on her screened porch and watching their bright canoes drift through the pines and oaks.

She sips hot hazelnut coffee and smokes a cigarette. The house is packed up. Walter and two of his Mexican hands, both older and polite to a fault, saw to that. Lois draws deep and long on her cigarette. Her own hand and arm look like someone else's, for she has lost so much weight over the winter and spring. And she's tired all the time. Just getting out of bed and driving to the shop has become a chore she can no longer pull off. But Marianne will take good care of the place. And Lois didn't even have to ask her not to change its name.

Susan's visit last September, it had been only a few weeks since Lois had seen her, but Suzie looked healthier than she had since she was sixteen, her legs and hips fuller, her skin with more blood in it. Her hair had begun to grow out too, and she had the distracted, joyful look of someone deeply in love. She said her book was going well, but that wasn't her best news, and when she told Lois, Lois wished at the time that Susan had kept quiet about it till she was further along, though thank God Lois hadn't said that, not that she could speak anyway, the kitchen going all blurry as Suzie rose from her chair at the table and came around and hugged her and wouldn't let go.

Whatever had lifted from Lois when she was exiled back here has stayed lifted, and she doesn't like not having a gun in the house but she no longer feels so afraid. No, that's not true. Her old fear of someone taking her Susan away is still there, but it has shifted to something else: what Lois fears even more is that by locking in on all that can go wrong, she will miss—in whatever time she has left—all that has gone right.

Before Susan drove back home, she went up to her old bedroom and came down with the two Dresden lamps Lois had given to her and Bobby, her pregnant forty-three-year-old granddaughter smiling as openly as when she was a kid, and Lois said: "Just tell me what he was like."

It was not what Suzie had expected, but she took a half breath and she nodded and said, "Sick. He was very sick, Noni. And he didn't stay long."

Two nights before Christmas, too tired to travel to St. Pete, Lois poured herself a tall glass of red wine and smoked a cigarette to the filter. She took a deep, shaky breath, opened her computer, then typed his name onto the keyboard. A hundred Daniel Ahearns came up. She drank off a third of her glass then typed: *Daniel Ahearn, Massachusetts. Death notice.*

And there it was. In the *Port City Daily Gazette.* Just five or six lines:

Daniel P. Ahearn

Nov. 28, 1949–Nov. 30, 2013

Daniel P. Ahearn, age 64, of Salisbury. Born in Palisades Park, New Jersey, the son of the late Liam C. and Mary (Orlowsky) Ahearn. Served 15 years in the Massachusetts Department of Corrections for the second-degree murder of his wife, Linda Dubie, 24. He is survived by his daughter, Susan Dunn, of St. Petersburg, Florida. He was buried in Long Hill Cemetery, Salisbury.

Yes, Lois thought, **survived**. *That's all any of us have done.*

Lois stared at that notice for a very long time. He'd just turned sixty-four. Exactly forty more years of life than her Linda got to have. Lois could feel that old rage turn inside her, and she shut off her computer and moved to the kitchen to do nothing in particular. She had thought that when this moment came, she'd feel some kind of—what? Satisfaction? But she just stood there staring at an old cigarette burn on the edge of her kitchen table and all she felt was empty, as empty as the coffee can Gerry had hurled into the sea after pouring out what had lain inside.

Paul and Paul Jr. should be here soon with the truck. The addition Susan and Bobby had built for her is larger than she needs, and Lois feels badly about it taking up most of their backyard. A child needs a place to play. A child needs a safe place to roam.

But the pictures Susan sent her on the Internet are nice indeed. Lois will have her own kitchenette and a sitting area, her bedroom behind a half wall made of glass bricks that were so common when she was growing up. The floors are glossy new oak, and her bathroom has big blue tiles on the floor, and she has a walk-in shower with stainless steel rails for her old liver-spotted hands. There's a pedestal sink, too, built up against a white marble backsplash that matches her countertop in the kitchen. It's the kind with gray veins in it, again like what was popular so long ago.

Many times in the last few months, Lois has emailed Suzie that she's spending too much money on her, that she needs to save it for her little one. But Suzie always writes back the same thing: "Bobby inherited some money, Noni. *Stop.*"

And over Lois's bed is a skylight. She has never lived in a house with one of those, and she's looking forward to lying on her mattress in the dark and looking up into deep space. She will miss her old things in her shop, but what's older than what she'll see up there? And besides, this is the time for the new, for Susan's baby daughter born just three days ago at just over seven pounds.

Again, Susan sent her pictures over the Internet, and there's one

Lois keeps staring at. It's of her great-granddaughter's tiny pink face up against the brown nipple of her granddaughter, the infant's eyes closed tight. Lois has never seen Susan's breasts, at least not since she was ten or eleven years old, and seeing them now opened a door inside her that led to another, Linda's bedroom door open, Paul gone somewhere, and Lois had walked in. It was early morning in late summer, and her daughter was standing near the curtained window holding the bra she was about to put on. Her face and shoulders, her arms and flat belly and legs were deep brown, but her breasts were white. They were so lovely and so white, and she wasn't mad at Lois for walking in like that. Instead, she turned and smiled at her as if they'd just had a good long talk and now it was through, and she put on her bra then slipped her Penny Arcade T-shirt over her head. She brushed her dark hair back with both hands, then she grabbed her coin apron hanging on the doorknob and she said goodbye to her mother, and she kissed her, she kissed Lois on the cheek, and then she was gone.

Lois stubs out her cigarette and slowly stands. The river hisses through the trees. There are the smells of damp pine needles and the clay banks of Bone River. She got a good price for this place, and she set aside quite a bit of it for Linda's granddaughter, for Suzie's little Woo Woo, Corina Linda Dunn.

For there is so much she needs to pass on to this child, that our lives are brief, even long ones like hers, and the one thing we should do is take care of each other. That's all. *But honey, it's so hard. Why, child, is it so hard?*

A voice through the trees. A canoe slipping quickly down the river. Lois can make out three people in orange life vests. There's a woman in the front, her hair tied back, and it looks like her paddle lies across her knees and her husband in the rear is using his as a keel. He wears a cap and sunglasses, and low in the center of the boat is the child, a boy or girl, Lois doesn't know, though she can hear the child's high, earnest voice, "I think I *see* one, Mom. Dad, *stop*. We're *here*. See? We're *here*."

Acknowledgments

I would like to thank my friends and family who read early drafts of this book and gave me invaluable insights into it: Stephen Haley; my mother, Patricia Lowe Dubus; my sister, Suzanne Dubus; my oldest son, Austin; and especially my wife, Fontaine, my first reader for all these years, who read and commented on every incarnation of this novel and made it better by doing so. As always, I am deeply grateful for my friend and agent, Philip Spitzer, as well as Lukas Ortiz and Kim Lombardini. And lastly, no one worked harder on helping me bring this story to fruition than my longtime editor, Alane Salierno Mason. I feel most fortunate to have her in my corner.